PRAISE FOR JOHN FRANCOME AND *OUTSIDER*

"Gets off to a galloping start . . .
with a surprise twist in the final straight."
—*Evening Standard*

"Displays all his racing knowledge to the full."
—*Oxford Times*

"Francome writes an odds-on racing cert."
—*Daily Express*

"The racing feel is authentic. . . . An entertaining
read."
—*The Times* (London)

Books by John Francome

OUTSIDER *

ROUGH RIDE *

STONE COLD *

STUD POKER *

(with James MacGregor)

BLOOD STOCK

DECLARED DEAD

EAVESDROPPER

RIDING HIGH

*Published by HarperPaperbacks

OUTSIDER

/////

John Francome

HarperPaperbacks
A Division of HarperCollinsPublishers

HarperPaperbacks *A Division of* HarperCollins*Publishers*
10 East 53rd Street, New York, N.Y. 10022

An edition of this book was published in 1993 in Great Britain by Headline Book Publishing PLC.

Cover illustration by Ken Rosenberg

First HarperPaperbacks printing: January 1996

Printed in the United States of America

HarperPaperbacks and colophon are trademarks of HarperCollins*Publishers*

10 9 8 7 6 5 4 3 2 1

A long, tortured scream echoed through the tops of the beech trees swaying above me.

The pain was so vicious, so unexpected, at first I didn't know my own voice. Before I could identify the epicenter of the agony, let alone its cause, someone grabbed me from behind where I stood, swaying knee-deep in fronds of fresh, green fern. I tried to turn, screamed again as naked pain burned through my right leg. A pair of hands like sandpaper plastered heavy sticky tape across my eyes and round my head, stuffed a rag in my mouth, choking off another yell, and taped over my lips. The same deft, hard hands lashed my wrists together behind my back. I couldn't run; I couldn't retaliate; I couldn't kick out—the torture in my right leg wouldn't let me.

But the man—it had to be a man—was trussing me

up tight as a turkey. Through a thick, black fog of pain, I groped for a reason; but I gave up before I started. I knew I was being offered a preview of hell but I didn't care why. And the turkey trusser wasn't going to tell me; he restricted himself to a few heavy breaths and a grunt while he tugged the knot on my wrists until the cord cut hard into thin flesh. For a farewell gesture, he toppled me over like a tenpin into the ferns and bramble, and he was gone.

I had seen nothing of him; I couldn't tell how big he was or how strong. It wouldn't have taken a lot of muscle to deal with me in this condition, but the job had been done by a man who knew what he was doing.

Whatever it was that had been slicing pieces off me was still there. I shifted my leg and felt something scrape my naked shinbone; I squeezed a scream through the rag in my throat and the tape across my mouth and fell back on my side with the smell of damp beech leaves and fern fronds in my nostrils. Bramble thorns pierced my jacket and my arm, but that didn't compare with the red, throbbing pain in my leg.

With pain howling through my head, I didn't hear the man go. But after a while, I found a way of lying that took some pressure off my leg and let me think in short snatches about what the hell had happened.

In these moments of semi-clarity, I thought of the girl. She probably didn't know it, but I had really wanted to see her this time. If she had turned up at my house and hadn't found me, she wouldn't hang around; and she probably wouldn't come again—ever.

I shifted again and the painful thought was displaced by painful reality in my lower limb.

I tried to figure out what was round my leg. It felt as if there was sharp metal clamped either side of it, buried deep in my flesh. I wasn't even sure that the bone hadn't snapped or splintered—it hurt enough—and that mattered a lot. Broken bones, injuries that stopped you riding—those were a jockey's real enemies, far more than the cohorts of crooked bookies, myopic stewards and unschooled horses that butt in and try to stop you winning races. Amid the confusion that wracked my brain, I found time to groan at the thought of losing weeks of racing, and the best Derby prospect I'd ever had.

Piece by piece, my thoughts turned practical. I guessed it must have been an hour or so since I'd set out from my house at seven that evening for a walk up my favorite track through the woods.

As usual, I'd taken a shotgun with me—a cheap Spanish over-and-under—to pick off any pigeons that I flushed. I guessed it was gone now, and anyway I had no way of looking for it, for all the help it would have been.

I was up at the top end of my valley, half a mile from the house, and another half-mile from the lane which ran along the ridge above. I jiggled my wrists to see if there was any hope of freeing them that way, but they were too well trussed. I attempted a yell but produced only a muffled grunt that might have carried a few yards through the brush. I tried to flex my jaws; they were stuck fast with some kind of heavy-duty industrial tape. And every time I exerted myself, the throbbing in my leg seared into a crescendo of pain. I lay back and tried to think of reasons not to panic.

There weren't many.

Scarcely anyone besides me came up through this woodland. It was my own private domain, away from the permanent people-crush and publicity of thoroughbred racing. I didn't encourage visitors; that was part of my policy for preserving its privacy. It might be weeks before another human being came up here. People who knew me were used to me hiding myself away when I could and they didn't often seek me out uninvited. This was the downside of privacy; the irony didn't escape me.

Someone would miss me eventually, I guessed, but it was Saturday evening and I wasn't due to ride until the evening meeting at Windsor on Monday. It might be the day after that before anyone official took any notice of my absence.

To get a kick-start out of apathy, I forced myself to look at the worst possible outcome. I could be lying out here in the woods for two or three nights. So far, there didn't seem a lot I could do about it and the damage to my leg could only get worse. I found myself staring at the possibility that I might die, here in my own woods, within yelling distance of my own house, from simple exposure.

Physically, I was in better than good shape; people don't easily survive in my job if they aren't, and they certainly don't win races. But the kind of pain I was being dealt weakened everything, physically and mentally. I didn't know how much blood I had lost and I didn't know if I would have the courage or the strength to last three days and nights.

I was in total darkness and it was getting hard to breathe. Everything made me want to submit to panic, but I forced myself to think calmly, to try and work out a plan.

First, if I could see, that would help—so I told myself; that would give me some confidence, let me know what I was dealing with.

Very slowly, very carefully, I turned my torso so the side of my face lay on the ground. I pressed it into the undergrowth and started to rub my head up and down. My face was scratched to shreds before I felt something, a twig or bramble, catch the edge of the sticky tape and lift it a millimeter from my cheek.

It was a big moment. I paused for a rest, sucking air through my nostrils. Very slowly, I scraped my head along the ground and felt the tape lift away from my face. It began to take some of my hair with it. I welcomed that small pain and persevered until I caught a sudden, glorious flash of light in the corner of my right eye.

It took another ten minutes to get the tape clear of both my eyes though it was still wrapped round my head like a sticky crown of thorns, tangled in my hair. The right side of my face felt as if it had been well worked over with a cheese grater. But I could see.

I propped myself up, trying not to move my right leg. At last I could look down at what was holding me.

I didn't want to believe what I saw.

My leg was clamped between a pair of rusty iron jaws three feet wide with short, jagged teeth welded every few inches. One tooth was buried in a bloody hole in my jeans at the back of my calf. Another, in the front, had sliced through the thin flesh beside my shinbone. I didn't need to see the rest of the contraption to know I had stepped right into an ancient, outlawed and well-primed mantrap.

I had seen one once before in a country museum up in the Cotswolds. Eighteenth-century landowners had used them to discourage poachers, the label had said. If I'd been a poacher, I would have been discouraged.

These things were supposed to be able to snap a man's leg in two. I must have had a little luck, then.

Looking at the trap again, letting more of the details come into focus, I saw the reason for my luck. Caught between one of the angles of the jaws and stopping them from closing completely were the barrels of my Spanish shotgun, dented but still intact with the stock buried out of sight in the bracken. I'd been walking with it broken across my arm, barrels to the ground. I'd always known it was a useful sort of a gun. Now it had saved my leg. I was struck by an absurd, incongruous thought—thank God I hadn't brought one of my Purdeys out this evening.

Looking back, it seems strange that, right then, I didn't give a damn about *why* someone should want to trap me in my own woods, or who that someone was. All I cared about was getting out of the horrific thing.

I already knew that whatever I did, I had to do it

slowly if I didn't want to aggravate the vicious throbbing in my leg. I judged from the angle of the sun that it was around eight or eight-fifteen. I had maybe an hour more of daylight. The next thing to do was to try and free my hands. The only way I could see of doing that scared the hell out of me. It meant somehow twisting over onto my front, then leaning back and hooking the twine that bound me over one of the rusty teeth of the trap and sawing at it until I frayed it through.

I tried to turn, but I couldn't do it without twisting my right leg between the teeth of the trap, and that was a maneuver way beyond my pain threshold. I tried again and failed. When I gave up, I was pouring sweat and my jaws ached from gritting my teeth. The only other way was to stay on my side and arch myself backwards. I could do that. I'd always been an acrobat as a kid, and it was part of my job to be supple and have short legs.

But I wasn't used to doing this kind of thing with a few inches of rusty iron cutting into one of those legs.

It took me five tries to loop the twine over one of the teeth, and when I started sawing, I was doing as much damage to my wrists as I was to the twine. But I began to feel it fraying. It had been wound several times round my wrist and when I felt the first strand break, it didn't loosen much. I sweated on with my back aching and my stomach muscles screaming for relief, but I didn't dare take my hands away from the jagged tooth—I didn't think I would ever get them back there. After fifteen agonizing minutes of concentrated sawing, I felt the bonds coming free. I kept at it, and a few moments later, my hands sprang apart and I could straighten my aching body.

I lay for a while, exhausted and trying to control the pain that seemed to be visiting every corner of my being. The light in the woods was grey, all color gone now. Soon, all shape would go too; there would be no big moon tonight. But having my hands back gave me a lot of hope. I peeled the tape from my mouth and spat out the piece of musty rag that had been trying to choke me. I gasped a few clean breaths and felt that now I had some control over my own destiny.

Once the ache in my back had settled down, I arched my body forward—the easy way—and got hold of the trap. Feeling through the ferns that covered the end of it, I found it was attached to a chain which I guessed was in turn attached to some kind of peg in the ground. Using my left leg, I managed to drag the trap round so that I could feel further up the chain. Inch by inch, I crawled my hands up it until I reached the end, and more bad news.

The chain was fixed into the ground by a thick iron hook, driven in at an angle of about forty-five degrees. When I was sure it would take a healthy man with all his limbs and a crowbar to get it out, I laboriously straightened myself until I was back where I had first fallen. I wanted to weep with frustration. In spite of the last two hours' pain and effort, I was scarcely any nearer releasing myself. At least, though, I could howl now.

I took a few more deep breaths and bellowed into the black woods like a Nebraska hog-caller. I scattered a few birds and small beasts of the night but only the wind getting up in the tops of the beeches answered me.

I hollered again and heard my voice fade up the coomb, away from my house and the farm in the meadows below the woods.

I listened for any human reaction. The wind brought up the sound of a tractor going home from a hay field, a mile down the valley. In a burst of optimism, I yelled again. Twenty minutes later, I was still alone and close to hopelessness. But I filled my lungs and tried once more.

Nothing.

I wasn't disappointed. I had expected nothing. From some dusty filing cabinet in a forgotten corner of my mind, I recalled a phrase from boyhood Bible class: "The voice of him that crieth in the wilderness." My voice. Echoing into emptiness.

It all seemed like a terrible waste of painful effort. What I really wanted was unconsciousness, release from aching pain, weariness and uncertainty. When it beckoned to me, I welcomed it and smiled as I drifted into oblivion.

////////////// CHAPTER 1

There's something about hot sunshine that always makes me feel randy. I guess it's a kind of primeval stimulus to procreate in favorable conditions or something.

It was mid-April and one of those freak spells of high pressure and still, sultry days that come along every so often to mess up England's reputation for blustering sogginess. Everyone was saying global warming was going to change the weather patterns for good; as it turned out, they were wrong and it rained as normal, pretty much for the rest of the summer.

But that day it was hot, and I felt a stirring in my crotch. There was what you might call a supplementary reason for this, or maybe the real reason: I was on my way to keep my first date with one of the best-looking girls I'd met since I'd first set a size seven foot on this damp little island, three and a half years before.

I had arrived, aged twenty-one, feeling as green as the tidy, white-railed English racetracks, and blue as they say the grass is back home where Kentucky meets West Virginia. My father had just died, aged fifty-two. It had been quick, and the way he would have wanted —cracked his skull and broke his neck coming off the back of a bucking thoroughbred colt. Crazy to be on a yearling horse at his age, crazier to be wearing no more than a battered old stetson on his head.

He'd been the biggest waste of a natural talent I'd ever seen. Granted—at birth, it seemed—the gift of being able to do just about anything with a horse except talk to it, he had grown up to abuse this rare privilege. He could and should have made his mark as a leading jockey of his time by riding winners. Instead, he'd taken a short cut to easy money and fame, or rather infamy, by riding losers, or—more precisely—by stopping horses from winning.

I was eight years old, notably slight and just learning to ride when the droppings really hit the fan and rebounded on my father.

The FBI had to tap our phone for just a few weeks to gather enough evidence to arrest and indict him.

He got four years and served two in the easy regime of an open jail. Whether this sojourn among the softer criminal classes did anything to change his attitude to life, I doubt, but it shredded every ounce of my mother's self-esteem and turned her soft brown hair prematurely grey.

She hadn't had any idea of what he'd been doing. And she never really recovered from the revelations at his trial. But there was no question of her leaving him; despite the disgrace, she stayed fiercely loyal and never stopped loving him. She was determined, though, that I wouldn't repeat his crimes. I had it drummed into me, day in day out, that honesty was everything and if I ever did the same as my father, I would cease to be her son. With no father around at that sensitive time of my life, I badly needed and wanted a mother.

When Dad came home again, he more than made up for his time away. He couldn't go near the racetracks again and was home all day, every day.

Whatever he'd done, I guess he'd done it for the right people and at the right price, because money never appeared to be a problem in our household. Dad carried on making a living by "spelling" horses on the beautiful West Virginia farm where we'd lived since before I could remember. Almost from the start of Dad's new activity, our yard was full of young horses waiting to be sent into training, a lot of top quality thoroughbreds among them.

From the age of ten, I spent most of my daylight hours in the saddle of up to a dozen different horses every day. By the time I rode in my first race in Louisville six years later, I was already an old hand. With my father's vigilant, all-seeing eye on me, and all the experience and knowledge he was able to pass on, I could hardly have failed to be a success. My career took off from that first day on the track and by the time my father died, I had achieved a lot more than most jockeys dream of in a lifetime. But I was already making plans to move to England when my father took his last, fatal fall.

My mother did everything she could to stop me leaving; I was her only child and she wasn't happy even if I was no further from home than the next state. But I had to do it.

I didn't know if I was running away, or just looking for somewhere healthier to live. People had told me that the English ran the straightest racing in the world, and in the States, success and eight million dollars' worth of races won had put a lot of pressure, very unhealthy pressure, on me. People were beginning to want to pay me more to lose races than to win them, and they didn't like that kind of generosity to be refused. Either I danced to their tune, the way my father had and my mother hated, or I took the risk that I would end up with no legs to dance on.

They didn't exactly greet me here with open arms. A lot of people in British racing, from the Jockey Club stewards to the men in greasy flat hats in the Silver Ring, felt they didn't need a Yankee pipsqueak who rode with a hunched back and only his toes in the irons; especially not a pipsqueak who had already won more prize money than most of their senior jockeys. But I had just enough sponsors to make me welcome.

It was Captain Toby Ellerton who had first suggested I come and ride in England; I'd unexpectedly won two races for him in Kentucky on English horses. I didn't take to him much, or to his arrogance, but I respected him as a trainer. He offered me a retainer worth less than the interest I made on the money I'd already saved. Two weeks after he had gone back to England, I phoned him to say I'd take it, starting at the beginning of March.

It wasn't until I'd been here for six months that I realized just how badly people had wanted me to fail. It seemed that almost everybody in British racing thought they could do anything with horses better than anyone else in the world—breeding, feeding, training and riding. They didn't like to see some American kid show them there might be other, better ways of doing things. They'd forgotten that half a century earlier Todd Sloane had shown them that the American way of race riding was better. While they had jeered at it—"Like a monkey on a stick," they had called him—they'd copied it, and never looked back.

I rode two winners my first day out in a couple of Mickey Mouse races at Warwick. To give Captain Ellerton his due, he'd made sure of it; he'd sent out two high-class but unraced horses for me to do it on. He hadn't done it for me, of course; he just didn't want to listen to other people saying what a fool he'd been to take me on.

Ellerton's yard was in form that season. He'd been sent a dozen good yearlings from the previous High-Flyer sale by a Kuwaiti prince, ten of which had won, two in Group class. He also had a good string of older horses. I ended up with sixty winners by the end of that first season. In my second season I passed the ton, and in the third I won a hundred and twenty races and the Oaks, my first classic. The racing hacks stopped jeering; they decided to tell their readers it wasn't all fluke, Jake Felton really could ride.

It was big of them. I was still feeling so insecure among the brittle backbiting of British racing that I was actually grateful to them!

I went back to West Virginia for a month each winter, but I was really getting to like the English way of life—fly fishing, pheasant shooting, even, occasionally, fox hunting—as well as the way they ran their racing.

The owners were always more friendly than the professionals. I think some of them even took time to understand and appreciate my reasons for leaving the States—after all, I hadn't left under a cloud or in disgrace—and they were only too happy to invite me into their homes. Well, most of them. Not some of the earls and other aristocrats, if they had daughters of my age, though gradually even they had melted.

And now, on a hot Saturday afternoon in mid-April, I was driving from Kempton to have dinner and stay the night at Aldrich Manor, the home of Sir John and Lady Fielding and their daughter Camilla, a very hot-looking 21-year-old.

I was feeling good. I'd just ridden a winner, my weight was steady at around 8st 2lb, stripped, and at this early stage in the season I was only a few winners behind the two leaders in the jockeys' table. I'd just about managed to come to terms with my natural dislike of my guv'nor, Toby Ellerton; my dark green convertible Aston Martin DB6 was running like a hare on ecstasy, and I'd just got my twin-engined private pilot's license. This evening I was looking forward to spending a bit of time with a girl who had more to say for herself than the stable girls and East End horse-owning butcher's daughters who had, up till then, been my main source of female company.

The only minus in the evening ahead was that I'd agreed to stop off on my way to the Fieldings at a pub in Midhurst to give a quick interview to one of the least friendly and most influential of the racing hack pack. One has to do these things, or so Ellerton said; good press attracts owners. Personally, I know that what attracts owners is a lot of winners or, in certain circumstances which did not apply to Ellerton, an affable, likeable trainer with a happy yard. But Ellerton had pointed his finger at me and said, talk to this man about your Guineas ride, so that was what I was going to do —for one hour, no longer.

I walked into the old coaching inn. It was so old that even I had to duck to pass through the door into the main bar, a sprawling room with low, thick, smoke-blackened beams, Persian rugs on a well-worn elm floor and a lot of rickety country chairs tucked into nooks and corners. There was that nice quiet buzz of conversation you get in the better type of English pub; no jukebox or fruit machine.

The journalist was sitting, waiting for me. He was wearing a grimy linen jacket and his usual surly manner.

He had the kind of face that could relax only into surliness—not so much lived in as squatted in. An artist painting his portrait would have found himself reaching for the *eau de nil* to capture his complexion, along with light charcoal for the furrows that lined his forehead like a cornfield in autumn beneath dry, lank hair the color of sludge streaked with pewter.

"What'll you have to drink, Jake?" he asked grudgingly, rising slowly from his chair as I approached.

"Valis'd be good, Geoff," I said, pulling up the chair he hadn't offered me.

"What the fuck's that?"

"Vodka, a dash of lime, ice and soda."

He looked pleased and wheezed up to the bar, leaving an opening for a couple of racegoers to come over and ask for autographs and a tip. I ought to have been used to it by then, but I still found it slightly embarrassing, and just smiled dumbly, signed and told them that they'd be broke backing my tips. I was almost glad when Geoff got back to the table with two tall glasses. I wondered why he had arranged to see me here and not at the races, but I noticed he had tucked us into a corner where a private conversation was actually possible.

He pulled a dog-eared, spiral-backed notebook from one of his baggy pockets, and started talking to me about racehorses.

On the whole, I'm always happy to talk about horses; I enjoy the hundreds of subtle differences in mood and performance that they can show to those who understand them. To most people, including a lot in racing, there's an incomprehensible mystique about the state of a horse's mind and health, but to that small percentage who can read the signals, it's an intuitive knowledge to be proud of. And there aren't many people I know who don't sometimes like to show off their special knowledge.

Geoff looked around the bar, for a bit of background color I guessed, and scribbled away in a messy scrawl of hieroglyphics which I doubted he was going to be able to read when he got home, but that didn't seem to worry him. Maybe it was just a front and he had a recorder in his pocket and a mike in his button.

"I told my editor you'd win the championship this season," he said, "so he asked me to do a bit of a feature on you sometime."

If he thought I was grateful, he was wrong. I just nodded and waited for him to get on with it.

"D'you know something, Jake? Most of my colleagues in the pressroom reckon you're uphill work to interview."

I laughed. "Good. It keeps 'em off my ass."

"And it's not just the way you talk. Though God knows, you've ended up sounding like a cross between Elvis Presley and Eddie Grundy."

"Whoever the hell he is," I said.

"He's a sort of English rustic folk hero. But no, it's not your accent they find difficult, it's just that you never seem to tell us anything."

"Well, it's your lucky day today, Geoff. I'm feeling chatty."

He looked quite surprised for a hardened hack. "Great! So tell me what you think of Captain Toby's prospects this year."

So, I told him.

Of course, there were a few horses I was specifically not allowed by Captain Ellerton to mention. But Dawn Raider, my prospective mount for the Two Thousand Guineas, had already been seen out, racing and on the gallops. We had no secrets about him.

Dawn Raider was among my favorite colts in the yard. He was exceptionally well-mannered and had improved steadily throughout the winter. He had an enormous stride which was always going to carry him a mile but which, in my private view, wouldn't be suited to Epsom come June. So, yes, I was feeling confident about him for the Guineas, but I couldn't say the same for the Derby. Anyway, everyone's focus was on the mile race until it had been run.

I told Geoff about our fillies and the older horses in the yard, who would go handicapping. Captain Toby had a bit of a name for getting these right. As that was how he earned the better part of his wages, information about his handicappers—the truth, anyway—was strictly taboo; but I had some fun pretending to give away a little that I shouldn't have done. I'd be surprised if he didn't get a few of his naps wrong later in the season.

To give Geoff his due, he knew what he was talking about and asked the right questions. I'd got into my stride and was loping along comfortably at a speed that would have suited a two-and-a-half-mile Cup race. Geoff got up every so often to replenish our glasses, and I didn't pay too much attention. It was Saturday evening; I wasn't riding the next day; I only had to make it to the Fieldings, no more than five miles away, and then I had nowhere to go until morning. I deserved a few vodkas.

Back in the car, slewing my way through the sunken lanes toward the Fieldings' grand house halfway up the downs, I knew I'd had more than a few vodkas. I felt as if I'd drunk a bottle of it. Geoff must have been priming me for some indiscretions. I hoped to God he hadn't succeeded. I didn't think he had, but then I was finding it a little difficult to think at all.

The land began to fall away steeply to my left, where a piece had been gouged out of the smoothly rolling downs, like a giant had scooped the first spoonful from a great, green blancmange. There was only a rickety post-and-wire fence between the lane and the cliff. With the exaggerated caution of drunkenness, I steered my car round a tight bend. The road widened but it was blocked with road menders' debris where a new, galvanized-iron crash barrier was being erected, and a set of temporary traffic signals showing red.

I pulled up just in time. The road works obstructed the way round the bend ahead.

I put the engine in neutral and sat waiting for the lights to change. It was still warm; there was an old favorite Chicago tape playing in the Blaupunkt; I was getting drowsy and I was trying to keep my eyelids up.

But I guess I didn't try hard enough.

The next thing I knew, my car was on the move, only it wasn't heading up the road; we were going straight for the fence at the side of the road, jerking sort of sideways. I didn't even have time to think what the hell was going on when we splintered one of the posts and I was looking through my windshield across three hundred yards of nothingness to the other side of the giant's spoonful.

I stamped on my brake pedal like it was a rattle-snake's head but I was doing nothing to stop the car. I felt it tip forward. I gazed around wildly to see a semi-circle of sheer cliffs a hundred and fifty feet high, and a mass of rocky quarry workings below.

Nothing was going to help me now.

I screamed the first prayer I'd said in ten years and watched in terror as the rocks leaped up to meet me in my shiny, dark green, convertible coffin.

I've tried a hundred times to run my mental video of the scene, but there's just about ten seconds before the tape goes blank; ten seconds that felt like ten minutes when, half asleep, I must have seen the lights turn green, put my gear shift into first, gunned the throttle and skidded off the road, over the edge of the quarry where Sir John Fielding's ancestors had got the stone to build his house.

I never did get to see Aldrich Manor that weekend.

I came round I don't know how much later. The records suggest, taking the time I left the pub, and the time it probably took me to drive four miles, that it was only another ten minutes or so. I don't know. I don't know how long I'd been asleep in the car before I drove the thing over the edge.

I came round with a lump on my head the size of a

Christmas pudding, both legs trapped beneath the steering column in the long, shallow well in front of the driver's seat and a strong smell of gasoline irritating my nostrils.

It was a miracle, the policeman said, that the car hadn't landed upside down. Maybe my prayer had worked, I thought; I should try it again sometime. It was a bigger miracle that the fuel hadn't ignited and burned my wrecked car to a black, steel skeleton.

I was feeling very lucky, lying in a hospital bed listening to the policeman.

I told him.

"You are, Mr. Felton, very lucky. Much luckier than you deserve."

He didn't sound as if he was making a joke. I turned my head, painfully, to see for sure. He wasn't. He looked like a first-grade schoolteacher about to stand me in the corner.

"Do you know how much you'd had to drink?" he asked, dryly.

"Too much," I said contritely. "But it wasn't my fault. I thought I had two, maybe three single vodkas, really not enough to make me do what I did. The guy I was with, he was buying the drinks." I shrugged, and winced. "He was a reporter, trying to get information from me. I guess he was getting me a lot more to drink than I thought. You can't always tell with vodka, not till it's too late, anyway."

"Was the reporter called Geoffrey Haslam?"

"That's him," I said.

"Hmm. If he was buying, he must have known how much you'd had. He turned up a few minutes after us, taking pictures while we cut you out."

I smiled cynically. "The greedy bastard. He already had all he needed from me for a good Monday story."

"It's not funny, Mr. Felton, driving in that sort of condition. You may be very lucky to be alive, and none too damaged, but you won't be driving for a year or two. We feel very strongly in this country that people in the public eye should set an example."

Thank God I'd just got my pilot's license. But I kept that thought to myself, and tried to look contrite. It was hard, though. I was so darn happy to be alive.

I spent half an hour attempting to give the policeman an accurate statement of what had happened. By the time he left, I was feeling pretty foolish, and almost contrite. I was exhausted, too, from what people like to call the trauma of the whole incident. I gazed around the room at a few bunches of flowers that had already turned up, and fell back into a sound sleep.

I was woken by a cozy-plump nurse messing around with my pillows. She apologized and looked embarrassed. Maybe they didn't get too many famous customers in this hospital.

"That's okay," I said with my best friendly smile. "I was getting bored sleeping anyway."

"You've got a visitor waiting for you outside. I didn't let her come in while you were still asleep."

"Her?" I asked.

She gave a shy grin, nodded and bustled out of the room in that special way nurses have.

A moment later, she was replaced by a tall, well-bred-looking sort of a girl. Her jaw and cheekbones were strong without being too strong, framed by a mop of bobbed, natural blond hair. Her big blue eyes were forthright but slightly defensive. She was a blend of Bambi and Amazon hard to resist.

Someone like Henry James would have described her as statuesque, except she had the longest, most visibly provocative legs I'd ever seen at close quarters. Of Camilla Fielding's height of six feet, the first four were below the waist.

The sight of those legs, then the half-smiling, soft-as-sponge lips quickly undid all the effects of the tranquilizers they'd given me to keep me calm and make me sleep.

I propped myself up and smiled. "Hi, shorty," I said. "How are you?"

"Hungry, you little worm."

"Not such a little worm," I corrected her. "Did you miss dinner for me?"

"Yes, but I've brought our first course with me." She pulled some smoked salmon and skinny slices of brown bread out of her bag. "They said I couldn't give you any Chablis to go with it. Apparently you'd already had rather a lot to drink."

"You've been talking to that policeman, haven't you?"

"No, just eavesdropping. Should be on the front page of the *News of the World* tomorrow."

"Oh my Gahd!" I said with exaggerated dismay, not too worried about the fact that of the ten thousand or so people who might be caught drinking and driving that evening, only my blameless, victimless misdemeanor would be reported on the front pages. I'd long ago reconciled myself to take the rough with the smooth that the British press liked to dole out.

"You might not mind," Camilla said, "but Captain Toby Jug will."

"Good. I hope he bursts a blood vessel over it. It was his bloody idea that I saw Geoff Haslam and it was that little toe-rag trying to get me oiled up and indiscreet that did the damage. I don't suppose the policeman told that to the gentlemen of the press?"

"I didn't hear him," Camilla said. "It sounds like a fairly pathetic excuse, anyway. I'm sure it's not very original."

"It may not be original, but it's true, dammit. I know what I should feel like after three short vodkas; when I drove away from that pub I felt like I'd been swimming in the stuff. Look, I'm not asking for your sympathy. I admit I should have noticed what he was doing—it's not the first time it's been tried. But I would like it if you believed me, even if no one else will."

"All right, I believe you. Now, do you think that chubby little nurse would get us a couple of plates for our smoked salmon?"

"I'll ring her," I answered and pressed the button over my bed. The nurse came right in, as if she had been outside the door. I hoped she hadn't heard Camilla's description of her, though I could have explained that Camilla was basically envious of short women.

I asked for knives and plates and the nurse smiled and went to get them.

Camilla sat down in the ugly, vinyl-covered chair beside the bed and stretched out her magnificent legs.

"My mother was sorry not to meet you," she said. "She wanted to talk to you about Corsican Lady. So, she's coming to visit you tomorrow. I thought I'd better warn you."

"Warn me? Why, does she bite or something?"

"Only in fun, you know, like a puppy."

"Should I stroke her?"

Camilla laughed. "You could try. Anyway, how long are you going to be a guest of the National Health Service?"

"A few days at the most. I got a bump on the head and what the copper called 'minor cuts and abrasions.' I don't think I ever had an abrasion before. I was lucky."

"When you go back and have a look where you crashed, you'll see that you were more than lucky. Someone must like you up there." She glanced at the ceiling.

"It's funny you should say that. I just had time to put in a quick supplication as I headed for the rocks. You know, I really thought I was on my way to the meat factory."

"They wouldn't have got much meat off you," Camilla said with a smile that only lightly overlaid her obvious horror at what had nearly happened.

The nurse came back in with two trays and two plates for us.

"Visiting time's over really," she said, "but it doesn't matter, so don't hurry yourselves."

She left and Camilla took three long slices of pink fish from her packet and laid them on a plate for me. Beside the salmon, she put two slices of brown bread and two quarters of lemon. She plucked a large wooden pepper mill from her bag. "Would you like me to grind for you?" she asked.

"Very much," I answered with overstated sincerity, and she scattered pepper over the smoked fish.

She passed me the plate and I pounced on it hungrily. I hadn't eaten since the night before.

Camilla picked at hers, and told me about the other people who were staying the weekend at Aldrich Manor. They didn't sound a lot of fun, and I wasn't too interested, but I was grateful to her. I didn't actually know her that well; we'd never even been out to dinner alone, but in her aloof sort of way I could see that she really had been worried about me, and that gave me a bigger charge than I would have thought.

The whole time she was in the room with me, though, she didn't touch me. In a way, I was quite relieved, because I don't think I could have stood the excitement, and not being able to do anything about it.

I was sorry when she left after half an hour, promising to come back the next evening with some dinner and telling me again to be careful of her mother.

I already knew a little about Lady "Bunty" Fielding; and what I knew, I liked the sound of. She was one of those great, hearty ladies of the turf who make racing in England as special and honorable as it still manages to be.

I had noticed that women owners were often likely to be more genuinely sporting than the men. Women seldom own horses for reasons of vanity or status symbol. They are usually much less concerned about the commercial viability of their animals, and they tend to love them more than the men do. That makes them much easier owners to ride for. They understand, for instance, that a filly might not always be feeling in top form. And once they've chosen you to ride, provided you do your best and don't knock their horses about with your whip, they tend not to criticize your riding. They don't feel the need to assert their authority in the way most male owners do.

Bunty Fielding was, by all accounts, a fine example of this type of lady owner, and she had recently sent Corsican Lady, a three-year-old filly of Classic potential, to Toby Ellerton's yard. Corsican Lady was entered for the One Thousand Guineas—the first fillies' Classic of the season, but I felt she would do better in the mile and a half of the Oaks. She had never yet run beyond a mile, and in the early stage of her races she always struggled to lay up with the pace. I felt that the further she went, the better she would be. But we would have to decide next week if she was going to run in the Guineas.

Lady Fielding had been to the yard a few times since Corsican Lady had arrived, but it happened that I hadn't been there when she had. As Ellerton's first jockey, I was the obvious choice to ride her filly, and I knew that was why she wanted to meet me.

She came into my room shortly after ten next morning. When I say "came into my room," I should say "arrived and filled my room." It wasn't just that she was physically a large woman—Camilla's height and twice her volume—her personality flooded into the place and took up residence in every corner and cranny.

She had good, high cheekbones, well fleshed and colored by the open air. Below honest grey eyes, she had a surprisingly neat, slightly upturned nose. Her face was framed by a practical, pudding-basin mop of black and silver-streaked hair. Her clothes—made for dog-walking, not cat-walking—showed that her interest lay in quality rather than fashion. She gave an impression of forthright dependability and I liked her on sight.

"Morning, Mr. Felton," she boomed as she came in.

Her appearance made me want to stand up to greet her. I started to swing a leg from under the sheets.

"Don't be so silly," she ordered as she reached out a hand to give mine a vicious tug.

"Good morning, Lady Fielding," I muttered with unusual meekness.

"How are you feeling?" she asked as she lowered herself into my visitor's chair.

"Not too bad, thanks," I replied.

"You're jolly lucky to be feeling anything. Sounds as though your chances of being a corpse were odds on. Camilla says you were pickled."

"Well, er . . ."

"It's all right. She told me why. Must be one of the hazards of the game these days, though I daresay they were doing it in Fred Archer's day too. Well, I'm sorry to be meeting you like this, rather put a damper on my dinner party last night, but I did want to talk to you about Corsican Lady. D'you want to ride her in the Guineas?"

"I'm not sure, Lady Fielding."

"What do you mean, not sure? What's wrong with her?"

"There's nothing wrong with her. I just think we'd do better to concentrate on the Oaks. It's a better distance for her, it'll give her more time to find her feet."

"She was bred for twelve furlongs, of course, but she looks as good over a mile as any of the other fillies I've seen."

"Maybe she is, and maybe she could do it, but I just think it might take so much out of her, she might not recover in time for the Oaks. She's quite a delicate filly, you know. Anyway, Lady Fielding, that's just my opinion. Maybe Captain Ellerton thinks otherwise and it's up to you and him."

"I'd always rather hear a good jockey's view first. The next question is, will you be ready to ride in ten days anyway?"

"The doc says yes," I replied, "and he looks like an honest man."

"You're still looking pretty peaky, though. And my main reason for sending the filly to Ellerton was that I'd be guaranteed to get you to ride her."

"That's very flattering, Lady Fielding."

"Call me Bunty; and I'll call you Jake, if I may."

"I'd better not call you that in front of the Captain. He'd have apoplexy."

"Pompous little twit!"

I assumed she was referring to my guv'nor, not me.

She stood up abruptly. "Well, I'm glad to have met you, Jake. I hope you're up and about soon. I have your home phone number so I'll give you a ring about the filly. Best of luck, and steer clear of the vodka from now on."

She took a couple of ground-covering strides toward the door, stopped and turned round. "Oh," she said, "I nearly forgot." She fished into a large floppy straw basket she carried, pulled out the biggest bunch of grapes I'd ever seen, smiled and placed them on the bedside table. "Don't eat them all at once," she commanded. "'Bye."

"Goodbye," I said as her back disappeared through the door.

I was elated by her visit. You couldn't really fault the old battleaxe, and I could appreciate, beneath a few surplus layers of fatty tissue, something of her daughter in her.

And, like I'd told her, I was flattered. I guessed she must have seen me riding dozens, if not hundreds of times, so she knew my style and, above all, she knew I always tried. She obviously appreciated that, and it was for that that I had come to England.

At least, that had been one of my more positive reasons for coming.

/////////// CHAPTER 2

An hour or two later, they brought me a full-blown English Sunday lunch, well-meant but with all taste cooked out of it. I didn't want it, but I didn't want to upset my chubby little nurse either. I managed to eat most of it before falling back into an uncomfortable doze. I was feeling scratchy when my next visitor was announced, and a lot more scratchy when he sidled into the room.

"Er, hello, Jake," Geoff Haslam said. He was wearing the same clothes as he had been the day before. He looked as though he had slept in them.

"What do you want?" I asked, letting him know that whatever it was, he wasn't going to get it. "You've had all the interviews you're ever getting from me."

"Just to find out how you are."

"Just to round off your story for tomorrow, you mean. Why didn't you ask the nurses? They'll tell you more than me. You've got a nerve, coming here after what you did."

Geoff tightened and looked nervous. "What d'you mean?"

"Getting me pissed like that."

He relaxed, even gave a nasty grin. "Come on, Jake, you're old enough not to have fallen for that."

"Yeah," I nodded. "But I thought you wanted to interview me, not kill me. I don't even want to know what I told you. Just get the hell out of here." I clammed my mouth shut and turned away.

Geoff took his cue, quite happily I should think, and left the room without a word. His skin was as thick as a nun's winter drawers.

After he'd gone, I reflected for a while that I'd let him off lightly. He'd probably cost me a week's racing, a year's driving, and a brand new Aston Martin. One day, I thought, he'll pay.

Meanwhile, I heaved myself out of bed to wash and shave before Camilla came. I was feeling a lot better now, and it showed in the face that stared back at me from the mirror. Like anyone else's, it was a face I had taken for granted all my life, though I knew I'd been lucky to inherit more from my father than just his talent with horses.

Dad had straight brown hair, good clean-cut features and mischievous hazel eyes. And his looks didn't deteriorate over the years after he had come home from gaol up until the yearling dumped him in the yard for the last time. Although he had been a little larger than I was, the face I was looking at now could have been Dad's thirty years before. I grinned at it and began to scrape two days' growth of stubble from it.

Camilla came later. This time she touched me, just once, with her luscious lips on my warm brow. My lips envied my brow and I felt a nice, reassuring tingle in my groin, but that was my ration for the night.

She asked how it had gone with her mother, who had evidently liked what little she'd seen of me. Then she sat down on the bed and chatted about where I'd grown up, and what I'd done as a kid. It made a change.

People here never usually asked me about that sort of thing. They only ever wanted to know about my racing experiences in the States, and I was sick of even thinking about those.

I told her about West Virginia and the farm where I was raised; about the thoroughbreds and working horses I'd been around all my young life; the hogs, the turkeys and the wild deer. I told her about my hunting expeditions to shoot duck, geese, pigeon—anything I knew my mum knew how to cook—and about swimming in ice-cold creeks in rocky valleys, and the colors of the Appalachian autumn.

She listened and seemed honestly interested.

"You must take me over and show me sometime," she said.

I smiled at the prospect until I realized it was her exit line. Maybe she was just putting on a show of good old English upper-class manners. But she blew me a kiss from the door.

Captain Toby Ellerton didn't blow any kisses when he next saw me.

I drove to Lambourn in the Berkshire Downs on the evening of my third day out of hospital. I parked my hired Jaguar XJS on the Captain's elegant, flower-lined gravel drive in front of his copybook red-brick Queen Anne residence, Melbourne House. He was in the yard when I let myself in through the front door, but his wife, Janey, was in the kitchen as usual, looking harassed and overworked. Poor Janey.

"Hello, Jake," she said with a self-erasing smile in her watery blue eyes. "Are you better?"

I stretched a few limbs and inspected them. "They all seem to work, and my abrasions are almost gone."

"Abrasions?" Janey looked slightly alarmed.

"It's okay, they're not contagious. You're looking sort of . . . lovely," I tried.

"Rubbish, Jake. If I ever looked lovely, it was a very long time ago," she said, and she was right.

I tried safer territory. "Miranda's looking lovely."

Janey smiled, with more conviction this time. "Yes, isn't she," and she looked down with pride at a dark chocolate Labrador, lying in a basket with her eight teats swollen in pregnancy.

"Not too long now," I said, sounding knowledge-able.

"Next week, I should think," Janey said.

"Should be a good litter," I said. "Now, where's the Fuhrer?"

"Out in the yard, giving someone hell probably."

"Worse than usual?" I asked.

"Much," she nodded. "*And* he had two winners to-day."

"Yeah, I heard on the radio. Lucky Garry."

"Not so lucky Garry. One of them wasn't supposed to win."

I winced. "Oh well, these things happen. I'll go and find him," I said, and let myself out through the back door.

I took a short cut through the Ellertons' large, tidy kitchen garden, through an arched gateway in the brick wall into the original cobbled courtyard where half a dozen of the best horses were stabled alongside the tack rooms and Ellerton's office.

There were signs everywhere reflecting the Captain's personality. Everything was just so, all historically and architecturally correct, he was proud of telling me. He'd had every window in the house replaced the year before because they were a century out of sync. In the old yard, all the new guttering and drainpipes were cast iron, made just the same as the Victorian ones they had replaced. It was an obsession I could appreciate, but I guessed it was a very expensive one.

I never talked to the Captain about money, except mine, and that was only once a year when we negotiated my contract, but I had a pretty good idea of his income from training racehorses. Right now, with the recent falling off of owners caused by Britain's particularly vicious recession, I reckoned it wasn't enough to pay for his expensive indulgences.

He was an ace at pulling off legitimate coups in handicaps. He gambled hard then. I had no quibble with that. What I couldn't come to terms with were horses being stopped for bookies. I'm not saying that there weren't times when I deliberately didn't give a horse a hard ride if it was lined up for something bigger later and was short of peak fitness. But I never stopped them to order. I still heard the message my mother had drummed into me as a boy. I never had stopped a horse, and I never would. So far, this had cost me the right to do my job in my own country, but I had hoped it was never going to cost me more than that.

Captain Toby knew this, and respected it—at least, he had. But his respect seemed to be a little more grudgingly given lately. Just a couple of days before my crash, he'd jocked me off a fairly certain winner at twenty-four hours' notice. He said he needed Garry's five-pound claim. So my junior, the apprentice, had got the ride, and the horse had come in a fairly plausible fourth.

At least Ellerton hadn't had the gall to ask me to stop the horse, but I guess it wouldn't be long before he asked me not to try too hard on another.

And that would be when he and I would part company.

It was a typically busy evening in the yard, with

horses back from the races being unloaded, lads doing evening stables and the head lad, Tony Heaney, checking on the next day's runners. In the middle of it all, clutching a leather-bound clipboard, stood the Captain.

He was barking orders, insulting the lads, haranguing the driver. It was hard to keep your eyes off him, and it was hard not to be impressed with the way he seemed to know everything that was going on in every corner of the yard, every minute of the day.

He had once been an amateur rider himself, though his physique was against him, and if he had trouble doing the weights then, now he'd have needed six months in a fat farm to do them.

He stood there like an angry beetroot wearing a fawn suit with a shapeless piece of battered brown felt perched on the top of his black curly hair. Not a pretty sight. Even less pretty when his eye caught mine.

But he had more sense than to bawl me out in front of the rest of them.

"I want to talk to you, Jake," he said. "So don't go anywhere."

"Ready when you are," I said lightly. "I'll be in the office."

"No, go back to the house. I'll see you in the library."

"Yessir," I shrugged, and threw a quick smile to a couple of the lads before walking back through the hole in the brick wall.

The library was a real library. Every piece of wall that wasn't taken up by door and windows was lined with bookcases, floor to ceiling. I'd had to fill in time there once or twice before and I'd taken a look at some of the shelves. There were thousands of books about every subject you could think of from stock rearing in the seventeenth century to Wittgenstein, Chaucer to Tom Wolfe. I guess for the most part they were inherited from the grand old family house in Yorkshire, which Ellerton liked to talk about, and I would have said that, apart from the books on architecture and bloodstock, he got more of a kick from just looking at their well-bound backs than he did from reading them. But a library was something an English gentleman ought to have, so he had one.

There was also a large partners' desk with a brass lamp on it, and a couple of deep, threadbare easy chairs. On a low table between the chair were scattered a few months' worth of racing magazines, *The Field* and *Private Eye*. I knew Toby would leave me sitting here for at least twenty minutes so I picked up the latest issue of the *Eye* and settled down in one of the big chairs to try and catch up on my self-instruction course in Understanding The English.

When finally he arrived, he looked as mad as he had back at the yard. He stomped in and banged the big solid door behind him. He didn't waste time on small talk.

"Jake, what the hell have you been doing? Do you realize just how much damage you've done to this yard by behaving the way you have? I've already had owners on the phone asking me to find other jockeys to ride their horses."

He was going to go on but I cut him off with a loud laugh. I hadn't got up from where I was sitting, but I did now. "Which owners?" I asked. I was curious to hear what he would say. I dropped the magazine back on the table and walked over to sit on the desk where he'd planted himself and looked him straight in the eye.

"It's irrelevant which owners," he answered. "Every owner with a horse in this yard is as important as the next. What matters is that my senior jockey gets himself so drunk that he drives off the edge of a bloody precipice; it might just as easily have been a million-dollar yearling. Your contract with me states quite categorically that it becomes invalid if you bring this yard into disrepute."

I stood up. "You're right, Captain. I realize what I must do. I quit."

Ellerton's tomato head gave a quick sideways jerk on his fat neck. "What?" he snapped.

"I said I'll do the decent thing, save you from all this embarrassment. I'll resign." I gave him a big, bland smile. "Where do I sign?"

Ellerton started back for a moment. I enjoyed watching him struggle. With an effort I had to admire, he produced a good pretence of a genial smile.

"Now look here, Jake," he said, oozing reasonableness.

"No, you look here, Captain." I gave it as much edge as I could. "You sent me to see that Geoff Haslam."

"You'd walk away from Dawn Raider and Corsican Lady?"

I shrugged. "Corsican Lady would follow me. And I think I'd pick up a few more rides. So I've brought your yard into disrepute—I'll resign, like you were about to suggest. Where do I sign?"

"Come on, Jake, I wasn't going to ask you to resign. I had nothing to do with Geoff Haslam getting you pissed, believe me. I don't know what the hell he was trying to do, and I don't mind admitting you're an important part of the team I've built up here. We work well together, we understand one another."

"Correction: we used to understand one another."

He didn't reply for a moment. He spun his desk chair round and looked out of the window where an evening sun lit his formal rose gardens between low, scudding rain clouds.

"Okay, Jake, I'm sorry. I don't want you to leave. He turned back to see my reactions.

I didn't give him much to go on. "I'll sleep on it," I said. "I'll tell you tomorrow." I turned and walked out of the room, across the flagstoned hall and out of the front door to my hired Jaguar. I started the car, cruised slowly round the wide sweep in front of the house, looking straight ahead, and drove out between massive brick pillars. On the top of each pillar crouched a stone dragon, glowering across at its opposite number. Like the Captain and me, they evidently thrived on conflict.

When I showed up at seven next morning to ride out with the first lot, Toby didn't let anyone else in the yard see the relief on his face.

He told me with his usual bluntness to ride an unraced, very expensive two-year-old filly called Rock Beat.

"She's only ever had a girl on her; she looks useful but I want her to do her first piece of work over five furlongs and for you to teach her something. She doesn't know what the game's all about yet."

I nodded. Usually I drove up in the Land Rover with Toby and took over from one of the lads when they reached the gallops. But sometimes it was useful to get to know a horse on the way up.

There was a lot of kidding and innuendo from the lads and girls as we walked our horses out of the yard and turned up a wide green lane that led to the top of the Lambourn Downs. Apart from my brief appearance the evening before, I hadn't been seen in the yard since my accident. But everyone there had heard the story and read the Sunday Trash, and reckoned they knew me well enough to rib me.

"Nearly got boxed in permanently," one shouted from the back of the string.

I took it, relieved to find that my bruises were giving me no grief now I was in the saddle again. But I had my hands full. The filly I was on was nervous and wouldn't relax. I tried the old tricks of taking my feet out of the irons and pinching the skin on her wither to make her walk, but neither worked. She still refused to settle when I took her to the front of the string, so I resigned myself to an irritating jig-jogging ride the whole way up to the gallops.

The south wind that had been blowing all night had seen off the smudgy clouds of the evening before. Now it had done its job, it had become a gentle breeze in a bright, sharp, blue morning. The larks were up and doing their thing and as we broke from the hedges and woodland of the valley onto the open green grassland that swept up toward the ridges, I was sharply conscious, as I often was, that here was one of the things that made racing in England so special for me. Back home, every worktrack looked the same—flat left-handed dirt.

We found Toby at the top of the gallop with one of his less prestigious owners, a big man named Smethwick with a face like a side of under-done beef and hands like legs of lamb. Someone had told me he was in construction, warehousing and meat. I guessed he wasn't too choosy what he did as long as it made big money and didn't get him indicted. He had half a dozen animals in Toby's yard, including the filly I was riding. Both men, wrapped in sheepskins against the chilly morning, were leaning on Toby's Land Rover with binoculars at the ready. The ancient turf on the gallop had been lightly mowed and pegged with markers at every furlong from bottom to top.

We walked past in single file. Toby carefully inspected each animal as it passed him and we carried on walking around in a twenty-yard circle.

Toby and his owner strolled up.

"How is she?" Toby called out to me.

"She's a little more settled now, Captain, but she's been on her toes for most of the way up. I don't think she's nervous; she's just pleased to be out."

"Well, whatever it is, I'll be interested to see what you think of her. Take her down with Sun Surf and Yareel and just sit in behind them for four furlongs. Try and keep her settled, then if she's good enough, join up with them and let her sit upsides for the last furlong or so."

I nodded and turned with the two fillies in front of me, away from the circle, and headed off toward the bottom of the gallop. Behind us, we heard the Captain splitting the rest of the string into work groups of twos and threes, which followed us down.

Selecting which horses should work together is a positive skill, and one at which the Captain excelled. A horse worked with another which is too good for it gets disheartened, the good horse doesn't do enough, and neither benefits. The idea is that they enjoy the work and the better horses pull the others along with them.

The two fillies in front of me had both already raced and won, which meant that the Captain thought something of the one I was on. We walked and hacked down a dirt track flecked with white chalk and glittering flint. It took us fifteen minutes to reach the end of a belt of old beech trees where the gallop began. When we stepped off the track back onto the grass, my filly couldn't contain herself. With a loud squeal, she put in a couple of small bucks to let me know how she felt.

The lad on Snow Surf looked round.

"Ready?" he shouted.

We lifted our backsides out of our saddles and were away at a good sharp canter, heading back up the slope toward Ellerton and Smethwick.

The Captain had been right about Rock Beat; she was very green. In the first couple of furlongs, she alternated between running away and being off the bridle. It was only when we passed the three-furlong markers and the two horses in front joined upsides that she got the message and settled into a beautiful, smooth action.

As the other two quickened the pace, all I had to do to keep in touch was shorten my reins a fraction and squeeze with my knees. We were working at a really good pace now, but my filly was barely ticking over. For her size, her stride was enormous, yet when I asked her to quicken up and join the others, she stretched even further and got up to them as if it had cost her no effort at all.

I didn't want her to overdo herself; I sat alongside the others, keeping a firm hold on her head. But when I glanced across, I saw that they were both struggling to stay with me. And I knew I was on something a little special.

We shot past the Captain and Rock Beat's owner at the six-furlong marker.

"That'll do!" he shouted at the top of his voice.

We let the horses ease down in their own time to the end of the gallop. In small groups, the rest of the string arrived from behind us and we all walked round in a big steaming circle while we waited for the Captain to join us.

"Well?" he called when I came in earshot. "How did she feel?"

"What do you think?" I laughed.

"Fuckin' lovely!" bellowed her owner with none of Toby's reluctance to praise.

"She ran a little green," Toby said. He didn't like owners to think their horses could do it all by themselves. "But with a bit more education she'll learn."

" 'Ere, Jake, what d'you think of her, then?"

I was beside them now but the filly didn't want to stand still. I walked her in a tight circle round them. "I'd say you haven't wasted your money, Mr. Smethwick."

The owner boomed with laughter. "I'm not famous for wasting money." He'd forgotten that Toby had told him to buy the horse, and even then, buying yearlings is about as chancy as putting your money on a roulette number. Trouble was, so far he'd always been lucky.

"I'll see you back at the yard." Ellerton nodded to me with more curtness than normal.

I shrugged and set off behind the rest of the string

who were already walking back down toward the track home.

I untacked my horse and chatted to a couple of the lads before I went into the house for breakfast. Janey greeted me with a wispy smile.

"I'm glad you came back," she said.

"I thought I'd miss you." I gave her a quick kiss and a follow-up squeeze on her behind which she ignored.

"Toby would have missed you," she said.

"That wasn't one of my problems. Where is he?"

"He saw Smethwick off, then Penruddock rang, ten minutes ago. I think he's still on the phone."

Mike Penruddock was the Kuwaiti prince's racing manager. He was nobody's favorite, having become embarrassingly arrogant since taking over the job. But Penruddock wielded his second-hand power very dextrously. These days, owners with money to spend were rarer than white rhinos, and Penruddock's boss appeared to have it in limitless quantities. And though he was no more than a 35-year-old ex-cavalry captain, people stood when they spoke to Penruddock on the phone.

When Toby walked into the kitchen, I could see that Penruddock had not made him happy. His face had turned a pale strawberry roan and there was a glazed look to his eyes as if he was fighting back tears. Even Janey was startled into sympathy.

"What's the matter?" She stopped prodding the sausages in the frying pan.

Ellerton didn't answer. He picked up a large jug of orange juice, poured himself a tall glass and knocked it back as if it had been Scotch.

"The ignorant little shit!" he said to no one in particular and flopped into his high-backed elm carver.

"Penruddock?" I prompted.

He nodded. "He knows bugger all about racing and tries to tell *me* my horses aren't running straight. Sheikh Ahmed's already had twelve winners this season. Who else would have given him that?" We were supposed to know the answer, so he didn't tell us and went on. "I'd like to know where the hell he's going to send them now."

"You mean he's taking some away?" Janey asked in consternation.

"Not some. All! Twenty of the bastards. For Christ's sake, that's a third of my yard. He knows fucking well I'll never replace them this season." Ellerton stared about him wildly then slammed his fist on the table.

I wasn't too pleased about it myself. I had ambitions too and Sheikh Ahmed owned Dawn Raider. But I didn't want to hang around and be part of this discussion. Penruddock had grounds for saying what he had, and I wasn't prepared to take Ellerton's side against him.

I stood up. "I'll pass on breakfast, Janey. Sorry. I hope you sort it out, Captain. I'll see you at the races."

He stared at me like I was Brutus with a bloody knife in my hand, but said nothing. I walked out and through the front door. I closed it behind me with relief, got in my car and headed for home.

///////////// CHAPTER 3

My home, Coombe House, sounds English and old but looks Swedish and new, so most of my English friends don't like it. They don't say so, but I can see their lips pucker when they first arrive. But I love it.

It's set close to the head of a small valley and the main rooms all have clear views through tall plates of glass, down the valley to the big wide meanders of the Test. I have my own brook to fish in, which feeds the Test, and two hundred acres of beech woods and pasture running down to it.

It's not such a beautiful house I admit, but I reckon I spend more time looking out from it than I do looking at it. It's cool in summer, warm in winter and everything works. The man who sold it to me went bust before he had finished it, which was lucky, because he wasn't planning a gym, a swimming pool or a squash court.

Everyone thought I'd want some kind of stable yard too, but I didn't. The place had everything I wanted now; above all, privacy and peace.

When I reached the big white gates, I opened them from my car and checked in the mirrors that they closed behind me. I carried on down the drive curving away through beeches and oaks to the dell where the house sat. The garage door slid up and the Jag purred in.

I walked straight through into the comfortable kitchen where the friendly buzz of the deep-freeze welcomed me home. My kitchen wasn't just for cooking. The phone, the fax, the TV, the video, the sound system and a small PC were all in reach of my big oak table.

I ground some coffee and put it in a pot to percolate and hit the "play" button on the CD player—Paul Brady, "Trick or Treat"—then sat down to check my faxes and my answerphone. Nothing too important there, though a message on the phone from Bunty Fielding sounded interesting.

I flipped through the pages of *Sporting Life* to find the declarations for the rest of the week's racing and checked my rides. Out of thirty possible till Saturday night, I was provisionally booked for sixteen. But five of those were on Sheikh Ahmed's horses. I'd have to help myself to a piece of humble pie and phone Penruddock.

I keyed his number and was answered by a girl who sounded like Camilla with adenoids.

"This is Jake Felton. Is Mike there?"

"Oh, hi. How're you? Michael's popped out."

"Will he be long?"

"Well, actually, I just saw him go into the loo with the *Telegraph* so he could be twenty minutes."

"Great. Can you get him to call me back?"

"Okay, yah. Has he got your number?"

Aren't you meant to be his secretary? I thought.
"Sure," I said. "Thanks. Goodbye."

"Byee."

I put the phone down and shook my head. This man
ran fifty million dollars' worth of bloodstock for the
Sheikh and he had some upper-crust dumbo taking his
calls and broadcasting his bowel movements.

I rang Lady Fielding next.

Someone at Aldrich Manor told me she was in London. I dialed the London number and Camilla answered.

"Hello, Jake. How are you?" Unlike the girl at
Penruddock's office, I think she wanted to know.

"I rode work this morning. Nothing hurts."

"At Toby's?"

"Yeah. I rode a really good filly of Big Jim
Smethwick's."

"We thought you might not be going back."

I laughed. "So did I. News travels fast. Is that why
your mother rang me?"

"I expect so. I didn't know she had. So it's her you
want?"

"I wouldn't say that. I'm just returning her call like a
good-mannered boy. But while you're on, are you racing today?"

"I doubt it. I think I'm on my own in the gallery."

"How about dinner?"

"In London?"

"If you want."

"Okay."

"I'll come round about seven."

"Do you know where we live?"

"I've got the address and I can read a map."

"Great. I'll see you then. Do you still want to talk to
Mum?"

"Sure."

"I'll get her. 'Bye."

A few moments later Bunty Fielding's voice was filling my ear.

"Morning, Jake. Camilla tells me you were back at Ellerton's this morning."

"That's right."

"We heard there was a bit of a disagreement."

"No. No disagreement. He thought I'd disgraced him by getting drunk and nearly killing myself. I agreed and offered to resign. Then he changed his mind."

"Of course he didn't want you to resign. He's got enough problems already, and I hear he's got a few new ones this morning."

I grunted my confirmation.

"What are you going to do if the Sheikh does take his horses away?"

"There's no 'if' about it. They're going. But I guess Penruddock will still give me the rides."

"What should I do about Corsican Lady?"

"Leave her where she is. She'll be fine. Whatever happens, I'll ride her."

"You'll let me know if you think there's a problem, won't you?"

"Of course I will, Lady Fielding."

"Call me Bunty, for heaven's sake. Thank you very much, Jake."

"Don't mention it, Bunty. I'll let you know if things change, okay?"

"Good. We'll see you at Newbury, then, this afternoon. Got any winners?"

"Yeah. Pink Pigeon in the maiden."

"Best of luck. Well, goodbye."

She put the phone down before I could answer.

She may have been grateful to me; I thought she was, and she probably realized it was mutual. Getting rides was never a problem for me, but getting on horses that could win was becoming a lot harder. Big owners were employing jockeys to ride all their horses, no matter who trained them, and no matter if a particular trainer had a retained stable jockey of his own. It was a relief to know that, whatever happened, I would keep the ride on Corsican Lady, but my main task was to make sure I still had the rides on Sheikh Ahmed's big string of horses.

I spent the next hour loading data into my PC. My program, Optimequus, had been written by a computer wizard who was a racing fan in his spare time. He had considered it a privilege, he said, to do it for me; I think he'd already been turned down by just about every other jockey at the top of the league.

It was basically just another way of handicapping horses, using speed ratings combined with the rating of its trainer. The Captain would have been pleased to know he had one of the highest.

Out of habit and to clear my head, I walked through to my covered pool, stripped off and swam twenty lengths. I followed this up with fifteen minutes on the Nautilus gear in the gym and five minutes on the punch bag. My natural weight was a good fourteen pounds higher than I kept it. I'd found the best way of keeping it stable was by swimming, running and eating to a strict, boring diet. But, although I preferred hard exercise to sitting in a sauna, I had to go easy to avoid putting on a lot of heavy muscle that I didn't need.

I was just drying after a quick shower when the phone rang.

I wrapped myself in a towel robe and went through to the kitchen to take it.

"Morning, Jake. Michael Penruddock here."

"Morning, Michael." I tried his cavalry officer accent; he hated it. The English jockeys didn't do that sort of thing.

"I take it you've rung me about the Sheikh's horses."

"I didn't ring to check on your bowel movements."

"What?"

"It doesn't matter. I wanted to know if I'll still keep

the ride on Dawn Raider in the Guineas, and all the others."

"Yes, of course. Provided Toby doesn't try and claim you for something else."

"He's only got Latin Dancer and he won't be ready in time. He's been held up with a bruised foot."

"Good, then you can ride Dawn Raider. I'm afraid the Captain didn't take it too well this morning. How was he when you saw him?"

"Like a dog that's just had its bone taken away. But then that's not surprising, is it?"

"He brought this on himself, you know," Penruddock said with his famous pomposity. "He can't really think I'm going to pay training fees for good horses so that he can fiddle with them to feather his own nest. However, I may suggest to His Highness that we leave Dawn Raider where he is, at least until after the Guineas. It would be foolish to move him so close to the race, and I can't see Ellerton trying anything in a Classic, and I'm sure I can rely on you to keep your eye on him."

I was beginning to feel like everyone's spy at Toby's yard.

"Anyway," Penruddock went on, "let's have a chat sometime. I'd like to know your plans for next season."

"Yeah, okay. I'll see you at the races."

I put the phone down with a smile. At least I was keeping the rides, even if the Captain was losing his fees. The phone was hardly back in its bracket when it cheeped at me again.

"Hello, Jake?" A quick, sharp Irish voice that originated from the boglands of central Ireland.

"Hello, Mick. Do you want a lift to Newbury?"

"I thought I might as well take advantage of you, before you fall from grace like me."

Mick Hagan had been banned from driving earlier in the year. My case wouldn't come up for a couple of weeks.

"Sure, I've got a ride in the first, so I'll pick you up in an hour."

"You're a charitable fella, Jake. See you later, then." He put the phone down.

I wasn't being charitable with Mick so much as repaying his charity. Since my arrival in England, he'd taken more trouble to tell me what was going on than anyone else. And it wasn't just that he was an old jockey on the way down making himself feel better by helping a young jockey on the way up. He had always seemed to me to be a real nice man. Unfortunately, he was also a crook. A wily old horseman who knew countless undetectable ways to stop a horse winning. He always made sure he rode just enough winners each season to carry on getting the rides, but he had surrendered long ago to the reality that losing often made more money than winning.

But they were his morals, not mine. He was an Irish version of my father.

If I'd been a trainer, I wouldn't have given him a ride with any confidence, unless a horse was starting way down the betting. But he'd never done me any harm, and I enjoyed his company more than a lot of the other jockeys'. He lived six miles away, and I often gave him a ride to the races. I was always glad to do it.

I put down the phone and noticed the answering machine flashing again. Someone had left a message while I'd been in the gym. I played the tape.

"Hello, Jake." It was a husky, female voice, confident with a hint of an American accent; so confident, the speaker didn't bother to say who she was. "How are you? I was hoping I might have seen you before now." Meaning—why the hell haven't you been in touch? "This must be the third message I've left. Anyway, I'm over in England for a bit, and I think we should get together, don't you? I'm staying at the Connaught. The old fellow's bought a house in Curzon Street, and I'll be moving in there in a couple of weeks."

The old fellow was her husband, Leonard Zimmer. "But ring me at the Connaught before then." She wasn't asking me, she was telling me. "'Bye."

Her message was followed by another from my valet, Martin Fletcher, to check a detail about the afternoon's racing. I dealt with that before allowing my thoughts to return to the previous caller, Sandra Zimmer.

And I found her demanding, voluptuous voice still tingling my ears as I drove to Mick Hagan's. I'd met Sandy the year before in Kentucky. The stewards at Ascot had given me a week's holiday for overusing my whip. I hadn't been, but there had been a lot of fuss about that kind of thing in the papers, and I guessed they were trying to show the great British public that they occasionally listened to them. I was sore about it. Like I've said, I always tried to win, and there are definitely some horses that need reminding; sometimes you get a little carried away. So, with a week on my hands, I'd taken the opportunity to go home, see my mother, and look in at the Keeneland sales.

As usual around the premium sales, there was a lot of social activity, maybe five parties a night to go to. I had arrived feeling pissed off and sorry for myself, so I didn't take too much trouble not to overindulge. I ate too much, I drank too much, and I slept with more women than I should have done. Sandy was the final fling before I went back to England to sober up.

Some fling. Some woman. I didn't know anything about her when she took me home with her. She'd found me in one humungous Blue Grass mansion and led me to another, three times the size, where she said she sometimes lived. She didn't mention a husband, though somebody told me later he was away, tending the Far Eastern end of his vast chain of burger restaurants. She didn't seem too worried about the few dozen assorted servants and flunkies around the place, so I guessed she was a free agent; anyway, she was a grown-up girl so I didn't see any reason to ask. By the time we were between her golden silk sheets, I didn't give a damn. She made love with the committed zeal of a ten-year-old boy confronted with a knickerbocker glory, or maybe ten knickerbocker glories. Her appetite, her skill and her sheer dedication to the job would have alarmed me if I hadn't been too excited to notice. She must have had at least fifteen years' more experience than I had, but I did my best to keep up, and I didn't hear her complaining.

After spending a night without sleep in a vast, carved four-poster bed imported from some French chateau, she insisted we went out as soon as the sun was up. From a pristine stable yard we took two horses that would have looked at home in the parade ring at Royal Ascot and rode across rolling parkland to a Palladian folly set beside a lake a mile or so from the house. The beautiful little building, no doubt transported brick by brick from a matching English mansion, had a single room furnished with Persian rugs, vast sofas and a fridge full of champagne.

It wasn't long before she wanted more ice cream, and I was ready to supply it.

A few hours later, a silent chauffeur drove me in a maroon Rolls-Royce back to my hotel in Lexington. I packed and flew back to England in such a daze that the stewardesses could have been naked and I wouldn't have noticed.

In the ten months since then, there had been two messages, left when she had been passing through England, I supposed; and then today's.

And I was going to do the same as I had with the first two—ignore it.

Sandra Zimmer had been the best lover I'd ever known, and it would have been frustrating that no girl I had yet met measured up to her performance in bed if I hadn't known, instinctively, that she was a dangerous woman to get involved with. Especially after I'd learned a bit more about her.

She had started her adult life, at seventeen, as a dancer in the Raymond Revue Bar in London. She scrambled up the ladder very fast after that. She had set her sights on marrying the richest man in the world, and in Leonard Zimmer, give or take a billion, she'd found him when she was still only twenty-five. Found him, and persuaded him to trade in his old wife for something with better lines and fewer miles on the clock. I reckoned that such brazen gold-digging took a lot of determination and a skin like an elephant's. It was obvious that she was somebody who liked to use people on a grand scale, and didn't like to be denied. That was why I was going to ignore this message like the others. But as I drove through the hot summer lanes, I couldn't ignore a small twinge of regret in my groin.

I pulled up outside Mick's brick and flint cottage and gave a blast on my horn. He came out with his wife, Mary, as he always did, and gave her a kiss goodbye. Three of his six children, playing on swings and slides in the front garden, waved and wished him luck. He walked up to the car with his jaunty little stride, opened the passenger door and hurled his battered old leather bag onto the back seat of the Jaguar.

"Well then, how are ye?" he asked as I pulled away.

"No pains," I replied. "And nearly no job last night."

"He never tried to blow you out?"

"No. He wanted to scare me, so I thought I'd get in there first."

Hagan turned to me with his funny little crooked grin. "He was trying to bring you into line, was he?"

I nodded.

"And doesn't he know yet that it's a saint he's dealing with?"

I laughed. "There's nothing saintly about my plans for tonight."

"Oh my God. What poor virgin is to be sacrificed tonight, then?"

The little Irishman really didn't approve. He could justify to himself his total lack of ethics on the race-course because, as far as he knew, the Pope had never made any pronouncements about stopping horses.

"I don't think I should tell you that, Mick. I don't want you to get overexcited."

"I just thank the Lord my girls are too young to interest the likes of you."

"I don't know," I wound him up, "Maeve's begin-ning to look a bit tempting. Like spuds, you know what they say, when they're big enough, they're ready."

"Just you keep your horrible little jockey's hands off her; she's only fifteen, for Christ's sake."

I laughed. "Okay, okay. You'd be the last father I'd want coming at me with a shotgun." And I tried a less volatile topic. "Talking of shotguns, you know my place was broken into last week, while I was in hospi-tal?"

"Sure. It made the front page of the *Newbury Ga-zette*. They said nothing was taken."

"At first, I didn't think anything had been. I'd checked everything I thought they'd be interested in. But the trophies and all that garbage hadn't been looked at. There was no sign of tampering with my gun cabinet, but I took a look in there and my big case that holds the Mewar Purdeys was there, so I locked it up. Last night, I wanted to take out a good gun for a shot at the pigeons. I unlocked the case and found one of the Purdeys missing. Now, why the hell would anyone bother to go to all that trouble just to take one of a matched pair? And close the case back up again. It's crazy, they're worth a lot more as a pair. Of course, I've claimed, but those guns are unique. They were made by Purdeys in the 1870s for the Maharana of Mewar; he had the details of his greatest days' shooting with the Prince of Wales engraved onto the action. They're beautiful guns, real works of art. They were the first big present I got in England and they're the best guns I've ever had. They mean a lot to me. I'd give plenty to get the missing one back."

Mick was well known as an enthusiastic amateur shot. He didn't bother with live birds; he wasn't into the social element of game shooting. He just liked to aim at moving targets and hit them. In this sport, he came across a wide and questionable crowd of gun freaks and dealers on and beyond the legal fringes of shooting.

"Are those the guns the Arab gave you? What's his name?"

"The Emir of Bhaqtar. Yeah, he gave them to me after I won the Oaks for him on Shooting Star."

"Did many people know about them, then?"

"Yeah, sure. They were no secret. I did an interview for the *Sunday Times* a few months ago. They asked me what was my favorite possession and I told them the guns. They used a picture of me holding one of them for the piece."

"That wasn't too clever, was it?"

"Why the hell not? If I'd had a favorite Canaletto or something, nobody would have been surprised if I'd been photographed in front of that, would they?"

"It's different with guns," Mick explained unsatisfactorily. "But I wonder why these people went to all that trouble and took only half a pair."

I shrugged. "They'd gone before I had a chance to discuss it with them. The police weren't a lot of help. They just said I must have disturbed them. But if that was the case, they wouldn't have had time to lock everything up again."

Hagan didn't have anything useful to add and tried to be funny. "Maybe they were just opportunists doing a recce for *Through the Key-hole* or *Hello* magazine; you know, seeing if the place was flashy enough, like, because your accent definitely isn't."

He wasn't the first to tell me he didn't like my hybrid accent. These days, Americans assumed I was English, and vice versa. I didn't mind; I found this limbo land gave me a useful perspective.

I laughed. "It suits me, and the women love it. Anyway, what poor brute's chances are you going to mess up today? I see you've got a filly first time out in the maiden."

Hagan nodded. He seemed glad of the opening. "She's a good horse," he said. "I've ridden her in all her work. She gives you a real good feel. Mind you, I've been keeping a fair bit up me sleeve, so even Wooton doesn't know what he's got. I've a pony on her at sixteens, so if you think you're going to win, just remember it's the baby's christening Sunday; I would ask you to be a godfather if you weren't a bloody heathen. But I've the whole family to feed and water and that'll cost me a monkey at least."

Mick knew I didn't respond to this kind of blackmail, but it never stopped him trying. "If I win," I offered, "I'll chuck a couple of hundred in the kitty if you ask me to the party."

"Your fella, I haven't looked him up. He's from some little yard in the back of nowhere, isn't he? He wouldn't ever have a bit of a chance, would he?"

The tone of his voice worried me. There was more anxiety than usual in it. I got the feeling he stood to lose a lot more than twenty-five pounds.

"I don't know. It's his first time out as well, and I've never been on the animal," I told him truthfully.

He glanced across at me sharply. "Look, Jake, as you know, life isn't so easy for an old jockey; it's sort of important that I win that race. You've buggered up my chances enough times before, so you'll not do anything to spoil a good thing today, will you?"

I looked at the road ahead. I hated these discussions, and Mick knew it. Usually, he had the sense not to push it.

"I've already told you, Mick, I've never been on the horse; I've never even seen him," I replied quietly. "But if he's good enough to win, he will."

I had never sat on Pink Pigeon, but I knew a lot about the colt. He was bred and trained by Tommy Preece, a Herefordshire dairy farmer who had had an extraordinary run of wins with three generations of his home-bred animals. Tommy had phoned me a few minutes after I'd arrived back from hospital to ask me if I would be sober enough to ride his colt. I'd told him I probably would be.

"Good," he'd said, "cos this'un's the best yet."

This man, wary of saying anything that might shrink the odds, wasn't known for exaggerating.

As soon as I saw the horse walking round the pre-parade ring at Newbury, twenty minutes before the first race was due off, I knew he hadn't exaggerated. Almost as eye-catching was the girl who was looking after him. She had one of those neat little back ends, nectarine shaped in a pair of stretch jodhpurs, with breasts to match and a pair of randy black eyes in her fresh young face. She looked better for being flustered. She'd obviously arrived late and was doing her best to rub out some of the straw marks on the animal's neck as she led it round.

"Don't bother with that," I said. "If one of Tommy's horses comes into the ring groomed and plaited, the stewards will think it's a ringer."

The girl blushed beneath her dark fringe. "But I want him to look his best."

"He looks fit as a fiddle. That's all that matters." I gave her a smile and walked on to the new changing room which was beginning to fill up. Martin Fletcher, my valet, was looking at his watch in panic.

"Mr. Preece hasn't come with your colors yet, Jake," he lisped.

"Don't worry, he'll be here."

And a moment later he was, standing at the door, still wearing a khaki milking coat.

" 'Ere, Felton," he growled, and proffered a plastic carrier bag containing a set of grubby colors. "Hurry up, I'm late," he said, as if it was my fault.

I changed and weighed out under the testy eye of the Clerk of the Scales then handed the saddle to the trainer who was standing impatiently by the rail.

"I'll see you in a minute," he said and snatched the saddle to hurry out of the door.

I walked back into the changing room and a bell rang for jockeys to get ready. I pulled on my hat and goggles and strolled with the other jockeys out into the parade ring where my trainer was gazing inscrutably at Pink Pigeon being led round by the fresh-faced girl.

"Who's your new groom, Tommy?" I asked.

"Never mind about my fuckin' groom," he grunted out of the side of his mouth. "This 'orse needs ridin' careful, look. All these other buggers'll be runnin' green and lookin' around 'un. 'E's drawn in the middle, so leave him there and get him in front. If he catches sight of anything comin' up either side of 'im, he'll go on. Allus you've got to do is keep 'im straight. Shouldn't be 'ard—I'd've put that bloody girl up if she 'ad a license."

"Got a bit on, then, Tommy?"

"The price of two good heifers, so mind you do your fuckin' job."

I was glad to hear it. I looked at all the runners again, and hoped Bunty Fielding had had a worthwhile punt. She was the only person I'd given the tip to.

When the bell rang to get mounted, I found myself beside Mick Hagan. "I hope you're wearing your lucky emerald jockstrap," I said, just before his trainer legged him up into the saddle. Once he was up, he turned and shot me a look that seemed to combine vitriolic spite with a final plea for loyal co-operation. I looked away with a twinge of guilt, and pointed Pink Pigeon at the exit from the ring.

The procession of two-year-old colts and fillies bounced and jogged from the paddock, along the tarmac walkway which led to the course. Most of the horses were at the races for the first time, but generally well-behaved. I still found it surprising that two-year-old debutantes could be so mature, as one by one they walked on to the course and felt the grass beneath their hooves. Their ears were pricked and their eyes were taking in everything as we set off in groups toward the start.

Mick Hagan joined me with his filly, Miss Minster, waving her pretty head all over the place in an effort to go faster than her jockey wanted. But my colt was settled and collected. Like all Tommy Preece's horses, he had a down-to-earth, practical attitude to the job. It must have been growing up in a field full of bellicose cows that did it.

We reached the start of the straight five-furlong course and circled untidily behind the stalls. Handlers in green bobbled hard hats eyed the horses as if they were a bunch of untrustworthy school kids—school kids who could pack a vicious punch with their back ends if they felt rebellious.

One by one, each was loaded. Pink Pigeon and I went early into stall seven between two colts ridden by apprentices. Mick on his filly was in last, drawn number fifteen against the stands rail. As soon as he was in, the starter dropped his flag, pulled his lever and the front gates flew open.

I grabbed a handful of mane and leaned forward as we sprang from the stalls and went straight into a narrow lead. I could sense that some of the runners had got away slowly and looked to my right to see if it was clear for me to track across to the rails. I remembered just in time that the trainer had told me to run straight down the middle. It would have made sense to run against the rail, but it was risky to ignore Tommy Preece's instructions.

He may not have had an all-weather gallop, or even a good grass one, but Tommy's horses were fit and strong and they knew their job. Pink Pigeon let his long stride take him along easily; he felt as if he was still in third gear, with a lot more to come if needed. He was perfectly happy out on his own. If anything came near him, he took it as a personal challenge and quickened without any asking from me. Tommy was right; the horse was a born front-runner.

Two furlongs from home we could hear the bellow of the crowd in the silver ring. Pink Pigeon pricked his long ears, raised his head and propped slightly. A sharp slap down his left shoulder quickly had him back on an even keel but that short lapse of concentration had been enough for a couple of the others to make a challenge. I looked over both shoulders and saw nothing that was going to cause a problem, but I still hadn't seen anything of Mick Hagan, either. The thought of his expensive christening party flashed through my mind; I hoped he hadn't lost too much money.

We passed the furlong marker, and Pink Pigeon began to pull clear of the horses on either side, but the roar of the crowd told me that someone else was throwing down a challenge. I shortened my reins and squeezed a little harder with my knees. The horse quickened at once. I knew without having to look back that whoever had been challenging wouldn't have come with us. In the shadow of the post, I sneaked a look over my right shoulder and as I turned, Pink Pigeon swung with me, straight across the nose of a small chestnut head. Urgently, I straightened my horse and we crossed the line in front, but I cursed myself for a dumb mistake.

A dozen strides later, the chestnut head appeared again and, beyond it, Mick's face grinning nastily at me.

"I think you just won that for me," he called across as we began to pull up.

I swore again at my own carelessness. "Are you going to object?" I asked.

"If the stewards don't do it off their own back," he said with no hint of apology.

I couldn't blame him; I'd have done the same.

"You wouldn't have won," I said.

"I know. But it won't look like that on the head-on," he crowed.

The stewards' inquiry was announced before we were off the course. I could hear the bookies in front of the grandstand shouting odds on the outcome. That was encouraging; at least there was some doubt about it.

The girl with the big breasts caught hold of Pink Pigeon's reins to lead him back in. "What do you think?" she asked.

"I think if I lose it, I'm in for a major bollocking from your boss."

She patted the horse on the neck. "He's lovely, though, isn't he?"

I agreed, but I was going over what had just happened and trying to picture it from the stewards' point of view. I knew Mick was right; it wouldn't look good.

Tommy Preece was a man of few words at the best of times. As he met us in the winner's enclosure, he could barely bring himself to grunt. I unsaddled quickly and went to weigh in.

I'd just settled on the bench under my changing-room peg when the stipendiary steward came in and summoned Mick and me to the inquiry.

Over in their room, the three acting stewards, under the chairmanship of a local farming colonel, sat behind somebody's cast-off dining table.

Mick and I stood side by side in front of them, with our hands behind our backs like a couple of naughty schoolboys.

We were each invited to give our version of what had happened. The stewards listened but didn't comment. The stewards' secretary dimmed the lights and started a video tape. All eyes locked on to the screen.

First we watched the head-on view of the final two furlongs. It was embarrassing. Pink Pigeon had veered a good two yards to his right as I had turned to look behind me. Mick's chestnut was immediately hidden by my horse. It was pretty conclusive.

Then we watched the side view. We saw Mick move his mount out from where they had been lying a few feet behind me in my slipstream. He came up close on my outside and got his animal's nose level with Pink Pigeon's quarters, then quickly began to fade, just as I turned to find him. We saw Mick take a tug—a hell of a tug that almost stopped his animal in its tracks and cost him three lengths before he got down to ride his finish.

I smiled to myself. Mick, ever the opportunist, had over-played his hand with a lack of subtlety unusual in him.

The secretary switched off the video and turned up the lights. The three amateur stewards looked at the stipe who asked us if there was anything more we would like to say.

I told them again exactly what I'd done, but I didn't tell them I thought the result of the race hadn't been altered by it. I'd found to my cost in my first season in England that they liked to reach their own conclusions.

Mick was far too wily to antagonize them by offering his opinion. "I don't know if I'd have won or not," he said. "You'd be the best judges of that." He sounded as if he really meant it. He'd have made a fine actor.

The senior steward asked us to leave the room and wait outside while they deliberated.

In the corridor, Mick bit his nails and wouldn't look at me. I simply didn't know which way it was going to go.

We didn't have long to wait. The door opened after less than a minute and we were called back in.

The senior steward looked up.

"We've decided that the positions of the race will remain unaltered."

I heard Mick utter a strangled grunt while I thanked the stewards. He and I left together for the changing rooms.

"Sorry about that, Mick," I said, though I didn't see why the hell I should be apologizing.

"Not half as fuckin' sorry as you will be." The venom in Mick's voice took me by surprise.

"Listen, it wasn't my fault . . ."

Mick quickened his step and showed me his back for an answer.

Back in the changing room, Martin was ready with my next set of colors and saddle. The result of the inquiry had already been announced over the tannoy and Mick was standing by his peg on the other side of the room with a small group of sympathizers.

"There are a few people here who are a bit upset about the result," Martin whispered hissily.

"Yes, I know."

"Hagan had a bundle on it, and all his punters, too."

"That's their tough shit," I said.

"And Hagan's in trouble."

There were several other jockeys nearby. I had to whisper back. "What kind of trouble?"

"Harry Devene—over six figures, they say."

Martin liked his gossip, but he liked it accurate. I believed him. Poor old Mick. He'd tried to bribe me as subtly as he could, knowing my well-broadcast dislike of stopping horses. I thought he'd tried to let me know it was important to him by bringing up his kid's christening. But I hadn't read the code, just taken it at face value. And he had grossly underrated Pink Pigeon.

I had two more rides, and Mick had one in a different race. I didn't see him again that afternoon. I had told him on the way to the races that I was going on to London later. I presumed he had made other arrangements to get back home. I didn't know if I wanted to see him or not but I wanted somehow to say sorry. If he had told me it was that serious, I'd have sprained an ankle for twenty minutes and let someone else ride Pink Pigeon. But it was crazy that I should have to feel so bad about winning a race I had a perfect right to win.

As it turned out, it was my only prize that day. After the fifth race, my day's work was over. I changed into my Tommy Nutter tweed jacket and headed for the seafood bar; if Bunty Fielding was in a public place, that would be it.

She was. She was a gregarious creature and she'd got bored sitting in the box with Sir James.

I walked up to her.

"Afternoon, Lady Fielding."

"Jake!" she bellowed. "Well done in the maiden, though you nearly cocked it up. You were bloody lucky the stewards gave it to you."

I looked hurt. "Lucky? Mick was already going backward before I crossed him."

"Tommy Preece was looking very shirty in the winner's enclosure afterward; just as well you kept it. And I shouldn't think Mick Hagan's very pleased with you either, is he?"

"No, but he'll get over it," I said lightly, though I wasn't so sure this time.

Bunty prodded a tall, thin man with no chin who was drooping behind her. "Hey, James, get a glass for Jake and give him a drink." She turned back to me.

"Champagne, I'm afraid, not vodka," she chuckled.

James Bullough-Ferguson, in a Guards tie and an antique suit, was one of those underfunded, upper-crust Englishmen who feel that their breeding exempts them from normal honest behavior in their attempts to find enough money, without doing much work, to keep up the standards which they imagine other people expect of them. Bullough-Ferguson did this by hustling around the fringes of racing, trying to organize owners' syndicates and introducing people with money, impressed by his brand of arrogant, unjustified superciliousness, to trainers and breeders. He bridled at being ordered by Bunty to fetch and carry, but he obeyed. Bunty Fielding could see right through him, and she was an important person to be seen with.

"Awful man," she said as he squeezed resentfully through the crowd toward the bar. "He's had the nerve to start trying to fascinate Camilla. Bloody fool, as if she'd look at him."

I hoped Lady Fielding didn't say that kind of thing about me behind my back.

James came back with a glass which he handed to me.

"Good result, Jake," he said. "You'll be glad to hear I had a nice little wedge on that."

I wasn't at all glad to hear it, but I didn't bother to say so.

"I knew that tricky little Paddy was up to something, though," Bullough-Ferguson was saying. "Bloody fool's already up to his neck in faeces and now he's just buried himself." He gave a short bark of nasty laughter.

"James," Bunty said impatiently, "if you don't mind, I wanted a word with Jake alone."

"Oh." Bullough-Ferguson looked miffed, but he wandered away, trying his best to preserve his dignity.

"I meant what I said on the phone this morning," Bunty said when he had gone. "Keep an eye on my filly, won't you? There's a lot of nasty talk flying around about your guv'nor."

"Bunty, he's not going to suddenly forget how to train horses. Dawn Raider's staying in the yard for a while, at least till after the Guineas; that'll keep him firing. But I will take special care of your filly."

She gazed down her nose at me, with one eyebrow

lowered. "You're a good-looking chap, for a jockey," she said. "And I hear you're taking my daughter somewhere this evening. Make sure you take care of her, too."

/////////////// CHAPTER 4

The Fieldings' London house was in one of those quiet streets in Kensington that stay private by leading nowhere. It was one of a terrace—white, smooth-textured and filled with British discretion. There was a space to park a car in the patch of ground—you couldn't call it a garden—which separated the house from the pavement; I nosed the Jaguar into it.

There were six stone steps up to the front door. I hopped up them and tugged at an unpolished brass handle. I hadn't expected anything to happen, but I heard a faint, tinny clanging from somewhere down in the lower floor.

There was no response or sign of life in the house. I looked at my watch and tapped my toe. I'd told Camilla seven, and it was seven ten. More annoyed than I wanted to be, I was just thinking about making other plans when the big door opened. Camilla stood with one hand on the door handle and the other on her hip.

"You're a bit early," she said, but she didn't sound too vexed. She was wearing some kind of oriental robe, and not a lot else.

"Okay," I said, "I'll come back later." I turned to go back down the steps.

"Come back, you cretin," she said with a laugh.

I came back. "What the hell's a cretin?"

"I don't know. Some kind of retarded mountain man, I think."

"Sounds right," I said, and stepped into the hall of the house.

Camilla shut the door behind me. "Go on into the drawing room. Help yourself to a drink while I finish changing." She waved her hand at an open doorway on the right.

I nodded and went on through. I heard her running back up the stairs.

Beside a pair of French windows which gave on to an unexpected, large garden behind the house, I saw a table with a clutter of bottles and a few glasses. I walked over, poured myself a weak vodka and looked around the room. There was a pair of large, gloomy seascapes —a lot of grey sky and foaming, slurry-green sea—either side of a lumpy Victorian fireplace and overmantel. There were some fine old portraits of racehorses and a couple of ham-fisted new ones. The curtains looked straight from the set of *Upstairs, Downstairs,* but not so new. Most of the furniture was good, Georgian mahogany, classic English stuff and hard to beat. Everything in the room looked as though it had been there a long time. Probably there had once been a team of servants to look after the place. I guessed there wasn't one now. There was a kind of beaten-up, musty look to it all, and I'd been living in England long enough to recognize this kind of faded elegance as a sign of real, old money.

I picked up a two-week-old copy of *Horse and Hound* from an inlaid side table and wedged myself into the corner of a high-backed sofa. A couple of minutes later, Camilla reappeared.

I stood up. "What did you want to get dressed for?"

"Why not? Or are we going to a nudist colony for dinner?"

I gave her a kiss; felt her lips linger a moment on mine. "No, I wouldn't be able to get near the table if I were sitting opposite you."

"Stop boasting. And let go of my bum."

I hadn't really noticed that my hand had strayed, but I removed it from her lovely quarters with exaggerated regret.

"Actually," Camilla breezed on, "I'm glad you're early. We're going to have a drink with a painter at the Chelsea Arts Club."

"We are?" I said. "Who's the painter?"

"You wouldn't have heard of her."

"Not all Americans are cultural pygmies," I protested.

"No, but most jockeys are."

I didn't rise. The truth was that I quite enjoyed Camilla's needling. "Okay, let's go then."

I opened the door of my car for Camilla and watched her long legs jack-knife into place.

As we drove through sultry evening streets to Chelsea, my eyes kept wandering back to those shiny brown, naked legs stretching out from a scrap of a black jersey skirt; it was beginning to interfere with my driving. But I kept myself under control until we pulled up in Old Church Street, right outside the low white building that had been a watering hole for thirsty artists for over a hundred years.

Before I could get out, I tried surreptitiously to disentangle my rigid hard-on from the elastic of my shorts.

Camilla noticed.

"Carrying a bit of overweight, are we?" she said, looking sideways.

I wanted to say, "Yes, and you look the best diet I've seen in a long time."

Instead, I gave her a fatuous grin and scrambled out of the car.

Camilla's artist was sitting at a table in the club's gardens where the sun still shone and birds hopped among the shrubbery.

Terese de Rosnay was a lot of things which Camilla wasn't. She was short with big, mobile breasts; she wasn't fat, but she was well covered. There were implausible blond highlights in her short-cropped duncolored hair. She looked more like a down-market cocktail waitress than an artist. When Camilla introduced us, I shook hands with her. She gave off an indefinable, sexy aroma. I almost felt as if she had turned it on for me. Her big eyes, on the same level as my own, suggested that she would not have put many obstacles in my way if I'd wished to remove her clothing and fondle her moving parts.

"Have a drink," she said, with her eyes still on me. There was a bottle of Sancerre on the table among a mess of papers. Terese's reaction to me had not escaped Camilla.

"Could you get a couple of glasses from the bar?" she asked me.

I walked out of the bright sunshine into a tall gloomy room. There was a lot of loud talk and laughter mixing with the click of snooker balls and someone fooling around on a grand piano. I headed for the bar. As I reached it, I was accosted by a tall man in his late fifties, still wearing a camel-hair coat and a maroon scarf. His eyes were bloodshot and malfunctioning; there was a lot of liquor on his breath. I backed off with what I hoped looked like tolerant good humor.

"Oy, you," this character slurred at me. He lurched closer and I caught some heavy spray. "You weren't supposed to win that fucking race today."

This wasn't the first time I'd been harangued by total strangers, disgruntled punters who reckoned because they'd backed me and I'd lost that they had some kind of claim on my sympathy. But this man was coming on stronger than most. Mick must have sold the tip far and wide.

"I am sorry," I said, trying to get past him. "I guess the horse forgot to tell me."

The punter had evidently got it off his chest. " 'S all right. It's that fucking little Paddy I'd like to get my hands on." He turned back to the bar to find his drink.

I asked for the glasses and fought my way back out to Camilla and Terese. They were too thick into their conversation to take a lot of notice. I poured myself some wine and wondered how the hell Mick Hagan had become so desperate that he was selling tips to drunken clowns like the one I'd just met.

Before we left, Terese suggested she should have dinner with us, but Camilla wasn't having that.

"That would have been great, Terese, but we're going on to a friend's house and we can't really bring anyone with us," she said before I could say anything.

"That's a pity," Terese said. "I really wanted to talk to Jake about horses. Look, here's my number, Jake. When you're next in London, drop in if you've got time." She scribbled on the back cover of a show catalogue, tore it off and handed it to me. Camilla pretended to take no notice and gave Terese a short goodbye.

When we were back in my car I asked Camilla where we were going.

"I don't know," she answered. "You're driving."

"What about your friend's, for dinner?"

"Oh, that was just to dislodge Terese. She was looking at you like a ravening tigress."

I laughed. Camilla was jealous; I was encouraged.

But that was all the encouragement she gave me. I took her to a place in Victoria Grove, near her home. The restaurant was run by a racegoer who had often asked me to come.

They were full, but they found us a space. There was a quiet, sophisticated crowd there. If they knew who I was, they weren't letting it show and I was left alone to concentrate on Camilla.

She kept up her usual defensive banter, but occasionally she was dropping her guard a little more now. She told me about her work in the Cork Street gallery in which her father had bought her a small share. She talked to me about the pictures they dealt in with an enthusiasm I hadn't often found in girls of her type. It was obvious that she knew a lot about the current art scene and, unlike a lot of people who worked in that sort of field, she didn't talk down to me. I was impressed.

Besides that, through her parents she'd been around racing people all her life and she understood my world well. She still rode when she went to stay at Aldrich, she said, and maybe I'd like to come hunting with her next season with the Beaufort where she had friends who kept hunters. I told her I could think of things I'd prefer to do with her on a cold winter's day but the comment was ignored.

She'd traveled, too, and had lived for a year in Florence. She'd spent a lot of time there ogling marble male genitals, she said, but she didn't want to tell me about her experience with the non-marble variety.

"Italian men think they're all God's gift," she said. "They're not, though. As far as I can see, they're all top dressing. But then so are most men."

"You've been reading too much Germaine Greer." I laughed.

"Maybe, but look at you—good looking, loads of superficial charm and a pint-sized sporting hero, and you probably never expect anyone to turn you down; you probably think that any woman who does is a loony or a lesbian."

I nodded.

"Well, I want you to know that I'm neither," Camilla went on.

"And are you going to turn me down?"

"Not until we've finished dinner."

I walked back with her to her parents' house afterward. She asked me in for a drink, and then she turned me down.

She did it as if she were giving a small child some nasty medicine to cure a juvenile complaint. I swallowed it like a man and went off down the street with a jaunty stride, until I was round the corner and out of sight.

I reminded myself that everything comes to he who waits, found my car and pulled Terese de Rosnay's piece of paper out of my pocket. I looked at the number and, beneath it, an address.

The *A to Z* confirmed my view that I would be mad not to look in on Miss de Rosnay; I would practically pass her door on my way out of London.

I rang the bell of the strange Edwardian studio in west London and waited in excited anticipation. I didn't need to be too conceited to think that I was not going to encounter much reluctance in Miss de Rosnay, and the flagstaff in my pants agreed.

We were both getting a little deflated when we'd waited five minutes, rung the bell several more times and no one had answered it.

I gave it a little longer, made a face at the closed door and slunk back to my car, resigned to a lonely night.

I'd paced my drinking carefully during the evening,

diluted by a few pints of Perrier, but I kept to the speed limit on the way back; I didn't want to risk facing two drink-drive charges.

I pushed a Crowded House tape into the slot and thought about the best way to handle Camilla Fielding. But as I reviewed the evening's conversations, I remembered the drunk in the Arts Club, and the totally unexpected vindictive glare in Mick Hagan's eyes after I'd won the first race that afternoon.

I worked Dawn Raider next morning over six furlongs with one of our five-year-old sprinters. Toby Ellerton had done his job well. The Two Thousand Guineas was being run in eight days' time, and he had the colt in top condition. His glossy coat bulged over hard, rippling muscle. His eyes were bright and he had learned to concentrate on racing. He felt, to me, as good as any horse I had ridden at that stage in his career. I was confident, but I'd been around racehorses long enough to know how quickly and easily an injury could wreck a horse's chances, however much care was taken. I also knew that there were probably half a dozen jockeys at that moment, between Lambourn and Newmarket, who felt exactly the same about their mounts.

But I wasn't worried about Dawn Raider's stamina over the Guineas mile, or his speed. In the end, it was going to be about his desire to please and his will to win. I didn't have any doubts about his ability, but at the back of my mind I had the niggling feeling that when it came to the shake-up at the end of the race, he might be happier to finish second. But I wouldn't know until the day.

At the end of the gallop, I dropped my reins ahead of the other horse and wheeled round to walk down to Ellerton.

Michael Penruddock had turned up and was standing beside the Captain. His crinkly blond hair, sticking out from under a flat tweed cap, waved untidily in the breeze. A loose-fitting fawn coat flapped around his long thin body as his supercilious, muddy-green eyes acknowledged my greeting. It was one of the less enjoyable sides of my job, having to be friendly to people like him.

He didn't often come to see the horses work, but I wasn't surprised to see him that morning.

The lad who had ridden Dawn Raider up to the downs came and took his head. I jumped off, legged him onto the saddle and walked across the lush, dewy turf to the two grim-faced men. I guessed that conversation between them hadn't been too free and easy—they weren't either of them jesters at the best of times.

"How did he feel?" Penruddock asked first.

"Never better."

"He still doesn't look as though he's striding out properly," Penruddock commented.

"Balls!" Captain Toby coughed.

I agreed with him. I felt like asking Mike if he knew which end of a horse to feed. If I'd thought it would have achieved anything, I would have done.

"He moves great," I said instead. "He's a bit pottery in his slower paces, but when he's warmed up, he's perfect." I noticed that Ellerton still had his stopwatch out. "What time did he do?"

"He covered the last two in just over twenty-three," he said with a trace of smugness.

I could see that he hadn't told Penruddock, who looked impressed. "That's certainly encouraging," he said.

"Do you still want to take all the others away?" Ellerton asked him sourly.

"The decision's been made, I'm afraid, Toby. The truth is that His Highness wants to keep a lot more horses in France. Let's face it, there's rather more incentive there."

We all knew that most of the horses that were

leaving the yard that morning would not be going to France.

"If they win anything," Ellerton grunted.

I was amazed he didn't say more, but I guessed he was on his best behavior. I also guessed he knew the main reason Dawn Raider was staying at Melbourne House was me. He was almost polite when he asked me if I'd like to work Corsican Lady in the second lot.

I left the Captain's yard as four six-horse lorries rolled in to take away a third of the lodgers. Ellerton stomped off back to the house, unwilling to watch, knowing he wouldn't keep his cool if he stayed; Penruddock would only have had to give the nod for his lads to load Dawn Raider with the rest of them.

The sun was already hot enough to remind me of Kentucky summers as I got into the Jaguar and headed south. The roads through Berkshire were empty and visibility was good. It took me twenty minutes to reach Mick Hagan's cottage.

I knew as soon as Mary came to the door that things had changed between Mick and me. Normally she was full of Celtic greeting and open-hearted warmth, but this morning she couldn't look me in the eye.

"He's not here," she said.

I didn't even have time to decide that she wasn't telling the truth before Hagan's voice bellowed from the room at the back of the cottage, "Yes, I am."

A moment later he appeared. He was wearing a pair of grimy jodhpurs and beaten-up elastic-sided boots. He nodded me into a small front room, the only room in the small house not cluttered with his kids' toys. The walls were almost entirely covered with photographs and citations covering Mick's thirty years in racing. The mantelpiece and a gross, overcarved sideboard were cluttered with trophies—crystal-glass rosebowls, mounted medallions—all irrelevant now; memorabilia of past, unrepeatable honors.

"I've only asked you in because I'm not wanting to bawl you out in front of my kids."

I didn't reply. This seemed to aggravate the strain that showed in Mick's eyes and his short, twitchy movements.

"D'ye realize what ye've done?"

"I won a maiden on the best horse in the field, for Christ's sake, Mick. It's not such a terrible thing to do."

There were tears in his eyes. "I fuckin' begged you not to. I told you it was important. Six kids, I've got, the littl'un to be christened Saturday. Y' bastard. You're already a fuckin' millionaire. What difference would it have made to you, just once, to get off your fuckin' high horse? Don't answer that, I don't want any of your high-minded bloody clap-trap. I looked after you when you needed lookin' after, and you just kick me when I'm down."

I couldn't think of anything to say that would change his mind or convince him that he was talking nonsense. I certainly didn't want to harangue him on the pitfalls of gambling and taking money from book-makers. I put my hand on the door latch to leave.

Hagan looked as though he would explode, or burst into tears, but he controlled himself. "If you think you can do what you've done and just walk away, forget it. Life is not that unjust."

"Look, I only came to give you the two hundred I said I would if I won."

Now he did explode. "D'you think I'd take your fuckin' money now? D'you think I'll ask you back into this house again? Just get the hell out of here, and God help you if you get in my way again."

I turned and walked through the door. I didn't think it would help for him to see how bad I felt. I didn't think he'd have believed it anyway.

I glanced apologetically at Mary who was waiting outside the door with damp eyes and a small child clasping her hand. I left the house and almost ran up the short gravel path to my car in the road outside.

The sun was still bright. I damned it as my eyes itched in the glare for most of the six-mile drive home.

The next day, to Toby Ellerton's disgust, I won the Group Two event over a mile at Sandown on Al Jiwa. The colt had won the Royal Lodge Stakes the year before and was Dawn Raider's chief rival in the market for the Derby. I'd got the ride by default from a jockey who'd had a small confrontation with the stewards the week before. If all went well Dawn Raider's Derby prep race would be at Lingfield.

But I was able to offer the Captain some solace. I was the only jockey who had ridden both animals, and as far as I could judge at that stage in the season, Dawn Raider was easily the better horse. Al Jiwa wasn't taking in the Guineas, and I was quietly confident about Dawn Raider's chances at Newmarket the following week. I was less enthusiastic when Ellerton told me that he and Lady Fielding had decided definitely to run Corsican Lady in the fillies' Classic.

But I drove away from Sandown feeling pleased with my day's work, and wanting a bit of company. I phoned Camilla from the car. There was no reply from the London number. Bunty Fielding answered the phone in Sussex. We talked for a few minutes about the day's racing and Corsican Lady. I tried not to sound too pessimistic. When I asked, she told me her daughter wasn't there; she didn't know where she was.

I cursed my own laziness and the habit I had of expecting my social life to run itself. Girls like Camilla didn't come on tap.

I carried on home in a bad mood and shut the world out of my life for the rest of the weekend, resisting the temptation to call her again.

On Sunday, I was feeling sociable enough to ask a fit young farmer's son to come up and play squash with me. I liked playing with him because he never said a word and usually beat me. After he'd gone, I did my round of the woods with a gun, then settled down for a couple of hours with a rod and a box of the grey and yellow flies that the trout in my stretch of river usually favored. That evening, they weren't taking anything from me. I trudged back up the valley convinced that Camilla and the trout were conspiring against me. We all make these irrational connections from time to time.

I didn't feel much like seeing anybody for the next few days. I drove to Lambourn each morning to ride work at Melbourne House and in the afternoon drove to the races alone. Three more winners—though only one of them for Ellerton—didn't do a lot to improve my mood.

I saw Mick Hagan, raced against him three times, but he didn't say a word to me. Most of the other jockeys in the changing room seemed to be on his side. I didn't blame them; Mick was one of the great characters of British racing. They respected him still for what he had done, not what he did now.

Each evening, I got away from the races as soon as I could. I went home to fish or walk my woods and hedgerows with a shotgun. The pigeons were always good sport, better in my view than the driven shoots I was invited to in the English winters. I never could get much of a buzz from blasting into a cloud of pheasant driven across a line of guns for ritual massacre.

I had a favorite route through the beech woods, where I felt I knew each of the great trees personally. The fern and bramble were growing thick across the woodland floor now, covering the faint paths that I had made. The jays and squirrels that lived there weren't used to being disturbed. They scattered as I came, while the evening breezes rustled a million leaves above me and the late spring sun's rays picked out the green-brown treetrunks in dappled light. It was the best possible therapy and I loved it. By the time I had to pack and head up to Newmarket for the Guineas meeting, I had my head together and felt ready to deal with all the hassle I was likely to get from Toby Ellerton, Mick Hagan, Penruddock and the gentlemen of the press.

News of the times Dawn Raider had been clocking on the gallops hadn't taken long to leak from the yard. Now he was firm ante-post favorite for the Two Thousand Guineas. I was used to that responsibility; I dealt with it by not thinking about it. If the horse could win, he would. Corsican Lady had also attracted support. A few hopeful journalists had phoned, but I gave them the usual, "She's a good filly and has every chance"—a meaningless stand-by. Personally, I thought she would do well to be placed; she was up against some sharp fillies at that distance.

I had been invited to stay the three nights with James Candy, one of Newmarket's more civilized, less spectacular trainers. I'd had other invitations too, but James was always the perfect host and didn't expect me to go to every single party that this big meeting spawned. The only concession I'd made was to accept an invitation to dine with Sir James and Lady Fielding, and Camilla, at the large house in Exning which they always rented for the spring meeting. The invitation was for the Thursday evening, after the running of the One Thousand Guineas. "Win or lose," Bunty had said, "but the champagne will be better if she wins."

And win she did.

Horses can make a fool of you every day of the week. I'd never been more pleased to be proved wrong than I was about Corsican Lady.

Far from being outpaced early on, as I'd thought she would be, she made every yard of the running and never came off a tight rein until we hit the rising ground coming out of the dip. But everyone else was struggling by then and she passed the post with a good two lengths of daylight between her and the second home.

She was running on really strongly; there was no doubt in my mind that she would get the extra half-mile of the Oaks comfortably.

It was a good evening. Sir James and Bunty didn't talk down to me in the way I had heard other, less aristocratic owners with their jockeys. I knew the fact that I was American helped—put me outside the strict, arcane rules of British social classification.

Camilla, though, was less forthcoming. She was polite, joined in all the conversations but was definitely aloof. After a while, she mentioned our last evening out together.

"I wondered what happened to you, Jake, as I hadn't heard from you. I thought maybe you hadn't recovered from visual rape by Terese de Rosnay."

Sir James looked interested. "What's that? Visual rape?"

"Terese is having a show at the gallery. I had to meet her and I took Jake with me. She couldn't take her eyes off him. She wasn't just mentally undressing him, she was tearing his clothes to shreds trying to get them off." She turned to me. "I thought she might have been in touch with you."

I laughed. "Did you? Well, she hasn't and I don't think she'd get through the first line of defenses if she tried."

"You've evidently got your defenses pretty well organized," Camilla said.

Bunty came to my rescue. "Leave him alone, Camilla. Poor chap's probably been getting himself ready for today, and thank God he did."

I looked at her gratefully while her husband topped up my glass with the dry, white Burgundy we were drinking in deference to my weight.

It was a good quality, old-fashioned sort of an evening. The Fieldings were delighted to hear my exclusive report on Corsican Lady's condition at the end of the race. I could tell them that the second fillies' Classic looked a real prospect from where I had been sitting. A lot of other people had evidently come to the same conclusion and I wasn't surprised to hear that Corsican Lady was Oaks favorite immediately after the race.

I left shortly after eleven. I wanted to be up on the heath early next morning. My hosts were well lubricated by now and would probably have gone on for a few more hours but they understood.

Camilla didn't come to see me off with her parents. Bunty Fielding shrugged her hefty shoulders. "I'm sorry Camilla was in a bit of a bolsh. She's not used to making the running."

"Would you mind if she did?" I looked at her; I wanted to know if she was going to tell the truth.

"No, of course not. Frankly, given some of the half-baked army officers who come round with their tongues hanging out, I couldn't care less if she fell for a builder's laborer as long as he had balls."

That was putting me in my place, I guessed, but at least she meant what she said. I wouldn't have been put off if she hadn't, but I liked her, and I liked riding for her; I was glad that there wasn't going to be any animosity about my plans for Camilla. The only problem was that I didn't seem to be making great headway with Camilla herself.

I didn't brood on it and woke up next morning in James Candy's house feeling fit for anything. I was up on the famous Newmarket gallops as small birds were breaking wind. I had arranged to have a pipe-opener on my mount in the Jockey Club Stakes. Captain Ellerton didn't have a runner, and I'd taken the ride on a locally trained six-year-old called Sapper. I'd not ridden him before but I'd seen him run often enough and, in my opinion, he'd become a thief. His trainer thought the same and had decided to put blinkers on him to keep his mind on the job. He also felt that an early morning blow-out might do him good and I had agreed to turn up.

The racing press that morning were, predictably, banging on about a Classic Guineas double for Jake Felton and Captain Toby. The more imaginative ones were even talking about triple crowns. I wished they wouldn't. It was just the kind of thing that turned your luck.

I wasn't even in contention in the Jockey Club Stakes. Sapper had made up his mind that, blinkers or not, he'd had enough of racing and finished a comfortable last. That second day of the meeting yielded me no more than a very hard-won second in the mile handicap. Friday of the spring meeting was always something of an anti-climax—most minds were concentrating on the next day's big race.

The big four bookies shortened Dawn Raider from 7/2 to 5/2 overnight. Some of the large independents were more generous in an attempt to attract more money. Anyway, 5/2 looked stingy to me; I wasn't totally confident—there are very few races where you can ever be, and certainly not about a Classic. But Dawn Raider had arrived in Newmarket the day before and I gave him a canter up a fresh strip on the limekilns at seven o'clock on the morning of the race. I thought that if I'd been Mick Hagan, I'd have had a big wedge on the colt. Even Toby Ellerton was more relaxed than I'd seen him for a long time. Corsican Lady had done a lot to replenish the Captain's self-esteem. Up on the gallops, his face was redder than usual and a few more veins had broken during Thursday evening's celebrations. According to James Candy who had been out with him and his friends the night before, the Two Thousand Guineas was already in the bag.

By lunchtime, the cold wind that had been coming in from the North Sea had blown itself out, leaving Newmarket awash in warm spring sunshine.

I left James sitting around in the garden with some friends and drove the few miles to the Rowley course. My face twitched into a smile at the slight fluttering in my guts; that didn't often happen these days. As a kid in Kentucky, I'd felt it before every single race; it took the ride on a hot favorite in an English Classic to bring it on now. But I enjoyed the sensation of excitement and nervousness seeping through my body. It focused my attention. Functioning under pressure was what separated the best from the also-rans in any sport and I thrived on it. The more money that was riding on me and the more that was expected of me, the better I liked it.

Unlike Corsican Lady two days before, Dawn Raider was expected to win. His campaign had been carefully planned, but I knew that anything could still go wrong.

I pulled into the jockeys' car park outside the west entrance and tried to push Dawn Raider to the back of my mind. I walked over to the weighing room, thinking about the two horses I had to ride before the Guineas.

The form book said that neither had a chance, and as it turned out they both ran true to form.

I didn't have a ride in the race before the Guineas, so I stayed in the changing room, sitting under my peg, going through the race one more time. I tried to take into account every possible danger and concluded that, as I was drawn two away from the stands-side rail, my only real risk was that I might miss the break from the stalls and lose my position at the start. If that happened, I would have to get round a wall of horses to come through and make my challenge. Usually, a gap would appear from somewhere to save going all the way round, but you could only wait so long for it to appear.

In the parade ring before the race, the Captain was a little more subdued than he had been early in the morning.

"Watch that front-runner," he said, pointing at a colt which we both knew was being run only to crank up the early speed for his stable mate.

I nodded, but I'd already discounted him as a problem. Leaving the paddock, I was still concentrating on my tactics when I heard my name called. There was nothing unusual about this. There were always a lot of punters milling about shouting advice and support on the way down. I was used to it and, on the whole, I didn't take much notice, but there was something familiar about this female voice.

I looked to where the call had come from, and nearly lost my balance on Dawn Raider's back. There, wearing a dress that showed off every curve of her body, was Sandra Zimmer. Caught on the hop, I gave her a smile. I'd never seen her at the races in England and I wondered what had brought her here today. I also wondered what she could possibly be doing with James Bullough-Ferguson, who was standing beside her, looking like the proud owner. But I had more pressing things on my mind, and forgot them both as soon as I was out on the course.

After months of planning how to win the final Colts Classic, everything went right for us. Until we hit the front with a little over two hundred yards to run.

Dawn Raider suddenly lost his action. He went from being all over the winner to going nowhere in four strides. I hit him hard twice behind the saddle. It gave me a quick pang of guilt, but the Captain and the punters who had backed me couldn't feel the signals Dawn Raider was giving me, and they would want to think they'd been given every chance of winning.

I managed to cling on to the lead for another fifty yards and for a brief, unlikely moment, I thought I might just manage to keep it. But the winning post seemed to be getting further away as I was joined, then overtaken, by a big brown colt, and I knew I'd been beaten.

The Captain met me in the unsaddling area looking drained and shattered. All the benefits of Corsican Lady's win had been neutralized. He must have had a hell of a bet. Worse, the colt had probably represented the second half of a double.

He tried to smile like a good loser, but when I jumped down from the saddle he put his face close to mine and spoke through clenched teeth.

"What the hell happened?"

"Sorry, Captain. He just died on me. He went there to win but didn't get home."

Ellerton knew it wasn't my fault, or his, that the animal hadn't won. I unbuckled my saddle and walked away toward the weighing room. I'd gone a few yards when Michael Penruddock collared me.

He accepted that the horse had run well, but he was sour about losing it. I didn't think Dawn Raider would be returning to the Captain.

The Guineas meeting gave me three wins from twelve rides. Not a bad score, only bettered by the reigning champion. I was disappointed about Dawn Raider, of course, but philosophical. The winner was, obviously, an outstanding colt and on reflection it was no failure to have been within a length of him at the finish.

The press, with no shame, reversed their opinion of twenty-four hours earlier and were now questioning Dawn Raider's stamina for the mile and a half of the Derby. But I was less worried about that. The Newmarket race had been run at a cracking pace, just a fraction of a second off the record. The Derby was an entirely different sort of a race, and provided I could get the colt to settle and conserve his energy up the hill in the slow, early stages, I thought there was a good chance he'd have more to offer in the last two furlongs up from Tattenham Corner. If the Guineas hadn't taken too much out of him and he trained on well over the next month, I was hopeful for his chances. What I didn't know was who was going to be doing the training.

///////////// CHAPTER 5

Michael Penruddock phoned me at home the Monday after the Guineas. I was about to leave for Melbourne House at half past six in the morning. I wondered what had got him up and functioning so early.

"Morning, Jake," he said. He sounded as if he needed a good cough. Something made me think that maybe the Sheikh—a few hours ahead of us in Riyadh —had already been on the phone to him. "His Highness wanted me to let you know that he definitely wants you to ride Dawn Raider in the Derby."

"Good," I said simply. "I presume you're taking him away from Ellerton's."

"Yes, though to be fair to Toby, I don't think there was anything wrong with the way he trained him."

"Where's he going?"

"Giles Seymour's. I'm putting out a press release in an hour or two. Kindly don't mention it to anyone at Ellerton's until I have."

"Captain Toby's not going to be a happy man this morning," I commented.

"That's his tough titty," Penruddock said. "He should have known better than to do what he's been doing."

"You know, sooner or later you're going to have to come right out with it. He could probably sue you for slander right now." I wondered why I was defending Ellerton; I didn't like him a whole lot more than I liked Penruddock.

"I think it's pretty unlikely that Toby would want to stir anything up, don't you?"

"I don't know. He's got his butt to the wall. He may not have much to lose."

"The only thing Toby Ellerton can do is train horses and you need a license to do that. He couldn't risk losing it. Anyway, it shouldn't worry you. With fewer horses in the yard, you'll be able to take any spare rides you can find, won't you?" The line went dead. He hadn't bothered to say "Goodbye;" after all, I was only a jockey. I held on to the phone for a moment, trying not to be goaded by his bone-headed ignorance.

The next few days at Melbourne House were hell. Ellerton raged at everyone all day. When I had to go into the house, Janey looked totally defeated. I tried to show her some sympathy, but she was sort of punch-drunk—emotionally, not physically; whatever other failings he had, I was pretty sure Toby wasn't a wife beater. Six lads had been laid off without notice or compensation, and the rest of them were wandering about looking over their shoulders to see where the axe was going to fall next.

Penruddock had been right about one thing. With Ellerton's string so truncated, my agent, Phil White, and I were kept busy juggling schedules and taking our pick of the better spare rides that came up. Some of the rides weren't so spare; a few owners had no compunction about jocking off a stable jockey if they thought I could produce a better result for them. When the rides looked right I took them, but it didn't improve my popularity in the changing room. And winning the Lingfield Derby Trial on Dawn Raider the following Saturday didn't help.

Giles Seymour's stable jockey, one of the top six, should have known better than to bitch about it. After all, the Sheikh had made it a condition of Dawn Raider's transfer to Newmarket that I should go on riding him. Ellerton had made noises about claiming me for an entry of his own, but since both he and I knew it was going to be a waste of time to run it, he backed down. Besides, he realized that everyone would have known he'd done it out of spite.

I was more pleased than I was prepared to let on in a post-race grilling for television. I always rated the Lingfield trial the best test for the Derby; the course is closer to Epsom in shape and contour than any other in Britain, and the trial is closer in time to the big race. It was impossible not to feel confident after the way the colt had strolled up past the opposition in the last two furlongs.

When, two days before and in my absence the Midhurst magistrates deprived me of my license for driving drunk into a quarry, the offers of sympathy from my colleagues didn't come flooding in.

I tried to shrug off their attitude; their hypocrisy was in direct proportion to their lack of winners. The senior jockeys, at least, showed no animosity. They reckoned that the fewer horses there were in Ellerton's yard, the less of a threat I'd be in the upper end of the league table. The main problem I had to deal with was getting to work every day.

I had given the Jag back to the hire company, and the insurers had paid out on the Aston. I didn't want to ask too many favors from racing people who lived near me, and I couldn't rely on my agent or my valet. I came to a temporary arrangement with a driver from Newbury, but I'd made other, more ambitious plans for my personal transport.

After I'd been driven home from Lingfield on the day of the Derby trial, I jumped onto the small red tractor I kept for messing around on my patch of land and drove through the green lanes to see my neighboring farmer. He had something I didn't have, which I was going to need—a dead-level strip of dryish meadow.

John Calloway was what they called a gentleman farmer. In other words, he didn't really care very much if his farming made a profit as long as it paid for his shooting and the three or four National Hunt horses he had bred and now trained at home.

He was a nice, simple man; medium height, middle-aged and not too clever. I'd done him a few favors, schooled a couple of his horses, aimed him at a half-honest bloodstock agent. I think he found me a little too much of a celebrity to feel totally at ease with me, but he was always ready to oblige when I needed a favor from him.

I found him leaning over a paddock rail by the house looking glumly at a mare and foal who had just come back from stud. I looked at the foal; I could see why he was glum. The foot on the foal's near fore stuck out almost at a right angle. No amount of treatment by a blacksmith was ever going to put that right.

"That's a shame," I said.

He nodded without looking at me. "Sausage factory job, I'm afraid. Five thousand quid down the drain."

I couldn't contradict him. "That's the way it goes. Is she in foal again?"

"Yes, thank God." He turned to look at me. "What brings you down here then?"

"I want to rent a bit of meadow from you."

He looked surprised. "What for?"

As I didn't yet have any stock on my own pasture, it was a reasonable question.

"I'm off the road so I've bought a plane. I need somewhere to fly it from."

His eyes lit up. "That's no problem. How much do you need?"

"Six or seven hundred meters should do."

"That's fine, you can use the strip along the side of the drive. You needn't pay anything, we'll work out the odd quid pro quo."

I knew that meant he would expect me to take him to the races in the plane from time to time. That was fine; he wouldn't get in the way. As it was I already let him have the hay from my own fields for nothing. "Yeah, sure. Thanks. I'll need somewhere to keep it under cover, as well."

"No problem. I'll move the hay out of the barn down there. It should be big enough." He seemed more excited than me at the prospect of the plane.

"I'll pay for that," I said quickly. I didn't want him too much in credit at the favor bank.

"It won't cost much. What sort of plane is it?"

"Twin-engined Piper Comanche; six-seater, thousand-mile range."

"That'd get you to Deauville," Calloway said with glee.

"Easily," I agreed.

"You leave it all to me, Jake. Just let me know how long and wide you want your strip. I suppose you'll want it mowed and leveled as much as possible. I'll run the roller over it a few times."

"That would be great, John. Thanks a lot."

I left him in a much happier frame of mind than when I arrived and I promised to phone him with details.

* * *

I rang my mother on Sunday, as I did every Sunday, and told her about my new toy. She was horrified. I could see her sitting out on the rickety old verandah on a short-legged rocker, gazing across the valley where she had lived all her life. She'd never traveled further from home than Lexington, and certainly not in a plane. She begged me to promise that I'd always fly with a parachute. I laughed, and told her she had more chance of being killed by a snake bite than I had of killing myself in a plane crash, but I promised her, and kept my promise.

The Piper arrived the next day. Now that Dawn Raider and several other outside rides were stationed up at Newmarket, it soon put in useful service as I flew up there twice that week and took it to the races when I could. I loved the flying, especially in the early summer mornings, and it was saving me a lot of time each day.

Dawn Raider had settled into his new yard, and I was confident that Giles Seymour, his new trainer, would produce him at least as well as Toby Ellerton. Seymour, like me, had been discreetly excited about the Lingfield win. I had to give him credit; he was spending a lot of time on the animal to increase its stamina, and it showed.

Mick Hagan still glowered every time he saw me, but I thought maybe the other jockeys were sick of hearing his gripe. My relationship with them was returning to normal. At the same time, I was getting some good rides and had managed to hang on to third position in the table, despite Ellerton's reduced number of runners. The Captain, though, was feeling so sorry for himself he was almost bearable. I was making the most of a messy situation and listening to some of the people who sidled up with propositions for the next season.

Now things had settled down a little, I was beginning to feel my solitariness. I still didn't know what had made Camilla so uncooperative when I'd seen her in Newmarket. Whatever it was, I thought maybe, now she'd had time to think about it, she might have come round a little. On a wet Wednesday evening, I finally picked up the phone and dialed her number.

This time, Sir John Fielding answered.

"Hello, Jake," he woofed affably. "How's Bunty's filly?"

Patiently, I gave him news, mostly good, about Corsican Lady. When I got round to asking if his daughter was there, he grunted.

"Camilla? No, I'm afraid she's not. James Bullough-Ferguson came round and took her to some party." He didn't add anything, but I had the impression Sir John didn't think any more of Bullough-Ferguson than his wife did. But that didn't help me much.

I put the phone back, pretending to myself that I didn't really mind. After all, I'd only had dinner with her once on her own, and the closest I'd come to physical contact with her was little more than a kiss on the forehead. It had hardly been one of the great love stories.

Hell, I thought, trying to be philosophical, there were other options. And to prove me right, the phone rang beside me and one of those options was on the other end of the line.

"Hello, Jake?"

"Yeah?"

"It's Terese de Rosnay here. Do you remember, we met at the Chelsea Arts Club?"

"I remember. What can I do for you?" The mood I was in, I could think of a lot of things I could do for her.

"This probably sounds like a feeble excuse, but I wanted to talk to you about horses. I'm doing a series of sketches for a client, and wanted to talk about their personalities with someone who really knows them."

I didn't think it was a feeble excuse; I thought it was nonexistent.

"Sure," I said, "I'm your man. I know all about

horses' personalities and all their little character defects and disorders."

"Great," she said breathily. "When could I come and see you?"

"You can come now if you like. I caught four big fat trout yesterday evening; I want to grill them while they're still fresh so I could offer you a little dinner too."

"Fantastic," she said. "Tell me where you live and the best way to get there."

I was gutting a trout when the phone rang again twenty minutes later. I wiped my hands on my jeans and picked it up, hoping it wasn't Terese backing out for some reason.

It wasn't; it was another of those options I'd been telling myself about earlier—Sandra Zimmer.

"At last," she said, "Jake Felton in the flesh."

"How do you know I'm in the flesh?"

"It doesn't matter if you are or not; I'm just imagining you are. How is that trim, hard body of yours?"

"Still trim, still hard."

"And when am I going to see it again?"

"I don't know."

"Come on, Jake. What's wrong with you? You don't have to play hard to get with me. I'm in London for a few weeks and I want to see you, Jake. And I don't believe you wouldn't like to carry on where we left off last year."

I got a hard-on just thinking about it, but I was hoping Terese would deal with that when she got here.

"Yeah, I'd like to. I'll give you a ring. I've got to go now; my almond sauce is bubbling over."

"I bet it is," she said. "Just make sure you call this time. Goodbye." She sounded nettled. I shrugged and hung up.

Terese showed up an hour later in one of those small

French cars that bounce a lot and have a roof like a deckchair. I was impressed. She looked a lot less like a cocktail waitress than she had last time I'd seen her. That was mostly because she got soaked in a summer downpour, running from her car to the house. She was wearing only a filmy white cotton top over multicolored leggings and a pair of trainers. She could have won a Miss Wet T-shirt competition anywhere against all comers. It took a real effort to keep my eyes off her big, inviting nipples, so I didn't.

I showed her to my guest bathroom to dry off. She came out a few minutes later wearing just a short toweling robe.

We ate the trout, drank two bottles of dry Hampshire hock, and talked about horses for a while. She really did want to know about individual character traits of animals I'd known. I told her what I could and illustrated it with videos and photographs when we had finished eating. She listened and sketched, cross-legged on a chair in my drawing-room. The toweling robe gradually fell open.

Later, we stopped talking, and horses' personalities were forgotten.

Terese was an uncomplicated, full-blooded lover. She knew what she wanted and demanded no more—just the sort of woman for the gloomy, self-doubting mood I'd been in.

In the morning, she kissed me goodbye with warmth, not passion, and she didn't ask for any commitments. She'd got what she wanted; maybe we'd do the same again, maybe we wouldn't.

I watched her bounce up the drive in her funny little car with a satisfied smile on my face. Something told me I ought to be feeling a twinge of guilt, but I dismissed it and went off to work at Ellerton's yard with a bounce in my stride and a warm glow inside.

I phoned Camilla the next evening.

This time, she was at home. It was the first time I'd

spoken to her since the evening after Corsican Lady had won the Guineas.

"Hi," she said, sounding neutral. "How are you? I see you're still winning races."

"Here and there. Look, I'm sorry I haven't seen you. I've been kept pretty busy, and I lost my license. I have to get around by plane now, and there's no airstrip in Kensington."

"And you've been busy discussing equine psyches with oversexed artists."

"Er, yeah. Your friend, what's-her-name, wanted some first-hand views about thoroughbreds. I was able to give her a bit of help."

"I expect you were. And how's that friend of yours who was at Newmarket?"

I tried to think who she was talking about. I had spent a particularly celibate few days over the Guineas.

"Who?" I asked.

"Sandy someone. A really bad-taste tart. The one you screwed the night before Corsican Lady won."

"Who the hell told you that?"

"James B-F."

"And you believe him?"

"As a matter of fact, I don't now. I think you've got too much taste."

"That's right," I agreed, glad to know at last what had been getting up her nose at dinner that night. "And I hear James has been hunting you."

"Yuck!" she said, encouragingly.

"Look, I'm sorry I haven't got hold of you before," I said. "You've been out when I've rung and it's been a difficult time, with Toby going ape shit about the Sheikh's horses departing. I just haven't felt like I'd be good company."

"And you do now?"

"Yeah. Will you come out to dinner Saturday? I'm riding at Newmarket, but I'll be back by seven."

"Do we go out to dinner in your plane, then?"

"No, you'll have to pick me up from here, if that's okay."

She didn't answer for a moment. Maybe she thought I deserved to sweat.

"All right," she said. "Tell me how to get there. I'll see you around eight."

The glare stunned me for a moment. I couldn't think where I was.

Why wasn't I waking in my own bed—any bed? What the hell was I doing, lying on a bed of leaves among bramble and bracken?

I moved. A stab of vicious, naked pain shot up my leg and reminded me.

The mantrap!

It wasn't just some abominable dream. It was real—all that pain and despair!

I'd been snared, caught like some wounded fox in a gin, left to bleed, starve and die.

I opened my mouth and my sore face cracked. "Why?" I grunted into the undergrowth that surrounded me.

A voice from behind the glare wanted to know too.

"God almighty, Jake! What the hell's happened to you?"

Camilla's voice; the voice of a thousand angels.

"Thank God!" I croaked with more relief than I'd ever felt in my life.

She was kneeling beside me now, beaming a big flash-light up and down my body. She gasped.

"Jesus Christ! What in God's name is that?"

I could see her face now, her eyes horrified as she gazed at the blood and shredded jeans between the teeth of the trap.

I grunted at another spasm of pain as I moved.

"It's a mantrap! Shit! It must be hurting like hell."

"It is, but look, you'll never get me out of it on your

own. You'll have to find somebody to help—John Calloway next door. Get him up here in his Land Rover with a crowbar and bolt cutters—anything he can think of."

She didn't waste any time. She stood up. "Right. Will you be okay?"

"I'm a whole lot better already since you showed up. I thought I'd be here till next Tuesday."

"Well, I wasn't going to hang around that long for you to take me to dinner."

"You knew I wouldn't have let you down if I hadn't been caught up, didn't you?"

"I knew," she said. "I'll be back as fast as I can, and I'll get an ambulance."

She took the torch with her and I listened to the wonderful sound of her going for help. I lay back and thanked the Lord that she hadn't thought I'd stood her up.

The private hospital in Newbury smelled the same and looked pretty much the same as the NHS one where I'd lain after my crash in Sussex. The big difference was that this time, if I wanted smoked salmon, Camilla didn't need to bring it; it was on the menu anyway.

She had found John Calloway at home and bundled him into the Land Rover, trying to convince him as they drove back to my place and through my woods that I was stuck out there with my leg in a mantrap. He hadn't believed her; thought she was indulging in feminine hyperbole. When he arrived, he was more shocked than she had been. But he'd brought the right tackle with him. He heaved the hook out of the ground, rammed it back in over the jaw that was on the ground and levered the top jaw open with an inch-thick wrecking bar.

I drew blood from my lip, biting it against the pain

and the urge to scream as the rusty tooth was plucked from the deep wound it had made.

"Pull your leg out, quick," he yelled.

I gritted my teeth and dragged my mangled limb out. John tugged my dented gun out and let the jaws spring back together with a clash that chilled my blood.

The limb I brought with me to the hospital wasn't a pretty sight. Apart from the deep flesh wound, the bone was bruised but not broken. A lot of serious stitching dealt with the torn calf muscles, along with a massive tetanus jab in my behind. There was some gloomy head-shaking about recovery time. I'd be very lucky if I rode at Epsom in two and a half weeks, they told me.

Luck wouldn't come into it, I told myself.

I asked them to go easy on the painkillers—not out of heroism, but because I've always reckoned that pain plays the useful function of telling you that something's wrong, where it's wrong and when it's getting better.

As a result, I didn't have a lot of sleep that first night in hospital. I thought I'd just dropped off when a nurse came in to discuss breakfast with me. I suddenly realized how hungry I was; I'd barely eaten a thing the day before, saving up for my dinner with Camilla.

I was making headway into a pile of wholesome wheatgerm toast when my first visitor arrived.

Charles Powell was exactly the man I wanted to see. He was one of those men who seem to know a little about a lot of things. My connection with him was through a couple of horses he kept in training and a small breeding operation, but this was just one facet of his varied existence. After ten years in the army, spent doing unmentionable things to terrorists around the world, he had become a landscape photographer, a travel writer, an amateur archaeologist, as well as the father of four stunning teenage girls. He was a rich, affable dilettante who, in his younger days, had loved the glamor and danger of steeple-chasing, twice becoming amateur champion.

I hadn't seen him for a few months. He'd been on a fishing trip in Tierra del Fuego, followed by a digging trip at an Inca graveyard in Peru. But he walked in as if he'd seen me the day before, with his bright blue eyes shining below a tangle of wavy black hair.

"Morning, Jake. How are you feeling?"

"Rough. How did you know I was here?"

"Next door neighbor. What the hell have you done to your face?" He was gazing with distaste at the scratches and lacerations the bramble had caused as I'd struggled to get the sticky blindfold off my eyes.

"It's not as bad as it looks; surface stuff."

"Take a tip from me though, don't appear on television for a while. Did you sleep much last night?"

"Not a lot." I waved him at a chair. He shook his head but heaved his large shoulders out of a rumpled linen jacket which he chucked on my bed. He carried on wandering around the room, looking out of the window at the cedars lit by the morning sun in the park that surrounded the hospital.

"I hear the leg's rather nasty."

"D'you want to see it?"

He laughed, displaying a set of gleaming white teeth. "Not unless you're going to take the bandages off and show me properly."

"Take my word for it, it's not comfortable."

"They tell me," and I could see that this was what really interested him, "you were caught in a mantrap."

"You like that, huh?"

"Well, it does pose some intriguing questions. I mean, I don't suppose they get too many mantrap victims in here."

"So they tell me," I said.

"Do you know who set it for you or why?"

I pushed the remains of breakfast to one side. "As a matter of fact, I don't have a clue. The police talked to me last night for an hour. I was throbbing with pain and I couldn't tell them much. My neighbor saw an old

Subaru pick-up he didn't recognize parked in the top lane at the back of my woods, about half a mile from where it happened. But that's all they've got."

"Who found you?"

"A girl. She came to take me out to dinner. When she didn't find me in, she guessed I was around because the house was open and my plane was back."

"Plane?"

"I got myself a little Piper Comanche; lost my driving license."

"How did you do that?"

"That's a long story. A hack got me smashed and I drove my car over the side of a cliff."

"My goodness, you have been busy." Charles was impressed; he even raised an eyebrow a fraction. "What took the girl into the woods?"

"She was looking for me, getting impatient, I should think, and she heard me hollering. I was lucky; that was my last try, and I'd passed out when she got to me."

"Where's the mantrap now?"

I shrugged my shoulders. "I don't know. I guess the police have got it for forensic stuff."

"I'd like to see it."

"I'd like to throw it in a furnace and watch it melt. Why don't you ask the police? They need all the help they can get."

"I will. When I heard what had happened to you, I looked up a few precedents. Those traps were normally used to catch poachers, but occasionally they were used as instruments of revenge, back in the eighteenth century before lawyers had learned to persuade everyone to go to litigation. Could the trap have been set for anyone else?"

I shook my head. "Nope. I'm the only person who ever walks those woods. I go through them most evenings this time of year, if I can, maybe for an hour or two. And I often take the same track. I guess someone must have checked it out. It was definitely me they were after, they gagged and tied me as well."

"Who would want to do this to you?"

"I told you, I don't have a clue. I've been thinking about it most of the night. I'm not saying I'm everybody's flavor of the month, but I haven't done anything bad enough to deserve this."

"You must have done something. There's no other reason anyone should do what they did. If they just wanted to kill you, there are dozens of more efficient and reliable ways. Whoever set that trap didn't care if you lived or died. He probably thought there was a good chance of your being found, but he would certainly have expected you to be off games for a while. A mantrap in good working order should have broken your leg and the nurse tells me it didn't."

"No, thank God. My gun got caught in it, so it didn't close completely, but my calf muscle's pretty well lacerated."

"Do you know yet how long you'll be off?"

"No more than a week if I have anything to do with it."

"You don't want to miss your ride on Dawn Raider."

"No, I don't. And I've got Corsican Lady in the Oaks."

"A big week."

"You could say that."

Charles had been looking out of the window again. "I see a tall girl with legs like a pair of shapely rugger posts making her way from the car park. A tenner at even money says she's coming to see you," he said.

I felt a pleasurable flush. "No bet."

Charles laughed. "You're a jammy bastard. I don't know how you get away with it." He spun round decisively. "I'll leave you to it, then. Would you mind if I dug around a bit, to see what I can find?"

"Be my guest," I said.

"Good," he nodded. "I'll be in touch. We'll have to talk more about possible avengers. In the meantime, could you write down the name of everyone you can think of who might remotely have it in for you, and why?"

"Sure."

"Right. I'll be off."

He was out of the room in a couple of strides and banging the door behind him. I was glad he had come. For no reason that I'd cared to analyze, I hadn't made any really close friends since being in England, but Charles came nearest to it. In a world rife with bull, I had never heard Charles say anything he didn't mean, or offer opinions on anything he wasn't very well informed about. He inspired more confidence than any other person I knew.

Camilla came in looking ridiculous.

Why was a girl who looked as though she had just stepped off a Paris catwalk clutching a brown paper bag in a hospital room containing one small, smashed up jockey?

I asked her.

"God knows," she said with a smile that would have weakened a stronger man than I was. "You look absolutely terrible. Anyway, I've brought you some fresh passion fruit."

"Passion fruit I don't need right now."

"That bad, eh? Mum's very worried."

"I bet she is."

"Are you any better this morning?"

"A little. Give me a day. I'm getting out of here tomorrow."

"Can you walk yet?"

"Sure I can walk. And you can tell your mother not to worry, I'll be on Corsican Lady."

"She is concerned for you, too, you know, though I

don't think she's quite taken in that someone must dislike you very much to have done this to you."

"If my gun hadn't been caught in the trap, it would have broken my leg, which would have put me off for a few months, so I guess that rules your mother off the list of suspects."

"Oh, Jake, it's horrendous that anyone should want to do that to you. Have you had any more ideas about who did it?"

"Not really."

"What about that shifty Irishman, Mick Hagan? I heard he was really pissed off about you winning a race at Newbury."

"He was. He'd had a pile of money on it and I think he's broke. He's sore all right. He won't speak to me, but I just don't believe he's that upset."

"You never know, Jake. Losing that race might have been the last straw for him."

"Nope. It wasn't Mick Hagan, I'm absolutely certain."

But, as I didn't have any other options to offer, Camilla was less certain. I didn't want to think about it.

"Look, I'm alive, I've still got my right leg, BUPA's paying the bill, and I've lost a few days' racing. It could have been a lot worse, so don't worry about it."

"Of course I'm worried, Jake. Whoever set that thing, if they didn't want to kill you, certainly wanted to harm you. You can't just shrug it off."

"I know. Don't worry, I'll be waiting for them next time."

"And the other thing is that I'm going away for ten days. There's an art fair in Florence I have to go to, and I'm spending a couple of days down near Siena with some friends. To tell you the truth, I'd rather not go, not while you're in hospital, but I can't let them down. I hope you don't mind."

"Listen, I'm just glad to know you care."

"I care," she said. "But I've got to go now. So look

after yourself." She leaned forward and gave me a quick kiss on the lips. She left the room with a look that did a lot more to ease the pain than a shot of morphine could have done.

//////////// CHAPTER 6

After Camilla had gone, I got out of bed and tried walking for the first time since I had put my leg between the teeth of the trap.

As I eased my weight gently onto my toes, a sharp pain leapt from the wound to my crotch. I let out a yell and snatched up my foot. Standing on one leg by the bed, I hoped that no one had heard—my scream had been out of all proportion to the pain and I realized it was just my skin playing tug of war with the stitches. I tried again to stand on my bad leg. It hurt less this time, but I began to sweat, though nothing like the way I had the night before.

I took a few tentative, hobbling steps. Although I couldn't get full flexion in my ankle, I didn't think it would be long before I did.

Later, a doctor came to inspect the wound. It looked encouraging, he said. I would be laid up for only two or three days.

I signed out next morning and asked the hospital to call for a taxi in a fake name to avoid any hassle from the press. If the driver recognized me, he didn't let on. I slipped quietly into the back seat and asked him to stop at the first newsagents we came to and buy all the dailies. Five minutes later, I opened them and found with relief that none of them had picked up the story of me being found in a mantrap. I'd forgotten to ask Charles Powell or Camilla if it had been reported. They hadn't mentioned it, so I guessed the police had released nothing yet.

A few people in racing would have heard something, and my absence at Windsor that evening would be queried. I'd have to think of a plausible excuse.

The gates of my house were still open from my exit by ambulance two days before and I cursed Camilla for not shutting them. But I felt a stab of guilt for being so ungrateful; if she hadn't bothered to come and look for me, I'd very likely have still been lying out there in the woods.

I paid the driver off and then stood there. I wondered how the hell I was going to get in. I didn't have keys with me. I tried the garage door. It had a manual action and slid up and over, not locked. The side door from the garage to the house was open.

I shook my head, annoyed that the place had been left open. I stepped into my warm, humming kitchen and dumped a plastic bag of bloody, shredded jeans and torn muddy shirt onto the table. I glanced around. A lot of lights were flashing at me—the fax, the answerphone, the video. I didn't want to deal with them yet. First, I wanted to see how much punishment my leg would take. I walked through the hall and up the wide, open-tread staircase to my bedroom. The clothes I had been wearing at Newmarket on Saturday were where I had thrown them when I had changed to go out for my last walk.

I pulled on a tracksuit and headed back down to the gym. As I padded silently down the stairs, I heard a noise in the large reception room off the hall. There was a clunk as somebody put some heavy object onto a table. I stopped. The hair rose on the back of my neck and my body tensed with fear. Then I smelled a whiff of black French tobacco, and relaxed.

"Charles?" I said.

Two heavy footfalls; Charles Powell appeared at the door of the room.

"Jake! You're back. I didn't hear you come in."

"Have you been here some time, then?"

"Half an hour or so. John Calloway lent me the key and I walked up from his place. I wanted to have a snoop around. I hope you don't mind."

"No, that's okay. Have you been out to the woods yet?"

"Not yet. I don't know exactly where it happened."

"I'll show you."

"Can you? Is the leg up to it?"

"We'll find out, won't we?"

I limped the half-mile to the place where I'd been trapped. My leg didn't give me too much grief, but when we reached the spot where the bracken had been flattened by my writhing attempts to free myself, the memory of the fear I'd felt came sharply back to me.

The trap, of course, had gone now, back with the Basingstoke CID. They had evidently searched a pretty wide area.

"You were bloody lucky you had that gun with you," Charles said, not for the first time.

"I was lucky it wasn't my one remaining Purdey."

"What are you talking about?"

"That's something else that happened. When I was in hospital last time, after the crash, someone broke into the house and took one of the Mewar Purdeys. Nothing else."

"I wonder if there's a connection."

"I don't see how, or why."

"A lot of things have been happening to you, Jake. It could be coincidental, of course, or maybe a result of Jupiter entering your star sign, but I doubt it. You're not looking too good," he said abruptly. "Why don't you get on back to the house. I just want to have another look round."

I didn't object. "Okay. When you come back, I'll show you the list I've made of people who might have a grudge."

I left him and slowly made my way back through the woods, even in these circumstances gaining pleasure from them.

By the time I reached the house, my leg was sore and I abandoned my plan for a mild work-out in the gym. I went into the kitchen and rummaged in my plastic bag to find the list I'd made in hospital. I took the sheet of paper through to the drawing room, where I could look out of the huge windows down the sunlit valley while I thought.

I took another notepad from my bureau and wrote the list again, canceling some names and adding a few more. After a while, I was gazing at the view, trying to think back over the last few years, when I heard the door from the garage open.

"In here," I called to Charles.

I heard his footsteps cross the flagstone hallway. My subconscious told me they were too quick to be long-legged Charles's. I turned and froze. In the doorway, at the end of a very handsome shotgun, stood Mick Hagan.

Mick Hagan, with fear and remorse in his sharp little eyes.

I tried to hide my apprehension as I spoke. "What the hell do you want, Mick?"

He didn't have time to answer. An arm snaked round his neck and jerked him back out through the door. The gun fell to the floor with a clatter.

I jumped to my feet and hobbled as fast as my bad leg would let me through into the hall.

Mick Hagan was lying prostrate on the stone flags, with his arms pinioned up behind his back. Charles was sitting on him, grinning.

"Is this fellow on your list?"

I nodded. But I still didn't really believe it could have been Mick who had attacked me on Saturday night, or had anything to do with it. I didn't know what to think now.

"For Christ's sake," Mick squealed. "Get off me, y' bastard."

Charles nodded at the shotgun. "Cover him with that and I'll strap him to a chair."

I picked up the gun. It was the missing Mewar Purdey.

"For Christ's sake, this is mine!"

"Of course it is!" Hagan's panic pitched his voice up. "I was bringin' it back to you."

Charles Powell got to his feet, dragging Hagan with him. He lifted the Irishman right off the floor and dropped him onto an old oak settle.

"Good heavens! Mr. Hagan," Charles said with surprise. "This is an unusual sort of crime for you."

"What the hell are you talkin' about? Y'man told me he'd lost a gun. I asked around and bought it back for him."

"Bought it back?"

"Yes, for twenty-five grand."

I had instinctively pointed the weapon at Hagan. "You bought it back for me? Why the hell did you come in aiming it at me?"

Hagan got to his feet and walked straight toward me. "The fuckin' thing isn't even loaded. I just thought you deserved a fright." He reached for the gun.

Charles grabbed him and spun him round. He delved into the pockets of the canvas jacket Hagan was wearing and pulled out a handful of cartridges.

"What are these for, then?"

Still staring at Hagan, I broke the gun. The barrels were empty.

Mick was protesting to Powell, "I always have a few on me. I've just come straight from the club." He turned to me. "For God's sake, will you tell your friend to let go of me. What's he think I'd come to shoot you for?"

I tried to read the truth in the bright, ferret eyes. But Hagan had forgotten how to look truthful.

"Let him go," I said at last.

Charles looked at me, shrugged and released Hagan's wrists.

"I think you'd better go," I said to Mick.

"What about my money?" he almost shrieked.

"You'll get your money."

Hagan took a long look at me, begging and threatening. "I fuckin' better," he hissed and spun round to stomp across the hall and out through the kitchen.

We heard a door bang, and he was gone.

"You believe him?"

"I guess so. If he'd come to do me damage, the gun would have been loaded."

"He said he'd just come from a club. Would that have been a gun club?"

"Yeah. He shoots a lot. I guess that's how he got to hear where the gun was. Like he said, I'd told him it had been stolen."

"If he shoots a lot, he could have had two cartridges into the barrel of that gun and cocked it in a second or two."

"Yeah, I know, but I don't think he came to shoot me, anyway he'd have had it already loaded if that's what he'd come to do."

"You said he was on your list. Why?"

I told Charles about the race which had caused the problem, and the rumors that were doing the rounds after it.

"He didn't look as though he came here to do you any favors," Charles remarked, "but I agree I can't see that he'd have had it in for you badly enough to leave you festering in a mantrap."

"He came here to get twenty-five grand out of me. The gun's worth fifty and the insurance company would pay up anyway but he knew I wanted that gun back."

"Could he have known that before it was taken? Did he know about it?"

"Everyone knew about it. I did an interview with a guy from the *Sunday Times*. He asked me what I thought the British did best, and I told him making sporting guns. They took a picture of me holding one of mine and used it with the piece."

"Did they say how much the guns were worth?"

"No, but it wouldn't have taken much to find out."

"And Mick knew you were fond of them, that you'd want the gun rather than the insurance money?"

I nodded. "He knew that pair of guns was one of the few possessions that meant much to me."

"And will you pay him?"

"That depends on what the insurance company have to say. Now I've got it back, it might be tricky to persuade them they have to pay anything. I could ask the police to have a word with Mick. He might talk if he thinks there's a chance of getting his twenty-five, but that could be risky for him. And it's just possible he didn't have anything to do with stealing it. I mean, he may not be an honest man when it comes to riding races, but I wouldn't have said he was a total crook. In a funny kind of way he's sort of moral. I guess it would have to depend on how desperate he was. Poor bastard's got six kids to feed."

"It's a pity we let him go, though. We should have kept him here and called the police."

"Maybe, but I just couldn't do that to the guy. He'd been a good friend to me in the past. He taught me a lot. It's only since that one race that we fell out. And I had the feeling he'd sort of got over that recently. It's possible he did ask around about my gun, especially as I told him there was a few quid in it and whoever took it would know that he had a direct line to me. From his point of view, he was doing me a favor and making a few grand for himself on the way through."

Charles was less understanding. "You won't have heard the last of it. He was probably counting on that money. If he doesn't get it, he may get desperate. In the meantime, will you tell the police that I have your permission to inspect the trap? I'd like to see it, and tomorrow I'm going to take a look at your Aston. I've tracked it down to the fellow who bought it from your insurance company and he hasn't broken it up yet."

"Don't tell me that—I miss it."

"I'll give it your regards." He looked at his watch. "Hell! I've got to go. I'm taking one of the girls to the airport. I'll give you a ring and come back and see you about your list of suspects."

I was used to Charles's abrupt departures. I watched him stride off back to Calloway's and thought that I had more confidence in him than in the young detective sergeant who had come to see me in hospital.

I went back into the kitchen and phoned the police station to tell them that Charles would be coming over to inspect the mantrap. When I told them his credentials, they didn't object.

The little mail van delivered the usual bundle of post next morning. Out of habit, as I walked through to the kitchen, I flipped through the pile of brown envelopes for anything that might be more interesting or welcome than the rest of the official garbage that my job generated.

One small, white envelope caught my eye. It was postmarked London and my name and address were scrawled with a clumsy, thick felt pen.

I ripped it open and pulled out a single sheet of paper. On it were written, in the same scrawled capitals, five words: "POACHERS GET WHAT POACHERS DESERVE."

I felt fear ripple through me as I stared at words which took me straight back to those terrible hours in the mantrap.

Poachers, Charles had said. And sometimes revenge. I put the paper down with a shaking hand.

Who?

Why?

What the hell had I done to make anyone hate me that much?

There had to be a reason. Just knowing that was beginning to make me feel guilty. And yet, though I'd searched every neglected crevice of my conscience over the last three days, I hadn't identified a single badly injured party for whom I could be called responsible.

I pinned the paper to a noticeboard on the wall and stared at it some more, trying to recognize or understand something about it from the clumsy writing. But the words just stared back at me.

I didn't ring the police. Somewhere, some time, I'd done something bad enough to stimulate a violent attack of hate. I had to know what that was before I brought them into it.

I concentrated instead on repairing my leg, and my bruised ego. With a strict program of increasing exercise, I made more progress than my doctor could believe.

I was surprised not to hear anything from Charles for a few days. I guessed that if he'd had anything useful to tell me, he would have rung. But I found that I'd been counting on his support more than I'd realized. I had told no one else about the note, but I wanted to tell him.

At the end of the week, I rang his big, rambling Sussex farmhouse. He was away, his wife Susan told me, with one of their daughters whom he had promised to take to Seville for the Expo.

I was more let down than I wanted to admit to myself. But then, I shouldn't have been surprised. Charles somehow managed to compartmentalize his life between being the doting family man and being the outward-bound, macho action man. I told myself again that if he had found out anything useful, he would surely have told me. I asked Susan to get him to ring me as soon as he was back.

Mick Hagan, on the other hand, did keep his promise to come back.

He turned up after the races on Saturday. I'd been at home and watched him on the TV stealing a five-furlong sprint with all his usual guile. As I watched, I wondered how a man of undoubted skill and talent had let himself sink into the crazy, nerve-wracking game of racing his horses for the bookies. Then I remembered my father. It was an easier, more tempting route to take than most people realized.

When he arrived at my house that evening, though, he was a walking advertisement for criminal stress.

I was pretty sure he hadn't come to threaten me physically, but I made him empty out all his pockets before I let him in.

"Sorry to do that, Mick," I said as I unlocked the front door for him.

"What the hell's the matter with you?" he asked, then he noticed me limping slightly as I led him into my kitchen to talk. "What have you done to your leg to put you out of it for so long?"

"Don't you know?"

"No, of course I don't."

I had no idea if he was telling the truth or not.

"It's nothing much," I said, "I should be working again next week."

"More's the pity."

"If you've come here to get money out of me, you're not going about it the right way, Mick. After all, I've got the gun back now."

"You promised me, you bastard. I found the fuckin' thing for you, and I didn't do it out of charity, I can tell you. I've got to pay for it meself, and people are beginning to get heavy about it."

"How did you find it?" I asked.

"It found me. Now are you going to pay me, or do I have to pass you on to the fellas who want paying?"

"I can't give you twenty-five grand for it."

Mick stared at me with a sudden look of abject panic in his eyes. "What? What are you saying? You promised. If I don't get the money, I'll be shredded by these people. You can get the money back from the insurance," he babbled. "It won't cost you a penny, for Christ's sake."

"Don't be dumb, Mick. Of course I can't get it from the insurance. I didn't even report the gun stolen when I first had the break-in because I didn't know it had been taken. I can't go to them now and tell them I forgot to mention it, but it's okay because somebody's brought it back and they want half the value. I'd have to tell the police for a start, and then they'd want to talk to you."

"Jake, Jake, don't do this. I thought you were a man of your word." The little man's eyes were popping from his head as he pleaded.

It was absurd, but I found myself wanting to help. "Look, I can't get anyone else to pay this. How much money are you supposed to come up with?"

Mick didn't answer.

"Just tell me, Mick. How much were you adding on for yourself?"

He couldn't look me in the eyes now.

"Mick, if you don't tell me, I'll have to report the whole crazy incident. Whoever's selling you the gun won't be too happy about that. Just tell me what you owe."

Mick looked at me now, hopeless, knowing the lousy scam wasn't going to work. Perhaps he'd known all along it wasn't going to, but had kidded himself because he was desperate to believe he could find some money from somewhere to settle with his bookmaker. I guessed that Harry would only take some of Mick's debt in stopped horses.

"Fifteen grand I'm to pay, or God knows what they'll break. You've got to believe me, Jake."

I watched his eyes. I'd played enough hands of poker with him to know his bluff.

"Ten, Mick. You've got to pay them ten, haven't you?"

His eyes slid away. His face twitched. He nodded. I thought I believed him.

"I'll give you the ten," I said.

He relaxed a little. I guessed he really wasn't going to make anything on the deal; maybe he thought he could talk down whoever had given the gun to him. At least he would be off their hook.

"That's a load of trouble I've had for fuck all," he said.

"That's your problem. If you'd asked me for a loan, I'd have given you one, you know that."

"You smug bastard," he growled. "Just give me the ten grand."

"I haven't got ten grand in readies, here, now. I'll have to arrange it," I said reasonably.

"When?" He was panicking again. "I haven't got much time."

"End of next week," I said.

"That's too late."

"They'll give you till then, Mick. It's that or nothing."

He glared at me, still with no trace of his old friendliness. "Don't you let me down." He gave me a last look, half plea, half threat, and spun round to walk out of the house. I let him go, feeling sorry for him; wondering why the hell I'd said I would pay him. I guess I believed just enough of what he told me, and at least I had the gun back.

But I wasn't going to pay him for a week; there was a chance that might throw someone else into the ring.

Seven days afer leaving hospital, and with ten stitches in my leg, I rode work.

My doctor hadn't recommended it, but he didn't deny that the gash in my calf was healing well and it wasn't in a position where it would be rubbed by riding. Thankfully, the bruising and cuts on my shin were just far enough above my ankle to avoid coming into contact with the stirrup leather, provided I rode two holes shorter than normal. I called in at his surgery on my way back from Ellerton's, and he agreed to declare me fit to ride by the following Wednesday, Derby day.

Since my non-appearance at Windsor the week before, the press had been speculating wildly about the chances of my appearing on Dawn Raider for the Classic. I had to leave my phone permanently on answer mode to filter out the hacks. Despite the rumors that were circulating, my absence was officially attributed to a tendon strained while playing squash.

Charles didn't ring me. He turned up two days before the Derby. He didn't apologize for his absence in Spain. There was no reason why he should. But I had to ask him if he'd got anywhere with the inquiries he'd said he would make.

"Yes," he answered. "I'm getting there. But I'm not going to tell you about it until after the Derby. You concentrate on that and leave everything else to me."

He also looked at the note I'd received: "Poachers get what poachers deserve."

"English, adult, male, not educated," he said, studying the writing. "That narrows it down to about twenty million. But I very much doubt it was written by whoever is behind this thing. Odd, though, isn't it? This piece of paper which can't do a thing to hurt you physically has scared you more than the trap that caught you and smashed your leg."

I agreed. "Sure, the trap was just an impersonal object. This tells me that somebody has been watching me, planning; that they'll try again."

"They will." Charles nodded. "And there's not a lot you can do about it. You'll just have to be very vigilant, and not let it show. In the meantime, I'll do anything I can to help you find out who's doing this. We've got to try and get to them first. Now," he said, abruptly changing his tone and the subject, "you can't land your plane at Epsom, can you? So I'd better take you."

He also agreed to back up my story about the squash injury, owning up to being my opponent. He provided one persistent hack who rang that evening with a detailed and colorful version of the shot I had been trying to return when the damage had been done.

The sun was creeping over the ridge of the hill at the head of my valley when Charles appeared in his Range Rover to take me to Epsom.

Dawn Raider had been taken there the day before to avoid the race-day traffic and to spend the night with a few of his competitors and a team of security men.

"How's the leg holding up?" he said as he leaned across the passenger seat, holding the door open for me.

I threw my helmet, stick and jacket onto the back seat with a small suitcase and climbed in beside him.

"I wouldn't want to run a marathon on it, but I think it'll be okay for this afternoon."

I pulled the door shut and we started the forty miles to Epsom. Giles Seymour had asked me to meet his traveling head lad outside the stables at seven fifteen, so we had plenty of time. At this time of day, the journey would take about forty minutes; later in the day it would take anything up to three hours.

We turned into the stable entrance just in front of the tunnel which ran under the racecourse and drove slowly down to where Dan Costello, Giles's head lad, was waiting for us.

"Morning, Dan," I greeted him. "What are we doing?"

"Just a short canter to stretch his legs. That's all the guv'nor wants." He smiled. "How's your leg?"

"Fine, thanks. This is the man responsible for it." I turned and introduced Charles.

"Could have been an expensive game of squash," Dan said as they shook hands. "You two wait here while I go and fetch the horse."

As neither Charles nor I held stable passes, there was no question of us being permitted into the stable area.

A few minutes later, Dan reappeared, followed by Dawn Raider, led by his lad. The horse looked as well as ever, even sharper than he had at Newmarket for the Guineas.

"He looks fantastic, Garry," I congratulated his lad.

Dan lifted me into the saddle. The back of my leg was no more than slightly sore and as we made our way up to the racecourse, I shortened my leathers to be sure they wouldn't rub my shin.

Galloping on the course itself was forbidden after Tuesday morning of Derby week to give the ground staff a chance to repair the turf. We headed over to the gallops used by the local trainers on the far side of the one-and-a-half-mile start. There was a heavy dew on the long grass and Charles's feet were soaked, but he insisted on coming with us.

"Why didn't Giles send another horse to keep him company?" he asked.

Garry, who had looked after Dawn Raider since he'd arrived from Toby's, gave the answer. "He's more relaxed on his own. If he's with other horses he tends to show off."

The gypsies' site on our right was well awake and bustling as we passed. Some came out of their caravans to have a look and called out what I guessed—or hoped —were messages of good luck.

There was a bit of warmth in the sun by the time I walked Dawn Raider out onto the gallops.

"I'll go four furlongs and then walk back, so you may as well wait here," I said.

Dan nodded. "Okay. Remember he only wants to stretch his legs; he did plenty yesterday."

I set off at a good canter and headed up the slight hill, keeping just to the right of the marker discs to avoid the poached ground—no point in taking unnecessary risks at this late stage.

Dawn Raider felt magnificent and reminded me that it was always exciting to ride a really top-class horse. The power from behind the saddle was pushing us easily across the rich green turf and he took a keen hold for the first furlong or so before he settled into his rhythm and gave me time to think.

I knew that a jockey had very few real chances at the biggest race in the British calendar, and today I had my best yet.

Would the horse be good enough?

Everything about him told me he was, but I'd just have to wait until the race was run to be sure.

When we pulled up, I was more concerned about the pain in my calf muscle. Usually when I rode, I didn't notice a bit of pain but I was worried now that I'd pulled a couple of the stitches apart. But by the time I'd walked back to the others, the pain had worn off.

Garry was holding out a handful of grass to his charge. "How is he?" he asked anxiously.

"Couldn't possibly be better," I told him.

"Do you think he'll come down the hill okay?"

It was a question I'd already asked myself. "You'll know as soon as I do," I replied, "but I don't see why not. I know he's got a long stride, but he's very well balanced."

Normally, I would have dismounted and led the horse back to the stables, but I didn't want to aggravate my leg, so I stayed on board.

Back at the gates to the stable area, I got off carefully and Garry and Dan took Dawn Raider in. I sent Charles off to the lads' canteen for breakfast while I took my suitcase from the Range Rover and walked up the course to the jockeys' changing room. I showered and found that my stitches were all intact, though a little blood was seeping from the top of the wound. If nothing happened to make it worse, I reckoned I could get through the afternoon.

I changed into a lightweight suit and looked at my watch. It was just after nine, which gave me an hour to kill before a scheduled interview for an American TV station.

Martin was busy cleaning a pair of boots on a table, and I called to borrow his paper.

I picked up the *Sporting Life* and read the headline: "DAWN RAIDER TO STEAL THE DERBY." Beneath it, the entire page was given up to an assessment of the race and the reasons why I should win it.

I couldn't dispute most of the material, but I still thought a price of 7/2—in half a point from the day before—was ridiculous. Quite apart from the luck needed in the running of the race, the performance of horses could improve startlingly in the summer of their three-year-old careers. Add the peculiarities of Epsom's contours and practically anything could happen.

I read the rest of the paper, made a couple of calls on

my mobile phone to confirm rides later in the week then went out to find the reporter who was supposed to be interviewing me.

As I stepped outside, I was struck by the change that had occured in a couple of hours. The whole place was buzzing with the activities of ground staff, officials, caterers and the hundreds of traders setting up their pitches. The sun was well up now, dazzling off the white rails round the hallowed winner's enclosure and shimmering off the blades of the helicopters that were arriving in the middle of the course.

Charles was leaning against a rail, watching them.

"That's what we could do with to go home this evening," I said, still peeved that I wasn't able to land my own plane here and watching a yellow Jetranger lift off after delivering its wealthy load.

"I've just been down to the town for some film," Charles said, "and the tailbacks are building up already. It'll take for ever getting out of here."

"If I win the Derby, there won't be much traffic around by the time we leave."

"Jake!" a voice hailed me from behind.

I turned to see a man in his early forties, six feet tall and well-built, holding out a big hand and smiling.

"Hi. I'm Darren Brown from NBC."

After being in England for a few years, it took me by surprise to be approached by someone so openly friendly. I even hesitated a moment before offering my hand back.

"Thanks for agreeing to the interview," the American said. "We're ready when you are, just up in the balcony."

I arranged to meet Charles at the same spot after my last ride, and went up to the first floor of the stands. The interview lasted about five minutes and was due to be broadcast on the East Coast, just before the Derby went out live at eight-thirty, local time. The Americans were loudly enthusiastic at the thought that one of their own was about to stuff the Brits on their home ground.

After that, I thought a little relaxation would do me good. I went back to the changing room and joined a game of stud poker with a couple of the valets and two other jockeys.

Derby day was notorious for jockeys being held up by the traffic and not arriving in time for their races. Old hands always turned up with a lot of time to spare.

Dealing with large stretches of time with nothing to do before and between races was a perennial problem for jockeys. Portable phones had helped take up some of the slack, but for the most part, for those who didn't need to sit in the sauna to make a weight, time was passed by playing cards, reading the papers, or simply sleeping on a bench.

Apart from Dawn Raider, I only had one other ride, and that was in the sprint race that followed the Derby. That gave me a good few hours to kill.

I fanned out my second hand of cards—a pair of nines and a pair of threes—and lightly scratched my stitches. They were beginning to itch. Maybe luck was running; it was a good sign. If they were itching, they were healing.

It cost me £200 to discover that I wasn't holding the best hand, and another hour and a half to bluff back most of it. Half an hour before the first race, the valets gave up their places at the table. They went off to make sure that the jockeys they looked after had everything they needed. The empty seats were soon taken by two jockeys wrapped in towels and sweating from the sauna. I was shuffling for the next deal when Martin called to say I was wanted at the door—only jockeys and valets were allowed in the changing room. I left a stand-in to play my hand and went out.

Giles Seymour was pacing up and down. There was an angry frown on his normally placid face.

"Did you want me?" I asked.

"Yes," he said testily, coming to a standstill and pushing his binoculars behind him. "That bloody jockey of mine has just phoned to say he's stuck in the traffic and won't be here in time for the first. He must be the only fucking person in the whole country who doesn't know you have to leave early on Derby day. Can you ride this horse of mine? I think he'll just about win."

I immediately thought of my leg, and the real possibility that it would only stand up to one ride. And if I was only going to have one ride, that was going to be in the Derby. The problem was that, if I told Giles, he might not even let me ride Dawn Raider if he thought there was any doubt about my fitness.

"Okay. Thanks," I said, deciding quickly that I had to accept. "I'll go and get changed."

Giles's filly, Lorna Doone, had won both her starts easily, though she hadn't had to beat much to do it. It was anybody's guess how she'd handle the course and the step up in company.

I changed and weighed out before taking a closer look at the form of the race to see how it might be run and which were the fancied horses. In the week leading up to the Derby, there had, for once, been no rain. With the warm weather we'd been having, the official going was "good to firm." That would suit Dawn Raider, but I didn't know about Lorna Doone.

I was just getting into one of the official cars that transport the jockeys down to the distant parade ring when I saw Tony Adams, the jockey who should have been on Lorna Doone, running toward the weighing room.

I climbed out again, asking the driver to wait a moment.

"What's this filly like?" I called over to Tony.

"Good. She's a bit green," he gasped, getting his breath back after sprinting from the car park. "Make sure you keep a good hold of her coming down the hill, she'll definitely keep galloping."

"Great. I'll give you a drink if she wins."

I got back in the car and we were rushed to the paddock.

Giles's instructions to make plenty of use of the filly confirmed what Tony had said about her ability to get the trip. She looked a little weak in the paddock, but on the way to the start I was glad to find that none of the other jockeys seemed keen to go on. With luck, she might be able to make the running in her own time. She certainly gave me a good feel on the way down.

Giles Seymour's two-year-olds were always well mannered, which didn't help when it came to getting a quick start. To make up for this, just before the starter let us go, I gave her a good crack down the shoulder with my whip so that she knew I meant business.

It must have been the first time in her life she'd been hit; she came out of the stall like a rocket and raced away down the hill and round Tattenham Corner while I was still trying to settle her.

At the apex of the bend, I'd just got her to drop the bridle when I heard a crack like a hunting whip.

I knew what it was.

I froze, almost rigid for an instant, before her left shoulder collapsed and she crashed to the ground, turning a half-somersault and firing me into the plastic running rail.

With a male jockey's instinct to protect his genitals, I rolled into a ball while the following runners scrambled round me and their jockeys shouted warnings. By the time I looked up, the last horse was past, and poor Lorna Doone was hobbling on three legs with her cannon bone snapped clean, swinging wildly from her knee as if it were held on by a piece of thread. I got to my feet and ran to grab her reins to stop her from running after the others.

Then I felt the pain in my own leg. And my heart

almost stopped. I guess I knew I wouldn't be riding again that afternoon, but I wasn't going to give up my Derby without a fight.

I looked up at the sky and swore, using every obscenity I'd ever learned. The crowd, ten deep at the rails, loved it.

I fell back onto the grass, clutching my leg. Lorna Doone had already learned that running hurt too much; she stood still and let herself be caught. The ambulance arrived for me at the same time that the vet arrived to deal with her. She looked bewildered and frightened, I thought, I might be in pain, but at least I knew where I was going.

I climbed to my feet as the ambulance rolled up. I walked to meet it, desperately trying not to limp but the pain was searing. At the back of my mind there was just a chance. I was still hoping I might be able to bluff my way past the doctor.

Back in the small first-aid room beneath the stands, a nurse gently pulled off my right boot, and sucked through her teeth when she saw the blood that was soaking my socks and breeches.

"It's okay," I said light-heartedly. "Just scraped a scab off."

"We'll see about that," she said. "I'm just as concerned as you that you should ride Dawn Raider. I've got the biggest bet on him I've ever had."

Giles Seymour arrived before the doctor.

"Crikey, Jake, what the hell have you done?"

"Nothing. Just opened up a bit of a cut I had."

"Bit of a cut!" the nurse expostulated, which didn't help. "You've got about ten stitches in the back of your leg."

I didn't answer. Giles was peering gloomily at the damage. "How does it feel?" he asked.

"It's a bit sore, but it'll be okay."

He didn't look convinced, though he wanted to be.

"You can't ride like that. I'll have to get someone else."

"Like who?" I protested. "Anyone who's any good has already got a ride."

"I'll think of something."

"Look, Giles, don't make any decisions yet. I'll be okay. If I really don't think I can ride, I'll tell you. I don't want to screw up your chances too."

The nurse had cleaned up the wound by the time the doctor arrived. The stitches and the bruising showed, but the bleeding had stopped.

"I don't see how you've got any strength in that ankle with that cut," the doctor said.

"It wasn't too deep," I lied.

"It must have been for someone to sew you up like that. Let's have a look at you walking."

I swung my legs off the bed as nonchalantly as I could and managed not to grit my teeth as I put weight on my knackered leg.

It was almost the hardest thing I'd ever done, to walk round that small room without letting the pain show in my walk or on my face. From the expression on the doctor's face, it looked as though I'd done it.

Giles Seymour, a man famous for not leaving anything to chance, still looked worried.

"D'you really think he can perform properly like that?" he asked the doctor.

"If he's telling the truth."

Giles, more used to subterfuge in jockeys, wasn't convinced that I was. But he didn't say so then. "There's still an hour to the off. I'll leave it for another quarter, and then I'm going to ask to see you trot up that corridor," he said to me.

"But I've got a piece to do for the TV in ten minutes. I'll have to be changed by then, and go straight to the scales."

"I'll tell the producer you can't do it. I'm going down to see about the horse. I'll be back in ten minutes."

I knew he was going to see about another jockey.

The doctor made me lie on the bed again and felt around the cut. I winced, but didn't yell as he kneaded the tender flesh.

"It's still giving you a little pain then?"

"Only when you prod it. I'll be fine with my feet in the stirrups."

"But there's a hell of a lot of pressure on your calf when you're racing. I'm not really happy."

"Look, doc," I pleaded, "it's fine. I wouldn't want to ride if I didn't think I could do the job properly."

"On the favorite? In the Derby?"

"Specially in the Derby. There's too much riding on it to risk losing it through my own fault. I wouldn't go if I thought I was going to let the punters down."

"I'm going to fetch my deputy, see what he thinks," the doctor said with decisive indecision. He went out.

The nurse shrugged her shoulders and shook her head.

I didn't want to admit it, but she was right.

I looked at a clock on the wall. The Derby was due to be run in fifty-five minutes. I had to change my colors and my breeches, weigh in, mount up in the parade ring, parade in front of the stands and ride with the rest of the runners down the track to the start.

I shook my head too, resigned. It wasn't going to happen. My first really big hit at the world's greatest Classic, and I was going to have to back out.

I wondered who the hell would get the ride. There was a big field for the race that year, twenty-one runners, and no spare jockeys of any quality. A few minutes later, I found out.

Giles Seymour came back into the room with real apology on his face. "Sorry, Jake," he said.

"Who have you got?"

"Mick Hagan."

For some reason, though I knew he didn't have a mount, it hadn't occured to me that Mick might replace me on Dawn Raider. I had to admit there was a kind of ironic justice to it.

"At least no one will have had a chance to get to him," I said bitterly.

"He'll give the horse as good a ride as anyone, you know that."

I nodded. "I'll bet he's been praying for a miracle, and now he thinks he's been answered," I said, while I tried to blank out the thought that maybe, just maybe, Mick had been involved in the scam which had crippled me. I'd spent the last week convincing myself and Charles Powell that it wasn't an option. I didn't know what the hell to think about a coincidence that could be so callous.

Giles apologized again and rushed off to do his job, his biggest that year, of saddling the favorite.

I thanked the nurse, picked up my boot and hobbled down to the changing room. On the way, I saw the doctor hurrying back with his second opinion. I told them they were redundant, and they commiserated.

"It's okay," I said. "I think I knew I couldn't go through with it."

But they understood.

Bunty Fielding practically ruptured herself with sympathy when I found her. I had hoped I might find Camilla—she should have been back from Italy—but she wasn't in her parents' box. A dozen loud and affable land-owning types were there among the debris of a well-watered lunch. Somehow, James Bullough-Ferguson had insinuated himself into the box, but Bunty boosted me, telling me Camilla was around and needed rescuing from James. She insisted I should watch the race with them.

That suited me. I really didn't want to be with Dawn Raider's trainer and connections.

The Clerk of the Course had been told that I wasn't riding again. As the Queen and her party walked back from the parade ring to the royal box, Dawn Raider's jockey change was announced. There was a deep gasp from the crowd at this last-minute change, though it couldn't have come as a complete surprise after my crash in the last race.

The Guards band marched off the end of the course, and two mounted policemen emerged from the paddock to lead the runners down past the stand. I wanted to turn away when I saw Mick Hagan in the colors I should have been wearing.

I heard Sir John's voice boom, "Ah, Camilla, I thought you were going to miss it."

I turned toward the door of the box, and met her eyes at once. She came straight over to me.

"Jake! What a fall! Are you all right? Have you opened up the cut?"

I nodded. "Giles wasn't having it," I said. "He was right," I added.

"But to give the ride to Mick Hagan!"

"He had to give it to someone, and Mick'll do his best."

"Unless he's had a big bet on another horse," Camilla said.

"Whatever he's had on wouldn't be worth more than winning the race."

"It's so unfair, after all the hassle he's caused you."

"Has he caused me hassle? I wish to God I knew."

The runners had turned and were cantering up to the narrow track which crossed the tip of the U of the Epsom course. I glanced down at them once or twice, less angry now that I had someone beside me who seemed to understand just how I was feeling.

She gave me a quick warm smile. "Have you backed him?"

"Of course not. I'm not allowed to, remember?"

/////////////// CHAPTER 7

A hundred thousand people having fun make a lot of noise, even spread out across the expanse of Epsom Down, but there was a perceptible drop in volume as the runners reached the stalls for the start of the Derby. Suddenly the voices of the bookies in the enclosures became more distinct as they tried to drum up some last-minute business.

Dawn Raider's price, I noticed, hadn't been affected by his jockey change, but odds on the second and third favorites had shortened.

Camilla thrust a pair of binoculars at me. "Go on, have a look. You know you want to."

I took them only half reluctantly and trained them on the horses and riders circling slowly behind the stalls. A sudden hollowness opened up in my guts, as I was there with them, sharing the tension and apprehension that even the most hardened old jockeys were feeling.

I picked out Dawn Raider and Hagan. I wouldn't have admitted it to anyone, but I was willing them to get beaten. The idea of missing a Derby winner was too unbearable to contemplate. It was a selfish thought, but I couldn't help it. I had to console myself with the thought that I would have the ride in the Arc. Right then, it wasn't a lot of consolation.

The handlers began to put the horses in the stalls. Odd numbers from left to right. First odd and then the evens. Dawn Raider was a good loader; they would be going in fourth. I swung the binoculars back to where he was approaching the back of the narrow iron cages. Mick Hagan walked him in and they stood quietly. It didn't take long for the handlers to get the rest of them loaded and as the gates snapped open, releasing twenty-one finely tuned racehorses to compete for the world's most coveted championship, a huge roar rose up from the crowd.

My binoculars were focused on Mick on Dawn Raider. I watched him bounce from the stalls.

And disappear.

My mouth opened slightly in disbelief as I scanned along the rest of the field and back. Then I found the familiar gold and chocolate colors again, this time in a heap on the grass.

There was a huge gasp from a hundred thousand mouths as the crowd realized that the favorite for the Derby was galloping without his rider. For a moment, all eyes were on the lump on the grass in front of the stalls before they gradually returned to the race.

I was still focused on Mick Hagan, wondering what had gone wrong. It wasn't impossible that a leather had broken, or something else had happened to make him fall off. Maybe he had had a heart attack. What worried me was that Mick was lying on the grass motionless.

I lowered the binoculars. Camilla was looking at me. "What on earth happened?" she asked.

"God knows. But Mick hasn't moved a muscle." I didn't tell her that whatever had happened, I had a crazy suspicion it should have happened to me.

The Derby was still being run. I watched; listened to the commentary in a kind of trance. I didn't care about the race any more. I swung my glasses back to the start. An ambulance had arrived and a stretcher was being loaded into it with reporters jostling for snaps and quotes.

I handed the glasses back to Camilla. "I'm going to the first-aid room."

She nodded.

I limped out of the box and along the empty corridors to the side of the stands where I had been only twenty minutes before. I could hear the race commentary echoing through the building, but it was as if it was taking place in a different world.

There was already a policeman standing outside the room, listening to instructions on his walkie-talkie. He stepped across the door to bar the way as I approached.

"I'm a friend of Hagan's," I said, almost meaning it then.

The policeman looked harder at me and, recognizing me, relented slightly. "He's not here yet. They're bringing him round the course. It's the quickest way. They may even take him straight to hospital. He's very bad; they've sent for some blood."

I waited and half listened to the commentary, revving up now that the runners had hit the bottom of the home straight.

I wondered how long it would take the blood-wagon to bring Mick from the start back up to the stands.

The course commentator bellowed as Al Jiwa took

up the running inside the last furlong and crossed the line a clear winner.

A moment later there was a commotion at the double doors at the end of the corridor as a trolley was wheeled in, surrounded by ambulance men and police trying to keep the reporters back. The policeman on the door flung it open and Mick was wheeled through. His eyes were open, but all the brightness was gone from them. His face was pale grey. There was a patch of matted bloody hair on the back of his head.

"Bad," the policeman had said. He looked more than bad to me.

The door closed behind him and his attendants. A minute later, it was opened again and the doctor who had examined me earlier came out. He saw me and nodded vaguely. He said to the policeman, "Are you in contact with central control?"

"Yes, sir."

"Tell them we don't need the blood. It's too late."

"You mean he's dead, sir?"

"I'm afraid so. He was dead when he got here."

The doctor was joined by another man, not in uniform but, I guessed, another policeman. He spoke to the man on the door. "Don't let anyone near here and get rid of anyone around that exit." He nodded at the end of the corridor. He turned to me. "I'd like to talk to you, Mr. Felton, so don't go away."

He didn't wait for my questions and ducked back into the crowded room.

I tried to absorb what had happened.

The wound in my leg had stopped me from riding Dawn Raider; Mick Hagan, a possible, but by no means obvious suspect for the cause of the wound, had taken the ride, and now he was dead.

I didn't know how he had died but unless it was a heart attack of exquisite timing, I was certain that neither he nor the colt was responsible.

There was a clattering of footsteps down the passage

that led from the stands. From round a corner, a small posse of morning-suited men appeared and bore down on the door where I waited. They were the Clerk of the Course, two of his minions and a senior steward. They saw me and nodded. The clerk said, "Okay, Felton?" as if I had been involved in Hagan's accident, opened the door and went in before the PC had time to stop him and his small entourage. The door closed behind them.

"Who was that?" the policeman asked me.

"Lord Buckingham, senior steward, and the Clerk of the Course with a couple of sidekicks. The Clerk runs this place."

The Clerk reappeared. "You can use my office," he was saying to the plain-clothes man.

The detective turned to me. "Would you mind coming with me, Mr. Felton."

I nodded and followed him back up the passage through a pair of wooden doors, into the large weighing room and up two flights of stairs. His office was just off the side.

A large mahogany partners' desk, cluttered with inappropriate-looking hi-tech paraphernalia, stood on a well-worn, once good, Persian rug.

The policeman was dressed in a drab grey suit, pale lemon shirt and some kind of club tie. He was indifferent to the surroundings. He waved me at a delicate Chippendale chair and seated himself in the large leather desk chair. He pulled a small black notebook and pen from his side pocket and put them on the desk.

"I'm DI Lawson, Surrey Police. I'm sorry to have to tell you your colleague Hagan has been shot—murdered."

"Murdered?" I gasped, even though I had expected it. It seemed such a ridiculous thing to happen, where it had, when it had.

"Yes. He was shot with a high-velocity rifle, from a range of two hundred yards or so and a height of forty or fifty feet."

"Where from?" I asked.

"The woods behind the start. We've already got fifty men sweeping up the south side of the down from Langley Bottom, and we're trying to do it subtly. There's quite a crowd over on that side and we don't want to start a stampede." He shrugged. "Frankly, the chances of clocking him aren't high, not among that crowd. But he'll have to do something with the gun. If we're going to get anywhere, we've got to sort out a motive, and bloody fast. Now I know that until quite recently you were a good mate of Hagan's, right?"

"Yeah, I was."

"But you fell out with him recently. Why?"

"Listen, Lieutenant—"

"Inspector."

"Inspector, if you want a motive, you're looking in the wrong place."

"Mr. Felton, I don't think you shot him or had him shot, I just want to know why you fell out with him."

"That's simple. I won a race he wanted to win."

"But you must have done that hundreds of times. Why did that one matter so much?"

"I don't know."

"Yes, you do. I think I do too, but I want you to tell me."

"I guess he had a bundle on his horse."

"How much of a bundle?"

"I don't know, for Christ's sake! But a lot of bread. Ask his bookie."

"Who's his bookie?"

"How the hell should I know? And a bookie's not going to shoot him for not paying his debts."

"No, but he might for not doing as he was told."

"That's possible, but I don't know anything about that."

"Hagan wasn't due to ride in the Derby. He only got that ride because you came off in the one before."

"Sure, but he was due to ride in the next. Maybe the

guy thought he'd take him out when he had the chance. I don't know, that's your department."

"Maybe the gunman thought it was you on that horse."

"Why the hell would he think that?" I asked. "Everyone knew I'd been injured in the race before and couldn't go, and I don't even look like Hagan, for God's sake."

"Maybe the gunman didn't know."

"Well he'd've had to be deaf not to have heard the Tannoy."

"You're probably right about Hagan being the target. That'll do for now, but I'll need to talk to you again. Would you write all your contact numbers here for me please?"

He pushed his notebook across the desk at me.

I wrote the numbers. We said a polite "Goodbye," and I left the Clerk's office to go back to the Fieldings' box.

The police, the stewards and the Clerk of the Course between them had decided to sit on the news of Hagan's death. The police had ruled out the possibility that they were dealing with an unhinged, gun-freak sniper. They felt that a public announcement in the circumstances wasn't necessary and might lead to major panic.

As a result, when I went back into the box, everyone still assumed that Dawn Raider had somehow dropped Hagan and the jockey had hurt himself badly enough not to be able to ride. These things sometimes happened.

I faked ignorance. To the gathering in general, I announced that Hagan was in a bad way and wouldn't be riding again that afternoon.

I needed to talk to someone—not Camilla, not yet—and Charles Powell was somewhere in the milling, morning-suited mass in the members' enclosure down below.

I took Camilla's arm. "I've got to find Charles Powell. I'll see you later, somewhere quieter."

She looked at me, and spoke so no one else could hear. "Is Hagan dead?"

I nodded. "Someone shot him."

Her face changed color like a traffic light. She knew what had happened. That was meant to be you; she thought for a moment.

"Be careful, Jake, please," she whispered, then smiled and said in her normal voice, "Bye, come back up before you go."

"Sure," I said, and nodded to her parents before leaving the box. It didn't take long to find Charles. He was looking for me, talking to Giles Seymour.

I hadn't seen Giles since he'd gone to saddle up Dawn Raider. He was looking very unhappy.

"Do you know what the hell's going on?" he asked. "The police and the doctors won't tell me. They just say Mick's in trouble and won't ride again today."

"That's true."

"But there's a rumor coming up from the handlers that he was shot!"

I took a deep breath. "That's true, too. But for Christ's sake, keep it to yourselves until the police announce it."

"But the Sheikh and Penruddock are going mad."

"And Mick Hagan's dead," I said.

Giles Seymour looked at me, totally knocked out.

Charles gave me a sharp, comprehending glance.

"We'd better talk, Jake." Alone, he meant.

"Right," I said, but I turned to Giles. "Look, there's no point you getting worked up over this. It wasn't anything to do with you or the horse. The best thing you can do is just carry on and deal with your other runners." I knew he had three more that afternoon. "I was supposed to be riding for my guv'nor in the last, but I'm out of it for the rest of today." The fourth race of the day was about to start. Charles and I set off across the course, unobtrusive and largely unnoticed, while I told him what little I had learned from the police.

"Looks like you were wrong about a connection between my missing gun and the mantrap," I said.

"Why? Because Hagan's dead? Hagan wasn't meant to be shot; you were. There was no way anyone was going to know he'd be on Dawn Raider for the Derby."

"But if he was involved, he'd have known it was going to happen and refused the ride. And I told you, I was going to give him his money at the end of the week. Maybe he was shot for not paying up."

"Don't be crazy! Nobody would assassinate him at the Derby for that. No, somehow he was involved in whatever's going on. He may not have known all the details; there may have been no need. He probably didn't know anything about your crash either."

"What are you talking about?"

"I told you I was going to look at the wreck of your Aston. Everyone—the police, the insurance company— assumes you drove off the edge of that cliff because you were pissed. They didn't have any reason to inspect the wreck particularly closely. But I did. And I went to check out the hole you fell into. There's no question about it, there was another vehicle involved."

"What are you talking about? There was no one else around, Charles. I may have been pissed, but I wasn't so far gone I wouldn't have noticed another car."

"There must have been. There's a big gouge along the driver's side that wasn't caused by the rocks in the quarry, or anything at the side of the road."

"How do you know?"

"Because whatever caused it was painted bright yellow."

I shook my head. "Charles, there was no other car."

"You stopped at some roadworks, didn't you? Traffic lights?"

"Yeah."

"Something else must have been there, and it was yellow, think!"

"Shit! Charles, you're right. There was a digger—a JCB!"

"I can't remember. I thought I'd just hit the gas too hard and skidded. It seemed pretty crazy, but there wasn't any other explanation. But if I was set up, that bastard Haslam must have had something to do with it. He knew where I was going. I'd told him when I fixed up to meet with him. And he got me pissed."

"Well I want to talk to him. After we've had a look around up here, do you think you can persuade him to meet you somewhere?"

"Sure. If I don't make it too obvious, he'll come running."

We didn't know what we were looking for up at the start. At first we didn't learn a lot. People were running around, getting ready for the next race. Neither the racecourse officials nor the public had any idea of the real extent of the drama that had occurred at the Derby start.

A couple of the handlers talked to us. They recognized me and commiserated with my bad luck in losing the ride. They had seen Hagan keel back over the horse's rear for no apparent reason. There were a lot of wild theories flying around, they said, but they reckoned Hagan must have had a heart attack or something. I didn't tell them he was dead.

We walked to the small wood behind the start which was now discreetly cordoned off. We stepped over the tape and through the scrubby sycamore, blackthorn and beech to find the place swarming with police. I went up to the most senior-looking and told him who I was before he could bawl us out. When I asked him, he didn't mind telling me what they'd found so far—which was a fat zero.

Coming out of the woods, we ran into a trio of old men who had positioned themselves in the shade of the trees to watch the day's racing. They glanced at me and almost keeled over in astonishment.

"'Ere, you're Jake Felton, ain't yer?"

I nodded. "Yeah."

"You wasn't hurt bad, then?"

"When I came off in the first? No, not too bad, just enough to stop me riding in the Derby." I grimaced and Charles and I started to walk away.

"What're you talking about?" another of the old boys called after me indignantly. "We seen you fall off fuckin' Dawn Raider and lose all our money."

We spun round. "You thought I was on Dawn Raider?"

"Well, you was, wasn't you?"

"No, I didn't pass the medical after Lorna Doone fell. Mick Hagan got the ride on Dawn Raider. Didn't you hear the announcement?"

The old fellows looked bemused.

"I told you it wasn't 'im," one of them said. "But we didn't 'ear no announcement. You can't 'ear nothing up 'ere. It's too far from them loudspeakers."

"So that was Hagan come off, was it? Blimey, I might have known it, slippery little bugger."

"I don't think he did it on purpose," I said. I turned to Charles. "Let's get back, for Christ's sake."

I nodded at the old men and we headed down the hill and made our way behind the start where the fourth race was beginning.

Walking back across to the stands, I couldn't even think about the race that was going on. Charles spoke my thoughts.

"If those old boys didn't know you'd been substituted, then nor did whoever shot Hagan. And he'd never have been able to tell you apart, not with your hat and goggles, unless he was very familiar with the way you sit on a horse."

"Sure. It was definitely meant to be me." My blood ran icy at the thought. Even though I had suspected it since I'd seen Hagan disappear off the back of the horse, I'd been hanging on to the hope that I was wrong.

"Why didn't we tell those police up in the woods?"

"Maybe they know, though the guy who spoke to me didn't. I don't want to talk to the police, not until I know what the hell I'm supposed to have done."

"For God's sake, Jake, you must know who you've upset in the last few years. Somebody's determined to kill you. They've got to have a reason."

"Let's see what Geoff Haslam has to say."

Back in the stands, we went straight to the press box to find the journalist. We had just reached the door when Haslam came bursting out and almost ran right into me.

"Mind out, you fu—Oh, Jake. How are you? Okay now? Christ, what horrible luck, eh?"

"Yeah." I pretended to shrug it off. "Worse luck for Mick."

"D'you know what the hell happened?" he asked, not really expecting anything from me. "I know you're pissed off about last time we met, but you couldn't just tell me something about it, could you?"

I surprised him. "Sure. I haven't got a whole lot else to do today." I turned to Charles Powell. "I'll catch up with you later, Charles, okay?"

He nodded affably and wandered off. Geoff could hardly stop himself from dragging me back into the press room. Most of his colleagues were too busy filing copy to notice me, and those who did were too wary of Geoff to come near us.

"This is the last place I'd choose to talk to you, but

we haven't got much choice today," Geoff said. "Look, we can sit in this corner."

We placed ourselves out of anyone else's hearing and Geoff pulled a spiral-back pad from his suit—half pressed today, in honor of the occasion.

"So, what can you tell me?" he panted.

"Nothing, here. If you want to talk to me you can come to my house at eight tonight." I stood up. Haslam glowered with frustration. He knew how many of his rivals would be pestering me between now and then. I relaxed him. "Don't worry. I won't be talking to anyone else, but I'll have more to tell you by then."

He didn't trust me, but he didn't have any choice.

"All right, I'll see you then," he said. His eyes reluctantly pleaded with me not to let him down.

I left the room, followed, I guessed, by a few dozen pairs of wildly speculative eyes. I didn't look back.

Charles was waiting outside.

"Hooked him?" he asked.

"Yeah. My place tonight."

"Good."

"Do you mind missing the last two races?" I asked.

"No. I've had a bit of a punt in the last, but I don't suppose my absence will affect the outcome one way or the other. What do you want to do?"

"I want to go and see Mary Hagan."

"Mick's wife—widow?"

"Yes."

"Fine, I'll take you. Why do you want to see her?"

"Because she'll be wiped out by what's happened. She's a lovely woman and she worshipped that little son of a bitch."

"Surely she won't be at home though; she'll be here. And anyway, will she want to see you, in the circumstances?"

We were out of the stands now, heading for the members' car park.

"I doubt she knows half the circumstances. I think

she'll be glad to see me, and she'll be at home. She never came to watch Mick ride; she hated leaving the kids. She'll have seen the race on TV, though, and I guess someone will have been to see her to tell her what happened. But she trusts me, whatever Mick might have told her. I guess I feel it's my duty to go see her, try and soften the blow. After all, it should have been me."

"I suppose she might be able to tell us something too," Charles said.

We had reached his muddy Range Rover. I looked at him across the hood and shook my head.

"No. She won't know anything. And even if I thought she did, I wouldn't ask her today."

We climbed into the vehicle and Charles drove us out onto the road and down to the M25.

I asked Charles to wait in the car when we reached Hagan's cottage forty-five minutes later. Mary opened the door red-eyed and bewildered. As usual, there was a small child clinging to one of her hands and a smaller one perched on her hip.

"Can I come in, Mary?" I asked her, as gently as I could.

"Please," she said in her soft Kerry lilt, and turned back down the narrow passage to the kitchen at the back of the house.

"Would you like a cup of tea?" she asked, then, remembering what Mick would have said, "A drop of Paddy's?"

"I'll have a drop of Paddy's, if you will. Where is it?"

She nodded at a dresser with a shelf full of bottles of obscure and varied origins. I found the Paddy's and a couple of glasses. Mary had sat down limply at the well-worn table. She was staring blankly at the window, not seeing the sunlit garden outside, ignoring the smallest child's demands for attention.

I put a glass by her and sat down opposite her. I

stretched out my hand and put it on hers where it lay on the table.

"I'm so sorry, Mary."

Her eyes met mine and, for a moment, some of the bleakness left them.

"It was good of you to come, Jake. I know you and Mick sort of fell out, but he always liked you really." The desolation returned and she looked away. "Why did it happen, Jake?" she whispered shakily. "I don't even know what happened. They wouldn't say; just there was an accident, and he's dead."

"Who told you?" I asked.

"A policewoman came out from Newbury, but she just kept saying it was some kind of accident, that was all. Then a policeman phoned. He said he would have to come and talk to me about it. I didn't even see it on the telly. He hadn't a ride, so I didn't bother. I watched the first race, when you fell off, then I went out into the garden with the kids. 'Twas a glorious afternoon . . ." Her voice trailed off as she contemplated the irony of such a tragedy occurring on such a perfect day.

I took a swig of whiskey. I needed it.

"Look, Mary. I wanted to tell you that anything I can do for you, you've only got to ask. I'll come by and see you every day, if that'll help."

"Why should you do that?" she asked. "You've races to ride, and horses to work."

"Because I want to. And because, Mary, I should have been on that horse today. Whatever happened to Mick should have happened to me."

It looked as though this was the first time that thought had entered her head. There was a brief moment's accusation in her eyes. But she shook her head. "That wouldn't be your fault. When I saw you come down, I was thinking how upset you'd be if you weren't to ride in the Derby. But you walked away from it and I thought it was no problem."

I shrugged my shoulders. "I was pretty angry about

it, but it doesn't matter a damn right now." I braced myself. "What matters is that you and the kids get all the support you're going to need. Don't worry about money or anything. Look," as subtly as I could, I pulled my checkbook from my pocket. "It so happens that I owed Mick ten thousand pounds. I'm going to pay it to you. Have you got your own account?"

She nodded, looking bemused.

"Fine. Well, here's a check; you put it in your account until you've got things sorted out."

"But I can't take that, Jake. Why should I take your charity?"

"It's not charity. I owed it to Mick, for a favor he did me, so it's yours by right. Take it, Mary, please."

"What sort of a favor would Mick have done for you?"

"He found something for me. It's a kind of commission he was due on a deal—nothing to do with racing."

I slid the check across the table at her. She looked at it. "Thank you, Jake. I can't say it won't help. Mick was always having problems, the kids costing so much and all. He earned a fair bit, but it all seemed to disappear."

"Well, don't worry about that now, and don't worry about the police coming to see you."

"Would you tell me why ever the police should be involved?"

I gulped. "There's a few questions to ask, I guess." She didn't say anything, just looked at me, waiting. I took her hand. "I suppose it'll be on the news sooner or later. It wasn't an accident."

She stared at me, horrorstruck. "You mean, somebody . . . killed him, on purpose?" she whispered.

I bit my lip and nodded slowly. "That's what they think, and I'm afraid they're probably right. But look, when the police come, there's nothing you can tell them. Just say that and they'll leave you alone. If you're worried about it, ring me and I'll come over. D'you promise you'll do that?"

She shook her head and her face wrinkled from the overwhelming sadness inside her. For the moment she couldn't cope with anything beyond the removal from her life of the man who had been its center.

I didn't speak until, after a while, she had absorbed the fact that the police would be interested. She nodded. "I would be glad if you were here when they came."

"Then I will be. You just call."

I let go of her hand and stood up. I knew I should have stayed longer, made her pots of tea and performed all the normal conciliatory functions. But I wasn't well equipped for that. I was too much in the habit of keeping my thoughts to myself to switch on instant communication and sympathy.

"Is anyone coming over from Ireland?" I asked.

She nodded. "They are. My sister, Siobhan, and two of my brothers. They'll be here in the evening."

"They'll be the best people to have around," I said. "But don't forget, anything I can do, let me know. Okay?"

"God bless you, Jake. And thanks for coming."

Charles was waiting in the Range Rover, drumming his fingers on the wheel.

"How was she?" he asked.

"I don't think it's really hit her yet. But she'll get through it when it does. She's a great woman and the kids will give her a lot of support. Thank God, some of her family are already on their way. But I told her to call me when the police come to see her."

"Will she be able to tell them much?"

"No. Mick would never have told her about anything he was involved in that wasn't straight. I don't think she ever knew his reputation, and other people protected her from it. Not that she's ever really mixed with racing people. I hope to God the police don't disillusion her too much. That's why I told her I'd be there when they come."

Charles had started the car and was cruising back up toward the A34. "Where to now?" he asked.

"To the doctor. I've got to have this leg tidied up. I won't be riding tomorrow. I only had one good ride anyway and the race doc would blow me out. But I've got to be okay for Corsican Lady on Saturday."

"I was wondering what had happened to your burning ambition. I'm glad to see it's still intact. And I don't suppose someone will try and shoot you again in the Oaks."

"I hope to God you're right."

"They're hardly going to try the same thing again, which is a pity really, otherwise the police might have been ready and able to apprehend them second time round."

"Yeah, well, that's too bad." I tried to laugh.

My own doctor, an ally and a realist, offered the opinion that, provided I didn't put any strain on it, the gash in my leg probably wouldn't stop me riding in the Oaks. He rebandaged it and told me to come back next evening.

Charles, still obliging, dropped me back at Coombe House around six. He said he'd be back by eight to hear what Geoff Haslam had to say.

In the house, I found that the afternoon's events had generated a pile of faxes and messages. Every trainer and owner I was due to ride for over the next three days —among the most important in the racing calendar— wanted to know where the hell I was and whether I would be riding for them.

I rang them all and gave them the bad news. Last of all, I phoned Toby Ellerton.

"I'm sorry, Toby," I told him, "I'm not going to risk

tomorrow or Friday. But I should pass the vet on Saturday."

"I suppose that's better than nothing, but I wish to God you'd told me about that cut in your leg before. How the hell did you do it, anyway?"

"On my tractor. I didn't think it would cause problems."

But Ellerton was milder than he might have been. I knew the reason for that. I'd heard the rest of the day's results on Charles's car radio and I knew Toby had won the last, unexpectedly and with a substitute jockey, at 25/1. He hadn't told me, the scheduled jockey, that he thought the horse was going to win, but I gathered from his tone of voice as he talked about it that it hadn't been a surprise and he'd profited heavily from the result.

"Too bad you weren't on it," Toby said when I congratulated him. "Would have made up for your bad luck with Dawn Raider," he added smugly.

"Not such great luck for Mick Hagan either," I said quietly.

"Little crook deserved all that was coming to him. I wouldn't be surprised if he'd done a quick deal to pull the horse anyway."

I shook my head in amazement at Ellerton's awesome hypocrisy. "I should have thought you'd be pissed off at losing a co-operative jockey. You didn't mind using him when it suited you."

"I don't know what the hell you're talking about." This was for the benefit of the eavesdropper who Ellerton imagined listened to all his phone calls.

"Just kidding, Captain. Personally, I'll miss Mick, and his wife is devastated. He's left her with six kids."

"Bloody irresponsible Catholics," Toby grunted and rang off with a curt "Goodbye."

I was really beginning to dislike Captain Toby Ellerton a lot.

Several journalists—mainstream as well as racing hacks—had called.

Did I have any idea why Hagan had been shot?

Had I heard the rumor that he was going to throw the race?

Was it true that I'd recently had some kind of dispute with Hagan?

I didn't call any of them back.

There was also one rambling message from a side-kick of Inspector Lawson's at Epsom police station. If I didn't mind, a deferential voice asked, they'd like to come over some time and check a few things with me.

I decided to return the call and was put through to Lawson.

"You're having a busy day, Inspector," I said.

"Yes, Mr. Felton. Thank you for calling us back. Would it be convenient if I came and saw you on Friday morning?"

"What about? Have you got anything to go on yet?"

"I'd rather talk to you about that when I see you, if you don't mind. Will nine o'clock be all right?"

"Sure. I'm not riding."

"I'll see you then, Mr. Felton."

I put the phone down, feeling that whatever track the man was on, it was the wrong one.

A moment later, the phone was bleeping at me again.

"Hello, it's Camilla."

"Hello. I'm sorry."

"Why should you be?"

"Well, I just ducked out without saying goodbye or anything."

"For God's sake, Jake, I don't care about that. I just wanted to know you were okay. I mean, somebody's trying to bloody well kill you! How do you know they're not going to try again?"

"I don't."

"But I hear you're still going to ride on Saturday. Mum's very relieved, but isn't it a risk?"

"I doubt it. And anyway, I can't hide for ever."

"I don't know how you can be so calm about it. And why the hell should anyone want to kill you? Is it the same people who set that trap for you?"

"I'm not calm about it. I wish to God I knew why someone wanted to kill me, but I haven't got a goddamn clue. All I know is that I'm supposed to have poached something from someone. Christ knows what."

"So the trap and the shooting were the same people?"

"I don't know. I guess so. There can't be two people who hate me that much."

"Shall I come down and see you?"

"No. No, you'd better not. Not yet. I'm going to lie low for a couple of days and give this leg a chance to heal so I can win the Oaks for your mum."

"Do you think you might?"

"If I get to the starting gate."

"Don't say that, Jake, please."

"All right. I'm sorry. I'll ring you tomorrow; see you Saturday."

"Take care."

"I will."

I put the phone down once more and groaned. What a way to launch a love affair.

/////////// CHAPTER 8

I turned on the television to see what they were giving out about Mick Hagan's death.

Once the racing was over and most of the crowds had gone from the Epsom, the police had released the news that Hagan had been murdered. They gave no details beyond the fact that he had been shot by a marksman from the woods behind the start, and the victim had been sitting on the favorite for the Derby at the time. The story was the lead on every news bulletin; the event had been watched on television by an estimated two hundred million people around the world, the most publicly witnessed assassination since Kennedy had been shot. It seemed to me an unlikely comparison; apart from their Irishness, Kennedy and Hagan hadn't had a lot in common.

Several "experts" of the racing world had been hustled into the studios and spouted theories that might have got them sued if Mick Hagan had still been alive. The most prevalent, and one of the most implausible, was that Mick was going to stop the favorite. No one, of course, suggested who might have been his paymaster for that kind of scam.

I watched some extensive coverage of the shooting on the *Seven O'Clock News,* including a slow-motion replay from three different camera angles of Mick falling back over Dawn Raider's rump as he leapt from the stalls. I hoped that Mary Hagan hadn't seen it.

Geoff Haslam turned up just before eight. Charles Powell hadn't arrived. I led the rumpled journalist through to my kitchen and sat him down at the table. I put a bottle of Wild Turkey—sweetly deceptive Kentucky bourbon—and a glass in front of him. He nodded appreciatively. I guessed it wasn't going to take too much to top him up; he was already half-drunk, as I'd hoped he would be. He must have made a hell of an effort to get from Epsom to my place.

I wanted Charles to be here to listen to what Haslam had to say about his part in the crashing of my Aston, so I talked first about Mick Hagan's murder.

Geoff Haslam poured himself a large slug of Wild Turkey and pulled out his notebook. I took my time to tell him less than he could have learned from the television news.

He was beginning to get truculent when the door from the garage opened and a frightened-looking man in his twenties and a purple anorak staggered headlong into the room. Charles Powell walked in behind him.

"Look what I found lurking in the bushes outside," Charles said to Haslam. "One of your junior competitors. You must be losing your sense of discretion in your old age."

Haslam had already registered this. I could see him searching his memory for something he'd said that could have been overheard.

"Sorry to intrude, Jake, Geoff," the younger journalist said, recovering some of his self-possession. "You know how it is."

Geoff knew. "Sure. Anyway, Mr. Felton isn't going to tell us anything we don't already know." He drained his glass and lumbered clumsily to his feet, knocking his chair backward. "Thanks for the drink, Jake."

"You're welcome," I said. "I owed you a couple. But don't go yet. There's something else I want to talk to you about."

"We don't want his fellow hack to hear, though, do we?" Charles said. "This story's exclusive to Geoff."

I nodded. "Can you get rid of him?"

"I'll lock him in your squash court, then ring the police and tell them we found him trying to break in."

"Ideal." I grinned.

Charles got hold of the man, who was maybe two-thirds his weight, and frog-marched him back through the garage to the windowless squash court.

Geoff Haslam had picked up his chair and sat down again. He wasn't sure whether he should be excited or apprehensive about this next interview.

I poured him another Wild Turkey which he picked up without thinking about it. Charles came back into the room and closed the door behind him to shut out a lot of banging and yelling from the squash court.

"He'll settle down soon," he said, and to Haslam, "What do you think? Shall we call the police?"

Haslam shrugged. "I don't care what you do with him, so long as he's not nicking my story."

"We'll let him off later," I said. "We don't want any interruptions from the police this evening. You can take him with you when you go, Geoff. He must have left a car somewhere."

Charles and I simultaneously sat down at the table

opposite Haslam. He looked from my face to Charles's and began to twitch nervously.

"What do you want?" he asked.

I smiled and spoke with false mildness. "Do you think there's any connection between what happened to Mick Hagan today and what happened to me nine weeks ago when I drove my car into that quarry?"

Haslam stared. He looked down at his glass, picked it up and took a slow swig from it before he could look back at me.

"What the hell are you talking about?" he challenged.

I felt my face harden. My hands, resting on the table, folded into fists.

"You know bloody well there's a connection." I couldn't keep the edge out of my voice.

For a moment, Haslam looked genuinely puzzled. But as my words sank in, his eyes shifted out of focus and slid back to his glass.

"You mean, if you'd been on Dawn Raider, you'd have been shot?" he said.

"For Christ's sake, don't pretend that you hadn't worked out that it was me who should have been killed."

"But why did they go ahead when Hagan got the ride?"

"Because whoever shot him was sitting up a tree in the woods and he couldn't hear the jockey change announcement from there."

"Shit! I didn't know that."

"No, and as far as I can tell, nor do the police, yet. And none of your noble colleagues seems to have picked it up. But they will, as soon as they've done a bit more work."

"If you know, why haven't you told the police?"

"Because this isn't the first time someone's tried to kill me, and I want to know who they are before I get the police delving. Also, I don't think they've got a cat in hell's chance of finding out what happened today—they haven't found a thing. We think we're in a better position. Now, do you see the connection between Hagan's shooting and my little 'accident'?"

"Look," Haslam said with bogus bewilderment, "if someone tried to kill you today—and I realize you're not feeling too happy about that—what's that to do with you driving over the edge of a cliff?"

"Paralytic pissed, remember?" I banged the heavy oak table with my fist. "Thanks to you. And I didn't drive over the edge. I was shunted by something."

Haslam gulped, but he decided to tough it out. "What is all this bollocks?" he shouted. "I've already said I'm sorry I got you pissed. I was just doing my job. I came and saw you in hospital to bloody well apologize, remember?"

"You came and saw me just after I'd crashed, too. That was a stroke of luck, wasn't it?"

"It wasn't luck. Some geezer came into the pub a few minutes after you'd left and said he'd seen an Aston Martin nose-dive off a cliff. I thought it had to be you, so I got straight up there. I wanted to see if I could help," he added.

"Of course you did." I unclenched my fists and leaned back in my chair.

"Anyway," Haslam went on, "if you'd been pushed over the side, the police would have known about it."

"No reason why they should. No one saw what happened, and I was three times over the limit."

Charles took his cue to join in. He leaned forward and looked hard at Haslam. "I examined the car, two days ago. On the rear offside wing, there are dents and traces of paint probably from a JCB or something. I bought the wreck from the breaker and I've already had it checked. I've had it locked up until we're ready for the police forensics to come and check it too." Charles stood up, walked round the table and stopped behind Haslam. "As soon as they have, they'll be wanting to talk to you. They'll be wanting to know why you were parked with your bonnet up in the middle of the lane half a mile below the roadworks where Jake was pushed off. You probably thought you were lucky, because no one tried to come up the lane, but the man spraying corn in the field beside the road saw you, or at least a car that matches yours. He remembers thinking, 'What a wally. Why doesn't he pull into the gateway if he's broken down?'"

Haslam, listening with wide eyes to Charles's voice over his shoulder, didn't move, apart from a slight twitching. There was a good coating of sweat on his unhealthy skin.

"This is all crap," he croaked. He tried to stifle a gulp. "Why haven't you told the police if you think it's true?"

"Jake's already told you why. He wants to know who's trying to kill him before he does, and if you tell us, maybe we won't tell the police about you."

"Why the hell not? If you really believe all this bollocks, tell the old Bill. I haven't got anything to hide. I've told you what happened." He appealed to me. "Jake, I don't know who your heavy friend is, but just tell him to leave off. You know I wouldn't be involved in anything like he's talking about. I'm just a humble racing hack, for God's sake. What he's talking about is pure bloody fantasy."

"The yellow paint on Jake's car?" Charles growled in his ear.

"You could have done that yourself. Now you've taken it from the breakers' yard, why should the police believe you?"

I glanced at Charles. Haslam had a point.

"I photographed it where it was," Charles said. "Right in close. It's not ideal, but it's enough to get you hauled in."

Fear seemed to have sobered Haslam. He was regaining some of his normal surly confidence. He twisted his shoulders to look round at Charles.

"Look chum. I don't know what the hell you're trying to say, but I've told you all I know, so I'd just trot down to the police station and give them what you've got, only don't be disappointed if they just laugh."

Charles grinned. "There is another reason why we don't want to tell the police about our new evidence. I can do things to you that they can't. Think about it. Jake and I find two prowlers around the house, and we have to give them a hell of a hiding before we get them inside and establish they're no more than a pair of over-inquisitive hacks." Charles bent down and growled in Haslam's ear. "A hell of a hiding!"

Haslam was not one of Nature's heroes. He was on the wrong side of middle age and out of any condition he might once have had. "If . . . if you lay a finger on me, I'll sue you."

"You could try," Charles conceded, "but before you do, you'll be hurting so badly, you won't be able to think straight enough to spell it."

Haslam turned back and took another swig of bourbon. His hand trembled as he picked up the glass.

In all the time I'd known Charles, I'd scarcely ever seen him raise his voice in anger, let alone his fist. But that didn't alter the fact that he looked as though he knew how to do a lot of damage if he chose to. He was a big, powerful man, used to calling on these resources in his travels around the less sophisticated corners of the world. If he was promising to hurt Haslam, I didn't doubt that he would.

Nor did Haslam.

Charles placed his gorilla hands on the nape of Haslam's neck and began to squeeze.

"Get your hands off me!" Haslam bleated.

Charles increased the pressure with his fingers. The journalist began to cough and wheeze. His eyes were starting from their sockets and his face was turning a pale purple. He didn't try to fight back. He already knew he was beaten.

"All right, all right," he hissed through closed teeth.

"Yes?" Charles prompted him, easing the pressure on the other man's throat.

"I can't talk with you lurking behind me like that," Haslam whined.

Charles took his hands from Haslam's neck and walked back round the table to sit beside me.

"I'm going to record this," I said and reached behind me for a pocket cassette recorder I used as an oral memo-pad. I put it on the table with the inbuilt mike aimed at Haslam's quivering lips and pressed the record button.

"Okay," I said, taking over the questioning. "What I want most is a name."

Haslam shook his head. "He didn't tell me his name; we weren't introduced."

"Tell us what happened, then—every detail."

Haslam took another quick slug of Wild Turkey and heaved a defeated sigh.

"A geezer came up to me at Doncaster, when you were riding in the Lincoln. We were beside the paddock. This bloke nods at you in the ring and says, 'You've written about Felton. D'you know him?' I didn't take much notice. There are quite a few punters who know who I am—they badger you for tips and that. I usually tell 'em where they can buy a copy of my paper, but this bloke was a hard-looking nut. I just said, 'Yeah, I know him.' He goes on, 'I want a message delivered to him. Could you do that?' I say, 'What's wrong with the phone?' He says, 'Don't get funny with me. I want this message delivered personal. Not here, not today, in a couple of weeks. If you can arrange to see him, privately, and do what I want, there's a month's wages in it for you.' I asked him how much. He says, 'A grand.' I said if all I had to do was deliver a message, I could probably find my way to doing it for that sort of money.

"He said he'd ring me to fix a meet to discuss the details, then he says, 'And don't tell anyone, right? Not if your health's important to you—know what I mean?' I knew what he meant. I'd never seen him before but I knew the type—flash, smell of money about him, and very hard; the sort of bloke you take seriously."

"What did he look like?" I asked.

"Fortyish, about five ten, small 'tash, well tanned, not bad looking and well turned out for a flash Cockney—camel coat and navy trilby. Not a regular racegoer—not the horses, anyway. No glasses."

"And he was from London?"

"Oh yeah. Mile End type, from his accent."

"He'd come to Doncaster just to look for you?"

"I s'pose so. Me or somebody like me who wasn't connected with you but could make contact with you."

"When did he call you next?"

"About two weeks later. I'd just got back home from Newbury. He said to meet him at Wimbledon dogs the next evening. There's a hell of a crowd there and we sat in a corner of the bar, nobody taking any notice of us. Then he tells me he doesn't want me to deliver a message exactly, just to arrange to meet you somewhere and find out where you'd be going after. And I had to put as much booze down you as I could. I know you have a drink now and again and I reckoned on a Saturday night you wouldn't be too fussy. And when I spoke to you about it, you very kindly told me where you were going after—saved me having to ask you. He phoned me up to get the details and told me to get on with it. So, that's what I did. He didn't say nothing about why he wanted me to do it. He just said, 'Keep him there for an hour and get him rat-arsed.' And that's it." Haslam splayed his hands palms up on the table to show that was all he had to offer.

Charles leaned forward across the table. "What

about blocking the lane with your car? And turning up at the quarry right after Jake had crashed into it?"

"I can't help you there, mate. That wasn't my car in the lane. There must be thousands of silver Montegos and they don't all belong to me. I told you, I went to the quarry because a bloke came into the pub and said what had happened. I guessed it was Jake so I went— it's my fucking job, isn't it, to know what's happening to our leading jockeys?"

I believed Haslam. I'd seen how he had behaved in the pub and in the hospital afterward. I put up a hand to stop Charles launching into another burst of interrogation.

"Didn't your man tell you any of what was going to happen after I left the pub?" I asked Haslam.

" 'Course not. Why should he? The less I knew the better."

"Did you see him again?"

"No."

"How did he pay you then?"

"He gave me the money at the dog track."

"What! Before you'd done anything?"

"He said the world wouldn't be big enough to hide in if I didn't do as I was told."

"Has he contacted you since?"

"No, not a word."

"And now you've told us, Geoff."

"Listen, Jake. I'd have told you before. I've got nothing against you personally. But whoever I was dealing with knows what he's doing. I didn't know he was going to try and kill you, for fuck's sake. After all, it's a bloody miracle you weren't. But if I have to tell someone, I'd rather it was you than the Old Bill. Now I've told you all I bloody know, and if they find out, I'll be in the same club as you."

"There's no need for us to tell anyone," Charles said. "As long as you're on our side. I expect you can understand that Jake would like to know who wants to kill him. They've tried twice, maybe three times. And they'll try again. So, if you hear anything else, you tell us, okay? And when the story breaks, you can have the best bits from the inside, exclusively." A big carrot to a scruffy little rabbit of a hack.

"If I'm still around," Haslam muttered.

"If," Charles nodded, "you're still around." He turned to me. "Got all you need?"

I nodded.

"Now," Charles said to Haslam, "you can go, and take that other arsehole with you."

Charles ushered him out and released his prisoner from the squash court. I heard them drive away, and Charles came back in. He poured himself a few mouthfuls of Wild Turkey.

"Do you want a lift to Epsom on Saturday?" he asked.

"Yeah. That'd be good."

"Do you want anything else followed up?"

"Haslam hasn't given us a whole lot, but there could be something, couldn't there? I'll call you when I've checked out a couple more things."

"What you need to concentrate on is staying in one piece until Saturday. I'm off now. I'll call you tomorrow." He left the house with an abruptness I was used to.

And he left me feeling very exposed. I glanced at the scrawled words pinned to my message board: "POACHERS GET WHAT POACHERS DESERVE."

They had hardly been out of my consciousness since they had arrived in the mail, but I still had no notion of what I had poached that would make someone want to kill me. I'd thought of every horse I'd ridden and every deal I'd done in the last few years. But there was nothing. Knocking on the back door of my mind was an uneasy feeling that maybe it went further back than that, to the people in the States who had begun to make life too uncomfortable for me there. But that had been more than three years before, and "poaching?" It didn't mean anything to me. Sometimes in my half-sleep, I came to the happy conclusion that it was all some kind of elaborate hoax.

But my wrecked Aston, the gash in the back of my leg, and Mick Hagan's corpse being wheeled on a trolley under my nose—they were no hoax.

All I knew was that somebody wanted to kill me, and I didn't have any idea where they were coming from, or when. I was a duck with its wings clipped, paddling in the middle of a rush-banked pool.

For the next two days, I felt like a condemned man. I didn't go out of the house and I discouraged anyone from coming to see me. I worked in the gym and I watched the racing on television.

On Thursday morning, Charles rang. He was on his toes and ready to do whatever needed doing. I asked him to go and see a few gun dealers, and find out if they'd had anyone inquiring about unusual Purdeys.

"That's not very likely, is it?" he said. "Not if yours was offered back to you anyway."

"I got an idea it might lead somewhere," I said. "Just see what you can find out."

I knew I should have been doing more myself, but I couldn't get myself to snap out of a fatalistic lethargy that was beginning to overtake me.

I left the telephone in "answer" mode all day. The calls kept coming but I ignored most of them.

With an effort, in the evening, I called my agent Phil White and my valet Martin Fletcher to confirm arrangements for Saturday. Then I made myself ring Toby Ellerton.

The Captain was full of hope for Corsican Lady. There was some desperation to his optimism. Winning the two fillies' Classics would go a long way to make up for the loss of Sheikh Ahmed's horses. And it would attract a few owners back to his yard, despite the prevailing gossip in a world where, in the final analysis, all that mattered was that a trainer produced winners. I put the phone down prepared to go along with his optimism.

After a long debate with myself, I tried to ring Camilla. I got her mother.

"Jake, how are you?" Bunty asked.

"I'll be fine by Saturday."

"Toby tells me Corsican Lady's jumping out of her skin."

"He's probably telling the truth. I'd go and work her myself if I didn't want to risk opening up this gash in my leg."

"You look after that leg," Bunty ordered. "Did you want to speak to Camilla, by the way?"

"As a matter of fact, I did."

"Well, she's out, I'm afraid. I don't suppose I'll see her when she comes in."

"Doesn't matter," I said as lightly as I could. But I was bugged by just how much it did matter.

"Shall I ask her to ring you?" Lady Fielding asked.

"No, that's okay. She'll be at the races Saturday, won't she?"

"Yes, and at the party afterward."

"At your place?"

"In London, yes. You're coming, of course?"

"Of course," I agreed.

I couldn't sleep at all that night. Camilla didn't ring back. I hoped that was because her mother hadn't told her I'd phoned. Charles hadn't called in or rung with any news, and his wife said she didn't have a clue where he was. In the middle of the night, I rang my mother. As usual, she tried to play down her pleasure in hearing from me. She had seen the shooting at the Derby, had even thought for a few minutes that it had been me, until the commentator had said otherwise. I was amazed at her restraint in not calling me before.

I reassured her; I told her all was well; I was taking a couple of days off to get over the fall I'd had on Lorna Doone. I told her I'd win the Oaks; she told me not to be so darn cocksure.

The next day, Inspector Lawson from the Surrey Police arrived at nine. He was wearing the same grey, tired suit and trailing a young detective constable. I made them some coffee and we sat in the kitchen, round the table where, the night before, Charles and I had grilled Haslam.

It soon became obvious that we were thinking along different lines. As far as they were concerned, Hagan had been the right target, and they were concentrating their energy on him.

I was tempted to tell them what I knew. But until I was certain I was in the clear, I didn't dare. I'd have to leave Lawson on the wrong track, and anyway, I reasoned, just for now we could get further than they could.

"We haven't found anything up in the woods by the racecourse," Lawson said. "We had a team up there all of yesterday, but so far nothing. He got right away. So we've got to start from the other end—motive. Now, I had the feeling you didn't tell me everything about your disagreement with Hagan."

"I told you everything about it."

"Did you, Mr. Felton? So why did you pay Mrs. Hagan ten thousand pounds the evening he was killed?"

The detective looked at me, with his eyebrows raised and a smirk on his face.

I stared back at him, trying to quell my anger at having a private act of good will questioned.

"I suppose it would be expecting too much for you to believe that I didn't *pay* Mary Hagan anything. I *gave* her the money, because she's a good woman, and Mick was up to his neck in debt."

"You knew about his debts, then?"

"Not specifically, but I knew he owed a lot. I told you I guessed he had a bundle on his horse when I beat him at Newbury. He was so mad afterward, I reckoned he'd gone double or quits. Unfortunately, it went the wrong way."

"You drove him to Newbury that day, didn't you?"

"Yeah. I often gave him a ride to the races since he got banned."

"As you are now."

"What the hell's that got to do with anything?"

"Nothing, Mr. Felton, but on this particular journey, when he knew you'd be riding against him, didn't he mention to you that he wanted to win?"

"Sure he mentioned it, but he didn't expect me to do a lot about it. He knew that I don't do that kind of thing."

"What kind of thing?"

"Stopping horses, of course. It wasn't a thing he often needed other people to do; usually he would bet against the horse he was on. This time I guess he thought he could have a real touch. He was on a good filly, but not as good as mine; he must have overlooked it, or maybe he didn't think I'd have the ride. I only fixed it the day before because Captain Ellerton's entry went lame."

"So he asked you to stop your horse from winning, and you refused?"

"Basically, yeah."

"Even though he was a friend of yours and you knew he was in trouble?"

"Yeah, but I can tell you, if he'd told me how much it was going to cost him, I'd have sprained an ankle or something, let somebody else stop it for him. At the time, I felt really bad about what happened, but Mick knew the score, he knew I wouldn't pull a horse."

"Well, that all sounds very noble, Mr. Felton, but it doesn't explain why you paid his wife off."

I stood up. "I've told you all I can, Inspector. When

they pass a law in this country against helping out friends in trouble, you come back and arrest me. Okay? Now, goodbye."

The policeman wasn't ruffled. He took the dismissal in his stride. "We'll be back, Mr. Felton, and in the meantime, if you feel you have anything to say, don't hesitate to call me." He got to his feet and beckoned his silent junior with a nod at the door.

I watched him go, wondering why the hell I was feeling like a criminal.

I kept myself busy for the rest of the day in the gym and the pool and tried to deal with my depression.

I'd always prided myself on my self-sufficiency, ever since I'd first known my dad was in gaol. Moving to England had been part of it. I still wanted to prove I wasn't like my father; I was my own man. It meant I had few really close friends, and the women I preferred were either the least demanding, softest of soft options, or, occasionally, like Sandy Zimmer, powerful predators with beautiful, well-kept bodies, turned on by my apparent lack of interest. It wasn't that I was scared of needing other people; I'd just got out of the habit of needing them.

The thought of phoning Camilla to talk to someone and help offload some of my depression came and went as quickly as it took me to turn at the end of the pool. When I'd finished working out, I rang trainers about my rides next day. I left a message for Charles to confirm that he was going to pick me up in the morning.

About five that evening, Mary Hagan phoned. The police were coming to see her. Could I be there?

I rang John Calloway to ask him if he could drive me to Hagan's cottage. He couldn't, but he sent up Nigel, his nineteen-year-old son who played squash with me sometimes. That suited me; Nigel rarely spoke, and right now, I wasn't looking for casual conversation. He turned up in his father's Mercedes and drove me in complete silence the fifteen minutes to Mary Hagan's.

The police were already there, sitting in Mary's front room, while her sister, brothers and kids were crowded apprehensively into the kitchen. I stuck my head into the cluttered room to see DI Lawson and his sidekick sitting at a small table.

I barged in, smiling at the Hagan clan as I went. "Mind if I join you?"

Lawson sprang to his feet. "I'd rather you didn't, Mr. Felton. I need to speak to Mrs. Hagan alone."

Mary glanced at me, then at the policeman. She looked confused and terrified. "Oh, please let him stay. He knows more about Mick's racing than I do anyway."

The detective raised his eyebrows. I guessed he'd been getting nowhere with the frightened little woman.

"All right."

I shut the door behind me and sat on a hard chair by the window, out of Lawson's direct line of vision.

"Now, Mrs. Hagan, I'm sorry to have to ask you these questions," the policeman said with a ponderous attempt at compassion. "I realize how distressed you are, which is why I left it a couple of days before coming to see you. But your husband was the object of a carefully planned, highly professional operation. We can't leave a stone unturned. Millions of people saw what happened and they're baying for results. Now, you've told me you can't think of anyone who might have had it in for your husband, but you can't be in the business your husband was in for all that time without making some enemies. There's a big pot of money involved in racing and no shortage of people wanting to get their hands in it. Your husband came across these people all the time, everyone in racing does to some extent, isn't that right, Mr. Felton?"

"Sure."

"All I want is the names of the people he saw most regularly."

Mary looked back at him wildly. "But I told you, I don't know. He never brought racing people back here. He said he liked to keep his work and his family apart. I seldom ever went with him; there's always too much to do here with the kids."

"Didn't you hear him talking to people on the phone?"

"Sometimes, but he never liked to use it, he said. Of course he talked to his trainers and his agent and so forth, just making dates and choosing rides, like. The only other racing person who ever came to the house was him." She nodded at me. "Jake was very good to Mick. He used to drive him to the races afer Mick lost his license."

"We know that. Mr. Felton and I have already had a chat. In fact, I've already asked him why he paid you ten thousand pounds. Now I want to ask you, Mrs. Hagan."

Mary Hagan had been doubtful about the money when I'd given it to her; now she was certain of its bad provenance. She gazed at the policeman with wide guilty eyes.

"Oh my God!" she wailed. "What is it you've done, Jake?"

I gave her what I hoped was a calm, reassuring smile and spoke to the detective. "Mary was as suspicious as you about that money. I guess that's the way in a cynical world." To Mary, I said, "Don't worry about it, Mary, there's absolutely nothing to hide about it. Otherwise I wouldn't have given you a check. I knew these guys would be looking at any bank accounts connected to Mick."

To my relief, Lawson looked half convinced. At least, he left the matter alone for the time being.

"We'll be having another chat about that, Mr. Felton. Now," he said, turning back to Mary, "we'll need to have a look at all your husband's correspondence, Mrs. Hagan. Where did he keep it?"

"Right there, in that desk behind you."

Lawson stood up and lowered the lid of a big mahogany bureau. Inside were piles of dog-eared papers and old envelopes, some unopened—the signs of a disorderly procrastinator.

"Don't you need some kind of warrant to look through all that?" I asked.

"Yes, Mr. Felton. And I have one. Would you like to see it?"

"Go ahead," I shrugged, confident that Mick would be unlikely to have left anything too incriminating among that jumble. Most of his misdeeds were arranged orally.

Half an hour's searching yielded a bagful of scraps of paper and old envelopes with phone numbers scrawled on them. Lawson and his minion took them away with them after a formal farewell and a promise to return.

When they had driven off, I asked Mary if we could search the rest of the house for anything Mick might have left lying around, since the police had given me the chance to get there first. Together we went through every drawer, emptied every box and looked under every rug.

For the first twenty minutes, it seemed Lawson had been right to assume anything worth having was in Mick's chaotic bureau. But then Mary struck lucky. She was in the hallway, going through the pockets of an old sheepskin jacket which I remembered Mick wearing to ride out, on chilly spring dawns up on the Lambourn Downs. She found a small, dog-eared pocket diary.

There wasn't a lot entered. On some dates, a simple figure, and at the back a dozen or so phone numbers. I asked Mary if I could borrow the diary, and I didn't tell her what I thought the figures meant. But when I asked her not to tell the police about it when they next came, I was sure she understood.

///////////// CHAPTER 9

The night before the Oaks, I went to bed at sunset, dreamed vividly and slept badly.

The implications of Mick's murder had really sunk in now, and in every dark corner of my subconscious lurked someone or something that meant me harm.

I woke early and pandered to my paranoia by pasting telltale hairs across doors and windows, and checking that my alarm systems all functioned. This activity went some way to putting me at ease with the world, and I was very glad to see Charles when he arrived at ten to take me to Epsom.

"You're looking very perky this morning," he said.

"Well, I'm still alive, there's no pain in my leg and Corsican Lady's still sound."

"And it doesn't look as though the racing will be abandoned either."

He was right. It was one of those clear summer mornings that reminded me of home and I was happy to forget for a while that somebody wanted me dead.

I concentrated instead on my chances of winning my second Classic that season. Normally my guts, all too empty, would have been churning by then, but other, greater fears had displaced that nervousness and the big race seemed more like a nice break from the angst that had been chewing me up since Mick had been shot.

"So," Charles said, "don't you want to know how I got on with the gun dealers?" He sounded pleased with his efforts.

In my preoccupation with conserving my own existence, I'd almost forgotten about the stolen gun.

"Yes, of course," I replied, turning off the radio. "What happened?"

"I went to Cox's of Bond Street. They had a visitor about two months ago, asking about the Mewar Purdeys. The manager there is a bit out of date; apparently he told the chap that they belonged to the Emir of Bhaqtar and there was no chance of procuring them."

"And?"

"Well, that was it. The chap looked disappointed. He asked Cox's to contact him if they found they could get their hands on the guns. He was an American; he left his name and gave the Connaught as his address in London."

"Could they do anything for him?"

"The manager did let something slip. What you've got to realize is that it took me about two hours of tactful probing to extract this information. I'd told him I was looking for rare Edwardian Purdeys with some history to them, which is how we got on to the Mewars. I asked him if he could give me the American's name and address to see if he had any to sell. He shouldn't have done but I think I bored him into submission. Anyway, I went round to the Connaught, and there had been a man of that name and description staying there for a couple of days. The chap in Cox's also mentioned that there was another, slightly disreputable dealer who occasionally came across interesting guns and with whom he had some kind of arrangement. He mentioned that he'd given the American's name to this dealer. He said he'd ring him and tell him I was interested in similar guns, not necessarily the Mewars. He picked up the phone on his desk and punched out a number. Evidently the man at the other end wasn't too helpful. The chap in the shop put the phone down quickly and said there was nothing doing there." Charles paused for effect and glanced across with a grin. "And, I clocked the number he'd dialed."

I didn't get excited. "Okay, so how does this help us?"

"I don't know yet. But I just felt from the way the telephone conversation went that this other dealer definitely didn't want to encourage inquiries about guns like yours."

"Have you followed it up yet?"

"Give me a chance. I'll get on to it on Monday."

"Just get his name and address, if you can."

"Right. Have you unearthed anything your end?"

"Not a lot. I went to see Mary Hagan yesterday evening. The police were there, but they couldn't get much out of her. They took away a pile of bits and pieces from Mick's desk, but I doubt there was anything useful there. I did a bit better."

"What was that?"

"His diary. It was in his old sheepskin. Mary found it after the police had gone."

"Anything in it?"

"Nothing of any interest. You can have a look later."

"If you want my advice, leave that until tomorrow," Charles said. "Maybe you ought to start concentrating on the racing today."

"And the party afterward," I added.

"Where's that?"

"At the Fieldings'."

Charles turned to look at me with a sly grin. "How are you getting on with the lovely Camilla?"

"Making a little progress."

Charles laughed. "That means you haven't cracked it yet. I'm glad to hear it. It's time you came up against a little resistance."

"Not that much resistance. It's just that I usually seem to be in hospital when I see her—or in a man-trap."

"She's a bit of an improvement on the tarts you usually go for. Which reminds me, I saw Mrs. Zimmer when I was in the Connaught. She must have come over for the races."

"Yes, she has. She rang me to tell me."

"She's still hot to trot, then?"

"She may be, but not with me for a jockey."

"Good heavens, Camilla must have made a big impression on you to make you turn Sandra down. When you got back from Kentucky last year, I remember you telling me she was the best thing you'd ever had."

"She was. But she expects a lot in return, and I don't like the idea of messing around with a married woman."

"Did you meet her husband?"

"No. He was away, but I guess Sandra had to square all the servants. I can do without all that kind of aggravation. Anyway, I'm not so interested in just screwing for its own sake."

Charles gave a burst of laughter. "What the hell is going on? Felton the Reformed Fornicator? I never thought I'd hear you say that, at least not for a long time yet."

"I'm not saying I've given it up, but you know what it's like—a kid in a candy store for the first few years after you discover what your pecker's for. I'm more selective now, that's all. And maybe looking for a bit more. I guess I've got bored going to bed with women who can't add two and two."

"Mrs. Zimmer can add, surely?"

"She can add all right but with her one and one make sixty-nine."

As we drove, I thought of Sandy and the twelve hours of unexpurgated sex I'd spent with her the summer before. I didn't regret it, not at all, but I didn't want to repeat it. At least, I told myself I didn't.

Sandra Zimmer was almost the first person I saw when we arrived at Epsom. She was with a wizened old guy in a baggy morning suit being let out of the back of a Phantom VI behind the stands. She looked spectacular in an outrageous short frock, and ten years younger than her thirty-five years. I thought of the hot body beneath the film of clinging silk and felt a sudden surge of blood to the groin.

She saw me, too, but she didn't raise so much as an eyebrow in recognition. I assumed the old man was Mr. Zimmer, but there were two younger men in their party. One was a square-jawed, stocky man in a shiny mohair suit. The other was younger, good-looking and seemed quite at ease in a crisp grey morning suit. I didn't get a lot of time to take them in. Sandra and the two younger men soon hustled the old fellow through the gates and up to a box somewhere.

As I watched them go, I remembered what another owner I used to ride for in America had once said to me. "Jake, there's only one thing that keeps beautiful young women horny for old men like me, and that's money." Zimmer, I thought, must have an awful lot of it.

We drove on and Charles dropped me by the stables before he went off to park. I found Ellerton. He was almost friendly as we talked about Corsican Lady and my two other rides for him that day.

"Still feeling confident about the filly, Captain?"

"Certainly. She's in very good order. Garry gave her some fast work yesterday and she went like a dream. Personally, I think she's got a very good chance."

"Have you backed her?"

He nodded smugly. "Oh yes, before she won the Guineas."

To some extent, this explained his good humor, though it amazed me that after all his years of training, he could still think there was such a thing as a certainty. But there had to be more to it than that to make him grin like a bookie who'd just seen a favorite fall.

I didn't ask. He had produced three fit, fancied animals for me to ride, which he wanted to win. That was all I needed to know.

I left him to keep my appointment with the course doctor. I'd taken the bandages off my cut and the skin was already knitting itself together. I didn't have to act comfortable as I strolled around the doctor's room.

"You've healed up well." He nodded. "No problems there. So, best of luck. Just try not to fall off this time." He laughed.

I didn't.

With a twinge of guilt, he became serious. "I hope nothing happens again, you know, like Hagan. It was the most horrific thing to happen at a Derby."

"It would have been just as bad for Mick if it had happened at a seller in Salisbury."

"Yes. Yes, of course. But the whole thing has left a ghastly taste in everyone's mouth."

"Well, I guess it won't happen again," I said, "Hagan's not riding today."

"No. Quite," the doctor said.

He signed my medical card and I left his room feeling sick. However much I had tried to reassure Charles and Camilla that it would be crazy for someone to try and shoot me in the same way as Mick had been shot, at that moment I'd have taken even money on it. Anyone could guarantee where a jockey would be at any given time during an afternoon's racing—an assassin's dream!

It was only after Corsican Lady and I had jumped out of the stalls and covered the first furlong that I felt safe enough to concentrate on winning the Oaks. I had every reason to feel confident. I already had a win and a third in the bag. Ellerton's horses were in peak form and I'd only thought good things about him since the racing had started.

Corsican Lady did everything we had hoped for. I knew before we hit Tattenham Corner that we were going to win. She sprinted up the hill, leaving the opposition trailing, and we crossed the line three lengths clear, but it could have been double that distance. That special surge of elation that comes with winning a big race on a great horse was increased for me by an extra surge of elation at still being alive. But I couldn't keep my eyes from wandering up to the roof of the stands as I chatted to the lad leading in Corsican Lady.

In the winner's enclosure, Bunty Fielding hugged and kissed me enough to arouse the interest of the more imaginative gossip writers. Seeing her pleasure added to my own.

"I see you've got a ride in the next," she said as she released me, "but make sure you come up and see us after that."

"I will. Thanks." I nodded.

"Camilla's here too, of course," she said with a twitch of an eyebrow which made me think I'd just passed my final test to gain her approval.

I looked around for her daughter; just caught her eye as I went back to the weighing room on a temporary high.

If I was high, Captain Toby was above the clouds. He was beaming like the happiest beetroot I'd ever seen. Normally a man who liked to keep information to himself until imparting it was unavoidable, he couldn't resist telling me about the cream on the top of the day's win.

"Winning this race has probably brought us a dozen more horses." He beamed.

"Already?" I asked with surprise.

He gave me a fatuous grin to show that was all he was prepared to offer at the moment. I didn't know whether to believe him or not. It seemed very unlikely that any owners would have had a chance to get near him since the finish of the Oaks to discuss that kind of thing, and anyway, nobody made those commitments in a hurry. But I wished him the best of luck, and left to change into the colors for the next race.

I rode the next as best I could on an outclassed animal—not one of Toby's. The owner had wanted an Epsom runner, and that was as much as he was ever going to get.

Afterward, I changed into the most English-looking suit I possessed and headed for the Fieldings' box once more. On the way I ran a gauntlet of back-slapping and hand-shaking for my Oaks win. I'd nearly reached the box when I ran straight into James Bullough-Ferguson.

I couldn't help thinking of him taking Camilla out, but I tried not to let that irritate me.

He didn't slap my back or offer me his hand. He gazed down his long nose and said, "Well done, Jake. Beautifully ridden. Of course, Toby's obviously in form despite his other troubles so I've arranged to send him fifteen more boarders."

I tried not to show my disappointment. If the horses that had so excited Toby were being sent by him, they were unlikely to be any good. If James Bullough-Ferguson owned any horses at all, which I doubted, they certainly wouldn't be worth training.

"Great," I said, as if I didn't mean it.

Bullough-Ferguson gave an oily grin. "You won't be disappointed with them, I can assure you."

"Glad to hear it," I said, and stepped round him to carry on to the Fieldings' box.

Camilla's kiss was softer, more apprehensive than her mother's effusive display. She was relieved to see me, I thought. But I wanted to push those problems to the back of my mind and get into the party mood that was expected of me.

Mostly, I managed it. The Fieldings' guests had all won money on Corsican Lady and wanted to thank me personally. I told them, with no false modesty, that most of the credit should go to her trainer. After a while, the trainer turned up to take the credit for himself.

I guessed Ellerton had a monster bet on his Oaks runner, but I couldn't criticize him for his confidence. At least it would help to solve some of his problems and let him enjoy being flavor of the day. He set about getting drunker than I'd seen him in a long time. I took advantage to extract more about his new charges.

"I saw Bullough-Ferguson outside. He says he's sending fifteen horses to us."

Ellerton laughed. "Does he? Self-important little sod. They're not his horses, they're Leonard Zimmer's."

That piece of news hit me right between the eyes, but Ellerton didn't notice.

"No," he went on, "all James did was introduce him. He's a funny old bugger, Zimmer. I'd never set eyes on him before today. He said he was bringing some horses over from the States to race here, and if we won the Oaks he'd be sending them to me."

I thought for a moment. "Did you tell anyone else how confident you were, before the race?"

"No. Not really, though I did mention it to James when he rang yesterday to arrange meeting Zimmer, but that was all."

"Right," I said unemphatically. In the circumstances,

it had been a reasonable indiscretion. "Well done, Captain. I hope there are some good animals among them."

"There are, and he wants me to buy him a couple more. He says he'd like to win a few group races this season." Ellerton, much drunker than usual now, leaned toward me and hissed champagne fumes at me. "And Zimmer has so much money he could buy every racehorse in the world and still have change. He's a billionaire, Jake, a bloody billionaire!" He beamed at me. I couldn't blame him; Zimmer didn't look much like a fairy godmother, but I guessed a few billion dollars gave him the capacity to work magic, or something close to it. "And have you seen his wife?" Ellerton went on with a leer. "I'd train her for nothing."

The Fieldings' London house had shed its mustiness for Bunty's party. Maybe it was just the sound of laughter, the smell of scent and champagne that roused it from its torpor. Maybe any collection of people celebrating shared good luck can imbue any place with a sense of occasion.

Beyond the large Victorian house, the garden was full of ebullient men and women, charged with drink and their bookmakers' money.

If I didn't know all the people, I felt I knew all the types that were gathered there. Normally, I wouldn't have had a lot of time for some of them, but it would have taken a stronger man than I was not to be flattered at least for a few hours by their overwhelming good will.

But when those few hours were up, I felt like Cinderella worrying about the chimes of midnight. It had been a great day, but the next day and the death sentence hanging over me weren't going to be canceled.

I wanted to go. And I wanted to take Camilla with me.

In the same way the sun encourages you to procreate

in favorable conditions, so danger encourages you to pass on your genes before it's too late. I badly wanted to be with a woman that night. And seeing Sandra had made me want to spend the night with Camilla.

I found her looking half asleep, boxed in by Bullough-Ferguson and another chinless wonder. It came as a relief to notice that, when she saw me, she woke up like a princess about to be rescued from a tower.

"Jake!" she said, and extricated herself from the two men. "You haven't spoken to me all evening."

"That's because I'm going to take you out to dinner now."

James Bullough-Ferguson scowled at me and turned on his heels.

"Thank God," Camilla said when no one could hear her. Outside she said, "I don't want dinner. Do you?"

"No."

"I'll drive you home then."

I played down the buzz her words gave me.

"Cheaper than a taxi," I said.

She looked at me frankly. "I think you'll find that a cabby would be less demanding."

A shock of pleasure rippled through me. I wasn't used to English girls like Camilla taking the initiative. But then I wasn't used to English girls like Camilla; or maybe she wasn't typical. Either way, she'd made up her mind what she wanted, and I didn't care whether it was out of love, lust or compassion.

Conversation on the journey down to Hampshire was comfortable, a kind of gentle verbal foreplay. I lay back in the passenger seat and watched her long legs changing gear, and her strong, lovely profile lit by the beams of oncoming cars.

But I had to change the mood, briefly, when we arrived at my house.

"I've got to check the place over before we go in," I

said and got out to inspect all the doors and windows for any signs of disturbance. There were none.

"I'm sorry about that," I said.

"It doesn't worry me. I'm not scared," she said, unconvincingly.

"I wish I wasn't," I half joked.

"Do you really think there might be someone here?"

"No. No one's here, I promise you. But we could go some place else, if you want."

"No, I don't want it to be in some hotel."

We went inside the house and I reset all the alarms. "We'll be confined to the bedroom and bathroom now," I said.

"Suits me." Her grin hid any fears she might have had.

But I turned off the alarms once more to go down to the kitchen and fetch a bottle of Krug and some glasses. I re-alarmed the ground floor and went back upstairs. I didn't open the bottle, in case we didn't have time for it.

We didn't.

We didn't need the Crowded House album I put on my CD deck, either, but the right music improves almost everything.

We looked out of the full-length windows across the moonlit valley. It seemed a pity to block it out, but I drew the curtains and turned to find Camilla sitting on the end of the bed, smiling wickedly.

I sat beside her, and we fell back on the bed, kissing each other for the first time with long, hungry kisses, and searching each other with excited, inquisitive hands, as if it was the first time for both of us.

Camilla laughed between kisses. "Somebody told me that you don't notice a jockey's height when you're horizontal, and it's true."

"You can abuse me later, if you still want to," I said. I reached out and switched off the lights.

Camilla reached out and switched them back on. "Oh no you don't. I've got nothing to be ashamed of."

She swung her long legs off the bed and posed with false coyness on the ottoman at the end of it, swaying to the music. I propped myself up on my elbows, and gazed at her with delight.

"If you goggle at me with your tongue hanging out, I won't go on," she said.

I carried on goggling; I had no choice.

As Camilla languorously loosened her short cotton frock and let it fall to her ankles, she revealed more than just a beautiful body; she showed me a side to her character which up till then she'd only hinted at.

In the time I'd known her, I had only been treated to tantalizing glimpses of this glorious body. The stark reality of her flawless, firm-fleshed physique took me by surprise and had me gulping.

She unclipped her bra and tossed it over her shoulder to let loose a pair of big, soft globes. With a wiggle of her behind, she slid her tights and pants down her long legs, straightened herself and kicked them across the room. She stood for a moment, as composed as a Greek goddess, then she smiled with frank concupiscence.

"Will this do?" she asked.

I was knocked out. This was a side to her, direct and lusty, that I hadn't even guessed at.

"That will do," I gurgled. "And you did it so well."

"Beginner's luck," she said. "Now, let's get you out of those awful trousers. Stand up," she ordered.

I stood, wobbling on the mattress, while she unbuttoned my shirt and slipped it back over my shoulders. She undid the waistband of my loose-fitting flannel trousers and slowly pulled them down, lifting my feet one by one.

"Socks next, I think," she said and rolled them off.

I was standing in nothing but a pair of small white briefs.

"And now the poser's pouch," she said.

With her hands creeping up my legs, there was no

way I could stop my bulge growing until it burst out of confinement.

Camilla's eyes widened. "Ah, someone's pleased to see me."

She gave me a shove. My legs buckled beneath me and I collapsed onto the bed. Camilla deftly removed my last remaining garment. A moment later we were wrapped together, legs entwined, rocking to the music, and absolutely nothing else mattered.

I made coffee next morning. We sat beside each other in bed and gazed through the glass wall in front of us at the peaceful valley beyond. I was finding it hard to believe that I could feel this kind of contentment in the midst of danger. It was like being in the eye of a storm, when you know what's going on all around you but for a while you can wallow in the peace.

I looked at the woman who was responsible for this respite from my troubles.

"Milly," she couldn't be Camilla from now on, "that was the most sensational night," I murmured.

"Awesome, wasn't it?" She grinned, gently mocking.

"I didn't imagine it would be so good," I said.

"Why the hell not?" She laughed.

"Did you?"

"No," she admitted. "It was amazing. It's amazing now, just lying here with you, looking at that view." Her hand, resting on my thigh under the sheet, began to squeeze and stroke. "It's a pity we can't stay like this for ever."

"You're right. It couldn't ever get boring, could it? Let's try," I said.

I felt like a king next morning, flying through an early morning dappled sky.

Our love-in had lasted thirty hours. We hadn't

dressed all day, though we cheated by spending a couple of hours messing around in the pool and the gym; we even played a game of squash wearing nothing but sneakers.

It was only twenty minutes since I'd left her in my bed but I found myself getting hot again, just from the smell of her body which lingered on me.

She said she'd still be there when I came back, so I'd left her with all the alarms on, and prayed that no one would come prowling for me. I was out of the eye of the storm now. Danger and the threat of death swirled around me once more. But I was a lot more prepared to deal with it.

I landed in Ellerton's front paddock and walked up to the house. The guv'nor was still glowing with the euphoria of his big win and the imminent arrival of his new owner. Janey Ellerton even gave me a long flash of her faded smile.

I couldn't believe that Toby was completely out of the mire yet. He would need more than just the Zimmer horses to put him back on the road, and I was still doubtful that those horses were really going to arrive.

But I went out to do my job; I rode Smethwick's filly, Rock Beat, in the first lot, and an old handicapper in the second. The improved atmosphere in the yard was obvious in the attitude of the lads. There was something of the old confidence returning. I listened to what they said, but I wasn't going to offer any opinions.

When I went into Melbourne House for breakfast, my pessimism was confounded. Leonard Zimmer, his wife and one of the younger men who had been at Epsom for the Oaks were sitting with Toby in his formal dining room, drinking coffee from his best Meissen. The remnants of a breakfast of croissants and marmalade were on the table.

"Come in, come in, Jake," Toby boomed effusively, like everyone's favorite uncle. "I'd like you to meet Mr.

and Mrs. Zimmer." He waved a hand between us. "This is Jake Felton, our stable jockey."

I nodded. "Hello."

Sandra looked at me as if she had never seen me before. There was a ghost of frightened apprehension in her cool eyes as she nodded back.

Leonard Zimmer's reaction was more enigmatic. The first flash of his steely eyes bore straight through me, but this was quickly replaced by the bland indifference with which the very rich tend to regard all but other very rich, wearing their wealth like an impenetrable cloak.

I also got the feeling that Zimmer was one of those rich old men who resent the power of younger men to attract their women, and envy any fit young athlete.

"Good to meet you, Mr. Felton," he said, politely enough, in American with a hint of middle Europe. "I saw you ride in your last season in the States. It was a shame you left, but you won a good race Saturday."

"Mostly thanks to Captain Ellerton's preparation," I replied.

"So he tells me," said Zimmer. "It was enough to persuade us that this is where we should place the horses we would like to run in England. As Captain Ellerton's first jockey, I expect you will be riding most of them." He turned to Toby. "Who will you use if anything happens to Felton?" he asked.

Toby looked stumped. "Why should anything happen to Jake?"

"No particular reason, Captain. But, after all, he was off for a few days before the Derby, and a few days a couple of months ago. I've always had contingency plans for all my businesses; surely you do the same?"

"Well, in the unlikely event of Jake being unable to ride for any length of time, we have Garry, our very able second jockey, who rides lighter than Jake and still has a five-pound claim, which can be useful. And, of course, there are always other top jockeys spare for most races."

"You're confident they'd ride for you?"

A cloud passed across Ellerton's face. I saw him struggle for a moment with his temper. But he overcame it. "Obviously, Mr. Zimmer, it's no secret that it was something of a blow to my yard when Sheikh Ahmed took his horses away. But even with a reduced string, we have consistently produced top-class winners. Every good jockey in this country knows that I only turn out horses that are ready to run, and win."

"Though sometimes, when they are most expected to, they don't," Zimmer said quietly.

"Well," Toby blustered, "nobody gets it right every time."

"Of course, that is true, Captain. We have taken that into consideration in making our decision. But I want to make it clear that my horses always go out to win. I don't like gambling, Captain, just winning. Now," he said to me, "I want you to meet my late sister's boy, Hal Symonds."

I looked at the man beside him, who hadn't spoken. He was a big guy, six three, over two hundred pounds and in good shape. Greased up and wearing a G-string, he'd have cruised through a Chippendales audition. He had longish blond hair, strong well-formed features and a full mouth with a confident, rich-boy shape to it. He was very good-looking in an arrogant, beefcake sort of a way. He wore loose, Italian clothing, that accentuated his well-developed torso and limbs. And from the way Sandra quickly glanced at him now, I guessed he was another of her extra-mural activities.

"Hi," Hal said to me in a lazy, West Coast drawl.

"I don't have a lot of time to run around looking at my horses," Zimmer went on, "so Hal will be over from time to time to check on them and report back to me, okay?"

Hal smirked at Toby.

Toby winced. "That's fine, Mr. Zimmer, as long as he has your written authority to instruct us, otherwise it can become acrimonious."

I smiled to myself. Training Zimmer's horses was going to keep Ellerton on his toes. Hal slid across the table toward me an impeccably produced brochure of the horses that were arriving at the end of the week. When I had looked at the pictures and read details of their breeding and form, I realized that they constituted a package that was a trainer's dream. Zimmer really had turned out to be Toby's fairy godmother.

The Rolls-Royce Phantom VI crunched smoothly down Ellerton's drive. Zimmer, his wife and his nephew didn't look back. Ellerton stared after them with a look of gleeful triumph.

"A lucky break, eh, Captain?" I said.

"Bugger luck," he said. "Zimmer's a man who always buys the best. He realized what a mistake Sheikh Ahmed made by pulling out of here."

"So he's a very rich Jew who wants to show a very rich Arab how wrong he was," I said thoughtfully.

Ellerton turned to me. "I hadn't thought of that. Well, we'll prove him right, and that silly bastard Penruddock will get his comeuppance." Ellerton grinned at the happy thought.

The grin was wiped off his face, and mine, when we saw James Bullough-Ferguson shoot between the dragons on the gateposts in a very new BMW.

"Christ," Toby said with exasperation. "He hasn't hung around. He must have been waiting down the road for Zimmer to go so that he could come and collect."

"Collect what?"

"He thinks he's due something for introducing Zimmer, greedy shit. Zimmer had already decided to send me his horses long before bloody Bullough-Ferguson got involved."

The BMW drew up beside us and James wound down his window to put his head out. He ignored me.

"Morning, Toby. Got your checkbook?"

I turned, walked away and left them to it.

Milly, at home in my bed, hadn't been far from my thoughts all morning. And I wanted to get back to her.

/////////////// CHAPTER 10

I landed the Piper in John Calloway's meadow and started walking back up to my house. There was a point on the way where the lie of the land let me see up the valley to the top of my drive. I glanced up. I had visitors. There was a big black Mercedes parked outside the gate, and I could just make out there was someone in the driver's seat. Abruptly, my pulse quickened and my mouth dried with fear. I wasn't thinking of myself, but of Milly, naked and alone in my house.

I broke into a run up the steep valley side which was the quickest route.

When I was near the house, I slowed down and crept toward it under cover of the bushes that grew right up close to the back door. Knowing that I couldn't be seen from any of the windows of the house, I darted across to it, with my keys in my hand.

The back door was unlocked. If anyone had opened it with the alarms on, the central station of the security company would have told the police, and they would already be on their way. I hoped they weren't going to be too late.

I pushed the door open, and tiptoed along the back passage, past my fishing rods and boots, to the kitchen. Slowly, I put my head around the door. There was no one there. I padded across the kitchen to the hallway, stopped and listened.

I heard voices, then male laughter from the drawing room. The laughter did a little to quieten my pulse. I crossed the flagstoned floor of the hall and went into the large, light room.

Milly was sitting on the sofa with her legs tucked up under her, wearing jeans and one of my shirts.

Opposite her, with a glass in his hand, was Smethwick, the Cockney meat merchant and owner of the filly Rock Beat.

"'Allo, Jake. How are yer?" he greeted me with a big upward movement of his lips that you couldn't call a smile.

I ignored him. "You okay, Milly?" I asked.

"Course she's okay, Jake. And she's looked after me handsome. You're a lucky boy, hiding this one away." He spoke as if Milly were a pet animal. Milly looked sick and shook her head.

"Hello, Jake," she said. "Mr. Smethwick said he wanted to see you urgently, so I let him in and gave him a drink."

"Do you know each other, then?" I asked.

"Course we do," Smethwick said. "Me and her dad's old mates."

I didn't think that, whatever their relationship, Sir John would have put it like that, but I didn't say so. "Oh, good," I said, aware at least that there had been no grounds for my fear. "What did you want to see me about?"

"Well, it's sort of private."

Milly hopped off the sofa. "Fine. I'll go for a walk."

"Be careful," I said as she left the room.

"You don't want to worry about 'er. She can take care of herself," Smethwick said authoritatively. "What a cracking richard! Now look, I come 'ere 'cause I knew you was riding up at Ellerton's this mornin' and they told me you'd more'n likely be back 'ere about now. Fing is, your Captain Toby's suddenly gettin' all unrealistic. He always used to be on for a bit of result control, know what I mean? But now 'e's being difficult. Rock Beat—she's running in the Coventry at Ascot next week, right?"

I nodded gloomily and sat down in a deep chair opposite him.

"And 'ow's she doing?" Smethwick asked.

"She's going well. She should win easy. You could have a big bet on her."

Smethwick gave a throaty chuckle and shook his head at me as if I were retarded and had to be humored. "Oh no, son. You and me and Captain Toby, we know she can win, and so do the bookies. They're offerin' a very unsportin' price. But she's entered for another competitive race at Sandown on Eclipse day, and if she's run a bit tacky at Ascot, she'll be a halfway sensible price by then. Right?"

I knew what was coming. "Just hang on a minute, Jim. I want to go and check Milly isn't lost."

I went to the kitchen, found my pocket cassette recorder and dropped it in my pocket. Back in the drawing room, Smethwick was getting twitchy.

"She's fine." I laughed. "But getting back to Rock Beat, she'll run well at Ascot," I said, all innocent. "I told you, she's in fantastic shape. I can't see her being beaten."

"Jake," Smethwick said with a harder edge to his voice, "you're bein' a bit thick this morning. You've got a lot of say in what 'appens; after all, you're riding the fuckin' animal."

I opened my eyes wide with astonishment. "You're asking me to stop her?"

"Yes."

"But Mr. Smethwick, we don't do that sort of thing at Melbourne House."

"Don't make me laugh! Ellerton's been havin' 'em tugged left, right and bloody center. Don't tell me you don't know that."

"I can tell you, Mr. Smethwick, that I've never deliberately stopped a horse from winning in my life."

"Don't give me that! And I can tell you, chum, you're not going to win on Rock Beat next week. And that's your bloody owner's instructions!" He glared at me for a moment, then suddenly remembered that he'd left out his principal argument. "Of course, there's a nice little bonus in it for you."

I thought for a moment. "I wondered when you were coming to that, Mr. Smethwick." I grinned. "How much?"

"Three grand."

"Three grand!? It's a fifty grand race; five for me if I win."

"All right, five—tax free."

I considered this. "And another five if I win at Sandown."

"You're a greedy little bastard, aren't you, but at least you're talkin' sense. I'll agree to that, but just make sure you do what you're supposed to, or you'll be in deep, stinkin' shit."

"You've got quite a way with words, haven't you, Mr. Smethwick."

Smethwick drained his glass and stood up. "Don't get cheeky with me, son. And don't forget what I said, whether you like the way I say it or not."

I shrugged. "No problem, as long as you don't forget your side of the deal."

"I never forget a favor. Right, I'll see you around. I'll be there to watch the race next Tuesday." He grinned. "I'll be lookin' very bloody disappointed, tearin' up my 'orse loses."

I went out with him and watched him walk heavily back up to the gate where his car was waiting. When the car had turned and driven away, Milly appeared from the side of the house.

"God, what an animal!" she said.

I laughed. "He could do with a few years at charm school, couldn't he?"

"I suppose he was asking you not to win, or something."

"How did you guess? I think it'll be the last time, though."

We walked back into the house, and into the drawing room. "Do you want to hear what he said?" I asked.

"How?"

I leaned down and picked up the small tape recorder which I'd tucked between me and the wing of the chair I'd been sitting in.

"Brilliant!" She laughed.

I shrugged my shoulders. "If I get a chance to use it. Now," I said, "how about another work-out in the gym?"

"If I'm going to be half a day late for work, I might as well make it worthwhile."

When Milly went, I was both sorry and relieved to see her go. I'd been able to forget my other problems for a while, but they came crowding back in on me now.

Though Smethwick had turned out not to be any kind of danger to Milly, he could have been. I didn't know much about his other connections, and it was just possible I hadn't pulled a horse for him before when he'd told Toby to do it. I didn't know, but I guessed he was a dangerous man, whose methods lacked subtlety.

Seeing that car waiting had given me a jolt and I decided that I couldn't risk having Milly down here again—not until I knew what was going on and who was responsible.

In fact, I thought gallantly, she'd be much safer not seeing too much of me anywhere for a while. Now I knew how good it was between us, I knew it would keep and not suffer from lack of practice.

The most important thing to do, if what Milly and I had started was going to last, was to clear up the doubt that was hanging over my future. From now on, that had to be the clear priority in my life.

Back in the house, I rang Phil White, my agent. Ellerton had no runners at Nottingham that day, but I'd got three outside rides, the first of them at two forty-five. Using the Piper, I wouldn't have to leave until around one-thirty. I rang Charles Powell's house in Sussex. His wife told me he'd gone to London early and was planning to call in and see me on his way back, around midday.

That suited me. I wanted time to analyze methodically everything that had happened since Haslam had first been approached by the London fixer at Doncaster. I made myself a large pot of coffee, and sat down at my kitchen table with a pad of blank paper in front of me.

I made a list of the events.

Haslam had arranged to meet me, knowing where I was going afterward.

He'd got me totally drunk.

I'd been pushed off the road in my car, with a ninety percent chance of being killed. But I'd survived.

Question: There had to be more certain ways of killing people, and less risky. Why had that method been chosen?

Answers: To make it look like an accident, not murder. That had been successful. And to make my death, or near death, as dramatic as possible? Maybe.

While I was in hospital, my house was burgled, very professionally, and only one of a very valuable pair of guns was taken.

Question: Was this connected in any way to the earlier and subsequent attempts to kill me?

Answer: Not necessarily, but as Charles had said, coincidence is the last resort of the empirical mind.

If it was connected, then so was Mick Hagan.

But Mick and I hadn't fallen out over the Pink Pigeon race until a week after that.

Four weeks later, I stepped into a mantrap. This time, there was at least a fifty percent chance of my surviving, and no way was it going to look like an accident. But there was also a very high chance I would have been injured badly enough to stop me riding for a month or so. Only the Spanish shotgun had prevented that.

Question: Had the intention been to kill me, or to maim me, or to stop me riding in the Derby?

Answer: Any of these. And again, a high-profile, publicity generating event. The attempt had failed on all counts, bar putting me off riding for a week. And getting me jocked off my Derby horse? That had to be an unplanned side effect.

The day I got back from hospital, Hagan turned up, pointing my gun at me. The gun wasn't loaded, but he had a pocket full of cartridges. He asked for twenty-five grand. He went away with nothing but a promise of ten thousand. I gave him no more than that promise while he was still alive and I'd heard no more from him in the week before the Derby.

Question: I'd mentioned to him that the gun had been stolen, but did he already know that? I didn't think so; anybody who had stolen the gun to sell it back to me would have known Mick would make a good middle man—despite our public disagreement over Pink Pigeon.

The next day, I got the first specific communication that someone had it in for me. "POACHERS GET WHAT POACHERS DESERVE."

That should have narrowed the field, but the more I thought about it, the more I felt it could mean practically anything I might have done that had spoiled other people's plans. As far as I knew, I hadn't done anything that should have upset anyone that much since I'd been riding in England. But I couldn't be sure, and I couldn't be sure that I wasn't implicated unwittingly in one of the dozens of potential conspiracies that can make a jockey's life a minefield—even when he's acting in complete innocence.

Question: Did whoever was responsible for the mantrap know I wouldn't want to talk to the police about it?

Answer: I reckoned they knew that, if I survived, I wouldn't. If I had died, the police would have been crawling all over the place, and it would have been on the front page of every paper in Britain and the States. So, they were confident the police wouldn't make any connections without me around to help them.

Question: Was there any connection between the crash and the mantrap?

Answer: On the face of it, none at all, but there couldn't be two people that interested in seeing me killed. That would be too coincidental.

I recovered, in time to ride on Derby day, which must have annoyed them, and goaded them into having the job done finally, infallibly and for the whole world to witness, at the start of the Derby. It was one of the most spectacular killings in recent history. And they'd hit the wrong man.

Or had they?

Maybe Hagan was involved. Maybe they had decided to silence him for some reason.

Or was it a crazy, sadistic plan to scare the hell out of me and put me on notice that I could go at any time?

I stared at the pages of scrawl I had produced and realized that I didn't have an idea, just a maze of disconnected, irrational events.

I was sure of a few things. Somebody was determined to punish me, then kill me. And that somebody suffered from an oversized ego, and wanted to make an example of me for outside consumption.

For the third time, I made my list of possibles.

At the top were four American individuals whom I'd upset in my first big year riding in the States.

But I didn't really believe it was one of them. That had been too long ago, nearly four years now. Unless they were making an example of me for consumption back home?

The only American element in the whole thing so far had been the gun collector. I had to follow that up, even though my instincts told me it was a blind alley.

At least it might eliminate the next name on the list, which was Mick Hagan's.

Hagan I didn't want to believe, but I had to accept that it was just possible he'd been bearing a grudge against me for a lot longer than I thought. I didn't want to think it, because I had considered Mick a close friend for several years, and nobody likes to see their judgement proved totally off beam.

The next name was Ellerton's, but that didn't make much sense.

Then Smethwick, simply because I knew he was a crook. I hadn't even had a disagreement with him, yet.

James Bullough-Ferguson disliked me intensely, but he had neither the resources nor a strong enough reason for the kind of things that had been done to me.

Next were the names of a few London bookies who had been annoyed when I'd turned down their offers, and a couple of mega-punters who liked to know results in advance. Haslam's Cockney contact could have pointed to any of them, but that was all.

I leaned back in my chair and groaned.

I started to concoct theories, trying to pull reasons out of the air.

Maybe, I thought, Mick Hagan had been approached, been asked to persuade me to take a few grand to stop a horse.

Maybe he'd taken the money, and failed to pass on the message—or the money—knowing I'd turn it down.

So, a horse had won which shouldn't have, and someone had lost a lot of money, and that someone was blaming me.

I shook my head.

I could have come up with a dozen more theories, all of them just as possible, and just as unfounded.

But, there had to be connections. And I knew I didn't have a lot of time to make them before the people hunting me hit their target.

I had thought they would try at the Oaks, and then this morning I'd been convinced when I'd seen the car at the top of my drive.

I was getting irrational and paranoid. I wished Charles would get here soon. I wasn't short of lines of inquiry but I was short of time, and I still had to try and win my six or seven races a week.

Charles didn't let me down. He arrived soon after midday and we went over and over everything that could have been connected with the three attempts to kill, maim or humiliate me in some bizarre way.

"Okay," he said, "let's deal with what we've got. I've just been to see the dodgy gun merchant that Cox's put me on to. I tracked him down through his phone number—I've made a little friend in British Telecom who charges fifty quid a number. This dealer's called Victor Constable, curiously enough. I caught him early this morning, leaving his house in South Norwood. I had to convince him I was a big collector, and I didn't care too much how I came by guns that I really wanted. He took me back inside his house fairly happily and asked me exactly what I was after. I deliberately didn't mention the Mewar Purdeys but, after a while, he did. He said he'd handled one recently, and he could probably get his hands on the pair.

"When I asked him where they were now, he said they were with a Middle Eastern collector who had fallen on hard times. Pretty implausible, but I pretended to believe him. He said they would cost me a hundred thousand, and I told him I'd get back to him. I think I should just tell him to get on with it."

"But that just means I'd have another break-in, which won't lead anywhere."

"It'll answer a few questions, though, eliminate some options. And," from his inside pocket, with a flourish, he produced a cassette, "I was wired and got the whole thing on tape."

"Great. Let's hear it."

Charles played back the conversation he'd described. The dealer had a half-educated, London accent. His delivery and high nasal voice gave me the impression he wouldn't be hard to deal with.

"We'll go see the man and lean on him a little. Can you fix up a meet with him? Tomorrow evening, after Kempton?"

Charles shrugged. "I'll try."

"Good. Now, let's take another look at Hagan's diary. I've got it upstairs."

I fetched the small book, and carefully wrote down every entry and every phone number on another sheet of paper. Then I opened my gun cupboard and locked the diary into the secret compartment where I kept my one, illicit handgun.

"I'll go and see my BT girl with these," Charles said,

jotting down all the phone numbers, "but it'll cost five hundred to check this lot."

"And save a load of time and hassle. I'll pay."

"Okay. What else do you want to follow up?"

"I think we should try Haslam again. See if he can give us some more on his contact. Also, can you check that it was definitely Harry Devene who was pushing Mick?"

"Sure." Charles nodded. "That shouldn't be hard."

"Another thing we've got to do is find out more about that car that was hanging around behind the woods the evening I got trapped—the Subaru four track John Calloway saw."

"I thought the police had tried to follow that up."

"They did. They checked the owner of every red Subaru pick-up in two counties. But that gave them nothing. Maybe we should talk to John Calloway, see if he can come up with more detail."

"There is something we could try," Charles said thoughtfully. "You may think it sounds a bit far-fetched, but it might work. I know a woman who's a hypnotherapist. She claims, and I've seen her do it, that she can put people into a trance and take them back to a specific event in their lives and extract total recall of that event."

"Yeah, I've read about that kind of thing, but it doesn't work too well; people get their facts in a muddle."

"Maybe, but sometimes she gets extraordinary results."

"So, who do we use her on?"

"John. Maybe he could tell us the car number."

I wasn't too impressed. "I wouldn't have said that John would be an ideal subject. He's not a very imaginative sort of a man."

"That makes him a better subject. Look, we can't lose anything by trying. If you can get him over here, I'll bring the woman down."

I shrugged. "Okay, we'll try it. Could you get her here Wednesday? I'll be back from Salisbury around six-thirty."

"Probably."

I picked up the phone and pressed Calloway's number.

"John," I said, when he answered. "I'm planning a little trip over to France sometime in the plane. I thought you'd be interested."

"Count me in, Jake," he answered without hesitation.

"Great. Could you come up Wednesday, around seven? We could fix a few details."

"Could I make it eight?"

"Yeah, that's fine."

"Great. I'll see you then, then."

"Okay, 'bye."

I put the phone down. "Eight o'clock, here."

"I'll arrange it."

"He'll have had a couple of drinks by then. Will that matter?"

"No, it'll help to relax him."

"It'd better. Now I suppose I'll have to get myself a few Sunday rides in Chantilly sometime."

"I'll come with you when you do."

Next morning, Charles came round to drive me to Kempton.

"Well done yesterday," he said.

I was preoccupied with our plan for that evening. I looked at him blankly for a moment.

"You had a double up, remember?" Charles laughed. "It paid about twenty to one."

I grunted. "Yeah. I hope you had some of it. I meant to tell you about them."

"As a matter of fact, I won a couple of hundred."

"Good. You can pay for the petrol today. And you could make some money on the last this afternoon."

Charles nodded. "Thanks. Then we're off to see Mr. Constable."

"In South Norwood?"

"That's right."

"Good." I smiled, glad to feel I was able to do something, even if it was only to eliminate Mick Hagan.

Charles thanked me again as we drove away from Kempton, alongside the river to London.

"Sorry it wasn't much of a price," I said. "I knew it would be an easy win, and so did everyone else."

"Small wins are more useful than big losses," he said. He wasn't really a gambler.

But we had other things to discuss.

"Did you get anywhere with those phone numbers?" I asked.

"Yes. I've got names and addresses for all of them. I made a few calls during the earlier races and I've eliminated some of the names already. Two are bookies, which might save us some further investigation. Two more are owners. I've checked them out and they're nigh on a hundred percent respectable, so I'm left with three names and addresses. Two of them gave no reply and I think the last one's a journalist, from what some sleepy woman said, though she wasn't too sure. He'd gone to the races and would be back later."

"So we've got two names to throw at your gun dealer."

"That's right. E. Lombardi of Deptford and Michael Wills of Streatham."

"Streatham? That's near where we're going, isn't it?"

"Yes. I'd have a small bet that he's our man."

"I like the sound of E. Lombardi. What do you say? An even hundred?"

"You're not allowed to bet."

"Only on the horses."

"Okay, but if there are no finishers, the bet's canceled."

"Done."

For me, this light-hearted exchange was all bravado. I couldn't get out of my mind the fact that we were driving to meet a man who dealt in weapons—whether as collectors' items or murderers' tools, I didn't care; gun dealers weren't part of a jockey's day-to-day experience. Charles, I sensed, was completely at ease.

"You're used to this kind of thing, aren't you?" I asked him.

"What kind of thing?"

"Arms dealers, professional killers, that kind of thing."

Charles didn't answer.

"Have you ever killed a man?" I pressed him, shamelessly wanting him to say "Yes;" wanting the confidence that his experience would give me.

"It's part of a soldier's job," he said.

"Even when there's not a war going on?"

"There's always a war going on somewhere. And more often than not, we post-imperialist Brits like to take sides and exert our influence. If that means sending in 'advisors,' then we do."

"You've done a bit of advising?"

"I helped out in Dhofar. I've looked after a few friendly heads of state."

"And you've had to kill people?"

"Of course."

"Does that worry you?" I hoped it didn't.

"Not as far as I remember. And if you think we're heading for some kind of armed confrontation now, you're going to be pleasantly surprised."

As we approached the gun dealer's house, I thought maybe he was right.

I couldn't think why anybody would live in Melrose

Road, South Norwood. It was a boring, featureless street, lined with dull, detached 1920s houses which looked as though they cost just enough to have allowed their owners to live somewhere a lot more inspiring. I imagined they were lived in by anonymous, solid Tory-voting clerks. Just the place to carry on a bit of illicit gun-dealing, if you could keep your front up.

At the door of No. 16, I stood behind Charles wearing a pair of dark glasses. When Victor Constable, who had been expecting Charles, opened the door, we were through it and inside before he had a chance to think about stopping us.

"You didn't say anything about bringing anyone with you," Constable snapped.

"It's all right. He's my partner."

The gun dealer could see me now. It was moment before he recognized me.

I hadn't ever seen a man's jaw drop, but I did now. His mouth hung open for a second or so, showing a few nasty brown teeth. Then it snapped shut and he turned to make a dash for the back of the house.

Charles had him by the scruff of the neck before he could get off the mark.

"Where are you off to? This gentleman's a fellow collector. He was very interested to hear about the Mewar Purdeys because he thought he had the only pair."

"Who are you, for fuck's sake? I know who he is—I was watching him on the telly half an hour ago."

"I'm a friend of Mr. Felton's and we would like to ask you a few questions. Perhaps you'd like to tell us where would be most comfortable for a quick chat."

Constable stared at him sullenly. Resigned, he shrugged. "You may as well come into the lounge." He nodded at the door to the front room.

"Jake, why don't you take a look inside that room, and make sure there isn't any of Mr. Constable's stock in trade lying around, ready for use."

I pushed past Charles and his captive and went into a small tidy room, furnished in dreary suburban British bad taste. I checked all the drawers, the shelves and the rest of the furniture for hidden guns. There weren't any.

"It's okay," I called.

Charles frog-marched the gun dealer into the room. He quickly frisked him, pushed him into an open-sided armchair and stood back.

"Now, Victor," Charles said affably. "I have here a tape of the conversation we had yesterday. Well, not the actual tape, but a copy which I'm going to allow you to keep. If you tell us what we want to know—the truth, the whole truth and nothing but the truth—we can probably avoid your having to do the same in front of a judge."

"I didn't say nothing incriminating to you yesterday. I just said I could probably buy a pair of guns for you from a bloke in the Gulf."

"For a start, you're not a registered arms dealer; and secondly, you'd have a hard time convincing a judge that you didn't know the Mewar Purdeys belonged to Mr. Felton. But, as I say, it shouldn't come to that. What we'll do is tell you what we already know, so as not to waste any time. Why don't you bring him up to date, Jake?"

I nodded. I hadn't taken my eyes off the weasel features since Constable had sat down. I adopted a less jovial tone than Charles.

"What I'm going to tell you is not what we assume, but what we know; it's not up for debate, okay?"

Constable blinked, but he didn't speak.

I went on, "An American calling himself Meyers, probably a New Yorker, late forties, expensively dressed, went into Cox's of Bond Street looking for fancy old shotguns. The assistant there, not being too loyal to his employers who probably don't pay him enough, couldn't help him but thought he knew someone who could. You were given the guy's name and told he was staying at the Connaught. You ring him and arrange a meet. He tells you he's a heavy collector and he wants one of the Mewar Purdeys. Somebody, probably not you, but on your instructions, breaks into my place and takes just one gun. I don't even see it's gone for a few days, though I knew I'd been burgled. By the time the police have got round in response to the central station alarm, your guy is gone, and that's that.

"Your American punter doesn't take delivery of the gun. You want to get rid of it as quick as you can. You know the gun hasn't been reported stolen, so you look for a way to offer it back to me. Naturally, you don't want to do this yourself, so you hand that job over to one of two specialists."

I paused, to let my words sink in, and to see how close to the mark I was so far.

Constable was looking jittery, but putting on a defiant face. "This is all bullshit," he said. "You don't know what you're talking about, and nor do I."

"I don't know which of the two fences you got to get rid of the gun for you, but I know it was either Michael Wills," pause, no reaction, "or Lombardi." That registered. The weasel eyes blinked, the sharp adam's apple jerked, the pasty complexion turned pastier.

I turned to Charles and grinned. "It was Lombardi, Charles. You owe me a hundred." I stopped grinning and looked at Constable again. "Did you tell Lombardi to try Hagan, or was that his idea?"

The man gulped again. "I don't know what the fuck you're talking about," he croaked.

My face hardened. All my muscles tightened as I dropped into a crouch in front of him and jabbed a forefinger within a few millimeters of his shifty eye.

"Don't fuck us around, asshole!" I spat. "We don't have a lot of time. If we don't get some answers from you right now, the tape and everything we've got already goes straight to the police."

I was play-acting. I guess it was more convincing than the real thing, because Constable bought it.

"All right, all right," he conceded. "If you're not bringing Plod into it, I'll tell you."

I straightened my legs to stand again. "Go ahead."

"It was the geezer at the Connaught who ordered your gun. He knew you had it. Christ knows why he only wanted one, unless he was planning on selling it back to you—I dunno. He gave me five grand down against twenty-five. That was all right. Getting it nicked only cost me two and a half. Then the Yank phones a few days later, must have been from the States, says he doesn't want the gun any more and to get it fenced back to you. He told me not to do it myself; he said to do it through Hagan and put someone reliable between him and me. Obviously, he says all this in a roundabout way, mentioning no names or guns. And then he says, if I do as he says, I can keep the five, and there's another five in it."

Constable shrugged. "I was on a winner to nothing, so I ring Lombardi, and tell him to try and get Hagan to offer the Purdey back to you, and give me half the proceeds. I took the gun round to him, and that's the last I've seen of it, honest. And I haven't heard a thing from Lombardi since. I was beginning to wonder, but I wasn't too worried. I'm already seven and a half ahead, and fences always pay you in the end, or you don't send them any more business."

Most of what he was saying tallied with what we knew.

"Okay," I said. "I happen to know that Mick Hagan was due to pay Lombardi ten thousand but I doubt that he did before he died; he wasn't going to have it until I paid him, and I didn't."

"You mean you've got the gun now?"

I nodded. "And I'm going to have to cook up some story for my insurers. They're ready to pay me out."

"Well, that's all right, then," Constable said appreciatively."

"Not for me, but that's another matter. I want you to describe the American, in as much detail as you can remember."

"He was like you said, late forties, well-dressed, quiet but hard. Not someone you'd take liberties with. And the contact number he gave me was in New York. I've got it somewhere. I wrote it in code—BAD HIDE, I think it was."

I thought for a moment. "214-8945?"

"Yeah, sounds like it. You're on the ball."

"It didn't take a lot of working out. Did you have to ring this guy?"

"No. When he rang me to tell me he didn't want the gun, he said not to contact him again. So I haven't."

"Just tell me more about this man. Height, hair and so on."

Vic Constable shrugged. "I didn't really take a lot of notice, but I suppose he was about five ten, a lot of grey hair, thick and tidy. He didn't look anything much—a bit like a bloke in an ad for encyclopedias."

Constable looked to me as if he'd been trying, so I didn't press him. "Okay." I stepped back from where I'd been standing over him. "Give him the tape," I said to Charles. "So he can play it and know what we've got; that'll remind him to tell us if anyone contacts him." With as much aggression as I could raise, I turned on Constable. "You tell no one we were here or what we know, understand? And you tell us if anyone contacts you, Meyers from New York, or Lombardi. Did you say that Meyers knew you were using Lombardi?"

"No. He didn't ask."

"Right." I turned my back on him. "Charles, let's go."

We drove away from South Norwood, pleased with ourselves, maybe a little nearer to knowing who wanted to kill me, but not why. We had a lot more work to do.

"Did you fix up your hypnotist for tomorrow night?"

"Yes," said Charles. "I'm picking her up at Basingstoke station at seven thirty."

"I hope to God she doesn't scare the shit out of Calloway."

"She won't, you'll see."

I was still doubtful about Calloway's powers of regression. "As long as he doesn't go off afterward and tell the press I'm nuts."

That got Charles worried. "Do you think he might?"

"Hell, no. I wouldn't risk it if I did. The next thing we've got to do is follow up Mick Hagan's bookies. What names did you get from his numbers?"

"Here." Charles took a piece of paper from his pocket and handed it to me. Next to each of the numbers I had copied from Mick's diary was a name. One of them was Harry Devene's.

"I'll start with him. He'll be at Salisbury tomorrow. I'll talk to him on his way home."

"Do it discreetly, though, Jake."

"I'll be discreet," I said.

///////////// CHAPTER 11

I sat beside Martin in his muddy, bronze Sierra station wagon. We were parked in a lay-by on the A303, the main road between London and the southwest. Beyond the pull-in, there was a clearing among the beech woods that surrounded it, where a thoughtful county council had placed a few timber picnic tables with plank seats. On the far side of the clearing, a green sign pointed a right of way which followed a path deeper into the woods.

"Are you sure this man's going to show up?" I asked Martin.

"Oh yes, definitely. He wasn't going to turn down a chat with you, was he? He moaned a bit when I said it had to be here, but I know he'll come."

I trusted Martin's judgment. "I wish he'd get here,

I've got a date back home. When he does, tell him I'll be a hundred yards up that track. He'll understand I don't want to be seen with him."

"And you want to see him alone?"

"Alone. Make that clear."

Martin nodded. I got out of the car. There was no one around to see me or recognize me, but I was taking precautions in case anyone else did decide to pull in here.

I walked across the clearing and into the well-worn track through the untended woods. I knew all the sights and smells that greeted me in this chalk woodland which was similar to my own. After a while, I looked around, following Charles's advice to be discreet.

I found an ideal spot where I could sit and wait without being seen.

Ten minutes later, a family—father, mother and two boys of nine or ten—came wandering past. I was watching them carry on up the track when I heard someone else treading heavily through the woods. I glanced back in the direction of the lay-by.

It was my appointment, not disguising his annoyance at being ordered into these woods by a jockey's valet. But he was alone.

When he had passed by me, and I was sure no one was following him, I dropped from where I had been waiting on a branch which spanned the track. I landed with very little sound. The man kept on walking.

"Hello, Harry," I said quietly.

He spun round. "What the hell are we meeting out here for?"

"You know we can't be seen talking together in public, much though I'd love to."

"What do you want?"

"Let's get off the beaten track a little," I said.

"We're off it enough already for me."

I ignored this and plunged through the undergrowth,

beckoning him to follow. After twenty yards or so, I stopped beneath an old, broad tree.

Harry Devene was wearing a sober, dark suit and a creamy clean Panama. He looked more like a lawyer than a turf accountant. His small black eyes glared beneath hoods of pudgy, white flesh, signaling surly impatience. He knew it was unlikely that I was going to tell him anything to his advantage—like which horses I thought would win—but he couldn't pass up the possibility.

"What do you want, Felton?"

"I want to talk to you about Mick Hagan."

The bookie's eyes narrowed. "I haven't got time to talk about him."

"You're going to have to make time, Harry. Not surprisingly, people are anxious to pin his murder on somebody. They're looking for a motive."

"There's a lot of people think that shot was meant for you," Harry Devene growled, "and God knows, I wouldn't be surprised."

"The police think it was for Hagan."

"So they told me."

"They've spoken to you?"

"They've spoken to every bookie in the country."

"Did you tell them about your arrangements with Hagan?"

Devene looked at his watch. "I'd like to stay for a gossip with you, Felton, but I've got a lot of work to do." He began fastidiously to pick his way back through the ferns toward the track.

I waited until he'd gone a few yards.

"Harry," I said quietly, "I've a list of every horse Mick stopped on your instructions over the past two years. And when the police investigate your books, they'll find that you took an awful lot of money at longer than SP on every single one of them. D'you think they'll think that's a coincidence?"

Devene turned round, looking absurd in his double-breasted suit, up to his waist in fern and bramble.

I met his piercing stare with bland, unblinking eyes. He didn't speak for a moment. He was weighing the odds. Then he picked the wrong horse.

"They'd never be able to prove anything."

I laughed, mostly with relief. "The Jockey Club aren't concerned about proof. They'll just look at the patrol films of every race, and see what happened. It really wouldn't help you to appeal against their decision; they'd only dig deeper, and they wouldn't stop digging until they'd found something."

"If you know it all, what do you want to ask me about Hagan?"

"I know when you started leaning on him. I want to know why, and I want to know who asked you to." I began to walk toward him.

He shuffled a step back, and saved me a job by tripping himself. He disappeared into the undergrowth with a rustle and a thud.

I pulled a short-barreled automatic from the pocket of my suede jacket and launched myself at him.

A second later, I was lying beside him in the bracken with my gun making a neat little circular indentation in the thin, white flesh at his temple.

"Right," I hissed. "You're going to tell me, *now!*"

"What the hell are you doing?" Devene squealed.

"I'm going to start squeezing the trigger of this neat little gun."

"What's it to you, what happened to Hagan?" Devene spluttered.

"I want to know who told you to lean on Hagan or I'm going to have to squeeze some more, *so tell me!*"

Devene's flabby body suddenly became limp. "I . . . I don't know who it was," he mumbled.

"Don't give me that. You know. Somebody told you. *Who?*"

"I didn't know him. I'd never seen him before. But it wasn't for him; he was just a gofer."

"Whose gofer?"

"Ow!" He gasped at the pain of the gun snout in his head. "I don't know, I tell you. But someone heavy. He sent me a fucking bomb—set fire to one of my offices. He said they'd fire the lot if I didn't put the pressure on Hagan, really push him."

"Was that why he had so much on Miss Minster at Newbury?"

"I suppose so; the dumb Paddy didn't even think about that horse of yours. We were getting impatient with him by then, he was getting out of order. We had to give him an ultimatum. Business is business," Devene whined in justification.

"For the last time," I hissed. "Describe the man who came to you, and get it right?"

"He was a sharp-looking bloke. Londoner, probably a punter, but I'd never seen him around. He looked as though he'd been in the sun a bit, brown as a Paki, with a black mustache."

"What was his name?"

"He never told me."

"When did you first see him?"

"Up at Doncaster, Lincoln day. I told him to get stuffed and mind his own business. Then we had the fire. He rang me, told me to meet him in the West End. He said all we had to do was go after our money. He said they'd told all the other bookies Hagan used. No one else was going to take Hagan's money or give him tick. Everyone knew which accounts he used."

"Did this man tell you why?"

"He said they wanted him desperate. I didn't ask why."

"Was it the same man who asked you to lean on Toby Ellerton?"

"Your guv'nor? He never dealt with us. He was with

Arthur Henderson and Arthur was told to put the boot in, but I don't know if it was the same bloke."

I knelt, still holding the gun to his head. "Turn and lie face down," I ordered.

He rolled on to his front.

"Right, I'm getting out of here. If you put your head above the bracken, I'll blow it off. There's someone waiting halfway down the track back to the pull-in. He'll be there ten minutes, and if he sees you, he'll blow your head off. So don't move for fifteen minutes. Understand?"

He nodded his head. "Yeah," he mumbled into the vegetation.

His Daimler was parked a few spaces away from Martin's Sierra.

I climbed into the Ford.

"Didn't he have anyone with him?" I asked.

"No."

"That was lucky. Let's go."

Martin drove us out of the lay-by and headed east up the A303.

I pulled the gun from my pocket and looked at it appreciatively. Martin saw it from the corner of his eye.

"Oh dear," he said.

"These replicas are fantastic," I said, releasing the empty magazine and showing him. "And the ammunition costs nothing."

Joan Robbins, Charles's hypnotist, looked and sounded like a middle-aged, suburban housewife, which, she told us, she was. But another persona was discernible from her eyes and there was an indomitable calm about her.

The three of us sat in my drawing room, drinking coffee. I'd briefed Mrs. Robbins on the date and events we wanted to explore. She had nodded and scribbled in a notebook. Now I'd met the woman, I was less skeptical about the powers which Charles attributed to her, but I was doubtful about John Calloway's receptiveness. This didn't worry her.

"If you haven't told him why he's coming," she said in her cozy London accent, "it would be best to pretend that you two have already been hypnotized, and why doesn't he have a go."

I nodded. "Yeah, he'll go along with that."

"Why don't you have a go anyway? It's amazing what you can find out about yourself."

"I'm not too happy with what I already know," I said, "but maybe some other time. Calloway will be here soon, and I'm not sure I want him or Charles hearing about all my hang-ups."

"Well, any time, dear. It's always a challenge to regress people who have got to the top of the tree in their careers."

John Calloway was knocking on the front door before she had finished. With relief—because I could see myself getting sucked into Mrs. Robbins' suggestion there and then—I went to let him in.

Calloway looked surprised to see I had visitors, but I gave him a drink and introduced him. He nodded shyly at Mrs. Robbins.

"You know what we've been doing?" I said to him. "We've just been hypnotized. Joan's a friend of Charles's and she has this incredible gift." I turned to Mrs. Robbins. "I bet you wouldn't get anywhere with John; he's much too self-contained."

"I'm sure I could," she said.

"Hey, John, let her try."

Calloway looked embarrassed. I thought he was going to put up a struggle. But he shrugged his shoulders.

"As long as you promise she won't plant any instructions to murder my mother-in-law or anything."

"We won't stop her if she does, don't worry," I said with a laugh.

"All right," Calloway said. "What do I do?"

"You'll be fine, dear," Mrs. Robbins said in a way he couldn't doubt. "Just sit on this chair, and I'll sit opposite you." She drew up two upright chairs for them.

The hypnotist and the farmer faced each other. Charles and I watched from where we sat in a sofa.

"Now, just look into my eyes, dear," Mrs. Robbins began quietly. "In a few moments you'll be asleep, but you'll be able to hear me and answer me. You'll wake when I ask you but you won't know anything that you've experienced. Now, you're feeling sleepy, very tired," she cooed in a breathy, contralto voice. She gazed unblinking into Calloway's eyes. "Your eyelids are getting heavy and you want to melt away into sleep."

Abruptly, Calloway's eyelids dropped and his head nodded forward slightly.

"Now you're asleep," Mrs. Robbins said gently. "But you can open your eyes and answer me."

Calloway's chin lifted and his eyelids rose again to reveal a pair of still, blank orbs like a zombie's. It was the first time I'd seen this kind of thing happen. It gave me a spooky feeling to know it could be done so easily.

"Now," Mrs. Robbins murmured, "we're going to travel back in your mind. We're going to go to places where everything you've ever known and seen in this life and before is stored. Do you understand?"

Calloway nodded slowly. "Yes."

"We're going to go to the day the girl came to tell you that Jake was trapped in the woods, and you went up to help him. Then we're going to go back a little earlier in that day, in the afternoon, when you were driving in your car, along the lane at the top of Jake's woods. Can you see it?"

"Yes."

"Tell me what you're seeing."

"I'm driving slowly," Calloway answered in a monotone. "There's a bright sun in my eyes. I reach the shade of the trees. I'm looking into the woods." Calloway stopped.

"You're driving, looking into the woods," Mrs. Robbins prompted. "Why are you looking into the woods?"

"I'm thinking why doesn't Jake clear them."

"You're still driving. What happens next?"

"I see a pick-up parked on the verge beside the woods."

I felt my grip tighten on the edge of the chair, knowing that Calloway was actually there in the lane. I didn't breathe when Mrs. Robbins spoke again.

"What kind of pick-up is it?"

"It's a Subaru, with a Truckman top."

"What color is the Subaru?"

"It's red and the top is white."

"What is its number?"

"A604 CVJ."

I couldn't believe what was happening. I glanced over at Charles who was calmly writing the number in his diary.

Mrs. Robbins was pressing Calloway. "Tell me the number again, dear."

He repeated the number.

Mrs. Robbins carried on. "Is there anyone in the pick-up."

"No."

"Can you see anyone near it, in the woods?"

There was a long pause before Calloway answered. "No, there's no one there."

"Now what are you doing?"

"I'm driving past the Subaru. I'm thinking I must tell Jake about it."

"Then what happens?"

"I'm driving on down the lane. I leave the shade of

the trees." His eyes winced at the brightness. "I have to pull down my sun visor."

"And then?"

"I reach the T-junction. Mrs. Mellor is trotting up the hill on her show-hack. I wait for her to pass."

"And then you drive home?"

"Yes."

"Do you see anything else to tell Jake about on your way home?"

There was another long pause. "No."

Mrs. Robbins turned to us. "I think he's told you what you want to know. Shall I wake him, or go on?"

"Wake him," Charles said. "We've no business to delve into anything else that might have happened."

The hypnotist turned back to her subject.

"Now, John. Close your eyes again."

Calloway did as he was told.

"I'll count to three, and then you will wake. One, two, three."

Calloway's eyelids jerked up, and he gazed around at Mrs. Robbins and us.

"Has she started?" he asked in his normal voice.

"She's finished, thanks, John," I said. "You've just told us the number of the red Subaru you saw parked up the lane the day I was caught in the trap."

Calloway was astounded. "I did what?"

"Mrs. Robbins put you in a trance and took you back to the day it happened, and you told us everything you saw."

Calloway looked startled. "Don't be ridiculous! I can't remember the number, I don't suppose I even noticed it."

"But you *saw* it, dear, so when I asked you to notice, you did."

"That's absolutely incredible." He stopped suddenly, looking embarrassed. "What else did I tell you?"

I laughed. "Only that you thought it was time I cleared my woodland."

220 / John Francome

"That's all?"

"Yes, why?"

"Well . . . I had a bit of a row with Ginny when I got back that afternoon. I didn't tell you about that, did I?"

"No, dear." Mrs. Robbins put a reassuring hand on his arm. "We wouldn't pry into anything personal like that unless you asked."

"But you could?"

"Not always; people can sometimes close up even their subconscious with guilt."

"But I don't understand how you do it."

"It's an amazing thing, the human brain. It stores vast quantities of information, like a computer with its disks. You can remember everything but you can't always recall it. Some people can recall being born, the feel and the smell of it. In fact we all remember it, it's a question of getting access to the information. You have to open the right doors. That's much easier to do under hypnosis."

"That was a marvelous demonstration, Mrs. Robbins," Charles said. "I'm only amazed the police don't use you."

"They do, sometimes, unofficially. But the trouble is, in those circumstances, subjects can be under a lot of stress and they're hard to hypnotize properly. And of course the public doesn't really trust it because they don't understand it."

"Right. Well, it was certainly successful today. Now, would you like a drink, or another cup of coffee?"

"No thanks, Mr. Powell." She looked at a small gold watch on her wrist. "If you wouldn't mind driving me back to Basingstoke, there's a train at half-past eight. I've got another client coming round at ten."

Charles stood up. "Of course."

Mrs. Robbins said goodbye and left the house with a busy stride, as if she'd just popped in to do a bit of cleaning. Charles saw her into the Range Rover, climbed in himself with a nod to me and roared up the drive.

I went back into the house to offer my apologies and explanations to Calloway for setting him up.

Charles was back forty minutes later. "That went well, didn't it?" he said.

"I don't have a way of checking the number plate John gave us. I phoned the police and they won't help. I guess they would if they knew who I was and why I wanted it, but I don't want to get them involved yet."

"No, you mustn't, not until you know what the hell's going on. But don't worry about the number. There was an ex-copper on the dig in Peru with me. He'll get a name and address for me. I'll ring him now."

Two phone calls and twenty minutes later, Charles had them: A. Smith, The Caravan Site, Ross Road, Hereford.

"Sounds like a traveler," Charles said. "That could make things tricky. And a bloody long way from here."

"We've got to find him, though," I said impatiently.

"Don't worry, I'll find him," Charles said, placating me. "You can't. Hereford's up near Wales."

"But I'm riding at Chepstow tomorrow evening, that's in Wales, for God's sake." I pulled a road atlas from a shelf and found Chepstow and Hereford.

"You'll be going straight there from Newbury," Charles said. "You won't have time to do anything. Stop getting excited; just relax and leave it to me."

"Look, I'm only riding in the first three. I'll get a taxi up and meet you in this place Hereford. I could be there by eight thirty. I want to see this man myself."

"Okay. I'll go up early tomorrow and try and track him down. If I find him, I'll make sure I know where he's going to be later. If I don't, I'll tell you when I see you. Now let's fix a place to meet."

Charles took my Michelin from the shelf and leafed through it. "Right," he said after a moment. "There's a big hotel called the Green Dragon in the center of the town. I'll see you there. Now, I've got to get back. My family are beginning to complain that I'm not seeing enough of them after being away in South America for three months."

I felt a quick stab of guilt at the amount of his time I was taking up. "I'm sorry, Charles. I should just be looking after this thing myself."

"And give in under the pressure, be seen to stop riding? For all you know, that's what they want."

"I wish I thought that was all they wanted," I grunted.

"You carry on riding. I'm really glad to help. I'll find A. Smith, don't worry, and we'll get something out of him."

I wished I was as confident as I watched Charles scatter the gravel up my drive for the second time that evening. But I went back into the house feeling that maybe we were getting nearer. Some of the pieces were beginning to make a pattern.

I was certain that Geoff Haslam and Harry Devene had been recruited by the same man. There was no obvious connection yet with the theft of my gun, though Mick Hagan was a strand common to both threads.

If A. Smith was responsible for setting the trap and trussing me up—now that I knew the Subaru was from halfway across the country, I was convinced he was— he could give us another critical lead. I felt myself quiver with frustration that it was going to be twenty-two hours before I knew if Charles had even found him.

There was no way I was going to sleep early that night. I made an effort to catch up on my racing homework. I settled down to pile two weeks of results into my computer. I'd been at it fifteen minutes when the phone rang.

"Jake?" The voice took me by surprise, warmed me and set every nerve tingling.

"Hello, Milly. How are you?"

"Lonely, and a bit pissed off."

"Why?" I really didn't know.

"Why do you think? We had a fantastic weekend then you wave goodbye and I don't hear another thing. Is that it? Just another scalp to hang from your belt?"

"Milly, for God's sake, no. Look," I said, trying to convey what I really felt, "I haven't seen you or rung you because I want to clear up this shit that's happening to me first. I don't want to screw up what we've started by being caught with my pants down; you know what I mean, but I'm not going to say it over the phone, okay? But I promise, that's what I've got to do. I'd love to have you with me right now, but you know I can't, don't you?"

There was a few moments' silence on the other end of the line. I didn't rush her.

"Yeah," she said at last. "I understand. It's just that . . . I didn't let anything happen with you until I felt I was sure, and then I felt sort of let down."

"You're not let down," I told her. "And you never will be by me. Look, I'm riding one of your mother's horses up at York Saturday. She'll be coming up. Why not come with her and I'll see you then? Maybe we can stay somewhere."

"Okay." She sounded happier, but disappointed it wasn't going to be sooner. She wasn't the only one.

"I'm making progress on my problem. It shouldn't take too long now."

"I don't know how you can be so calm about it."

"No point getting excitable," I said, wishing I could follow my own advice, "I'll tell you about it when I see you at York."

"All right," she said. "And just make sure you get there."

"I will," I said lightly, before promising to see her on Saturday and then putting the phone down.

/////////////// CHAPTER 12

I rode eight horses at Newbury and Chepstow next day —two favorites and no winners. If I'd believed in omens, I'd have been doubly depressed on the journey up to Hereford.

A battered taxi came out to Chepstow racecourse to collect me. The driver was one of those punters that knows more about racing than any living jockey or trainer. He kept up a barrage of views and criticism on the subject. Occasionally he broke off to point out features of the spectacular river valley we were following —ruined monasteries, castles and the best salmon pools. Impatient to meet Charles, I was grateful for the distraction. When we reached the Green Dragon Hotel in Hereford, I gave him a horse to back the next day, which he rejected disdainfully while accepting my more tangible cash tip.

Charles was waiting in the bar of the hotel. He leapt to his feet when I came in.

"Right, we've got to get a move on," he said.

I felt a prickle of excitement as we walked back out into the street where his Range Rover was parked.

"What have you got?" I asked.

"Enough to keep us busy."

"Have you found the man yet?"

"No, but I've found where he lives, and his pick-up —John Calloway was spot on. He's on a pitch two or three miles out of town now, on the road to Worcester. There was a car for sale there, a terrible old rust-bucket of a Morris Minor. I could only find an old woman there and she said the man it belonged to wasn't around. I asked about the Subaru, and she said it belonged to the same fellow, who was in his truck delivering scrap metal to Birmingham. She said he'd be back late this evening."

"And you're sure that was A. Smith?"

"No, I'm not sure, but he registered the pick-up very recently, so I'd say there was a good chance."

We were heading out of the small, quiet city by now, with the sun sinking into a sea of livid, streaky cloud above the Black Mountains. We reached a kind of ox-bow of road where the main highway had been straightened. Parked in it were four caravans, clad with shining chrome, two small trucks, a Portaloo, a washing line with a string of grey underwear flapping in the breeze, and a red Subaru pick-up.

Charles drove by slowly and pulled up round the next bend.

I started to open the door.

"Don't go anywhere yet," Charles said. "There are going to be three or four other men there. Let's wait and see if he goes off again and try and deal with him alone."

"But he may not go anywhere."

"He will. I left a number for him to call me about the

Morris. I said I wouldn't be home until after nine, but that I had the money waiting in cash if he wanted to sell it. He'll have to go to a phone box to ring. The nearest one's just round the next bend."

"He may go somewhere else to phone, though," I argued, anxious not to miss our chance. "I'll get out and walk back to where I can see him leave and still see you. If he goes the other way, I'll beckon and you come back and pick me up quick. If I give you a thumbs up, he's coming this way, and I'll run back. Okay?"

I climbed down, and walked fifty yards back toward Hereford. There was a steep bank at the side of the road. I scrambled up and followed an overgrown hedge at the top of it until I could see down onto the pitch. I tucked myself back into the hedge and waited. And wondered what the hell an American jockey was doing, grass-stained and dusty, keeping watch over a gang of gypsies out near the Welsh borders.

I checked to make sure I was in clear sight of Charles. I didn't make any sign, in case he misread it, but he waved at me. I was glad to see that the traffic was so sparse on what appeared on the map to be one of the main roads across the county. It shouldn't be too difficult to cross if our man went the wrong way.

While I waited, watching a few grimy kids fooling around with a long dog on a chain, I was more aware than ever that whoever was planning my persecution was doing it carefully. Bringing in a traveler from this distance to set the trap and strap me up was always going to make it difficult to follow up. The only mistake had been to leave an unknown vehicle parked less than a mile from the scene. I guessed he'd thought it would be far enough away, and not attract any attention; and how many people remember car numbers? I thought, thankful to Mrs. Robbins the housewife hypnotist.

After ten minutes, a man appeared from one of the caravans and walked toward the Subaru. He reached it and climbed in. My heart pounded at the knowledge that I was so close to him. He started the car, drove out of the lay-by and turned to drive off away from Charles.

I ran back along the top of the bank, beckoning Charles, who spun the Range Rover round, roared back down the road, and slowed down while I ran across to get in.

"He must be going to make his call from somewhere else," I said. "But he won't be too far ahead."

We came into view of the gypsy site and shot past it. A hundred yards on, we could see the back of the pick-up. Charles decelerated a little.

"I won't get too close, though I don't suppose he'd take much notice of a dirty green Range Rover; there are enough of them round here."

"Don't lose him, though," I said quickly, as the Subaru turned off to the right.

We followed it into a narrow lane, and came out onto another main road, heading east now. A mile later, the pick-up indicated to the right, and pulled across the road into the car park of a pub standing on its own, but busy, judging by the number of cars outside.

"Bugger!" Charles said. "He's gone to have a drink."

"Too bad," I said. "Anyway, he may have gone to call you from there."

We pulled up where we could see the car park and tried to contain our frustration. We both knew there was no point in trying to deal with him in a country pub.

"What do we do when he comes out?" Charles asked after a minute's silence.

"If he drives straight home, it may be difficult to stop him."

"Not if we're in front. I can block the lane easily enough."

"But if he goes another way, we'll be stuffed. We'll have to wait for him in the car park. There's a space next to him; drive over and park there. With a bit of luck we can take him by surprise, get him in here and drive him away before he knows what's happened."

Charles smiled. "That'll do."

But we were too late. As we started up the road toward the pub, the driver of the Subaru came out and climbed into his vehicle.

"Shit!" I yelled. "We'll just have to see which way he goes and play it by ear."

Charles shook his head as the pick-up drove back past us. He swung the Range Rover in a tire-screeching U to follow it.

"Get your head down, Jake; he knows you. I'll get him to pull up. When I've got him out of his car, get out and help."

He dropped a gear and pulled out to pass the Subaru, blasting his horn and flashing his hazard lights. I was ducked out of sight before he got past.

Charles pulled up, and I guessed the other had done the same. Charles jumped out and left the motor running.

"Hello," I heard him say. "Are you the person selling the Morris Minor?"

I didn't hear the reply, but I guessed the man had fallen for it because I heard Charles say, "Great. I'll just turn off my motor."

A moment later, his head appeared through the window.

"He's out of his truck!" he whispered from the side of his mouth. "Get out as quietly as you can. I'll set him up."

He turned the ignition key and in the silence I heard him crunch back down the road to meet the Subaru driver.

"I was looking for a Morris Minor for my son," I heard him say. I reached for the door handle, and pulled it down, tugging it in toward me. When it was down, I slowly let the door swing open. I picked up a fat, rubber-clad torch from the glove compartment and stepped out onto the grass verge. Doubled up, I crept along the side of the vehicle. When I reached the end, Charles was still giving the man a load of bull about what marvelous cars Morris Minors were, and how suitable for teenage boys with too much energy in them. The vendor was probably rubbing his hands with glee at such an easy prospect. I couldn't see because he was standing on the edge of the road with his back to me.

I trod silently across the few yards of turf that separated us, lifting the torch as I went. I checked up and down the road for any traffic or other witnesses, then raised my arm and brought the torch down with every pound of energy I could give it.

There was a thud, the noise of splintering glass, and a tinkle as the broken lens landed on the tarmac a fraction of a second before my target.

He'd barely hit the ground before Charles grabbed his shoulders and I took his feet. We half dragged, half carried him behind the Range Rover, just before a family in a camper wagon drove by, checking out the scenery.

When they were gone, we heaved the groaning gypsy into the back of the car. I climbed into the rear seat to watch over him with the broken torch, and Charles gunned the vehicle back into life.

"Do you know where the hell we can take him?" I asked.

"Yeah. I've checked out a couple of places. There's a derelict farm with a few wrecked barns about a mile down this lane."

As he spoke, we swung into a narrow lane with high verges. We didn't meet anything coming the other way, and turned off up a short track which led round to the back of a boarded-up, brick farmhouse.

When we were out of sight of the lane, Charles

pulled up, and turned the motor off. He came round to the back and opened the tailboard.

Our hostage had come round now and was ready to fight. He swung a vicious kick at Charles's groin. He didn't connect and gave Charles time to land a large fist squarely on his nose.

I was still on the rear seat and winced as the blood spurted, but flung an arm round the man's neck.

"Let him go," Charles shouted, and grabbed the man's ankles.

I released his neck, and watched him shoot out of the back and land with a crunch on the ground. I scrambled straight out after him.

Charles had spun him over on his face and was forcing his arms up between his shoulder blades.

"Grab some of the binder twine," he grunted, nodding at a mess of orange plastic baling cord in the back of his vehicle. "And tie his legs and arms."

I remembered what this man had done to me and, trussing him up as tight as I could, didn't feel a lot of guilt.

When we were sure he couldn't move, Charles let go of him and we dragged him across a mess of farm debris and rubble to a stone barn whose doors were hanging off their hinges. Inside, we dropped him face down on the earth floor and sat on a pair of black, rotting straw bales.

The man twisted his head sideways to see us. The small black eyes glared at us like an angry stoat's.

"Who the fuck are you blokes?" he said huskily.

"Don't you remember?" I asked.

He twisted his head round a little more to see me clearly, opened his mouth to speak, but stopped before any words came out.

"You do, don't you?" I said.

"Course I do," he said. "I seen you on the telly."

I stood. "And in my woods, remember?"

"Don't know what you're talking about."

"Don't you," I said, getting angry. "Well, I'm going to kick holy shit out of you until you do know what I'm talking about, and then I'm going on until you tell me who paid you."

"You're off your fuckin' 'ead, you are!"

I swung my leg back, closed my eyes, and piled my foot into his scrawny ribs so hard that I thought I'd broken it.

From the yell that followed, I guessed I wouldn't have to do it again. I waited and listened. The defiant snarl had become a whimper.

"Right. Are you ready to tell me?"

"It weren't nothin' to do with me."

"What wasn't?" I swung my leg back again, to encourage him.

"The trap. That was 'is idea."

"Whose idea?"

"The bloke what asked me to do it."

"Who was he?"

"Never seen him before. La-di-da sort of bloke. Lots of money. Come from a big 'ouse round 'ere I should think."

"Did he tell you his name?"

"Course not."

"Did he pay you?"

"You think I done it for nothin'?"

I swung another kick at him, not so hard as before, but enough to ginger him up.

"How did he find you? What sort of car did he drive?"

Smith grunted. "I dunno. I didn't see no car. He just came to the site and found me."

"Right," I growled at him. "I'll be back. You find out the man's name, and where he lives. If you don't, I'll have you busted apart next time. Understand?"

He didn't answer.

I turned to Charles. "Got a knife?"

"Of course."

"Cut his legs free. He can walk back to his car from here."

Charles did as I asked, and Smith staggered to his feet. Curiously, he didn't seem too resentful of the treatment we'd given him.

"Is that all you want, then?" he asked.

"Sure, for now. You find out the name of the man who paid you, and maybe the police will stop looking for whoever set that trap. We'll give you till Saturday."

"You won't tell 'em, then?"

"Not if you do what I say. Now, enjoy your walk."

Charles was already in the Range Rover and had started it up. I climbed in.

"Feeling better?" Charles asked as we drove round the side of the farmhouse out into the lane.

"I'm not a vengeful type," I replied, "but I don't deny there was some satisfaction in kicking his ass."

"At least we found out something. Let's hope he can put a name to this chap."

"I've already got a hunch about that."

"Who?"

"You wouldn't know him, and I'm not sure yet. It'd be better to follow it up through that tinker first."

"All in all, not a bad day's work. Did you have any winners, by the way?"

"No, I did not." I dragged my mind back to the normality of a jockey's life. "But I will tomorrow, and Saturday."

"Are you riding at York on Saturday, then?"

"Yeah."

"I'll come back up here and follow up Mr. Smith. I'll be at your place in the evening to tell you what I've got."

"That'd be great. Are you going to have the time to do it, though?"

"Don't worry. I've promised the girls I'm taking them to Madagascar in July, so until then I'm all yours."

"I don't know why you want to help an ungrateful bastard like me, but I don't know what I'd do if you didn't."

Charles laughed. "Don't worry, I love it. I've had more action in the last week than I've had in a month up the Amazon."

Charles dropped me off at Coombe House after midnight. The knowledge that I was fighting back, and getting somewhere, was obviously good for my health; I went to bed and slept properly for the first time in the eight days since Hagan had been killed.

I landed at Ellerton's meadow before nine next morning, in time to ride second lot. We had three good runners at Sandown that day.

The Captain was in a state of high excitement. Zimmer's horses were arriving in the yard that morning. I was surprised it had all happened so fast, but I supposed a man as rich as Zimmer could get anything done as fast as he liked. At least there was a mood of optimism spreading through the yard. The sense of desperation that had been plaguing Ellerton all season seemed to have departed, and we were almost back on normal terms. Instead of being bitter and offensive, he was just rude now.

After riding two lots and schooling a backward two-year-old through the starting gates, I decided to hang around until Zimmer's horses arrived. I was as interested as anyone else in the yard to see the new intake.

I hadn't counted on Mrs. Zimmer turning up at the same time, though.

She arrived within ten minutes of the six or seven million dollars' worth of bloodstock that her husband had consigned to Melbourne House. Zimmer's nephew, Hal Symonds, was with her, trying to look authoritative. I managed to avoid them for a while, keeping a couple of boxes behind them as they inspected each of the horses with Ellerton and discussed their form. But Ellerton beckoned me to catch up.

"Come round with us, Jake. You may as well hear this now."

I caught up reluctantly. "I've already checked out all their form. There are some great animals here. We could have an Eclipse runner in Magnificent Mogul."

"Yeah," said Hal Symonds. "And we want to run Miss Pavlova at Ascot next week."

I smiled indulgently. Even Zimmer's money wouldn't get him by the Jockey Club's rules of entry. It was far too late to enter the filly now.

"I'm afraid you're going to be too late for that," I said.

"No," Ellerton said, "it's all right. They've had her entered from America."

That surprised me. It meant they must have been planning to bring these horses over for some time. Or maybe Zimmer had horses entered in races all over the world, in case he felt like running them on the spur of the moment. That didn't seem likely; it would mean a few hundred thousand dollars' worth of wasted entry fees.

After the inspection, I hung back as we headed toward the house. So did Sandy Zimmer.

Hal threw a quick inquiring look over his shoulder, but carried on walking and talking with Ellerton.

"Jake," Sandy said in her husky, submissive voice. "Why haven't you been to see me yet?"

"What for?"

"Come on, Jake. You know what for! We were fantastic together!"

I glanced around to see if any of the lads were near enough to hear this. Thankfully, they weren't.

"I hadn't forgotten, Sandy, but aren't you with Arnold Schwarzenegger?" I nodded ahead at Hal.

"No, of course not. I'm not saying that he isn't a bit infatuated but that's nothing, and he's Leonard's nephew, for God's sake!"

"And his sole heir, they tell me," I added conversationally.

Sandy's eyes snapped round at me. "Yes," she said slowly. "He's a very lucky young man."

"Hmm," I said. "And quite a catch."

Sandy ignored this. "You must come to dinner sometime. Now the house is ready, I'm giving a few parties after the races next week. I'll try and grab you for one of them."

I thought I ought to be safe at a dinner party. Maybe I would bring Milly along, just to let Sandy know once and for all that there would be no encore of last summer's performance.

When I phoned Milly after racing that evening, she didn't go for the idea.

"If you want to go to dinner there, you can do it without me," she said.

"Okay, but I'll see you at York tomorrow."

"All right," she said, sounding as though she regretted her show of pique. I wondered just what Sandy had told James Bullough-Ferguson, and what he had told Milly.

It was a damp, grey morning. I flew below the clouds, partly to relieve the boredom of flying through a thick grey blanket, and partly to make navigation easier as I followed the motorways up toward York. I thought of Charles heading out to Herefordshire, and wondered if he would be told what I thought I already knew.

The cloud began to break up, and the sun sparkled off the rivers in the Vale of York. I began to look forward to the day's racing. I had four good rides, including a nice four-year-old of Bunty Fielding's on which I had won earlier in the year. I'd promised her I would do the same again—a sort of reward for being Milly's mother. And I was looking forward to seeing Milly.

The last radar point before touching down at York

racecourse is about six miles east of Doncaster at Finningley. I had passed the small RAF base fifteen miles back. Casually, confident in what I was doing, I looked across at the instrument panel to check my bearings.

The next moment, I was hurled forward and my forehead smashed into the dashboard. An explosion somewhere outside the cockpit had shaken the plane violently sideways then downward.

There wasn't time to think about what had happened. I automatically jammed both feet hard into the floor of the cockpit; the seatbelts cut viciously into my shoulders as I jerked my body upward, frantically trying to counteract the first, terrifying sensation of plunging straight out of the sky. Fear tried to empty my guts, and throbbed adrenaline through every artery in my body. For the first time in my life, I lived through a moment of naked terror, before a deep-rooted instinct for survival screamed at me to get out—just get out!

I grabbed for the release buckle on the straps which locked me into the plunging coffin at the same moment that the windscreen crashed in against the control column. A blast of searing heat crackled across the top half of my body. Without thinking how, I wrenched myself over the back of the seat to get away from tongues of flame whipped on by the torrent of air. I tumbled sideways over the armrest, upside down on the floor. The wind howled through the plane, chilling the sweat which soaked me now. Battling against the wind and the angle of the plane, I scrambled over onto my knees and clawed under the seat for my parachute. My hand felt wildly into the empty space where my only means of survival should have been; I began to panic again, until I caught sight of the small, life-saving package nestling against the side of the fuselage. I scrabbled it to me and had it open and across my back in a single movement. I secured the harness as I leapt for the passenger door and kicked the handle furiously until the lock sprang apart and I recoiled onto the broken windscreen.

I knew that time to jump safely was running out and I lunged forward to be dragged back by the parachute caught up on something. I wriggled desperately until it freed itself and I could apply all my strength to pushing open the door against a 200 m.p.h. wind, just wide enough for me to squeeze out.

My first glimpse of the ground flooded me with relief as I let myself tumble headlong into space. Then I felt the utter joy of the strings and canopy catching me up in a gentle, floating spiral toward the ground.

I smiled, and found myself thinking of the lyrics of a Pink Floyd track. "In the space between the heavens and the corner of some foreign field . . . I had a dream . . ."

The sight of my plane crashing into an empty field below was no dream, but from where I hung suspended, safe in the air above, it certainly felt like one. I groaned to myself, resigned to the fact that the Piper was gone, but grateful for the promise I had made to my mother and blissfully thankful to be alive.

A minute or so later, the shock of what had happened hit me and I felt myself shaking within the harness. And I knew I had to make some decisions about where to come down. I was getting some idea of how to steer myself and I selected a harmless-looking field of pasture being grazed by a herd of black and white cows.

I aimed at the middle of the field. About a hundred feet from the ground, a gust of wind spoiled my aim and I was drifting down toward the cows clustered in the corner.

They panicked and galloped away from the pond where they'd been drinking. They were well clear of it when I finally came to earth in two feet of water and another foot of black mud.

The nylon billows of the parachute settled around

me and floated on the surface of the stinking pond. I floundered the few steps to the edge, dragging hundreds of square yards of wet material behind me. I ploughed on, up to my hocks in mud until I reached some solid, well-grazed turf. I unclipped my harness, dragged the rest of the 'chute off the water, and fell to the ground exhausted and quivering. I lay there pulling myself together for the best part of ten minutes before I got up and looked around. There wasn't a dwelling to be seen from here. I ran to the nearest gate and clambered up for a better viewpoint and was rewarded with the sight of a Land Rover bouncing across the next field toward me.

The ancient vehicle drew up and a farmer twice its age jumped out.

"Bloody 'eck! You're all right, then?" he shouted in broad Yorkshire.

"Yes, thanks," I said. "I came down in a pond back there."

"Aye, I can see that."

I looked down at myself. As far as I could see, I was covered in mud from head to foot. I laughed. "At least it was a soft landing. More than the plane had."

"I heard her hit the ground, but I didn't see where. What happened?"

"I don't know. I think the port-side fuel tank blew up." I shook my head. "I still can't believe I got out."

"It's bloody lucky you had a parachute."

"Yeah, you could say that," I nodded. "Though I nearly couldn't find it."

"Where were you flying to?"

"York races."

The old man stared at me for a moment. "Crikey! You're bloody Jake Felton, aren't you?" He gazed at me as if I were some kind of beatific vision.

"I guess so," I said.

"And you're riding this afternoon. We'll have to get you there bloody quick! Here, jump in, I'll take you."

I climbed into the Land Rover and scuffled a place for my feet among the accumulation of junk and rubbish in the footwell. The farmer took his seat and rammed the gear shift forward to spin the vehicle round and head back from where he'd come. We were bouncing around like a pair of rodeo riders until we reached a track on the far side of the field.

"There's not much hurry," I told him through gritted teeth. "How far is it from here?"

"'Bout fifteen miles. Half an hour in this old girl. But don't you want to get cleaned up a bit first?"

"No, I can do that in the changing room."

"Well, you hang on, and I'll get you there, don't you worry. Fancy taking young Jake Felton to the races. The wife'll never believe it when I tell her."

He told me his name was Fred Pickering and rattled on continuously for the half-hour he had predicted it would take to get to the racecourse. He promised to check out the plane and tell the authorities, as well as collect up my parachute. I said I'd come round and see him after the races to sort everything out.

"Don't you worry," he assured me for the tenth time, "I'll see to it all."

I didn't doubt that he would, and reckoned I couldn't have landed on a better farm.

At the gates to the racecourse, he grinned through the window of his battered vehicle and pointed me out to the officials there. He was waved through and, beaming with pleasure, followed my directions round to the jockeys' car park.

"Right," he said as I got down. "I'll get back and sort out your plane. I'll come back and pick you up after the races, if you like."

"No, don't do that, thanks. I'll get a ride over."

"It'd be no trouble."

"You've already done enough."

"You won't find the way. I'll be here after the races. I'll bring my son's car, more comfortable." He wasn't going to be dissuaded, and anyway, he was right; there was no way I could remember the way we'd come.

"Okay, thanks, Fred."

"Eh, you're welcome, Jake. By the way," he went on a little coyly, "d'you reckon you'll have a winner today?"

"You could try Perfect Pet in the second."

"Thanks, I will," he said gleefully, and I had another reason for trying to win on Bunty's horse.

Toby Ellerton saw me rushing to the changing room.

"Good God! What happened to you? I thought you were flying, but I didn't see you land."

"I did land, in a parachute, fifteen miles short of here."

"Christ! Are you all right?"

"Yeah, I'm fine. Not a scratch."

"What happened to the plane?"

"I don't know. I was out of it when it came down. I've got a guy looking after it for me."

"But what the hell happened? Was it an accident or what?"

"I wish I could tell you, Captain. I don't have a clue, except something outside exploded. I hope to hell the CAA will be able to find out from the wreck. They may turn up here this afternoon, but there's no way I'm going to miss my rides, so you can relax."

"I wasn't thinking about that, Jake."

"Oh yeah? Well, I am. I'm fine and I'm riding. Look, I've got to get out of these shitty clothes before more people start asking questions. I'll see you in the weighing room before the first."

Martin's eyebrows almost shot off the top of his head when he saw me. "Christ, you look a bit of a mess," he said.

"Never mind. I'll have a shower and a quick sauna. You got everything ready?"

"Of course. I haven't got your colors for the last yet,

but they'll be here. Mr. Wooton's lorry hasn't arrived yet."

I remembered that I was riding Miss Minster in the last, now that Mick Hagan wasn't available. I thought, ironically, that she'd probably win today. Ellerton wasn't in the weighing room when I got there, so I strolled out to the parade ring where the first runners were already being led round. On the way, I bumped into Hal Symonds. I was surprised to see him—Zimmer didn't have any runners at this meeting.

I caught a look of anger in his eyes before he covered it up with a makeshift grin. I thought it was a bit strong for this man to have already taken such a dislike to me, but I guessed it had to do with Sandy. As I gave him a grin back, I thought that I would be much better off sticking to my original plan to keep well out of Sandy's way.

Ellerton was waiting for me in the parade ring. His owner hadn't turned up, so we were able to talk privately for a few minutes. He was bursting with news he hadn't wanted to tell me outside the changing rooms.

"I've bought three cracking new horses for Zimmer," he said. "Two already entered for next week, so he'll have three runners now. If we can deliver, I think he'll come on a lot stronger." His manner became more deferential. "By the way, I may as well tell you he's made it a condition of his keeping his horses with me that you'll be available to ride them. We must have a proper talk about your contract for next year."

"We must, Toby. But it's one of my conditions that there'll be no more stopping."

"There won't be any more stopping, I can assure you," he answered confidently.

"Why, what's changed?"

"Zimmer's horses coming has helped, I don't deny."

"Isn't your bookie still after you?"

"I'm in the clear now, as it happens," he said cagily.

I didn't press for details. I intended to get better answers elsewhere.

I had a disappointing run in the first. The colt had peaked too early that season and I had told Toby I didn't think he should run him for a while.

I'd tried to make plenty of use of him, but he'd run all over the place in the last furlong, and earned me a session in front of the stewards for my trouble. When they played it back, I couldn't argue. I guess I'd been more shaken up than I'd realized by having to leap from my plane. It wasn't much of an excuse, so I didn't offer it and took their verdict of "careless riding" as stoically as I could—along with a sentence of one week's ban to start seven days from now.

In contrast, Bunty Fielding's Perfect Pet ran a stormer, led from start to finish and hit the bookies hard where it hurt them. Bunty was bubbling with pleasure in the winner's enclosure.

"Jake, I don't know what you do to that horse to make him run so well. He simply won't do it for anyone else. You really are a genius!"

"Now don't overdo it, Bunty, or I might start believing it. Where's Milly?"

"Ah," she said cautiously, "she said she couldn't come; she had to meet some people at the gallery this morning. But she did say she might drop in to your house this evening, as you said you'd be flying straight back from here."

"Did she? Well, I won't be flying back; I've had a spot of trouble with the plane. Unless I can get someone else to give me a lift," I added.

"Do try, because there'll be no way of getting hold of her to tell her now."

"Yeah, I will."

Milly's absence took the edge off the day for me. I'd

had no trouble keeping buoyant up till then, now I suddenly felt flat.

But I still had to do my job.

I put my mind to it, didn't let myself think about people trying to kill me, or Milly not being there.

And I won two more races for my effort. What a day to get a treble up! But I wasn't out of the winner's enclosure after the last before I was concentrating on other things.

Fred Pickering would be waiting for me in the car park, he had said. I'd just have to let him wait a little longer. First I had to see Arthur Henderson, Ellerton's regular bookie, and bookie to half the aristocracy of England.

I found him where I'd expected to in the champagne bar, despite the fact that my three favorites winning wouldn't have given him a very profitable day. But he was a well-mannered man, and showed no sign of resentment when he saw me.

"Hello, Arthur. I wanted a very quick word with you," I said to him quietly and unheard by anyone else.

"Is that wise?" he asked.

"You know me," I said, "I'm not going to tell you anything wicked."

"Okay, we'll take a stroll round the stands."

Outside, away from any prying ears, I could ask him what I had been wanting to for three days.

"You handle Toby Ellerton's account and it's no secret he was in much too deep with you. What's his position now?"

"It's not really ethical for me to talk to you about that, Jake. But I respect your position. It doesn't help us much when trainers start mucking about the way he was earlier in the season."

"You reckon he's stopped?"

"Oh yes."

"Why?"

"Well, as you say, he was in deep, and we were

getting worried. We asked him to clear his account before we'd take any more bets from him."

"That's what I thought. And I also happen to know that you were strongly encouraged to put the squeeze on him by some third party." I stopped and looked at Henderson, so he knew I wasn't bluffing. "I've got to know who that was."

Henderson walked on a few paces. "It was a simple business decision. We were told if we pressed him, and pressed him hard, threatened him with the Jockey Club, we'd get paid up." Henderson shrugged. "We don't much care who settles people's accounts, as long as they get settled."

"And who put this proposition to you?"

"I don't know. It was put by an intermediary."

"And who was that?"

Henderson nodded across the expanse of tarmac in front of the stands. "That gentleman just going through the gate."

I followed his eyes. And nodded with satisfaction. It was James Bullough-Ferguson.

"Thank you, Arthur. That's all I need to know."

I left Henderson and went back into the stands. I thought I might just catch Bunty Fielding before she left. I raced up the stairs and asked a waitress where the Fieldings' box was. She pointed me down the corridor. I tried not to run.

I needn't have hurried. The Fieldings weren't the type of people to rush off the minute the racing was over. They preferred to finish their afternoon in a civilized, leisurely way and leave when the crowds had gone.

"Hello, Jake. I thought you were getting a lift back."

"I am. But I just wanted to ask you something."

"What about?"

"James Bullough-Ferguson."

Bunty made a face. "What do you want to know

about him? If you think he's getting anywhere with Camilla, I can assure you you've nothing to worry about."

"It's not that. He's involved in some way with the Zimmers, Toby's new owners. Do you know where he comes from?"

"I think he lives in London—Chelsea somewhere. Why?"

"I don't mean that. I mean, where's his family from?"

"Now let me think. I used to know his mother; she was a Devereux-Johns. She inherited a rather splendid place, I seem to remember. I think she's lived there with James's father since they were married. I went there once just after the war." Her forehead wrinkled as she thought back. I had to stop myself from yelling at her to remember.

"Where the hell was it?" she asked herself. "You could always look it up, in Debrett or *Who's Who,*" she suggested brightly.

"Yeah, I could. But do you remember, was it in Herefordshire?"

Her brow cleared immediately. "Yes. That's exactly where it was. Practically in Wales, near a pretty village called Weobley. Athelstan Court—that's it!"

"Bunty, you're a star. Thanks." I started to leave.

"Aren't you going to stay and have a drink? After all, you don't get a treble up every day."

"Bunty, my lift's waiting outside, and Milly's coming round to my place later, remember?"

"Of course. Off you go. See you at Ascot."

I nodded goodbye to her husband and a few others I knew, and hurried back down to find Fred Pickering.

He was waiting in the car park, with his son, in a surprisingly new Mercedes. He got out and beamed at me as soon as he saw me. From the driver's side, a tall man, about thirty, emerged.

"This is my son, Bolton. He's already had the Civil

Aviation people and the police round to look at your plane. They're waiting there now to see you."

"Okay," I said, hiding my impatience. I'd known I'd have to go through some formalities. And I wanted to know why the plane had come down.

The formalities took an hour. I was almost beside myself with frustration at the end of it, answering a string of pointless questions. Then the inspector told me it would be a week before they knew for certain what had happened. His educated guess, though, suggested that something had ignited in the lefthand wing. He promised to get back in touch as soon as possible.

Maybe there had been a fault in the plane, but I doubted it. Coming after everything else that had been going on, it seemed just too much of a coincidence. But I didn't want to tell the police or the CAA my suspicions; not yet.

When the police had finished with me, I had to think about how I was going to get back home. I had made a loose arrangement to hitch a ride in a plane with two other jockeys, but they'd have been long gone by now.

Back in the car, Fred and his son asked me where I wanted to go. I asked about getting a taxi to take me back. Bolton wouldn't hear of it.

"I've got nothing better to do. I'll run you back."

"But it's about a hundred and twenty miles."

"That's nothing in this car. We'll drop Dad back at home first."

I protested some more but, to my relief, the young Yorkshireman was adamant. I gave in and let him drive me.

//////////// CHAPTER 13

Bolton was a good, fast driver who paid little attention to speed limits. The Saturday-evening traffic on the motorways was light enough to let us touch a hundred and thirty on the straight stretches. In the well-sealed interior of the big German car, it was quiet enough to talk at those speeds, and my driver was a talkative man.

Bolton—so named, he said, because he had been conceived among the ruins of Bolton Abbey—had joined the army after school at eighteen. He'd done ten years in the paratroops. After that, he didn't want the docile existence of farming—not yet, anyway.

He'd looked around and decided to open a small discotheque in Pontefract, then three more in South Yorkshire. Though he didn't say so, it seemed that he knew how to run them, and I guessed he didn't get too much trouble in them, either.

"I've just sold them," he told me, "for a lot of money. Of course, I could have hung on until after this recession's over, but there were a good profit in it, and I were fed up, so I took the money."

He said he didn't know what to do now. I thought he ought to meet Charles Powell.

With Bolton's driving, and his life story, it didn't take long to reach Hampshire. By half past nine, we were turning into my lane. I asked Bolton to pull up.

"This may sound strange," I said, "but I'll walk from here."

"You think there might be someone hanging around your place, don't you?"

"Why do you think that?"

"I could tell from your face, when you were talking to the CAA blokes, that you reckoned someone did it on purpose."

"You could be right."

"When Dad and me were waiting for you, we were talking about what happened at the Derby last week. We reckoned it were you should have been shot, not that Hagan bloke. After all, who's he? A has-been."

"He's a has-been now," I said. "And he was a friend of mine."

"That's as may be, but it were you they were after, weren't it?"

"As a matter of fact, yes."

"Right, I'll come and check your place with you, then. But we don't want to leave the car here, do we?"

"No. You're right. We'll go on down to the next farm."

We parked the car in John Calloway's yard. There was no one around. We slipped across the lane and worked our way up through the fields until we were opposite my woods. We checked the road, listened, and ran across to climb the high wire fence I'd had put up the year before. On the other side, in the dense, wild wood that Calloway had objected to, we stood and listened some more.

It was Bolton who first heard it. He nudged me, and whispered close into my ear. "That's not an animal moving down there."

I trusted his judgment. Since I'd realized the Piper had been sabotaged, I'd been pretty sure it would be followed up fast. These people must have been wild with frustration by now.

By tacit agreement, Bolton was in charge now. He indicated that we shouldn't speak any more and should stand completely still.

I strained my ears for more sounds. After a few moments I caught some, and then a distinct human cough echoed up through the trees.

Bolton smiled.

He signaled me to follow him as he selected a route through the undergrowth. Slowly, stopping every few yards to listen, we zigzagged our way down through the woods toward the cough.

It took fifteen minutes to reach the edge of a small clearing where I'd had a shed built. I kept a large logging saw and other bits of equipment in it. In front of it were a few stacks of beech logs with tarpaulins across the top, in the first stages of drying for my winter fires.

There was a man sitting on the ground with his back to one of them, where he had a clear view across two hundred yards to the front of my house lit by the setting sun. He was wearing jeans, trainers and a camouflage combat jacket. There was a cigarette in his mouth and half a dozen butts were strewn about the ground beside him. Across his lap lay a short rifle with a metal frame stock and telescopic sights.

Bolton turned round to me. With a large forefinger, he pointed at himself, then the gunman. In the same way, he conveyed that I should get further back into the cover of the trees. I didn't argue.

The ex-para came back with me and made his way

round through the woods to emerge facing the back of the shed. He seemed to glide silently from out of the trees, across the clearing until he was close up against the lap-timbered wall.

Pressing himself to it, he sidled along the back and down the near side of the shed. I could see the man sitting, stubbing out another cigarette, out of Bolton's sight.

Bolton crouched low and crept across to the back of the log pile. There he waited. I couldn't tell how long; it felt like hours, though it was probably more like five minutes.

The man coughed again and fumbled in the pockets of his jacket for his cigarette pack and lighter. When he pulled it out, I saw it was an American soft pack. He tapped out a cigarette and drew it from the pack with his lips. He flicked a flame from the lighter and drew through the tobacco.

While the man was concentrating on the business of getting some smoke into his lungs, Bolton climbed up the back of the log stack. Now he was crouched on it with his hands a foot above his target's head.

The man coughed, hacked up a gobbet of phlegm which he spat six feet ahead of him. He gave another cough, which turned into a choke as Bolton's forearm flashed under his chin and jerked him up by the neck. With his other hand, Bolton grabbed the rifle and flung it as hard as he could across the clearing.

"Get hold of it!" he yelled at me.

I broke cover and ran across to pick up the weapon. It was surprisingly light. I checked the magazine; it was loaded. I swung round to face its owner. His face was scarlet, eyes rolling in panic while his hands grappled uselessly with the hard-muscled arm that gripped his neck and jaw like a pair of oversized pliers.

Without losing his hold, Bolton maneuvered himself off the logs until he was crouching behind his victim.

Every time resistance got too lively, he squeezed harder, and the man grunted through tight-locked teeth.

Bolton glanced over at me. "Can you use that thing?" he asked, nodding at the gun.

"Yeah," I said with more certainty than I felt.

"Right. Keep him covered, in case he slips me. Where'll we take him?"

"In the shed."

I walked across to it and opened the door to let Bolton shove his groaning, struggling prisoner through. I switched on the one naked bulb and shut the door. Bolton now had the man prostrate on the floor with one knee in his back.

"What do you want to do with him?" he asked.

"I want to know where the hell he comes from, and who sent him."

"I don't think he'll tell you, but we can try." Bolton loosened his grip on the man's throat. "Did you hear that?" he asked him.

"Of course I fuckin' heard," the man choked. He had a strong Brooklyn accent. "And I ain't tellin' you nothin'."

"Okay," Bolton said easily and clamped his arm tight again. "Take everything off him. That'll give you summat to go on."

That wasn't so easy. I put the gun down, well away from the writhing body, and tried to dig my hands into every pocket I could find. Even debilitated by the ex-para's strength and expertise, the man put up a hell of a fight. But I was as determined as he was, and I had Bolton on my side.

The search yielded a wallet, cigarettes, more bullets, car keys on an Avis fob, a pair of shades and some chewing gum.

I flipped open the wallet. That produced a Master-Card in the name of Francis Xavier Kaminski, a New York State driver's license in the same name, several hundred pounds in fifties, and a few pieces of folded paper.

I unfolded the first. It had the name of my house, the registration number of my plane and a list of times that I recognized as the times of the races I'd ridden that day.

The next slip of paper had one number scrawled on it: 214-8945.

My system was already wallowing in adrenaline. That number gave me another, bigger hit.

I looked at Bolton and his seething hostage. "I've got all I need from this guy."

"Are you going to call the police, then?" Bolton asked.

"Nope. First, I'm going to take his picture, then we'll have to get rid of him somewhere."

"I can bung him in the boot of my car and dump him a couple of hundred miles from here. I'll get him pissed out of his head first, then aim the coppers at him. That'll keep him out of your way for a bit, if he still fancies coming back."

"I want him out of the way for longer than that."

"I'm not going to top him for you."

"No, no, I didn't mean that. Whatever it costs, if you can lock him up somewhere for as long as it takes for me to follow up this number, I'll pay. But it could be a week or so."

Bolton had had his fun, now his business instincts were aroused.

"Two hundred and fifty a day, and he won't go anywhere for as long as you like."

"You're on," I said. "Right, I'm going to get my camera, and then I'll drive your car back up here. Where are the keys?"

"In this pocket." Bolton nodded to one side.

I fished in and found a Mercedes key.

"Are you going to be okay?" I asked.

"I'll be fine, but bring the car up as close as you can to here, all right?"

"Right."

I left the shed, shutting the door behind me, and ran down in the post-sunset gloom to my house. I let myself in, turned off the alarms and picked up a small automatic Pentax from my study.

I carried on running down the valley to John Calloway's place. He was in the yard when I ran into it, looking at the unknown Mercedes.

"Hello, Jake," he said. "Is this anything to do with you?"

"Yeah. Sorry, John. You weren't in. I couldn't leave it up at the house."

I opened the car door and climbed into the driver's seat.

"What are you doing, Jake?" John burst out anxiously, as if he was worried I'd flipped my lid. "You're banned, remember?"

"It's okay." I started the car and revved it. "I'm only taking it back up the road to my place, for a friend."

"Oh, I see."

"See you later, John," I called as I drove out of his yard.

I reached my front gates a minute later, at the same time as Milly in her black Golf.

My heart sank. She saw.

"What's the matter?" she said, as I climbed out of the Merc and walked across to her.

"I've got a problem. It could be messy. You've just got to do as I say. Get out of here, and come back in an hour."

She looked at me hard, with her head on one side. For a moment I thought she was going to want explanations, and I didn't have time for that. But she shrugged her shoulders.

"Okay," she said neutrally. "I'll see you in an hour."

She put her foot down and skidded off the loose

gravel at the side of the road until she found traction and the car shot off like a stubby black bullet.

I sighed, opened my gates and jumped back into the Merc.

I skidded round in the sweep in front of my house and headed up the rough track which led to the wood shed. I turned the car so that it was facing back down toward the house and got out, leaving the engine running. I opened the boot and went into the shed. Nothing had changed.

"Okay, Bolton. Can you lift him so I can get some good clear shots of him?"

Bolton jerked the American to his feet and locked his arms behind his back.

"Will this do?" he asked.

"Great."

I was expecting the failed assassin to object, but he seemed to have accepted that he'd met his match in Bolton.

I shot six frames from three angles. I put the camera down and picked up the gun.

"The car's outside. I left the trunk lid up."

"Right."

The big Yorkshireman pushed his stumbling charge in front of him, out into the dusk toward the waiting car. He lifted the man off his feet and hurled him into the Merc's big boot. Before the man could retaliate, Bolton was holding him down with one hand and wrapping a pair of jump leads round his wrists with the other.

"Give us a hand to finish this off," he said.

I took over. When I reckoned the wires were secure, I stood back. Bolton stuffed a chamois leather in the man's mouth, stepped back and slammed the lid down on him.

"He can't do much in there. I'll have to fill up at a self-service when there aren't any other cars around, in case he starts kicking. But don't worry, he'll not be going anywhere without my permission."

"Bolton, you've been great. Here's my number." I scribbled it on the back of a check. On the front I made it out in the sum of one thousand five hundred pounds. I left the payee blank. "Here's the first six days of his hotel bill in advance."

Bolton took it. "Thanks. I'll ring you to find out what's happening. And if you want more help like today, there'll be no charge."

"That's good to know. I may need you."

I watched Bolton drive away with his dangerous baggage. I was confident that he could deal with Kaminski —if that was his name. I didn't have any doubt that if I'd arrived back home on my own, I would have been dead by now. Kaminski was a professional. He'd have made mincemeat of me. I liked the irony that the plane crash he'd caused had prompted the train of events which had brought me back to Hampshire with a hardened, highly trained ex-paratrooper. I guessed it was Kaminski's professionalism that had discouraged him from putting up too much resistance against Bolton; he must have recognized the Yorkshireman's skills and strength. But Kaminski looked a hard, wily little man; Bolton would have to be on his guard.

The sun had melted into the rolling hills to the west, painting the ragged remnants of the day's clouds a brash scarlet. It was after ten. I had hoped that Charles would have been back from Herefordshire by now. I didn't think he was going to be able to tell me much that I didn't already know, but I wanted the confirmation.

Milly came back first.

With the immediate threat removed in the back of Bolton's Mercedes, I was a lot more glad to see her than I had been an hour earlier and I was more relaxed than I'd felt since I'd stepped into the mantrap four weeks ago to the day.

When I went out to meet her, Milly noticed.

"You look a bit friendlier than you did," she said first.

I carried on smiling.

"I feel it. I'm sorry I had to aim you out. We found a man with a gun sitting in the woods."

"What have you done with him?" she asked, alarmed.

"He's on his way to Yorkshire for a short holiday on a health farm. I guess someone will be out looking for him soon, ready to carry on the good work, but not for a day or so."

"I wish I knew what the hell was going on, but does that mean it's safe to stay here for now?"

"It does," I said.

"And what about your plane? Why didn't you fly back?"

"Ah, well," I said lightly. "Bit of a problem there. It broke down."

"God! what a bore."

"You could say that." I didn't feel like going into more detail right then.

Back in the house, I told her I was waiting for Charles to get back. She hadn't eaten, so she sat in the kitchen while I prepared a couple of steaks from a young fallow buck I'd shot in my woods the previous autumn. When they were grilling gently with a few crushed juniper berries on top, I sat down and helped myself to a bottle of heavy Italian Barolo that I'd opened—the next day was a Sunday.

I didn't want to talk to Milly about what I'd been doing over the last week; she'd hear enough of that when Charles arrived.

"How's the London art world?" I asked.

"Not falling over itself to praise Terese de Rosnay, I'm afraid."

"The show's not a hit?" I asked.

"Commercially it is. We've sold most of it, but Terese wants critical recognition, too—you know the type."

"Yeah, I know the type," I said with a rueful grin.

"It's okay. I've forgiven you for that."

"It happened before I'd had a taste of the real thing."

I got up to take the venison steaks out of the oven. I was putting them on the table when Charles breezed in looking pleased with himself.

"Hello, Camilla. Hi, Jake," he boomed.

"How did it go?" I asked.

"We have a result," he said triumphantly.

"Let me guess," I said, unfairly taking the wind from his sail. "James Bullough-Ferguson."

"Bull's eye, but how the hell did you know?"

"I'd had a hunch, since Smith described him to us. Bullough-Ferguson's been acting strange with me for some time. I thought that was because I was getting between him and Milly here."

"As if that were likely," Milly interrupted.

"But I realized it had to be something more, well, something else. Then up at York today, Arthur Henderson, Toby Ellerton's bookie—"

"And mine," Charles said.

"—told me that B-F had come along and told him to lean on Toby and his account would be paid off, just as long as they pushed him hard for a while, threatened him with the Jockey Club. Lady Fielding was up there too, and she always knows who's related to who and where they come from, so I asked her about James Bullough-Ferguson. She told me his mother had inherited some big place in Herefordshire. It had to be him who aimed Smith and the mantrap at me."

"I was amazed when the traveler told me it was James B-F," Charles said. "He's such a prize prat."

"Yeah, but he's a prat with expensive habits and no money. He knows everyone in racing, even if they don't much like him. In a way he was kind of an obvious choice. What we have to do now is find out who chose him, who's paying him."

"And why," Charles added.

"Sit down and have a drink, Charles." He was still pacing up and down in his excitement, making the place look untidy. "We had a visitor here this evening."

"Good God!" he exclaimed, lowering himself into a big elm carver. "Why the hell didn't you say so before? Where is he now?"

"Don't worry, everything's under control. Let me tell you from the start. First, I think my plane was sabotaged. The port-side fuel tank blew up ten minutes short of York."

"Shit! How did you get down?"

"You know I told you my mother made me promise always to wear a parachute?" I shrugged. "She was right."

"You mean you jumped?"

"Yeah. I landed in a pond full of cow shit. The plane's a total wreck. There must have been a small time-bomb on the wing, and I reckon the man we found back here placed it."

"He told you that?"

"Of course he didn't. He didn't tell us anything. But it had to be him. When I turned up at the races, someone must have told him to get back here and finish me off."

"Any idea who that was?"

"No, not yet, I'm working on it. The man didn't say a lot, but he had a few things on him, including the same number as Constable."

Charles's eyes lit up. "The New York phone number?"

I nodded. "You've got it."

"So this thing must have been started in the States," Milly said.

"Not necessarily. Bullough-Ferguson was responsible for getting me caught in the trap, and he leaned on

Henderson; there's nothing to tie him in with New York. And this other Cockney bloke fixed up Haslam and my first crash, and he leaned on Mick's bookies. There's no New York connection there either. I think New York's a red herring. They've brought in this American hit-man to keep the thing at arm's length."

"You didn't tell me your hit-man was American, and where the hell is he now anyway? Did you get the police?"

"No, I was trying to tell you. I jumped out of my plane and landed in a farmer's field. He took me to the races, and insisted on collecting me afterward. I had to go back and see the police and a man from the CAA, then the farmer's son said he'd bring me back here. He's a great bull of a man, an ex-paratrooper, hard as rock and ready for a fight. He came in to check the woods with me, like I've been doing every day, and we snuck up on this man Kaminski, sitting waiting for me with a rifle. He could have taken out anyone coming down my drive. Bolton got him first."

"What do you mean?" Charles looked alarmed.

"We caught him, and Bolton took him away to cool him off."

"But where?"

"I don't know. Yorkshire, I guess. I agreed to pay two hundred and fifty a day for his keep. I tell you, if Bolton hadn't been with me, I'd have been shot. The man waiting for me was definitely a pro."

"Where do we go from here, then?" Charles asked.

"Do you feel like going to New York?"

"Why not? I haven't been for a while. But you said you thought New York was a red herring."

"I do, but we've got to find out who laid it. They're not going to tell us over the phone."

"Okay, I'll get over there and see what I can find out."

"Great, but make sure you're careful. I don't want you to not be able to make the girls' holiday."

"I will. I won't be able to go till Tuesday, but I'll ring as soon as I've found out anything. It could take a few days, though, if I've only got that number to go on; I don't have the same ready-made sources that I have here."

"That'll be okay. Look, I don't know when these people are going to realize their hit-man's gone missing, but it won't be long. I'm not riding Monday, but I've got a full card on Tuesday at Ascot, so they'll know for sure then that I haven't been hit. Anyway I guess their information is better than that."

"If you can ride at Ascot as if nothing had happened, that's going to help my end," Charles said. He drained his glass and stood up. "Right, I'm off. I'll give you a ring before I go. Look after yourself in the meantime."

"I'll still be here," I promised.

Charles banged his way out and left me with Milly. She was looking at me thoughtfully.

"Now I realize why you didn't want me around last week."

"Yes, well, you picked a bad time to get to know me. There aren't usually that many people around who want me dead."

"But surely, Jake, you must have some idea of why. Somebody's spending a lot of time and money trying to kill you and they keep missing. They're going to get desperate soon."

"And that's when they'll start making mistakes, so I wouldn't worry."

"Of course I'm worried, and it seems to me they've made enough mistakes already."

"Tonight, there's nothing to worry about. Let's go to bed and forget about it all."

"That shouldn't be hard," she said, smiling.

* * *

The next morning was glorious. All the grey of the day before had been seen off by a southerly breeze and the sun was already warm by the time we left my bed.

We swam and ate a big breakfast before we let our conversation revert to external interferences like frustrated hit-men.

It was Milly who brought it up first.

"Jake, the man you caught yesterday must have got here somehow. He must have left a car somewhere, and that could have some clues in it."

She was right; I'd already thought about it.

"And if you just leave it," she went on, "whoever's behind all this might find it and realize something's gone wrong."

"Do you want to come and look for it with me?"

"As you can't drive, I think I'll have to."

Ten minutes later we were out in the lane in her VW.

It took us half an hour to find Kaminski's car. It was a BMW with an Avis sticker on the back parked three miles away in a lay-by on the Newbury-Winchester road. I unlocked it with the keys I had removed from Kaminski's pocket the evening before.

There was a small leather grip on the back seat, and in the glove compartment a camera with a 500-millimeter lens.

"What shall we do about this car?" Milly asked.

"I'll drive it into Basingstoke and leave it in one of the big covered car parks there. No one'll do anything about it for a few days."

"Just don't get stopped by the police for anything," Milly said, "or you'll be off the road for a few more years."

"Sure. You take this gear, and follow me."

There wasn't much traffic around on a Sunday morning. But I still drove slowly and reached the ugly concrete cage of a car park without any problems. I parked the car in the empty ground floor and walked out to where Milly was waiting for me.

Back at home, we opened Kaminski's soft leather grip. He evidently hadn't been planning a long stay. The case contained one change of clothes and a wash kit. Besides this, there was his US passport. I couldn't tell if it was a forgery, but I assumed it was. Its date of issue was five years back, but it had only three entry and exit stamps: into London on 11 July, three days before; into London on 2 June and out again the next day, 3 June—Derby day. It didn't take a lot to work out the connection.

There was also a folder of photos from a one-hour processor. The shots were alarmingly familiar: my house, from half a dozen angles; my plane; me riding out at Melbourne House on Friday morning, and me leaving my house for Sandown a few hours later. Tucked in among them was a much older shot of me, taken while I was still riding in America, grinning over a vast cup at Saratoga.

The camera was a neat, professional 35mm tool. It wasn't loaded. Kaminski had only used it for his pre-hit recce.

Seeing the shots, knowing the reason for them, didn't do anything for Milly's peace of mind.

"For God's sake, you must get the police in, Jake. I don't know how you can let all this happen and expect to deal with it on your own."

"Look, I'm still around. I've got help. I don't think there's anything the police could do which I can't. And we can do things they can't. If they'd wanted to question that gypsy in Herefordshire, they'd have got nowhere. He'd have been demanding his rights to a lawyer and all that. We found out the number of his truck; we were able to deal with Kaminski; we can go and ask questions in New York, all much more easily than they can. And there's not a lot they could do to protect me; unless I never want to go out again."

"But you don't want them involved anyway, you said so."

"Look, racing is a business that thrives on suggestion and rumor. There are a lot of bucks in it, and always a few people trying to help themselves. It would only need a whisper that I might have been mixing with the wrong people to screw up my career here. It's like a man being accused of rape in a small town. Whether he's done it or not, nobody ever forgets; even if it's proved beyond any doubt he hasn't done it, the mud still sticks, and people steer clear of him, however illogical it might seem. I can't risk that. Until I know just why someone's trying to settle old scores, I've got to know what it is they think they're settling."

"Are you sure you haven't done *anything* you don't want anyone to know about?"

"No, I'm not sure; I can't think of anything serious enough, but I can't risk my career until I know."

"But if you're not careful, you won't have a career to screw up, and you're actually enjoying the whole thing, aren't you? I mean, I could tell when you were talking to Charles last night; you were like a couple of characters from a boy's adventure story."

I laughed. "You're sort of right there, too."

"What about other people getting caught in the crossfire?"

"That's why I told you I couldn't see you for a while," I justified myself.

"But Jake, I don't want you to die, not now, not when we've just got together. It's not fair."

"I'll make it up to you, I promise. And I still don't want you caught in any crossfire, so you'd better head out of here."

She sighed and looked at me, shaking her head.

"You're crazy, Jake." She put her lips to mine in a long, soft kiss. "Don't get killed, please," she whispered.

After she had gone, I sat silently for a while, gazing out across my quiet valley, wishing she had stayed longer; glad that she hadn't.

/////////// *CHAPTER 14*

There was a lot of work for me at Melbourne House on Monday morning. Captain Toby wanted me up on two of the new purchases he'd made for Leonard Zimmer, as well as Miss Pavlova, the filly which had come from the States and was running at Royal Ascot on Thursday.

As I always did, I became totally absorbed in my job, my preoccupations locked into a particular compartment from which they couldn't be budged as long as the horses were around. It was a kind of obsession, and undoubtedly a large part of the success I had on the racetrack; an unassailable single-mindedness and the reason I kept no horses at home.

I was brought back to the outside world by the arrival of Sandy Zimmer.

I was having a large cup of coffee with Janey Ellerton when she showed up. As she greeted me, her manner was more coy, less hectoring than usual, though there was a dangerous lusty glimmer in her eye.

"I hear you've been working Miss Pavlova. Does she feel ready for Thursday?" she asked.

"Yeah. I haven't seen all the opposition, but I would say we had a good chance."

"You must come to dinner in London afterward, Jake. You can't keep putting me off."

"If I win, I'll come."

"You'd better win, then," she threatened.

"You tell the horse," I said.

Toby and a young racing journalist who often rode out for him came into the kitchen and the talk inevitably concentrated on the runners that were going out from Melbourne House to chase the big prizes at Ascot that week. Rock Beat, Smethwick's filly, was one of the most fancied by the trainer and the lads. She was running the next day, the first of the royal meeting, and her ante-post price was shortening by the hour. I thought of my taped conversation with her owner, and smiled.

After twenty minutes or so, the journalist offered to drop me home and save me a taxi fare. He was a genuine type so I repaid him with a little genuine information.

I got back into my house after my customary check through the grounds to be met by a stack of faxes and messages. I tried to deal with most of them right away, behaving as normally as possible, and got talked into riding Pink Pigeon at Brighton that afternoon for Tommy Preece. I liked Tommy, and with a week's ban starting on Saturday, I needed all the winners I could get.

This would alert Kaminski's employers to the fact that they had failed yet again—if they didn't already know. That was too bad. And it might encourage them to think I still didn't realize I was anyone's target.

Tommy picked me up and drove me to Brighton in his cattle/horse box. It was unconventional transport for a top jockey and I liked that. Besides, Tommy had a lot to say about the training of horses that defied some of the industry's sacred cows, and I still had something to learn from his blunt country talk.

At Brighton, Pink Pigeon came out of the lorry needing a good bath and quiet as a mole.

On the dogleg track above the cliffs, I didn't even need to break sweat to notch up my first winner of the week. The bookies were grumbling about the amount of money they had taken before the late jockey announcement, but they knew Tommy; they should have been ready. They were ready for Rock Beat on the first day of Royal Ascot.

The filly was a terrible price now, worse even than Smethwick had predicted, 10/11 in a competitive field.

In the parade ring, Smethwick looked like a vaudeville act in a morning suit with his top hat tilted to the back of his head. When I went to get mounted, he gave me a knowing wink.

"Best of luck, Jake. You know you can do it," he boomed as I was led out of the ring.

I grinned at his lack of subtlety.

"What are my instructions again, Captain?" I asked Toby.

"Win the fucking race," he growled.

At least it looked as though I was only going to upset one of them.

Rock Beat would have made all the running if I'd let her. But I knew there were at least two others who normally led, so I tucked her in just behind them.

It was a close-packed field, no more than six lengths between the first and the last of the ten runners. I got her settled where I wanted, using the quarters of the horses in front as a buffer rather than the bit to hold her back.

Two of my main rivals were held up for a late run,

and when they broke at the furlong marker, I was caught flat-footed for two vital seconds and became momentarily boxed-in. When at last I got out I rained a dozen curses down on myself for the age it seemed to take for my filly to get going.

The leaders had already gone two lengths clear and were pulling away. Rock Beat was going to have to try like she never had before. I asked her; she obliged, straining every inch of her tiring body and stretching her neck to the limit as the finishing post came up on us all too quickly.

It was going to be very close.

Photo!

Smethwick put his large arm round my shoulder and pretended to commiserate as his filly was awarded second place.

"You fuckin' nearly blew that," he whispered angrily.

"It was convincing, though, wasn't it?"

"Nearly give me a fuckin' 'eart attack. Don't you do that to me again, son."

"I'll try not to, Mr. Smethwick."

I wasn't the punters' favorite either, not until after the next; I won that with ten yards of daylight to spare.

After I'd weighed in, Geoff Haslam sidled up to me to congratulate me on my first win of the royal meeting; then, more confidentially, when he was sure we couldn't be heard, he said, "That bloke's here."

"The man who set up the crash?"

Haslam nodded. "Yeah. I caught him talking to a man in the car park. They pretended they hadn't been, acted like they didn't know each other."

"Did you know who he was talking to?"

"Don't know him; know who he is."

"Who?" I asked impatiently.

He shrugged. "James Bullough-Ferguson."

"Great!" I nearly yelled.

"Is it?" Haslam asked. "What's that wanker got to do with it?"

"It makes a connection. Don't worry about it. And for Christ's sake, don't talk to anyone else about this."

"I don't bleedin' intend to. I'm sticking my neck out just talking to you."

"You owed me, Geoff. Let me know if you see anything else."

"All right," he said grudgingly.

I didn't think he would now. I got the feeling he thought he'd paid his dues. I didn't mind too much; at least he'd joined up one set of dots for me.

I managed to grab a half-hour with Milly, in a corner of the Fieldings' box. She looked sensational. It still surprised me that I couldn't find a flaw in her; it didn't seem possible. I guessed I was biased.

She almost persuaded me to let her drive me home, instead of Martin. But I knew I couldn't risk it.

Feeling half elated, half dejected, I listened to Martin's gabble on the way home. There had been parties to go to, but I wasn't in a party mood.

When I got back, Bolton Pickering had phoned and left a number. I rang it.

"Hello, Bolton. Everything okay?"

"Hello, Jake. No problems. He's not going anywhere, and I think he knows it. And I got something out of him today you'll want to know."

"Yes?"

"He shot Hagan at the Derby."

"Yeah, I already got that."

"How?"

"I found his car, with his passport. He checked into Heathrow on the second of June, and out on the third. It had to be him."

"Well, it were. And he done it by mistake, like we thought."

"Yeah. If you're getting anything out of him, can you

try him with the name James Bullough-Ferguson? Just see if he reacts to it."

"James Bullough-Ferguson?"

"That's right."

"Okay. I'll give you a ring, then."

"Thanks."

When I'd rung off, I sat at my table and added to the pile of scrawled lists and charts I'd already made.

I hadn't heard from Charles. He would only be arriving in New York that evening. But I had already decided that I'd make use of the holiday the York stewards had awarded me and join Charles in America at the end of the week—if I wasn't dead by then.

Wednesday went without a hitch and I won two races for Ellerton which we'd both expected, one of them on a colt he'd bought for Leonard Zimmer. Milly hadn't come to Ascot that day and afterward I accepted an invitation to a dinner party with an owner in Sunningdale.

When I got there, I wished I hadn't come. There was no one I really wanted to talk to, and I didn't feel like putting on the charm just for the sake of it. I didn't do my reputation a lot of good, but frankly I didn't care. My host sent me home in his Bentley, whose driver was puzzled by my request to walk the last few hundred yards home. I told him it was part of my exercise routine. He shrugged and opened the rear door for me.

My precautions weren't necessary. No one had come back to visit me yet, but I didn't think it could be long before they did. Without Charles or Bolton Pickering around to back me up, I was feeling more vulnerable.

Sitting alone in my big house, wishing Milly was with me, I felt my confidence dwindle. It took an effort not to pick up the phone and call the police for help.

I didn't sleep well, but the dawn gave me a boost. At six thirty I was outside watching the sun blaze up over the ridge behind my valley. A car called for me at seven to drive me to Lambourn. It had been a hassle getting around since the plane had crashed, but I'd had too much on my mind to do anything about replacing it.

There was a lot of excitement in the air at Melbourne House. Toby had got off to an incredible start at Royal Ascot, with two wins and a second, and we had two good prospects that day, including Leonard Zimmer's Miss Pavlova in the Chesham. I rode out two lots and did a round of inspection with Toby before leaving with him for the races.

Now I had him alone for a while, I took the chance to sound him out on his relationship with Arthur Henderson, his bookie. He wouldn't say much beyond admitting that he'd had a problem, but he'd sorted it out now. In a roundabout sort of way, he even apologized for having asked me to stop horses for him earlier in the season.

I couldn't see how all this linked up with the three attempts that had been made to kill me. But I knew it couldn't be a coincidence that it was Bullough-Ferguson who had asked Henderson to lean on Toby and arranged to have his account cleared. Unless it was some ham-fisted attempt to get the Captain to compromise me, to get me involved in stopping horses for him.

At least there was now no question that horses were going out from Melbourne House to win. Above all, that day, Toby wanted Zimmer's horse to win.

"You shouldn't have any problems in the Chesham. Miss Pavlova's in a different class from the rest of them. It was a good move by Zimmer to enter her."

"Do you know if Zimmer makes those kind of decisions himself?" I asked.

"No. That chap Hal Symonds seems to have acted as his racing manager for some time. Frankly, I don't get the impression that old Zimmer is particularly passionate about the game anyway. Of course, Mrs. Zimmer is, and she and Hal seem very chummy."

I knew what he was talking about. I'd come to the same conclusion.

"The fact is," the Captain went on, "Zimmer's got so much money, he can run his racing out of petty cash —and all from selling filthy hamburgers. It makes me sick to even think about it."

I laughed. "He's been feeding American kids for thirty years. I shouldn't think there's a single person in the States who hasn't eaten in a Zee-Burger Bar. They're in every hick little town in every state. You've only had them in Europe for ten years, but he was into Japan and all over the Far East way before that. He kind of followed in Coca-Cola's footsteps. You can get a Zee-Burger in over fifty countries now. He sells something like four million of them every day."

Ellerton laughed. "What an appalling thought. Still, I suppose I can't complain if he's passing some of it on to me. What I find incredible is the influence he has. Did you see the television last night?"

"Nope, just a couple of race videos."

"That's what I like to hear, but you know the last of the American hostages was released in Damascus last night?"

"Yeah, I heard."

"There must have been a thousand reporters all clustered around him when he came out of the American embassy to make his first appearance. When they asked what he most wanted to do after being locked up in a cell in Beirut for three years, he said, "I can't wait to get my teeth into a big Zee-burger." It's incredible. A free plug in front of God knows how many hundreds of millions of viewers. Old Zimmer must know the right people to pull a stunt like that."

"Yeah, well, I don't suppose it was exactly a *free* plug, but I know what you mean. Makes us look real small fry."

"And that's how he treats everyone, except that tart he's married to. He's absolutely besotted with her, thinks the suns shines out of her lovely little arse, even though she treats him like shit—probably *because* she treats him like shit. Do you think he knows the only reason she could possibly have married him was for his money?"

"Of course he knows," I said, entertained by Toby's abnormal foray into the realms of personal philosophy. "But I guess as far as he's concerned, his money is an essential part of him."

"Ah, well," Toby said, having exhausted the subject. "At least he pays his bills very promptly, unlike most of the richer owners I've had."

We saw Sandra Zimmer soon after we arrived at the racecourse. She had excelled herself for Ladies' Day, obviously determined to outdo all the wives of the big European owners. The Arabs, of course, didn't produce their wives for these occasions.

Sandy wore an elegantly simple royal blue silk dress wrapped round her in a way that pointed up the best parts of her beautiful body. Despite everything that I knew and thought of her, I felt a twitch in my groin as I watched her striding toward us.

She flashed a blunt instrument of a lascivious grin at me before she turned to Toby.

"Make sure he wins on my horse," she said to the trainer. "He's promised to have dinner with me afterward if he does."

Toby glanced at me in amazement. It was the first time he had noticed any kind of relationship between Sandy and me.

"Now you know why I want to win that one so badly." I shrugged at Toby.

Beneath a small-brimmed concoction of straw and net, Sandy's eyes narrowed as she tried to gauge the flavor of my comment. I didn't help her.

After a bit of small talk about the horse with Toby, she strode away with a flutter of blue silk about her long, brown thighs. It didn't take much imagination to see why a very rich old man might feel that he didn't want to lose a prize like Sandy.

I got on with my afternoon's work. It looked like it could be a big payday and, with one thing and another, my expenses were running high.

Race-riding's much the same as any other way of making a living; talent is maybe ten percent of the reason for success. Without it, you can't start, but the other ninety percent is dedication—to winning and, though it's not the sort of thing to tell an interviewer, to making money. I locked my brain into racing mode and got on with it.

Two and half hours later, I was seven grand richer, two winners closer to my rivals in the jockeys' table and able to switch my attention to other realities.

Sandy had given me a speculative wink as she had accepted the cup for Miss Pavlova's hard-earned win, and whispered, "See you later."

I guessed she would be looking for me now. But I saw her first. She was standing in a corridor in the members' stand, pleading with Hal Symonds. It was a surprising sight. She was clutching his arm and talking with more than her usual energy. He shook his head, shook her arm off, and walked away.

I ducked back out of sight before she could see me and let her bump into me outside the exit to the paddock.

In a feat of impressive acting, she transformed herself from the beseeching figure she had been a moment before. She beamed at me with wide, confident eyes.

"Do you want to come back in my car to London?" she asked.

"Sure. I'm not allowed to drive myself."

She laughed. "I'd forgotten."

"It's not so funny," I said. "I was getting around in a plane, but I crashed that too."

"I read about that in the papers. Wasn't it lucky your mother made you promise to wear that parachute?" she said with a quick disparaging smile. "I suppose being your mother, she knew how accident prone you are."

"Yeah." I nodded. "When are you leaving?"

"For London? In about ten minutes. Is that okay?"

"I've got a few people to see first. Can you make it half an hour?"

"Oh, all right," she said, annoyed but doing her best not to let it show.

She looked happy enough by the time I met up with her in the back of a Rolls-Royce big enough to hold a party. She was lying back among some animal fur cushions watching a video of Miss Pavlova's race. I was sitting beside her. She only looked away from the video once.

"You have got a lovely little arse," she said, nodding back at the TV screen just to the left of the chauffeur's head. It was showing a rear view of me bringing the filly back to a trot after I'd won the race.

"Thanks," I said.

"Drink?" she asked.

"Why not."

Sandy nodded at a handsome walnut cabinet below the television. "In there. Only champagne, I'm afraid. You can pour me a glass too."

The car was gliding out of the car park with the rest of the race traffic, part of it but separate, by virtue of its height and the efficient sound-proofing of the world's greatest coach-builders.

I leaned forward and opened the drinks cabinet. It held glasses and a small fridge with two bottles of Dom Perignon inside. I pulled out a bottle and two glasses. I eased the cork up with my thumbs until it gave a discreet pop, and filled the glasses.

I settled back in the deep, cloth-covered seat, prepared to join in the inevitable flirting banter that would take up the journey to London.

* * *

The Rolls drew up outside a large eighteenth-century, red-brick house set back in Charles Street. With the kind of money Zimmer had to spend, I'd expected something impressive, and this must have been one of the best private houses left in that part of London.

Curiously, because most of my friends were English, I knew very few people who lived in Mayfair. I know it had once been a ghetto for the rich and the aristocratic British, but during the sixties and seventies they had been pushed westward into Belgravia and Chelsea by a series of invasions from countries with less stringent tax regimes, and there were fewer British passport holders living there now.

The chauffeur opened the door for us, and Sandy led me out and up a short flagstoned path to a grand classical stone portico that would have had Toby Ellerton drooling.

The place was even more impressive inside, decorated in a way that was opulent without being flashy; Sandy's choice of decorator, no doubt, to give her her due.

She showed me up to an enormous drawing room on the first floor.

"I'm just going to change," she said, "and have a bath. Help yourself to a drink, then come up and scrub my back."

I gave a noncommittal reply and watched her go. I didn't want another drink yet. It was only seven, and I'd had half a bottle of champagne already. I wanted to keep my intake under control; with too much drink in the system, in the presence of a beautiful woman, a man could forget his priorities, however much of a bitch she might be.

I didn't go up and scrub Sandy's back. I went down and found an English cook with a trio of Filipino girls in the basement kitchen, and asked for a bottle of San Pellegrino water.

Sandy looked miffed when she came back down to the drawing room half an hour later.

"What about my back?" she asked.

"Sorry, I forgot," I said.

"Never mind, there'll be plenty of time for that later. I've told them to have dinner ready in an hour."

"Who else is coming tonight, then?" I asked.

"It's just us. Didn't I tell you?"

My heart sank. I just didn't know how I'd deal with several hours of Sandy on her own. She was a very determined woman.

"Let's watch a movie first," she said with a grin.

She evidently wasn't seeking my views on this; she picked up a remote control wand and pressed a button. A bookcase slid to one side to reveal a screen four feet wide. Giving me a quick, wicked leer, she activated a video player. A moment later the screen was filled with heaving naked bodies of both sexes.

As blue movies go, it wasn't anything too unusual. The dialogue was almost nonexistent and the plot predictable. It involved an American football player with the looks and build of Hal Symonds—though I thought it unlikely that Hal matched up to him in the genital region—and a team of drum majorettes of a sharing disposition.

I sat next to Sandy, sinking into a soft, deep sofa. She moved herself close up to me and put a hand on my leg.

"Do you want a line?" she offered.

"Nope."

"Some grass? I've got some great grass."

"Nope."

"I'll get you another drink."

I let her and carried on watching the film.

Sandy knew what she was doing. Only a saint or a eunuch could have watched the antics of the naked cast and not found themselves with an uncompromising hard-on; and I was neither.

It wasn't long before she started to undress me, and I wasn't doing much to stop her. At least I wasn't taking any initiatives, I justified to the small voice in my head trying to remind me about Milly.

Sandy had my zip down, her hands round my nuts and her soft, wet lips hovering over my tip. There was a knock on the door.

Sandy's eyes flickered up to mine; she groaned and looked over her shoulder. "Oh shit!"

She swung her legs off the sofa and, straightening her skirt, walked across to the door. She opened it.

"What is it?"

"You want dinner now?"

"No. I said at eight thirty, didn't I? Can't you understand English?"

The film had reached the last of its several climaxes and the television screen was blank. I was deflated enough to get my zip back up and my shirt tucked inside my waistband. I was suddenly glad of the interruption.

"Hey, Sandy, I'm starving. Couldn't we eat now anyway?" I called across the room.

She turned back and looked at me, all done up.

"Oh, all right," she said petulantly, and to the maid outside, "You can serve dinner now."

She shut the door and came back to sit beside me again. I had my arms folded to discourage her.

"What's happened to you?" she said, reverting to a kind of winsome seductiveness, stroking my ear with sensuous fingers.

"I thought I'd save it up till later," I said.

"Why? There's nothing single-barreled about you."

"And I don't like screwing on an empty stomach."

Dinner was tricky. I'd known it was going to be as soon as Sandy realized I wasn't going to make love to her afterward. But she showed an odd sort of disappointment. It didn't seem like sexual frustration, more like annoyance at having her plans go wrong. But I tried to keep a conversation going, realizing more than ever that beneath Sandy's lovely exterior lurked a spirit of utter selfishness; not just normal, everyday self-interest, but a total lack of concern for anyone else at all, unless they had something she wanted.

I also guessed, from what I'd seen earlier, that it was Hal whom she would rather have been engaging in her elaborate foreplay.

I tried to find out more about Zimmer, but she didn't come across with more than the fact that she only had to open her legs to get anything she wanted from him.

Straight prostitution by another name. As we ate and talked, Sandy drank, twice as fast as I did. And the more she drank, the more she felt sorry for herself, and accused me of treating her dirtily by not screwing her.

"Who the hell do you think you are, anyway?" she slurred while we ate a feather-light Armagnac soufflé. "What do you think gives you the right to run around the world screwing whoever you like, whenever it suits you, and not when it suits them? How many times have you turned me down since Kentucky last year? Don't think that I'm ever going to ask again. I've got bigger boys to play with."

"I'm glad to hear it," I said mildly.

"Much bigger," she said, "with cocks like bloody tree trunks."

I laughed.

"Don't you bloody laugh!" she said. "You should know the trouble you and your puny performance last year caused me."

"Like what?" I asked.

"I got damned pregnant."

I didn't believe her. "So? What happened? I see no diapers or baby clothes cluttering up the place."

"Leonard went mad when he found out. He said he

knew it couldn't be his and he made me abort it. Then he went madder because it was a boy. All his life he says he's wanted a boy, and he hasn't had a single child from five wives. Probably the old bastard's firing blanks, but he swears he isn't."

"How was he so sure he wasn't the father of your baby?"

"From the timing, dummy. He'd been away for a month, and then I wouldn't let him touch me for a bit because he wouldn't buy us a house in Gstaad. He couldn't understand why I should want a place in Europe. He only held out for a few weeks, though."

"Did you tell him I was the father?" I asked quietly.

"No," she answered quickly. "There was nothing he could do to get that out of me, I promise."

I wondered. But I didn't pursue it. "I'm sorry that happened, Sandy," I said. "Did you want the baby?"

"Not much."

"Then why did you let yourself get pregnant?"

"Don't you think I asked my doctor that, for Christ's sake?"

"Oh, I see," I said, trying to sound sympathetic, though I couldn't help thinking that if the child had been born, it would have had a hell of an existence to earn Zimmer's millions. "In the meantime, big Hal inherits the lot, does he?"

"Yes," she said cagily.

"Lucky boy, and good-looking, too."

"He's a spoiled brat, actually," Sandy said.

"Is he? Then you're just the person to understand him, aren't you?"

"Who the hell are you to talk?" Sandy almost snarled.

I shrugged my shoulders. "It's time I went. I've got some horses to ride in the morning."

"Oh yeah? And who are you riding tonight? The lonely Camilla I suppose?" she said sarcastically.

"That'd be nice."

Sandy grunted, resigned to the fact that whatever she had planned for that night with me wasn't going to happen. "There should be a car outside to take you home."

My surprise must have shown.

"I may be a spoiled brat," she said, "but no one can say that I'm not a conscientious hostess."

It was easy to be conscientious with billions of dollars at your disposal and an army of servants to carry out your smallest whim, but I didn't bother to say so. Anyway, I was glad I didn't have to look for a taxi willing to take me to Hampshire.

I stood up. "I'm sorry about the baby. Thanks for dinner."

Sandy lifted her eyes and stared at me sullenly. "Fuck off."

I walked out of her Georgian dining room, glanced back at her, hunched at the table, looking tragic and beautiful in the light from the silver candelabra.

"Good night," I said and left the room, closing the door behind me. I ran down the shallow stairs and picked up my small suitcase from where I'd left it in the hall.

I opened the front door. A large black Ford was waiting on the other side of the wrought-iron gate.

I walked out to it. The driver emerged from his side and came round to open the rear door for me.

"Evening, Mr. Felton," he said.

I nodded to him and climbed in.

When the driver was back in his seat, he said, "I've had a look at the map, Mr. Felton. M3 looks the best."

"Yeah, that's the quickest way."

The car pulled away from the pavement and glided through the quiet Mayfair streets, out into the bustle of Hyde Park Corner and headed west out of London.

I dozed in the back, and thought about Sandy and

the wretched billionaire life she led. I wondered if the baby had been mine; if there had been a baby at all.

I thought how glad I was that I wouldn't have to lie to Milly when I saw her.

/////////// CHAPTER 15

I woke when the motion ceased. The car had stopped; the engine had been turned off. We had left the motorway; there was only thick black night outside.

I was going to ask the driver what had happened, but a sudden suspicion crept into my already suspicious mind. I watched as he opened his door and heaved himself out of his seat, making as little noise as possible. The internal light which should have been triggered didn't come on.

Fear flooded my system with adrenaline. I was tense and ready when he opened my door.

I could make out his bulky shape now my eyes had adapted to the dark, but no more than that. I slid my hand up behind me and found the switch for the rear inside light.

I hadn't looked at the driver when he had let me into the car in Charles Street. Now I saw a heavy, square-jawed face, with dark eyes that blinked beneath bushy black brows. In the same second, I saw the gun he was clutching in his right hand.

My reactions were utterly instinctive; there was no time to plan strategies.

I lifted my right leg and drove it with every ounce of energy I could find at the place where his genitals should have been. I hadn't miscalculated.

He howled with pain and pitched forward onto me. I felt the hard metal of the gun on my knee and grabbed for it, yanking it from his loosened grip. I struggled and slid out from under him, across the seat to open the other door.

He roared and caught a fistful of my jacket. I got the door open and my legs out of the car, and ripped my clothing from his hand. I was free of him now, and out of the car. I slammed the door shut and sprinted along a narrow lane, just visible in the moonless night. After I'd run two hundred yards, I stopped and turned round.

I could hear him coming, but I couldn't see him.

I could make out high hedges on both sides of the lane, but I saw no gaps, or anywhere to hide. Knowing I had the advantage for the moment, I carried on running. Another hundred yards on, there was a discernible break in the hedge. I prayed for a gateway.

I could see enough of a big timber gate to clamber over it. On the other side was a field of deep pasture. I ran a few silent yards back down the inside of the hedge and waited.

I heard him coming, panting heavily and grunting every other pace. He passed the gate and kept on going. I waited another twenty seconds before climbing out of the field and heading back toward the car.

I was gambling on the likelihood that he had left the ignition keys in place.

He had.

I started the car and put my foot down. The head-lights showed me a single-track lane passing through some woodland. I had no idea where I was but I carried on until I reached a junction. An old finger sign told me I was three miles from Basingstoke. I took that route and was rewarded a few minutes later with a view of the lights of the sprawling town spread out below me. From there it wouldn't be difficult to find my way home.

But I had to decide what I was going to do with the car, and the gun.

I guessed if I'd had to I would have turned the auto-matic on the man who was surely going to use it on me. But, although I'd shot a lot of creatures in my time and despite the threat I'd lived under for the past month, I didn't know if I could have brought myself to kill some-one. I hoped I'd never find out.

I reached the old highway which ran from Basing-stoke to Winchester. It was eleven thirty, and there was still a trickle of traffic. I drove half a mile westward and pulled up in a lay-by. I grabbed my suitcase, flung the car keys into the nearest hedge and walked another few hundred yards to a big old coaching inn that was spending its latter years as a steak house.

I walked in, with my shades on and my collar up, hoping that no one would recognize a small, scruffy, mud-stained individual. No one did. I found a pay phone and called a car to come and pick me up from the car park outside.

While I waited, I wondered who, besides Sandy, had known where I was that evening.

Back home, I rang Charles in New York.

"I'm coming over on Saturday. How are you do-ing?"

"Fine. I've done all I can usefully do without con-fronting them."

"Wait till I get over before you do that, will you?"

"If that's what you want. But I warn you, it may not be wise for you to show your face."

"I'm going to show it if that's the only way I can get this sorted. Look, there's something else I want you to check. It may be difficult, but do what you can."

I gave him a few dates and details to work on, wished him luck and rang off.

After that I called Bolton Pickering in Yorkshire. "Sorry to call so late, but you should be able to let your man go soon. I'm going to the States tomorrow to knock this thing on the head."

"You think that's where it's coming from, then?" Bolton asked.

"I've an idea, yes. Did you try Kaminski with Bullough-Ferguson?"

"Aye. Nothing. I don't reckon he'd ever heard of him. He didn't bat an eyelid."

"That's a pity. But it may not matter. I'll call you from the States and let you know, okay?"

"Okay," Bolton said. "No rush."

The next day, the last of the Royal Ascot meeting, I heard that James Bullough-Ferguson had known I had been in Charles Street the evening before. Milly told me.

I knew something was eating her as soon as I saw her. She turned her cheek away when I tried to kiss her.

"I hear you had an intimate little dinner with your owner's wife last night," she said.

"Yeah, I told you I was going to. I asked you if you wanted to come."

"It's just as well I didn't. I'm not into gang-bangs."

"How do you know until you've tried?" I teased her.

"I have, thanks."

"Have you?" I was intrigued. "Who with?"

"I'm not going to tell you now, and stop trying to wriggle out of it."

"I'm not, Milly. I did nothing you could have

objected to." I wasn't mentioning what had been done to me. "I made sure of that. I only went there to extract some information from Sandy."

"What sort of information?"

"I was just following up an idea."

"And did you get anything useful?"

"I'm not sure. But I left at half past ten; an hour later, I had somebody waving a gun in my face again."

"Oh no!"

"It's okay. I dealt with it."

"Jake," she had forgotten her hurt pride, "you *must* tell the police what's going on, please. It's not a bloody joke."

"I will, I promise, when I get back from the States."

"Are you definitely going, then?"

"Yeah. Tomorrow, but you mustn't tell anybody, especially not your friend Bullough-Ferguson."

"Why not? He's already told me that your friend Sandy Zimmer's going back to the States today."

"Shit! She never told me that. Believe me!" I said in response to Milly's cynical look, and I think she did. "We didn't get around to discussing each other's future plans. Just don't tell James B-F."

"No, of course not. But for God's sake, don't do anything crazy over there."

"I won't need to, and Charles will be around. Don't worry."

"Just promise me you'll come back in one piece and tell the police."

"I promise. Now, I've got to go and win a race."

"I bet you don't," she said.

"The bookies are down there." I nodded toward the rows of boards and golf umbrellas in Tattersalls.

Milly told me when I saw her a week later that she'd bet against me, and she'd won.

I scored a row of duck eggs that afternoon, but I left the course glad that I wouldn't have to ride another horse for seven days.

* * *

Charles Powell met me next evening at New York-JFK. It was a Saturday and six o'clock local time. The clear blue sky above degenerated into a dirty orange haze which hung over Manhattan as we approached it across the Queensboro Bridge.

Charles had been staying with friends in an apartment in the East Sixties. They had gone up to the Hamptons in Long Island to get away from the humid midsummer smog. I didn't blame them.

Sitting in a small roof garden as the sun set, looking up East Sixty-Sixth toward the park, we drank very dry martinis which Charles had mixed. The noise of traffic ten storeys below drifted up to us while we talked.

"We can't do much until Monday, now," Charles said. "I've tracked that phone number down to a small lawyer's office in the financial district. I went and took a look at it today and the whole place is shut up."

"Have you got any names?"

"The firm's called Peabody Finkelbaum—a Wasp-Jewish set-up I should think."

"We know they had something to do with Kaminski, who came over on Derby day and last weekend; and we know Meyers, the gun collector, gave that number to Constable. I've been thinking about that. My guess is that was all to do with trying to implicate Mick Hagan somehow if they'd killed me. I can't see how it was going to work, but they were successful up to a point, putting the squeeze on Mick and giving him a sort of motive. I suppose it might have worked if I'd been shot on Derby day and the police got to hear of Hagan trying to sell my gun back to me. But," I shrugged, "all the other shit that's been happening leads back to Bullough-Ferguson."

"What about the Cockney chap who set you up with Geoff Haslam?"

"I was coming to that. Haslam found me at Ascot on

Tuesday and told me he'd seen his man talking to B-F. So the crash, the mantrap, paying off Toby's dues to Arthur Henderson all lead back to Bullough-Ferguson. There has to be some connection between him and these New York people."

"We've established one link," Charles said.

"What's that?"

"Didn't you tell me it was Haslam's chap who leaned on Harry Devene?"

"Shit! You're right. Why the hell hadn't I taken that on? Jesus, I've drawn so many goddam charts I don't know how I missed that."

"It links both sides of the operation," Charles said, "and it means either that Bullough-Ferguson and Peabody Finkelbaum are being employed by the same people in London, or B-F's being employed by Peabody Finkelbaum."

"Exactly."

"Like I said, I'm afraid we're going to have to wait until Monday to find out."

"How did you get on with the dates I asked you to check?"

"The abortion clinics? Not bad. It wasn't too difficult. In the upper echelons of society here, your abortionist has to be as exclusive as your couturier or your hairdresser. I didn't take long to find the right one, but it cost a lot of money to get the information out of it."

"But you got it?"

"Yes. Here it is."

Charles handed over a sheet of paper on which he had written a few dates and ages in his neat italic hand.

I glanced at it, and smiled.

I spent most of Sunday looking at my watch. Charles and I tried to pass the time in the Metropolitan, eating lunch for a few hours and watching a movie, but it was the longest Sunday I'd ever known.

We took a cab downtown at eight o'clock Monday morning and were deposited outside an old office block a couple of streets from the Chase Manhattan building.

Charles led us in and up the elevator to the sixth floor where a brass plaque announced that it was occupied by Peabody Finkelbaum, Attorneys-at-Law. Charles knocked on a door labeled "Reception," opened it and walked in.

Inside was a large oak-paneled room. The floor was covered with one big Aubusson rug on which stood two deep-buttoned leather chesterfields and a mahogany table. Sitting behind the table was a fashionably turned out mulatto woman. She glanced at us with guarded inquiry.

"Good morning, gentlemen. Do you have business here?" She posed the question in a way that suggested she thought it unlikely.

"Yes, we do," Charles answered. "We would like to see a gentleman called Mr. Meyers."

The girl blinked before recovering herself. "There's no one of that name in this office." She gave a good, and practiced, impersonation of a stone wall.

"Mr. Meyers has some connection with this office, I can assure you," Charles said. "However, I'm quite happy to see another partner on the same matter. My name is Bullough-Ferguson."

She gave him a look which said, "No it isn't." Out loud, she said, "One moment, please." She stood and strode across the carpet, with her hips swinging, to a door in the paneling.

A moment later, she was followed back out by a man who could have fitted the description we had for Meyers, but then so could a few thousand more Wall Street lawyers.

He looked first at Charles, and showed no reaction; then at me. Only a slight narrowing of his eyes told me he had recognized me, and wasn't happy about it.

"What can I do for you gentlemen?" he asked suavely, displaying no suspicion.

"We heard that Mr. Meyers was interested in collecting unusual guns. We have some to sell, and we were given this as a contact address. We assumed he was a partner in your firm. Perhaps he's a client?" Charles suggested.

The man was working out strategy on the hoof. He took a moment to answer. "We did have a client of that name, but I'm afraid we no longer have any dealings with him nor any means of contacting him. I'm sorry, gentlemen, I can't help you." He lifted one shoulder slightly in a gesture of apology. "So I'll say good day."

He turned and left the room. The receptionist, back behind her table now, glanced at the door by which we had entered.

Charles looked at me. "That seems to be that," he said. He turned back to the girl. "Thanks so much for your help." He led the way out to the elevator lobby. I closed the door behind us.

We didn't talk until we were outside the front door of the building.

"That didn't get us too far," I said, trying not to let my annoyance get the better of me. "I didn't even get a chance to flash a picture of Kaminski in front of him."

"I can tell you now, he'd have known Kaminski, and that wouldn't have helped us."

"You're right," I said. "All we've achieved is to let them know that we're on to them."

"We'll have done more than that. They knew I wasn't B-F, they knew who you were, and they know we know about their involvement with the Purdey. They're probably certain we don't know about their connection with Kaminski, so it's just as well you didn't show them your shots. After all, they'd have thought we were mad if we'd walked straight in there knowing about their connection with him. Don't get twitchy, Jake. We'll just wait nearby quietly and watch. We'll get a cab to sit and watch the door. When that guy comes out we'll follow him."

"But we could be here all day."

"I know but I can't think of an alternative."

"Neither can I."

Charles waved a hand at a cruising yellow cab while I tried to control my impatience. When the cab stopped, we both climbed in. Charles pushed a fifty-dollar bill through the grille to the surly Hispanic at the wheel. "We'll want you for at least that long. I'll give you the same again if it runs out."

"Okay, boss. Where to first?"

"Nowhere. Stay right here for as long as you can."

"That's easier up the street a little."

"As long as we can see that doorway clearly, that's fine."

The cab driver drove the wreck of a taxi to where the parking restrictions were less stringent. If we turned right round, we could still see the portico of Peabody Finkelbaum's block. We took it in turns to watch.

We had nearly used up the fifty dollars when a stretch Mercedes drew up outside the door.

"This could be it," said Charles who was watching. I spun round in time to see the Meyers look-alike climb into the back of the limousine.

Charles turned back to the driver. "Just follow that big Mercedes," he said, as the limo swept past.

"Okay, boss." The driver rammed the gear shift into first and lurched off behind the car.

The journey ended a few blocks south of where we had set off that morning, outside one of New York's supreme hotels on Grand Army Plaza.

We went into the lobby of the hotel keeping out of sight of our quarry.

He crossed straight to a waiting empty elevator and the doors closed on him. We reached it in time to see the indicator show that it had stopped at the fifteenth floor.

Another one opened beside us. We stepped in and followed Finkelbaum up. When it came to a halt, we emerged into a long, broad corridor and a line of closed doors. A chambermaid was languidly pushing a breakfast trolley toward us.

Charles walked up to her with his best, old-fashioned English charm.

"Good morning. We're lost. We were supposed to meet someone up here, but we've forgotten the room number. Would you happen to know any of the names of the people who are staying on this floor?"

"I should. But I don't always remember them. Let's see now . . ." Her forehead puckered as she began laboriously to recite a litany of names we didn't know.

As she talked, I glanced up and down the corridor. One of the doors at the far end opened and a thickset man emerged.

My heart thumped as I spun round before he had seen my face.

"Excuse me," I said quickly, "I need the bathroom."

I didn't wait to listen to the directions the maid tried to offer. I walked as quickly as I could without running, away from the man as he approached the elevator. I rounded a corner at the end of the corridor and waited out of sight with every nerve prickling, praying that I hadn't been seen or recognized.

It was two or three minutes before I felt it was safe to rejoin Charles.

The maid had disappeared, and Charles was walking down the corridor toward me. He asked a silent question with his eyebrows.

"Has that guy gone?" I asked.

"Yes, he took the lift."

"Did he look as though he saw me?"

"Not particularly. He gave me a good look as he went by, but he didn't seem too interested. I take it you know him."

"I don't know him, but the last time I saw him was

on Oaks day at Epsom. He was with Leonard Zimmer."

"Are you certain that was the man you saw with Zimmer?" Charles asked. We were walking back to the
apartment in Sixty-Sixth Street, already sweating in the
humid air.

"Yeah, I'm sure. I saw him another time after that, in
the car when Zimmer came to Toby Ellerton's. I guess
he's some kind of a heavyweight gofer."

"If that's what he is, he wouldn't ever be far from his
boss. You must be right, then. It had to be Zimmer that
Finkelbaum went to see. So where do we go from
here?"

"Now we know who's been trying to kill me and I
think I know why."

"Sandy's abortion?"

"It has to be."

"But why the hell would he kill you for that?"

"I don't know. You'd have to ask a shrink. She told
me the fact it was a boy really wound him up. It seems
to me a lot of mega-rich people get paranoid. The richer
they are, the more insecure they become. And I think
he's been fed some disinformation by Sandy. There's no
way I could have been the father of the baby she had
aborted. The dates don't fit."

I noted Charles stiffen up a little beside me as we
approached a street intersection.

"We're going to have to duck into that bar." He
nodded at a corner diner. "Just stroll in with me as if
we're going to grab a drink and a sandwich."

We walked into one entrance, elbowed our way
through the crowd of office workers on their lunch
break and out through another entrance on the
intersecting street. We turned right and carried on turning right until we were thirty yards short of where we
had gone into the bar. Charles stopped me.

"Zimmer can't have done much of this sort of thing," he said. "He's hired a bunch of amateurs. Do you see the man who was following us?"

I saw him; a small, pale man with greasy black hair, in jeans and a baseball shirt. He was standing a few yards from the entrance to the bar, gazing at it expectantly over a copy of the *New York Post*.

"He's been onto us since we left Finkelbaum's office," Charles said.

We turned round and made our way back to the apartment, back-tracking and checking every block. When Charles was certain we had lost our tail, we went up.

"Let's have a couple of beers while we decide what we do next," Charles said.

We took our cans out to the balcony where a tiny breeze fanned some of the sweat off us.

"That tail may have lost us, but he'll be able to report back that we went to the hotel and probably made the connection with Zimmer," Charles said. "Which means Zimmer'll be going crazy by now."

"Yeah, he'll be sore as hell. He's spent a fortune on cock-ups." I laughed.

"It's not so funny, Jake. There's no way you can go and see Zimmer to confront him with the facts. You wouldn't get near enough now. He's got to find out for himself it wasn't you who got Sandy pregnant."

"Sandy's been in on Zimmer's plans, whether he knows it or not. And that's because she's protecting someone else, someone who stands to lose a lot if Zimmer finds out."

"You mean Hal Symonds?"

"I do."

"You said Sandy came back to the States last Friday. Do you know where she was going?"

"No, but I doubt if she came to New York."

"Do you know if Hal Symonds came back too?"

I shook my head. "I should have checked."

"I'll see if he's at Eagle River," Charles said. He picked up the phone and rang the American Bloodstock Breeders Association. They gave him a number for Eagle River Farm. He dialed the number.

"Could I speak to Mr. Hal Symonds?" he asked, putting on an oddly familiar voice. "It's Captain Ellerton here, from Lambourn in England."

I grinned at him. Charles spoke again. "I'll wait. I would like to speak to him."

A moment later, Charles put the phone down. "He's there."

"Then Sandy's got to be there too. From what I've seen of them together when they were alone, she's heavily into him and she doesn't want him out of her sight."

"I think our best bet is to get down there, see what's going on and then invite Zimmer down to see for himself."

Packed into an internal flight from La Guardia to Lexington, we didn't have a chance to make plans. We hired a small BMW at the airport and headed north until we found a motel a few miles from the Zimmer mansion.

I kept out of sight now that I was back near my home territory. Charles went for some take-out food which we ate in our room. My palate was so used to European cooking, I'd forgotten how highly sauced cheap American food was. It reminded me that I was within a few hours' drive of my mother and the farm where I had grown up. But I couldn't let myself think about that now, not until we'd dealt with Zimmer. And that wasn't going to be easy without some risk and a lot of luck.

The next morning, Charles went alone to Eagle River Farm. I put on my scruffiest jeans and a pair of shades to take a walk in the fresh, clean air of the Blue Grass country.

This was a different place to the Appalachian hollows where my parents came from and I'd been raised, among tobacco farms and mountain people, where wealth lay under the ground and the profits went to big city stockholders. Here in northern Kentucky, the wealth was on the surface, in the land which could grow the best grass in the United States, where a single paddock might hold several million dollars' worth of bloodstock. It was a peaceful place that felt a thousand miles from the hustle of the racetracks it supplied.

When I returned to the motel, I dragged myself back to my own particular realities, picked up the phone, and hoped that Finkelbaum was out to lunch.

My call was answered by what sounded like the handsome colored girl we had met in Peabody Finkelbaum.

In a husky, Brooklyn accent that I'd been practicing, I said, "This is Kaminski. I gotta talk to Finkelbaum."

"He's not here." The girl sounded worried.

"I gotta to talk to him, tonight. Give me his number."

"You want his home number?"

"Yeah, right."

"And you're back in New York?"

"Yeah."

"I don't think I can give you the number," she said nervously.

"Look, doll, don't fuck with me. Give me that number now, or I'll be right around to get it."

I held my breath and hoped she was scared enough of what she must have known of Kaminski.

She was. I could almost hear her shaking as she gave me the number.

Charles came back around midday.

He had gone up on spec to the Eagle River stud farm, pretending to be an English racing journalist. He

had blagued his way through the security that surrounded the place and told a large black butler that he
was doing a piece on the Kentucky studs before the big
July sales. He said he'd particularly like to speak to Mr.
Zimmer.

Mr. Zimmer was away, the butler told him.

When would he be back?

Not for at least a week, and then he wouldn't see
anyone.

Charles didn't suggest that he should see Hal Symonds, nor did the butler. But he persisted until it was
finally agreed that the head groom would show him
around.

He looked at Zimmer's twenty or so mares and the
two stallions that had recently come to stand at Eagle
River Farm and tried to ask a few intelligent questions.

He left, he thought, without raising any suspicions,
but without having seen a sign of Sandy or Hal.

"If Zimmer's not expected for a week, there's no
reason why Sandy wouldn't hang around to screw
Hal," I said. "She didn't make much attempt to disguise
what was happening when I went there last year. When
I ring Finkelbaum and tell him what's going on down
here, Zimmer will be here in as long as it takes to fly.
He has a pilot on permanent stand-by at La Guardia."

"But if Hal's supposed to be running the stud, it
wouldn't be so odd if he was there."

"We'll just have to lay a scent for Zimmer and hope
he responds to it," I said.

"And we'll have to make sure there's something for
him to find when he gets there."

///////////// CHAPTER 16

Charles and I lay in the long grass beneath a stand of newly planted maples, looking down on the placid lake in front of Zimmer's mansion.

The setting sun lit the place like a bizarre backdrop in a fairytale movie. In the year since I'd been there, I'd forgotten the overstated grandness of the house. Zimmer's architect must have employed every classical device in the catalogue to assert his client's importance. It was a kind of Disneyland orgy of Palladian ostentation. Seeing it in this context, as an extension of Zimmer's vast, uncertain ego, it made sense.

Panning my gaze across the lake and over my right shoulder, I saw the small, English folly—a round, domed temple—where Sandy and I had cavorted that hot summer morning.

I turned again to watch her now, down on the lake in an elegant Edwardian skiff with Hal Symonds. The boat had been there when we arrived, so I could only assume that Hal had rowed them out, although that seemed like too gallant an act for him.

We had managed to walk a mile from the far end of the park unnoticed by farm workers and stud staff on the way. Our plan was still only half formed. It depended on what we found. So far, at least we knew that Hal and Sandy were around and didn't look as though they were going anywhere soon. Beyond that, we were relying on my past experience of Sandy's voracious libido.

"At some point, they've got to end up in bed together," I murmured.

"If Hal still has the energy," Charles answered. "All I can see now is a rocking boat and his naked arse."

"Is it his?" I asked. "I can't tell from here."

"It doesn't matter whose arse it is," Charles said. "Just look at the ripples spreading out from the boat. They're not playing Ludo in there."

"I hope he's fit and capable of rapid recovery. I don't want to hang about here all night waiting for them to go to bed and start again."

"From what you've told me, Mrs. Zimmer's rather good at arousal techniques."

"Don't talk about it. It gives me a hard-on just thinking about it. But I don't know if this is going to work. Even if we can identify which room they're in, I don't see how you can get up there without setting off the security."

"I can get up the outside of that building, no trouble. They won't have the alarms on in the bedroom, and probably the windows will be open. Getting out again may be tricky. I may just have to hang around until morning and take my chance then. But don't worry about that. Once they're in the room, I'll keep them there; you call Finkelbaum and tell him what's going on, and when Zimmer gets here, he can draw his own conclusions."

The boat stopped rocking as the sun finally dropped below the tree-covered ridge behind us. We watched Hal row back in the gloom, and heard the faint sound of Sandy's laughter drift up to us on the breeze.

We waited two more hours, growing less confident of the plan we'd made, more aware of the security arrangements that protected the perimeter of the park as well as the house itself. But it seemed a sound assumption that sooner or later, Sandy and Hal would be going to bed. We watched lights come on and go off in the ground floor of the house as they moved from room to room. But no lights shone on the first floor where I knew the main bedrooms were all along that west front, with the best views of the park.

The crickets were trilling and frogs down on the lake were belching quietly in the warm night air.

"What the hell are they doing?" Charles asked. "Could they be having it off on the drawing-room floor?"

"More than likely," I said, "but they'll go to bed sooner or later. Sandy likes her comforts too much to sleep on the floor."

"If she ever goes to sleep."

Suddenly, another light appeared on the façade of the house. It was the oblong shape of the front door behind its tall, Corinthian columns.

"Oh no! They're coming out again," Charles groaned as we saw two figures, just identifiable as male and female, walk down the steps and across the sweep of gravel in front.

Then the dark swallowed them up. We strained for sounds above the crickets. Five minutes later we were rewarded with a guttural burst of a big bike's engine, followed by the sight of its headlight sweeping round from the carriage block behind the house.

The bike sped along the drive beside the lake, then turned abruptly and started to bounce and jerk across the newly landscaped turf, its light reflecting wildly off the surface of the lake.

"Christ, they're coming up here," I said, suddenly thinking that we had been discovered.

Charles didn't reply for a moment, until it was obvious the bike was carrying on round the lakeside.

"No, they're not, but where the hell are they going?"

"I know! Up to the temple. Sandy and I went up there last year. It must be one of her favorite rutting sites."

"Perfect!" Charles said. "Let's go, then."

We ran down the slope in the light of a slender moon. The bike ahead of us was bucking and jerking up the long grass ride toward the circular English folly at the top. When it reached it, four hundred yards before us, we slowed to a walk. The bike stopped and the engine was turned off. A moment later, a light shone out from the small stone building's one doorway.

"What does that place have by way of windows?" Charles asked.

"As far as I can remember, none, just those double glass doors at the front, and they've got a heavy pair of outside shutters on them. I had to open them last year."

"That sounds very promising," Charles whispered.

We carried on walking as quietly as we could until we were within fifty yards of the temple.

We could see the double glass doors open, and a light shining brightly from the circular room within. The faint sound of a country music station drifted across the grass toward us.

We crept up, outside the shaft of light, until we could see one side of the room—the wrong one. I remembered there was a kind of Greek divan on the opposite side.

We worked our way round the back of the building,

stopping when the song finished. When the music started again and we were sure we hadn't been heard, we sidled on round so that we could see into the other side.

Sandy and Hal were stretched out, half-clothed, on the deep-seated Grecian sofa. In front of them on a low table was an ornate silver Moroccan hookah. Hal was clutching the mouthpiece. He drew up a deep draught of cannabis smoke, lay back and handed the pipe to Sandy. She took a suck before dropping it on the floor beside her.

Charles and I backed away and round to the side of the building.

"They're away," whispered Charles. "We'll give them a little longer to get seriously stoned."

I didn't find it easy, waiting out there, listening to the sounds of lovemaking above the music.

"Do we have to wait till they've finished?" I asked impatiently.

"No," said Charles. "Let's get on with it."

We worked our way round to a point where we had a clear view into the single room, without being visible from within.

"Good God!" Charles said under his breath. "They are going at it!"

They were.

Hal and Sandy were both naked now. Their bodies were entwined, twisting and thrusting. I could almost feel the waves of sensual pleasure they were giving off. It was my first experience as a voyeur; I was alarmed at how much I was enjoying it.

"Shit!" I whispered to Charles. "I can't stand this much longer. Let's get them locked in there and call Zimmer. Or maybe we should take their clothes first."

"No. Wait. What we've got to do is photograph them, now, like that. Where's your Polaroid?"

"Shit!" Guiltily, I told him. "I forgot to bring it. It's still in the car."

Charles controlled himself. "Oh. That's a shame," he understated. "A few shots of them like that would clinch it for us."

"If I know Sandy, they'll be there a while, and Hal looks as though he can keep up. I'll go back and get the camera. I could do it in fifteen minutes."

"No. I'll find my way better than you. You stay here."

"Okay," I agreed and watched Charles melt into the night and the trees on the far side of the temple.

I looked back at the sexual feast going on in the folly and gratefully found my thoughts turning to Milly. I didn't want to go on watching these two. I turned and sank deeper into the shadows and sat down with my back to an old oak, looking out across the park and the lake in the moonlight.

I could still hear the music and intermittent sounds of pleasure from behind me. I'd know soon enough if they were making plans to go.

If only Zimmer could turn up now, I thought.

But I knew it would need the call to Finkelbaum to get him there, and that could take anything up to three hours from central Manhattan. Maybe the cannabis would do its stuff and keep the couple fornicating in the temple until dawn. Meanwhile, I'd just have to be vigilant.

Some vigil!

I let my thoughts drift back to England, to what I knew I had waiting for me there, once Zimmer had been dealt with.

Now that I was so close to confrontation with the man who had ordered my hounding over the past two months, I was almost relaxed. At least it would all be over soon.

A sound from the black wall of trees, ten yards to my left, roused me with a prickle of fright.

It was no animal noise. It wouldn't be Charles, not yet; not from that direction.

I looked and could see nothing. Quickly, with my heart pumping, I got to my feet and sidled round into the cover of the broad old tree trunk.

I took a deep breath.

A hand was clapped over my mouth. An arm like a steel hawser wrapped round my waist, pinning my arms to my sides. I was lifted off my feet, tilted on my side and carried.

I struggled; my legs flailed uselessly in the air. I guessed the man who had me was twice my size and used to the job. I couldn't see where we were going but we must have covered a hundred yards or more before we stopped.

"What you got?" a voice in the darkness whispered hoarsely.

"I caught me a little prowler, no more'n a boy, I shouldn't think. Takin' a peek at Mrs. Zimmer's private life in the temple."

The other voice gave a chortle. "Bring him on down to the barn. We'll take a look at him there."

I was gasping breaths up through my nose, smelling the hard, oily hand still clamped across my mouth. It was going to be a waste of time and energy to struggle. When he whipped me off my feet again, I didn't resist.

We came out from the trees and down the grassy slope toward the lake, before bearing off toward the stud buildings a quarter of a mile to the north of the house.

I could just make out the second man a few paces in front of us now, leading the way. When we reached the buildings, he opened a door and let me and my abductor through into a small office.

At last the hand was removed from my mouth, I was dumped into a chair and I could see the two men for the first time.

They were both of them big, at least twice my weight

and built for action. From their battered faces, I judged
they had seen plenty of that in their time. I'd already
guessed they were security guards of some kind, not so
uncommon on a valuable stud, especially in the
grounds of a man like Leonard Zimmer. I had the impression they were pleased with this opportunity to
demonstrate their *raison d'être*.

"That ain't a boy, Dan. It's some kind of goddamn
midget."

"Who the hell are you? What you doin' here?" asked
Dan, the man who had carried me.

"I came to see Mr. Zimmer," I said.

Both men laughed aloud. "You thought you'd find
him up there, fornicatin' in the temple with Mrs. Zimmer?" Dan guffawed. "He'd like that if we was to tell
him."

"Why don't you?"

"Maybe we will. Let's see who you are first."

There wasn't anything I could do to stop him grab-
bing hold of me again while the other gorilla went
through my pockets.

"Looky here. He's brought his driver's license with
him. Jake Felton, from West Virginia. You don't sound
much like an Appalachian. What the hell are you doin'
here?"

"I came to see Mr. Zimmer."

Dan, who was the larger of the two and, I guessed,
the senior, abruptly lost his joviality.

"Now, boy. That's enough. You ain't come to see the
old man, we know that. You just tell us why you was
prowling before we have to beat it out of you."

"I told you."

Dan replied with a monster fist. He buried it in my
guts.

Every ounce of breath exploded from my lungs. I
collapsed forward, toppled off the chair, gasping, swimming in a red and yellow sea. I lay doubled up on the

floor aching with the shock of the blow, when that was compounded by a brutal kick in the back of my ribs.

"Dan, maybe we should get some more out of him first. Maybe we should call Zimmer, or Finkelbaum."

"Nope. A little guy like this, he'll be something on the racetrack, maybe workin' for a trainer or some such. Maybe they're planning to steal a horse."

"If he knows Zimmer, and we get it wrong, the old man'll have our asses. We gotta call him."

"If we call him, and he comes down, he's goin' to find Mrs. Zimmer up there with Hal, and all hell'll break loose. She's paid us a lot of money to keep the lid on her fornicatin'."

"So, we can tell her. The bitch'll have plenty of time to clean up before he gets down, if he comes."

"Okay. I'll ring Zimmer. Here, you keep this little bastard on the ground."

He walked across to a desk, picked up a phone and dialed.

"Hello, it's Dan Wright, security at Eagle River Farm. I gotta talk to Mr. Zee. I know it's past midnight in New York. But we've caught us a little fella sneakin' round, says he wants to talk to Mr. Zimmer . . . Hello, Mr. Zimmer, sir. This is security at Eagle River. We got a guy here, calls himself Jake Felton. Says he—" Dan stopped mid-sentence, listening hard.

I'd recovered my breath enough to look up from the floor where I lay. Zimmer was obviously still talking. After a minute or so, I saw a smile spread across Dan's face.

"Right, Mr. Zimmer. We'll do that. No problem. Goodbye, sir." He put the phone down, pleased with himself.

"You wanted to see Mr. Zimmer? You're in luck. Mr. Zimmer wants to see you." He grinned down at me. "He don't want you killed just yet. First he wants to see you, punish you a little bit. You know what they say in the Bible—if your hand offendeth, cut it off! Hey, Joe, I ain't done that to no one since 'Nam."

"Hell, Dan, who is this guy?"

"I don't know, but he ain't no friend of Mr. Zee's. We gotta peg him out somewhere. I know!" A big, nasty smile spread across his face. "The covering shed, where the stallions get their dicks out."

My head was spinning.

I couldn't take in what I was hearing. The whole scene was a crazy nightmare.

Why the hell had Charles suggested we come here? We walked right into it, and had nothing to show.

Now Zimmer had me right where he'd been wanting me; pegged out—ready for what? Castration? Or worse? I knew he was an eccentric, obsessed old man. But just how mad could he get?

The two guards, Dan and Joe, grabbed me by an arm each, lifted me and swung me like a school bag between them.

They carried me out of their pokey little office and into the barn situated between lines of stables. Over some of the doors, the heads of well-bred mares gazed at me with untroubled eyes.

I didn't even try to struggle. In the dark confusion of my mind, I still knew that I had two or three hours before Zimmer arrived. I was sure to have a better chance than now to escape from these gorillas and whatever treatment they were proposing.

They carried me through the far door of the barn, out into the night air, and across a dimly lit yard to a hexagonal brick building, about thirty feet wide. Inside, Dan switched on lights which flooded the wood-chip-filled arena where the stallions and mares were brought together to mate.

I was dropped like a sack on the soft surface.

Dan pulled a small automatic from a pocket of his leather jacket and pointed at me with a happy smile on his face.

"Joe," he said, "go get some cord and four of them iron fence pegs."

He didn't take his eyes off me for a moment, not even when Joe came back with a length of blue nylon cord and some angle-iron pegs about two feet long. He had also brought a large mallet.

"Okay, Jake," Dan said, sounding like an instructor on a kids' summer camp, "just lie back and spread your arms and your legs so's Joe can place the pegs comfortable for you."

I didn't move. I didn't want to and I couldn't.

Dan's eyes hardened. He gave me a nasty leer and prodded the air with the muzzle of his gun.

"Didn't you hear me, boy?"

He wasn't going to shoot me, though, I knew that—not before Zimmer got here. I didn't move.

"You help him, Joe."

The junior heavyweight dropped on one knee beside me, heaved my shoulders to the ground, took my arms and lay them at right angles to my body. When he'd done that, he moved round, grasped my ankles and shoved them until they were a yard apart.

I pulled my arms back in and raised my torso to look at him. He glanced up. I saw him bunch his fist.

It felt as if a rocket had exploded in my face. I felt the crunch and squelch of cartilage breaking in my nose as my head jerked back. I saw a flash of kaleidoscopic red and orange and my head thumped onto the firm soft-ness of the sawdust floor.

Amidst the sudden excruciating pain, I licked my battered lips and tasted blood and phlegm. Any idea of fighting back had left me.

I didn't open my eyes this time my wrists were grabbed and pulled out across the floor. I felt the metal of the iron pegs as they were hammered deep into the substrata of the flooring. Only when I knew each of my limbs was stretched and pegged so I lay pinned like a misshapen star did I open my eyes toward the glazed cupola in the center of the hexagonal roof.

"Comfortable, boy? Mr. Zee's going to be mighty happy to see you like this. What have you done to make him so mad at you?"

I heard, but I didn't answer.

I couldn't lift my head to see them, my face still throbbed from the impact of Joe's fist and the cool of the night air was beginning to seep into my stretched body. It was hard to think, hard to care what happened next.

I couldn't tell how long it was before I saw the first signs of day through the glazed skylight above me. I hadn't slept; I hadn't lost consciousness. Once or twice I had tried to wriggle my wrists and ankles in the cord that bound them. That achieved no more than a painful chafing of my skin and bruising of thin flesh.

And each time I moved, I brought forth a growl from one or other of my captors. I couldn't tell which of them was there but they hadn't left me on my own for a moment or allowed me any opportunity for the initiatives I had hoped for earlier; initiatives which, anyway, I no longer had the urge to take. I had been lying there for what must have been close on four hours. Every muscle in my body screamed for relief, aching with the unnatural stretching they had endured.

Shortly after dawn, Zimmer arrived.

"Sounds like Mr. Zee," Joe said, as a car pulled up. There was a bustle as he and Dan prepared themselves for his entrance.

"D'you hear that?" Dan asked me. "No more waitin'."

I heard people, two or three, come in from the yard. I strained my neck forward to see them.

There was Zimmer, and the man I had seen with him

at Epsom. Hanging behind him was another, similarly proportioned guard, and Finkelbaum.

"What the hell is he doing like that?" Zimmer growled.

"I thought you said you wanted us to cut his pecker off, Mr. Zimmer."

"I want to talk to him first. Then you can get rid of him."

With grunts of regret, the two gorillas cut me loose. Gradually, life and comfort throbbed back into my tortured limbs. I lay on my back for a while, savoring the luxury of movement.

"Bring him into the office," I heard Zimmer order. I looked up to see him and most of his entourage walk from the building.

Not Dan and Joe. They stayed to heave me up between them once more and carry me after their boss.

In the fetid atmosphere of the guards' small den, Zimmer was waiting. His old, bent nose was wrinkled in distaste at the smell of stale tobacco smoke and rancid burger fat. If he had granted a stay of execution, from the abomination in his pale, colorless eyes, I judged it was only a temporary stay, and not out of compassion or mercy. I was also conscious of being in the presence of an extraordinary personal power, though I couldn't tell if it was inherent or a product of my awareness of Zimmer's mega-wealth.

"Vermin!" He spat the word from his eyes and his dry, lipless mouth. "Like a rat, crawling out to scavenge, to thieve from better men. What are you? Nothing! A farm boy who can ride a horse, like a performing flea!" His American English was tainted by guttural, mid-European consonants. "You must be mad to come here." As he talked, he took a few paces toward me, until I could smell his sour breath and feel specks of his spittle on my face.

I wanted to back away, from the spit and the venom. But I stood my ground.

"You're wrong." I forced the words from my aching throat. "I'm not your poacher."

Zimmer laughed. There was a moment's insanity in his cackle. "You must be mad," he said again, shaking his head. "I've been wanting you for months. And what happens? You come to pay a call on me." He laughed some more. "So now I can deal with you personally."

I looked at him as steadily as I could, knowing that the moment I showed my fear, I would lose all chance of his listening to me. I needed all the bluff I could raise not to flinch from the fear and disgust I felt.

"It wasn't my baby."

Zimmer's eyes blazed. "Of course you say that! You think I'm just going to say, 'Oh, that's okay, then, forget it?' Are you going to tell me you didn't sleep with her?" His voice rose in volume and pitch. "That you didn't screw her like a mongrel dog in a farmyard? Cocky, pretty little jockey, think you can have who you want? Not from me you don't."

"It wasn't my baby," I said quietly. "It couldn't have been. It was aborted at twelve weeks—fifteen weeks after I saw her. I could prove to any court in the world it wasn't mine."

"I don't care about any fucking courts!" Zimmer's eyes were protruding from their sockets. "She told me it was you!" For the first time, he touched me; a bony finger stabbed my chest. "And nobody, nohow steals my treasures, uses that beautiful temple to propagate their filthy seed." He paused and sucked in a deep rasping breath. The anger in his eyes was replaced by bleak, deep misery. "I wanted her to have *my* child, my *son*. A boy like me to grow into a man who can do things, make empires, lead men." He focused on me again. "And she conceives a boy by nothing more than a midget!"

"She lied to you, Zimmer," I said. "I was nothing to her, totally expendable to her. She was protecting someone else."

"There was no one else! She swore to me!"

"She lied to you."

"She wouldn't. She knows I can give her everything she wants. She loves me for that."

"And who'll be able to give her everything she wants when you've gone? Who gets your money when you've gone?"

"There's no one else. You're just trying to save your own miserable little life."

"By coming here? To see you? I'm saving you too. Do you know why your wife came back here from London?"

"What are you talking about? She's still in London."

"Didn't anyone tell you? Didn't she tell you? Ask these gorillas if she's here." I indicated Dan with a jerk of my head.

"Is she?" Zimmer spat.

"Er . . . yessir."

"See how honest she is, Zimmer. She didn't want to tell you because she wanted to be with your nephew."

"Hal? Don't be crazy. He wouldn't do that. He knows I'd kill him if he did."

"That's why Sandy told you to kill me. If you don't believe me, and you kill me, all they have to do is be very careful and wait for you to die. Even you can't dodge death."

It got home. At last, doubt and misery flooded his eyes. But he still wanted to fight the idea.

"You . . . you're just making all this up, to save yourself. You used my wife's body to plant your own seed. It's time for you to pay!"

"She's duped you, Zimmer." I was more confident now. "She's made an old fool out of you, and so has your sister's son, your only living relative. You kill me, and one day they'll be dancing on your grave."

Zimmer fell silent for a moment. His eyes, uncertain, slid from mine. "You," he said to Finkelbaum who hovered in the doorway. "Get Dexter on the phone, then get back up to the house and check this jockey's dates."

Finkelbaum stepped across to the phone and punched some numbers. He waited until his call was answered, then handed the phone to Zimmer, before slipping out of the room.

Zimmer grabbed the phone and barked into it, "This is Zimmer. Is Mrs. Zimmer there? Is that so? And where is Mr. Hal? He is? Okay. Tell Mrs. Zimmer I want to see her, now in the great hall." He slammed the phone down and glanced at me. But he gave nothing away this time. Whatever emotions he'd been nursing, he'd brought them back under control. "Bring him to the house," he snapped at his guards, and they parted in front of him as he left the stuffy little room.

I was frog-marched outside in time to see Zimmer being swept away in the maroon Rolls which had brought Sandy and me here the previous summer. I was piled into a Jeep, which Dan roared up the road to the mansion. The house lay with its back to the rising sun, above a sea of mist which hung over the lake. In this light, it almost achieved the impression of grandeur and serenity for which its architect had probably aimed. It did little to reassure me though.

I guessed that Dan or Joe had been to warn Sandy and Hal of Zimmer's coming, and any signs of her infidelity would have been concealed or destroyed by now. I wondered where Charles was, and what he had been doing. If he had been caught like me, I would probably have heard some mention of it by now. All I was sure of was that I had cast doubt about Sandy in Zimmer's mind, and as long as I could keep that doubt alive, I'd keep myself alive. If not, he'd already made clear his wish to see me dead. If he still wished it, there would be no chance of failure this time.

I was hustled out of the Jeep and up one side of the double sweep of stone steps to the colonnaded entrance to the house.

Inside the hall, heavy with oak furniture which didn't match the architecture, I was kept standing between Joe and Hawkins, the man I had first seen at Epsom on Oaks day. There was no sign of Zimmer.

After a few minutes, Sandy appeared in a white silk dressing gown, fresh and flushed, at the top of the wide, shallow stairs that curved down gracefully from a gallery above. Beside her was an enormous black man, like a one-time heavyweight boxer and wearing perfect English morning dress. He drove her before him, without touching her. But when she saw me, she almost stopped dead, before recovering herself and reaching the bottom where she swept past without another glance.

I watched her go through a high, paneled mahogany door which closed behind her.

Nobody spoke out here in the hall. I glanced at the faces of the men on either side of me, but they told me nothing.

I had to wait ten more minutes before the door opened and Finkelbaum beckoned us in.

I was marched through into a cavernous medieval hall that looked as if it had been transported and dropped inappropriately within the neoclassical shell of the house. Suits of armor stood guard on each side of a vast open fireplace. Facing the fire, twenty feet back from it, was a tall upholstered throne of a chair. Sandy stood facing it, frightened and defiant. Zimmer sat in it, a wrinkled old King Lear, radiating rage like a wounded beast of prey.

He turned and stared silently at me.

After ten or fifteen seconds, he spoke. "You almost convinced me, jockey," he said. "I know my wife is not a saint, but you almost got me thinking that maybe she was a fool as well. Do you think she's a fool?"

"I think she's . . . a woman," I ventured.

"In my experience, women are pragmatic beings, once they're past puberty. I trust that pragmatism more than I trust a jockey trying to save his life."

I was going to have to come up with something good, and fast. But Sandy was holding all the cards. Maybe.

"Ask your men here what your wife was doing, right in front of this house, on the lake yesterday evening."

Zimmer shrugged and turned to Dan and Joe, beside me. "Well?"

"Mr. Hal took her for a row, sir," said Joe.

"That's all?" Zimmer snapped.

"Yessir," Joe lied.

Zimmer turned to the black major-domo. "Dexter, what did you see?"

"I wasn't lookin' out of the window at that time, sir." Dexter, I judged, was telling the truth.

"I don't say I like the idea, but I don't really think I can chastise my wife for rowing on the lake, do you, jockey? I'm a man who likes to look at all angles of a situation before I make a decision. I've looked at yours, and I think I've seen enough of it. Now I've made my decision."

Zimmer was interrupted by a clamorous clanging of bells from the front hall. He glanced at Dexter.

"See who the hell that is."

Dexter gave a nod and swept his graceful bulk from the room.

It was barely six o'clock in the morning. Even an eccentric like Zimmer would be aware that it was early for casual callers. We waited in silence for a few moments before Dexter came back into the room, ushering Charles Powell before him.

Finkelbaum looked at him with surprise and concern.

Charles glanced at me, but gave no sign of recognition.

Zimmer glowered at him angrily. "Who the hell are you?"

Charles was completely unfazed by his reception. "Are you Leonard Zimmer?" he asked.

Zimmer didn't think that was worth answering. "I said who the hell are you?"

"My name's Charles Powell. I'm a photographer. I've got some lovely pictures of your wife which I thought you might like to buy."

Sandy turned sharply and stared at him with horrified misgiving.

In Zimmer, too, I saw reluctant foreboding.

"What are you talking about? Pictures? At six in the morning?"

"I thought these might interest you. I only took them a few hours ago." He put his hand to the inside pocket of the Harris tweed jacket he wore and pulled out a clutch of Polaroid photographs. He walked from the door across to Zimmer's chair and stopped in front of him. He held out the photos to the old man, who grabbed them before Sandy's terrified eyes.

Zimmer glanced at the first photograph. I saw his bony fingers suddenly tighten their grasp as he looked up from under his heavy brow at his wife.

"Who's she with?" he wheezed.

"I managed to get some quite nice shots of her partner," Charles said, sounding like a society photographer after a wedding sitting. "They're a little further down. Of course, they would have been even clearer if I had been able to use a flash, but I couldn't really ask permission."

Zimmer started to look through the rest of the pictures. He groaned at each new confirmation of what he had dreaded to believe. The color drained from his face until it was a muddy cream.

When he reached the last shot, he looked at Sandy, who was immobile now, a rabbit hypnotized by a snake, gazing in horror at the pictures in her husband's hands.

"You bitch!" Zimmer breathed. "You do this here? With my nephew? How can you? When I've given you everything you ever wanted."

"Except pleasure," Sandy fought back now. "You just wanted to look at me, to own me!"

"I wanted you to have *my* son, not his." He stabbed a finger at a photograph of Hal's naked body.

"It wasn't his, I swear," Sandy pleaded desperately.

"Finkelbaum already checked," Zimmer snarled. "The dates are in the jockey's favor. I didn't want to give him the benefit of the doubt, but now, I believe him. These pictures aren't lying to me, are they?" His voice had grown into a harsh rasping shout. He thrust one of the photographs under his wife's nose. "Are they?"

Sandy looked, and recoiled with her face in her hands.

Zimmer sprang to his feet, scattering the photographs, and confronted her. He forced her hands from her face and grabbed her throat in his long fingers. "You were just going to wait for me to die, weren't you? OR MAYBE YOU WERE PLANNING TO BRING THE DATE FORWARD!" He began to shake Sandy. Her lustrous blue eyes bulged from her skull; her face turned livid. "Don't! You're killing me!" she choked. Without waiting to think why, I stepped forward and grasped Zimmer by his shoulders.

"Stop! Killing her won't solve anything. Get off her!" I dragged him back until his hands released the bruised and slender neck. It was easy, then, to pull him right away. I pushed him back into his chair, where he glowered at me uncertainly.

Dexter and the bodyguards looked on with approval. Sandy had collapsed onto a tall, Knole sofa.

Zimmer turned to stare at Sandy, hunched in the sofa, defeated, stripped of her weapons for the moment. He looked smaller, more withered, but still defiant. "I would like the whole world to know what a slut you are," he hissed at her.

Her head jerked up. "They won't care; they won't

believe it," she said. "They'll just say you were another old man who couldn't satisfy his wife."

I saw Zimmer tremble. He started to lift himself from the chair, then sank back.

"Get her out of here," he said to no one in particular. Hawkins and Dan stepped across to where she lay. Before they picked her up, she whispered, "What are you going to do with me?"

"You can get out of here, and take Hal with you. You probably won't want him so much now he doesn't have any money. Or maybe you can go back to wiggling your naked butt at dirty little men in London. You're going to have to find some way of making a living."

Sandy's eyes blazed as heavy hands descended toward her. "Don't think you can throw me out like that, you miserable old bastard! You had the Irish jockey shot, have you forgotten? By some bungling asshole acting on your instructions. I've got plenty to tell the British police about that."

"They can't touch me for that, dumb bitch! You were more involved than I was. You go tell them what you like."

"Now, Mr. Zimmer," Finkelbaum spoke for the first time, showing his panic, "Mrs. Zimmer's right."

"Shut up, Finkelbaum. She can't tell them a thing without incriminating herself. The only person we have to worry about is Felton." His eyes bore in on me. "But I think maybe we can do a deal with him."

"Maybe," I said.

Charles raised his eyebrows.

"Or maybe we get rid of him and this photographer now."

"You could do that, Mr. Zimmer," Charles said, "but then I wouldn't be able to get back to New York to pick up the other pictures. I mailed them, with a great story, to the Travelers' Club, to be passed on to a friend of mine at UPI if they aren't collected, by me personally, in the next twenty-four hours."

"It's okay, I was joking," Zimmer growled, and then he smiled. "You've done me a big favor. You just cured me of the worst piece of judgment I ever made in my life." He let out a great bellow of laughter that seemed to emanate from a far bigger body than his. He stood up and held out his hands to me in appeasement. "Will you accept my apologies for trying to kill you?" He bellowed with laughter again, and waited for me to take his hand.

I paid our bill at the motel, and Charles and I headed back down to Lexington in the BMW.

"Do you know, for a few hours last night, I thought I was dead," I said. "It was an interesting experience. Nothing has ever made me appreciate what I've got so much."

"And it's probably taught you not to sleep with other men's wives," Charles added.

"Maybe." I smiled. There weren't any other men's wives I wanted to sleep with right then.

"But I still can't see why you don't want to tell the police in England what happened here," Charles said more seriously.

"Okay, I know they killed Mick, but even if they ever got to Zimmer, which I doubt, that wouldn't bring Mick back. And it would mess up other plans I have."

"I think I'd want to get even with someone who'd tried to kill me six times," Charles said. "But I suppose that's up to you."

"I kind of feel it doesn't matter now," I said, trying to establish just what I did feel. "You see, I think Sandy drove old Zimmer insane with jealousy. And like you said, I was in the wrong; I slept with another man's wife. And I actually quite like the old bastard now, and I feel sort of sorry for him."

" 'When mercy seasons justice,' " Charles quoted, and shrugged his shoulders. "I suppose one shouldn't argue with that. Though personally I don't see Zimmer as one of life's natural recipients of mercy. I wonder what he'll do to Sandy and Hal. I shouldn't think he'll show them much mercy."

"Who knows?"

///////////// CHAPTER 17

Zimmer was in the Rolls that arrived to take me to Sandown.

I climbed into the back and saw him crouching in the corner, gazing at me from the gloom. His small, sharp eyes gleamed like a cat's.

I sat down beside him, sinking back into the soft woolen upholstery. The chauffeur clunked the door shut, got back into his seat and the car began to creep up my drive.

We swept through the open gates and out into the lane. We had left the boundary of my land before Zimmer spoke.

"I was very disappointed you couldn't ride my horse in the Eclipse today," he said.

"I'm sorry about that, Mr. Zimmer, but I had to take

322 / John Francome

the ride on Dawn Raider after losing the chance in the Derby."

"In the circumstances, I didn't feel I could insist that Captain Ellerton should claim you," Zimmer said. "But I wanted you to win this race for me; I felt it would be fitting. So, I bought Dawn Raider."

I felt my jaw drop.

I didn't know what the income of Dawn Raider's previous owner was, but I guessed it gushed out of the sand at a few million dollars a day; and I knew he was very proud of Dawn Raider and convinced that he would win today's race and have a great chance in the Prix de l'Arc de Triomphe at Longchamps in October.

"Jesus!" I blurted. "What did you pay for him?"

It was a naive question.

Zimmer smiled. "He wasn't cheap. But I'm going to need a good stallion for my mares in Kentucky, so, what the hell."

Not cheap! I couldn't imagine Sheikh Ahmed letting him go at any price, and even then Zimmer would have had to have pulled a few extra strings.

"I didn't think you were even interested in the horses, Mr. Zimmer," I said.

"I wasn't particularly. As I guess you know, it was my ex-wife who introduced them. But now that she's left, I thought I'd take a little interest in them myself. I have been an abject failure at breeding my own progeny; the idea of trying to produce a perfect horse is maybe more realistic."

I hadn't thought he was going to raise the subject of Sandy, but since he had, I asked what I'd been wanting to know since I had last seen her, cowering in the corner of the sofa a week before.

"She left?"

Zimmer nodded. If he felt any remorse or regret, he wasn't showing it. He laughed. "Relative values are fascinating. I gave her the same amount to go as I paid the Arab for Dawn Raider."

"Expensive week," I remarked fatuously.

Zimmer shrugged. "Loose change, that's all. But the week's not over, Jake, I owe you, too."

He owed me all right, but I started to protest.

He waved me down with a firm, wrinkled hand. "I owe you. You faced me out last week. I guess you had the chance and every reason to want to get me indicted. But you didn't. Maybe you're right; maybe it's better to understand and forgive than to seek revenge. Especially when you could never have made anything stick," he added, chortling.

"What did you do about Hal Symonds?" I asked.

"Hal will be reading an announcement in the *Wall Street Journal* this morning which I think will spoil his breakfast. He won't be sending me birthday cards any more. But you, I have to settle up with you."

I looked at him. Was he really thinking he could salve his conscience of everything he had perpetrated against me with a check? Maybe I'd be helping him if I let him.

"You can do one small thing for me today," I said. "You can put ten thousand pounds on a filly called Rock Beat in the second race. Try and get as much as you can on with a bookie called Harry Devene."

"Sure," Zimmer said, "but back in the States they all say you were too honest to bet, that you were the straightest jockey in America, and that's why you came here."

"Is that what they say? Well, you put that bet on for me, and if it wins, you can have the stake back."

Zimmer shook his head. "It's lucky you don't ride the same way you handle your personal finances."

There, he was probably right.

The car park was already filling up when we arrived at Sandown. There would be a big crowd for the Eclipse, the first major race of the season where the four-year-old Classic crop met the younger generation. For once, Toby Ellerton wasn't having a bet; he was counting on Zimmer sending Dawn Raider back to his yard. When I saw him, I thought I'd let him know the odds on that happening had shortened a little.

"I've told Zimmer I'll only be able to ride Dawn Raider again if he's trained at Melbourne House," I said.

Toby beamed at me and for an awful moment I thought he was going to hug me, but he stopped himself in time.

I saw Smethwick, smirking at Rock Beat's price of 3/1. It was a shame, I thought, that I was going to have to give this man his punishment some other day. Today, I was as certain as I could be, his filly was going to win.

I gave the tip to Charles Powell who was there, and Fred and Bolton Pickering whom I'd invited down from Yorkshire for the day's races. I told them to be sure to get their bets on before Zimmer's hit the bookies and bounced the price down to nothing. There was some small satisfaction in knowing that Smethwick thought Rock Beat's price would drift in the face of two hot favorites and he'd put his money on at SP.

I managed a few moments alone with Charles before the filly's race.

"How's Zimmer?" he asked.

"Sort of remorseful. He's relieved he instructed that Finkelbaum; it was Finkelbaum who recruited Bullough-Ferguson. All those crazy ideas were B-F's. Zimmer had said he wanted me humiliated and killed, but B-F had the idea to try and lay a false trail to Mick Hagan, getting Devene to lean on him and presenting him with the chance to make a lot of money selling my gun back to me. It was all kind of clumsy, but I suppose it might have worked."

"If you hadn't had the luck of nine cats."

"Luck?" I laughed. "It was constant vigilance and your resourcefulness."

"And your Yorkshire friend, Bolton Pickering."

"You've met him, have you?"

"Yes. He and his father are up with Bunty Fielding having the time of their lives. He told me that Kaminski was deported yesterday for carrying a false passport and you've still got a small bill outstanding for his stay in Yorkshire."

"No. That's been waived. I've told him to back Rock Beat."

I left Charles and headed for the changing room to get ready. Later, as I walked back to the paddock with the other jockeys, it crossed my mind that if Rock Beat didn't win, I wasn't going to be the most popular person on the course. I watched her being led into the parade ring. Her long, effortless stride restored my confidence. So did her lively fidgeting as we jigged down between the rhododendron wall and the stands to get to the course. She was obviously feeling very pleased with herself, and as her lad let us go onto the course, she prickled her ears, took a hold of the bit and bounded away.

At the start, we were three off the far rail in stall ten. When the gates sprang apart, Rock Beat came out running for her life. I called up every ounce of my experience and knowledge to settle her and conserve her strength and was thankful for the early uphill climb. We had covered a furlong before I was sure she was doing what I wanted. I'd managed to keep her from hitting the front and she was lying a length or so behind the two leaders. That was perfect. She was wasting no energy by straining for more speed or fighting me. I let her settle and stayed where we were until I asked her to get about her business, one and a half furlongs from home.

I didn't just ask, I pleaded and I prayed. I let the filly know that reaching the post first was the most important thing in the world to me right then; and I made damn sure this time she had plenty of warning.

Just as I had at Ascot, I experienced a moment's

panic between pressing the button and getting the response. But then she answered with a breathtaking surge of speed as she stretched her legs further and faster and we swept up the outside of the two horses who'd been battling it out in front. My heart pumped like a train as we left them in our wake a hundred yards from the post. And I muttered thanksgiving to every deity I could think of as we crossed the line with five yards of daylight between us and the nearest challenger.

Smethwick was not effusive in the winner's slot.

"You must have talked," he snarled at me from the side of his mouth, unaware of the cameras whirring and clicking. "Have you seen the price she come in at?"

"No," I said innocently, "I thought she was about threes."

"Fuckin' two-to-one ON!" he hissed.

"Maybe you shouldn't have taken SP," I said, removing the filly's saddle and wondering at the injustice of such an unpleasant man owning such a lovely filly.

I walked away and left the Captain to deal with him.

After that, the day couldn't go wrong.

Dawn Raider presented me with my double, though at predictably ungenerous odds. I didn't care about the odds; I had my ride in the Arc secure now.

Zimmer, guarding his customary privacy, took the unusual step of asking me to accept the trophy on his behalf. It wasn't until I'd clocked up a third win that I had time to go up and find him in the box he had somehow managed to hijack at the last minute.

To my surprise, he stood as I walked in. Hawkins, his chief minder, offered me a drink with more deference than I'd thought possible.

"Well done, Jake. What a splendid display of skill and timing."

I shrugged it off. "The skill was in getting the right horse to ride."

"And I have to retract what I said," he went on, "about the way you run your personal finances. I have a check here from Mr. Devene for forty thousand pounds. What shall I do with it?"

"The first ten thousand's yours, we agreed," I said. "I want you to lodge the balance in an account at the Bank of Ireland, City branch. Here's the account number." I passed him a slip of paper that I'd written it on earlier. "The account's in the name of Mrs. Mary Hagan."

Zimmer took the paper, folded it slowly and nodded before handing it to Hawkins.

"I have something else for you," he said. From an inside pocket of his suit, he pulled a sheet of paper which he handed to me. I unfolded it. It was a copy of a letter to Weatherbys, instructing them to register fifty percent of the ownership of Dawn Raider in my name.

I didn't speak for a moment. Before I could, Zimmer said, "I'm afraid you'll have to pay a bit of tax on that. But maybe I can find a way of helping you out there."

"I can't take it, Mr. Zimmer."

"You can't stop me giving you half the horse."

"I can't stop you, but the Jockey Club can. I'm not allowed to own horses in training."

Zimmer looked truly disappointed.

"But," I went on, "I'd be happy if you gave it to Mary Hagan instead. She'll have a few money problems since her husband was killed. He left her with six kids."

"Six kids, huh?" Zimmer nodded his head. "Lucky woman. Rich woman too, now." He grinned. He was enjoying being the fairy godfather. You could almost have forgotten that he was the person ultimately responsible for Mick's murder.

"You'll give her the half-share, then?"

"Sure." He nodded. "Are we square now?" He held out his hand.

I gazed at the extraordinary old man. Slowly, I lifted my hand to take his.

* * *

I stretched in the bucket seat of Milly's small, black Golf. She had pulled up outside the restaurant where we were going to celebrate.

"Just tell me one thing," she said. "Tell me you already knew Sandy was trying to kill you before you went to her house that night."

"I didn't know. I wasn't sure. I had a hunch, but I couldn't see why. After all, all I'd done was turn her down a few times."

"I shouldn't be jealous, should I?"

"Don't worry, I like a bit of jealousy; it makes me feel I'm wanted."

"You are." She laughed. "Now let's get in there and eat," she added impatiently.

"Eat? Eat? I don't want to eat. Do you?"

She shook her head slowly.

"Let's go home then," I said, and leaned back in the seat, closed my eyes and smiled.